Praise for Midori Snyder

"Any new book by Midori Snyder immediately tops my must-read list."
—Charles de Lint

"Midori Snyder is one of the finest writers to enter the fantasy field."
—*The Year's Best Fantasy & Horror*

Praise for *The Flight of Michael McBride*

"Midori Snyder succeeds in a grand way where other fantasists have failed. There is nothing in this book that doesn't work. . . . Highly recommended."
—*Starlog*

"A very good, very unusual fantasy."
—*The Hartford Courant*

D0019319

Praise for *The Innamorati*

"The hybrid of street theatre and fantasy seems to spin itself into existence before the reader's eyes."
—*Publishers Weekly* (starred review)

"Snyder's Renaissance Italy is a supremely entertaining setting, teeming with hustlers, poets, and lovers, and her shimmering Maze will work its magic on readers as well."
—*Booklist*

"Snyder's dreamlike novel resonates with overtones of the commedia dell'arte. . . . An allegory that is a priority purchase for fantasy collections."
—*Library Journal*

"A well-woven tapestry."
—*San Diego Union Tribune*

ALSO BY MIDORI SNYDER

The Flight of Michael McBride
New Moon
Sadar's Keep
Beldan's Keep

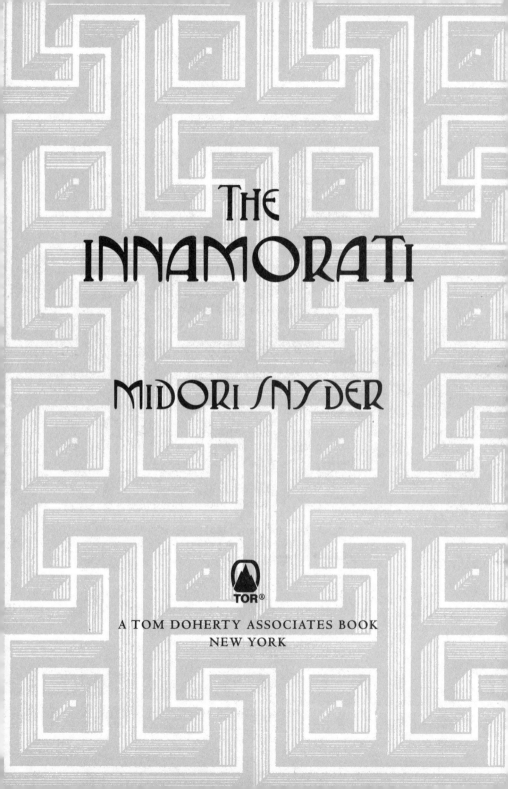

THE
INNAMORATI

MIDORI SNYDER

TOR®

A TOM DOHERTY ASSOCIATES BOOK
NEW YORK

THE INNAMORATI

Edited by Terri Windling
Designed by Nancy Resnick

A Tor Book
Published by Tom Doherty Associates, LLC
175 Fifth Avenue
New York, NY 10010

www.tor.com

Tor® is a registered trademark of Tom Doherty Associates, LLC.

Library of Congress Cataloging-in-Publication Data

Snyder, Midori.
The Innamorati / Midori Snyder.
p.   cm.
"A Tom Doherty Associates book."
ISBN 0-312-86197-4 (hc)
ISBN 0-312-86924-X (pbk)
I. Title.
PS3569.N89415 1998
813'.54—dc21   98-3039
                                                                                 CIP

First Hardcover Edition: July 1998
First Trade Paperback Edition: January 2000

Printed in the United States of America

0 9 8 7 6 5 4 3 2 1

For my father, Emile Snyder, in loving memory

Later

talk to the grandchildren/
about me/ that they come
to trust that a road does
go on/ far beyond the curve/
and that movement is another
form of eternity

—E.S., 1992

GLI INNAMORATI, THE LOVERS

I hate and I love.
Why? you might ask.
I don't know. But I feel it
Happening and I hurt.

—*Catullus #85*

1

The morning sun rose above the edge of a quiet green sea. Bright rays of light speared the waters of the laguna and transformed the canals of Venice into ribbons of flame. Burnished water splashed over the mossy walls of the canals, scattering droplets the size of sequins. A golden tide sluiced across the Piazzetta de San Marco and lapped at the white and pink marble columns of the ducal palace. The sun climbed across the pale sky, stopping when the golden light had reached high enough to wrap itself like a great cloak around the domes of the Basilica.

A bell jangled over the door of an artist's studio on the Campo de Barnabo. Three floors above, the maskmaker, Anna Forsetti, stirred, distantly hearing someone call her name. Half asleep, she attempted to rise but found she couldn't move her legs. A weight held them captive on the bed; her feet were numb. Anna swore, trying to work her legs into a kick.

"Get down, you damned cur," she grumbled, deciding one of Mirabella's dogs was stretched across her legs. "Go away." But the weight didn't budge.

As Anna raised her head from the pillows, the blood started to pound in her temples. Her tongue was thick and dry as old leather, and she tasted the sour burn of last night's wine. When her eyelids fluttered open, she was startled by intense blackness.

"Madonna Santissima! I've drunk myself blind!" she cried. Her hands flew to her face to discover something hard covering it. She clutched at the smooth carapace, her frightened fingers trying to discern its shape. Pantelone's mask; one of hers. Her hands felt along its familiar contours, up from the stiff brush of its mustache, until she found its long sweeping nose. Twisting the nose brusquely, she settled the mask correctly over her face. The morning light pierced the eyeholes.

"Madonna," Anna moaned, squinting in the painfully bright light. She struggled to sit up, her stomach protesting violently. Bile rose in her throat as the room seemed to slope to one side. The pounding in her temples had been joined by a high-pitched hum. "Too much wine," she groaned, holding her aching head. "Too much . . ." She stopped, seeing at last what was preventing her from rising.

A naked man lay on his back across her legs, the span of his thighs pinning her to the bed. The sheets were tangled around his legs and waist; the sunlight tinted his bare chest bronze. His arms were outflung to the far corners of the bed, and his head was nearly falling over the side. He was wearing a woman's half mask made of peach-colored leather, the wide eyes outlined with long lashes and delicate arched brows. The snubbed nose lifted over the rosy suggestion of a full upper lip. The man was snoring, his mouth agape beneath the feminine mask, the shadow of a beard darkening his jawline.

In spite of the throbbing pain in her temples, Anna gave a deep-throated chuckle. She pushed her mask up onto the top of her head, then, lifting the man slightly by the legs, she managed to free herself. She leaned down and rubbed feeling back into her lower limbs while she looked over the sleeping man.

Very nice, Anna thought, pleased by the sight of his muscular thighs wrapped in the linen sheets. His chest almost hairless, the smooth skin curving away from the breastbone like the pages of a newly opened book. Young, she scolded herself. Much too young for a woman of her age.

Anna gave a quick glance down at her own body. Not bad, she decided, brushing back the long, ash-blond hair from which the few grey strands had been carefully plucked and burned. There was a mark or two from childbearing, silvery streaks like dueling scars across her hips. Her breasts were still plump, though they lay lower on her chest, sloping more like pears than the hard green apples of her youth. She laid a hand on her thighs. The skin was still soft.

Seeing red streaks staining her thighs, Anna frowned. She worried for a moment that some aspect of their game had drawn blood. She touched the streaks with a curious finger. They were sticky, and when she tasted her fingertip it was sweetish and smelled like fruit.

Anna looked around her and saw the dried pulp and tiny seeds of dark grapes clinging everywhere to the sheets. She scowled at the purple stains. What did she make of it? she wondered, trying to remember the events of the night before through the haze of too much wine.

And who was he? Anna looked at his face half-hidden behind the mask. Biting her lower lip, she gently loosened the sheet from around his hips and lifted it. He stirred, but didn't waken. She gave the air a quiet kiss of approval. The olive skin of his flat belly was covered with purple smears and there were crushed grapes in the soft, curling black hair of his groin. She lowered the sheet and grinned at the woman's mask with its wide-eyed stare.

"Brava, carina!" she whispered to the mask, giving it a round of silent applause. "What a pretty young man you found."

"Mamma!" a girl's voice sang out from the stairs. "Mamma! Roberto's come! Do you hear me calling?"

"O'Dio!" Anna groaned and quickly slipped from the bed. Her stomach lurched at the sudden movement and she clutched the bedpost to steady herself. The room swayed, the light savage and bright. But the sound of her daughter's voice kept her moving. Anna pulled on her shift and her blue velvet cloak, which lay in a heap beside the bed, jerking the bed curtains closed just in time to shield her daughter from the sight of the sleeping man.

"Mamma!" the girl called as she pushed through the door. Two dogs followed her in, barking loudly. "Mamma, didn't you hear me? I've been calling and calling! Why haven't you—"

At Mirabella's abrupt silence, Anna turned from fussing with the bed curtains. She tried to assume a calm expression, but the pain in her head pinched her brow into a scowl. Bobo, an old arthritic hound, raised his greying snout and barked loudly. Lily, a small bitch mostly composed of long tangled hair, yapped shrilly at his side. The blood pounded in Anna's head in time with their duet.

"Lily, Bobo, basta! Be quiet!" Anna commanded. Bobo bowed his head with a final woof and Lily, though she ceased barking, tapped her claws nervously on the marble floor. In the near silence, the throbbing pain in Anna's head dulled and she smiled weakly at Mirabella.

"Yes, amore mio? What is it?"

Mirabella continued to stare, her expression wary. She was sixteen, her smooth face round and full as the moon. She wore small, gold-rimmed spectacles that gave her blue eyes an odd, fishlike stare. Her brown hair, dull as a sparrow's wing, had been braided carelessly into twin coils over her ears. Her dress was badly cut, too large in the shoulders, the bodice lumpy where the laces were drawn tight. Her shift bunched beneath her throat to cover the gaping decolletage.

"Amore, help me with my dress," Anna murmured, crossing over to Mirabella. As she approached, Mirabella's eyes widened in alarm, and she backed up quickly into the doorway. The dogs crowded around her skirts, and Lily, ignited by Mirabella's sudden flight, flamed into shrill barks. Anna squeezed her eyes shut in renewed pain.

"Wait!" called a man's voice from beyond the doorway. "You're all about to push me down the stairs. And after I've nearly lost my breath making the climb in the first place!"

Mirabella bolted back into the room, sidestepping her mother to hover near the carved wardrobe. Signor Roberto Farachi pushed his way through the barking dogs into the room, his face red with exertion but wearing a pleasant smile. A few strands of salty grey hair drifted up from his blushing scalp, snagged by a gentle breeze from the opened window. He took a white linen handkerchief from his sleeve and began to mop his damp brow as he caught his breath. "Hush, Lily, it's only me, Roberto," he said evenly to the small dog. "Go to your mistress now."

Her ears drooping, Lily quieted down and obediently joined Mirabella by the wardrobe. Bobo remained to lick Roberto's hand, and Roberto returned the favor by scratching the old hound behind the ears. Roberto looked up at Anna with amusement.

"A new profession, Anna?" he asked.

Anna blanched, trying not to look behind her at the closed bed curtains. "What do you mean?" she asked coolly.

"That," he said mildly, a finger pointing to his head.

"What?"

"On your head. Are you studying to be a Commedian now too? And Pantelone no less. I would have thought you would have chosen an Innamorata."

Anna reached up and felt the mask where it rested on the crown of her head. "Oh," she answered in a small voice. No wonder Mirabella had gaped. "Just a little game," she murmured, pulling the mask off her head. "To help me sleep." She tossed the mask on a chair that was covered with a heavy black robe. At the sight of the robe Anna froze, memories of the night before flooding back.

"Madonna," she whispered, appalled. "I'm ruined."

The drums rattled in her head again and a wail filled her ears. Her stomach heaved and she gagged on the acidic residue of wine.

"You've gone pale, Anna. Are you all right?" Roberto asked. He took a step toward her, but his shoes stuck to the marble floor. "What's this?" he said, glancing down. His shoes released with a squelching noise. "Anna, there's grapes everywhere," he said frowning. "What have you been doing?"

"Nothing," Anna insisted. "Really, Buffo—"

"You know I hate it when you call me that," Roberto protested absently, staring at his feet as he pranced, trying to rid his shoes of their stickiness.

"Roberto, please," Anna begged. "I need some time to dress properly and then greet you." She was pushing him rudely toward the door when a groan from behind the bed curtains stopped them.

"Hell! I'm in hell, damned for all eternity," a man moaned. "All the sins are mine. Perfidy . . . gluttony . . . lust . . ." The litany was interrupted by a loud belch. The bed trembled with an unseen movement, and before an astonished Roberto and a dismayed Anna, the young man threw wide the curtains. Lily's ears perked up out of the mop of her hair.

"Ma, che cos'e? What is this?" Roberto exclaimed, gaping at the sight of a swaying man, naked except for a sheet tangled around his legs. A woman's mask smiled coyly above his body, the eyes large and innocent.

Lily began yapping furiously from the shelter of Mirabella's skirts.

"Help me, Roberto!" Anna urged over the din. She snatched up the black robe on the chair.

"Help you!" Roberto said, shocked. "Help you do what?"

"I have to get him dressed and out of here before anyone finds out."

"Who is he?" Roberto asked. "Some nobleman's son? Really, Anna, a woman in your position . . ."

"He isn't a nobleman's son," Anna said grimly.

Roberto looked more closely at the black robe in her hands and the braided cord belt that had fallen from the pocket. He glanced again at the swaying man, his chin now drooping to his chest. Above the rim of the mask could be seen the clean-shaven circle of a priest's tonsure.

"Oh no. No, no, no," Roberto said, his hands trying to wave away the image of a naked, drunk priest in Anna Forsetti's bedroom. "Not even you, Anna, would stoop so low as to corrupt a priest."

"He corrupted me! Making wine like that was his idea!" she answered, shouting over Lily's frantic barking.

"Don't tell me," Roberto snapped. "I don't want to know any more. How drunk was he?"

"Very. He won't remember a thing."

"If he does and confesses, it will be expensive. You will be completely at the archbishop's mercy for years, paying out all kinds of 'contributions' to the church."

"Roberto, scold me later!" Anna exclaimed. "I think I can get us—"

"Us?"

"—me, out of this mess if you'd just help instead of complain."

"Lily shut up—be quiet!" Anna and Roberto shouted together. Lily cowered with a whimper.

The young man was trying to speak, trying to take a step forward toward Anna, who held up his black robe. But his legs deceived him, and instead of moving forward, he fell backward onto the bed, the slats groaning under the sudden weight.

"I'm dying. I'm dying!" he moaned. Bobo sat on his haunches and let forth a desolate howl.

Annoyed, Anna leaned over the fallen man and roughly pulled off his mask. She meant to toss it to one side, but stopped her hand in midair, dazzled by the stark beauty of his mournful face. Though his skin was pale and his dark eyes hollowed by a night of drinking, his face remained handsome, his profile clean and chiseled.

As she touched his cheek, her fingers imagining a mask shaped out of the perfect symmetry of his features, Anna tensed, feeling the sudden stab of a deeper, wounding pain in her belly that had nothing to do with the young man, nor the night of drinking. It was a secret she couldn't reveal, only suffer.

"Do you remember me?" she asked the priest, ignoring the pain. "I met you in the Campo Santa Margherita, near the Rio Foscari. We were talking about the wisdom of God and suddenly you were seized by a terrible fit."

"A fit?" he slurred, blinking back at her.

"Yes, foaming at the mouth and quaking. And then you cried out, like one possessed by a vision. Fearing that you might fall into a canal, I had my servants bring you to my home," Anna explained.

Anna saw a spark of recognition in his bleary eyes. "You!" he exhaled heavily. "You . . . we . . ."

"Yes, yes," Anna went on quickly. "You've been having terrible visions all night. Why, you mistook my manservant here for Satan himself." Anna grabbed Roberto by the sleeve and shoved him into the young man's face. "See?"

"Did I have to be Satan?" Roberto hissed.

Anna nudged him hard. "What must you have thought of me," she continued, "a serpent, a temptress from hell!" She grabbed the priest by the arms and pulled him upright. He wobbled, uncertain of his feet.

"Strange visions," the young man mumbled.

"Indeed," Anna agreed. "You have been battling the devil all night. My gentle nature can't bear to imagine your trials. Why look, is . . . is this what I think it is?" she whispered reverently and held up the young man's hand before his confused face. A long smear of grape juice had stained the palm a deep red. "And here too!" She held up his other hand, similarly stained. "You have been marked by God with the stigmata of faith."

The young man stared at his palms in surprise. With effort, he spread his arms out wide and looked down in drunken awe at the red streaks crossing beneath his ribs. He gasped, then exhaled slowly, and peace settled over his features. In the hushed silence, Bobo licked the grapes from the young man's feet.

"Signora, I have been called by God," the young man said, his voice cracking with emotion.

Anna threw the black cloak over his head and quickly angled his arms through the sleeves. She knelt down by his waist and tied on the rope belt. He glanced down at her with the faint glimmer of a smile and a sly

look stole into his eyes. As she watched, Anna saw the smile twist into
a grimace. His eyes closed and his body stiffened, his shoulders hunched
as though he'd been struck in the chest. He swayed, face contorted, eyelids squeezed shut. Anna steadied him, until his body slumped forward
and he sighed.

He laid his hand on Anna's head. She frowned, uncertain of the gesture. The young priest opened his wine-smudged eyes and held her gaze.

"Ego te absolvo a peccatis tuis," he said in a solemn voice. "I forgive
you, my daughter, and give you absolution." Raising his eyes again, he
stared out of the window into the blazing sunlight and the sea beyond.

"Che un pazzuccio!" Roberto muttered. "You've muddled this one,
Anna."

"How dare you," Anna said coldly to the young priest. Her pulse was
racing; her head burned where the priest's hand had lain. Forgiveness!
How long had she waited for that word? How long had she prayed for
its healing touch, a touch that might free her of the curse of thorns.
Even now those thorns stabbed her womb, even now they robbed her of
peace, of joy. True forgiveness did not come from a drunken, whoring
priest, she thought angrily. His absolution mocked her.

"How dare you, you insolent spawn of a crippled—"

"Anna, be quiet," Roberto warned. "You've got what you wanted.
The man's convinced, and with luck this little affair won't cost you a single soldi."

"I don't want his forgiveness," she spat. "He can shit his forgiveness
in the canal—"

"Anna, what's wrong with you?" Roberto demanded. Lily bristled
and began to bark wildly again.

Anna sat back on her heels and hugged her arms hard around her
waist to stop the stabbing thorns. A noiseless cry of grief filled her chest.
She turned away from the sight of the young priest's serene, sunlit face.
Her eyes met Mirabella's where she watched the trio, half-hidden beside
the wardrobe. The girl's face was white, except for two red spots flaming on her cheeks. Her mouth was pressed into a thin-lipped frown and
her eyes were an icy blue behind the gold-rimmed spectacles. Her hands
clutched her skirts, twisting the fabric.

Seeing the contempt in her daughter's eyes, Anna writhed as the curse
of thorns tore invisible wounds in the center of her being. All at once
there was too much pain to hold back.

"Anna, do something," Roberto ordered brusquely.

Groaning, Anna lunged to her feet, a hand clapped over her mouth,
and fled. She fled the priest's forgiving hand and Mirabella's unforgiv-

ing eyes, fled the deceiving masks, the barking dogs, and the odor of rotten grapes that permeated the air. She bolted down the narrow stairs, her hands barely grasping at the railing to keep herself from tumbling head over heels. As she ran along the corridor, the sunlight spilled from the tall windows to brighten the blue velvet robe coursing behind her.

Anna was gagging by the time she pushed open the door to the privy. She collapsed to the floor, crawling over the marble threshold on her hands and knees to a porcelain pot, its rim gilded with gold leaves. She grabbed it, and retching loudly, vomited out her misery, splattering the golden rim. Her back arched as she heaved, and her hair fell in a damp, stinking curtain around her face. Each time she vomited, another thorn seemed to bud and grow into a new spike, tearing at the sides of her womb.

"Cursed," she moaned when she could speak again. She lay down on the cold marble floor and curled her aching body beside the chamber pot. "Cursed from hell," she whispered hoarsely, and burning tears trickled down her cheeks.

2

Far to the west of Venice in a marshy field beyond Milan's towering walls, the bright morning rays of the sun shimmered over Rinaldo Gustiano's sword. It was a beautiful, ornate sword, with a gold relief of the rape of a pagan queen worked into the swirling bands of the handguard. The double-edged blade was etched with fruiting vines that at the moment were vibrating as a man, impaled on the blade's point, was in the act of dying.

"I curse you, you pox-faced shiteater," the man spat, blood forming little bubbles at the corners of his mouth. Blood-soaked gloves gripped Rinaldo's blade where it had pierced his chest. Standing above the dying man, Rinaldo smiled gallantly.

"Too late. Someone else has already had that honor."

Rinaldo gave the sword a savage thrust, driving the blade deeper into the man's body. He felt the brief resistance of bone before the sword's point sheared a path between the man's ribs. The man cried out and his back arched as the blade speared his body.

"Fuck the whore who brought me to this," the man groaned, his face drained white as blood gushed from his wound.

"I'll take that as your dying request," Rinaldo said, and jerked his sword free from the man's chest. The man crumpled to the grass and lay on his back. Rinaldo waited, listening to the rattle of the dying man's last breaths. When it was finally quiet and the fierce eyes had faded into dull stones, Rinaldo wiped his blade clean on the man's doublet and resheathed his weapon. He glanced up to where the seconds waited on horseback near a break of poplar trees, raised his hand to indicate that the duel was over, and then walked toward his horse, Lapone, grazing nearby.

Wearily, Rinaldo pulled himself up into the saddle and watched as the seconds gathered up the body and slung it over the back of the dead man's huge black gelding. The gelding shied at the scent of blood, ears laid flat against its skull. "Not a soldier's horse, that one, to balk at a little blood, eh, Lapone?" Rinaldo said softly. The stallion's grey ears twitched to catch the sound of his master's voice. Rinaldo continued to watch as one of the men was called to hold the gelding steady by the reins until the body could be secured to the saddle. And still Rinaldo watched, letting his horse graze until the seconds with their lifeless burden had finally ridden away from the field. Then Rinaldo gave the stallion's sides a light tap with his heels and rode back toward the city.

Captain Rinaldo Gustiano had no seconds, no men waiting to bring his corpse to a decent burial. Had he died while dueling, Rinaldo knew his opponent would have left him there for the crows and foxes to feed on. He might have tried to take the stallion, but he would not have been successful. Rinaldo smiled to himself. He possessed only two things of value in this world: his sword, which had never yet lost a duel, and his stallion, Lapone, who would carry no other rider but him.

As he neared the city, the rough stone walls surrounding the old Roman gates lifted out of the marshy plains. The morning breezes snapped the brightly colored pennants flying from the towers of the huge castello. Thin ribbons of grey smoke rose from the armories, wreathing the pennants in soft clouds before drifting across the low plains.

Out of habit, Rinaldo pulled on his earlobe, rubbing his fingers over an old battle scar. He recalled when these fields were cloaked with the black smoke of cannon, the poplars burning torches, and the wide plains were littered with fallen soldiers. Yet in spite of those horrors, war had been good to him. He had come to Milan from the countryside while barely a boy, in search of a future. He was the last son of an impoverished nobleman who had bequeathed what little land there was to Rinaldo's oldest brother. And without land, Rinaldo's noble birth was worthless.

In war he had come of age, proving himself smart and capable in battle. And his officers, discovering that he was ruthless with a sword, had rewarded him with the title of captain. He had fought for whichever side offered him the most reward, the French, the Italians, or the Spanish. And over the years, he had done very well for himself.

Though he was in his thirties now, and the worst of the fighting eight years over, Rinaldo could still remember clearly the last battle he had fought alongside an army of Italian nobles confronting Swiss mercenaries hired by the King of Spain. It was a furious battle, and Rinaldo had swept through men as a farmer through wheat, cutting them at the knees and the waist, threshing heads from shoulders as he fought. Then one man had stepped out of the charging throng of soldiers and challenged Rinaldo in a long and final contest.

He had worn Swiss colors beneath his chain mail, but he resembled none of the tall, fair mercenaries. He was short and heavyset, his skin deeply tanned, hair long and black, with greying locks braided at his temples. His craggy face was seamed with scars over one eye and down the side of one cheek. His nose had been broken and flattened against his face. But his eyes were razor sharp and never wavered despite the blows that Rinaldo succeeded in landing on his body.

The mercenary moved more slowly than Rinaldo, but with more precision, experience giving him insights into the rhythm of their battle. Rinaldo's last reserve of strength began to flag, for each time he struck, the old soldier blocked his blow and countered it. It was as if the man knew in advance every stroke they played.

In the end, it was a stroke of light that gave Rinaldo the final victory. As he raised his sword, his arms aching, the last rays of the afternoon sun glanced off the blade, and for an instant, his opponent was blinded. Rinaldo knocked the sword free from the mercenary's grip, and both men howled in astonished rage as Rinaldo's sword found its fatal entrance in the mercenary's side.

Dying, the man had gripped Rinaldo hard by the shoulders and laid his grizzled cheek against Rinaldo's face.

"Cursed to love the sword," the old soldier whispered in badly accented Italian. And then he bit Rinaldo hard on the left earlobe, his teeth drawing small beads of blood.

At the end of the day, when the victory had been decided, Rinaldo buried the old soldier in the battlefield. But he kept the mercenary's sword with its double handguard and vine-etched shaft in memory of the best fight of his life.

The sound of Lapone's hooves clattering noisily over the cobblestones roused Rinaldo from the haze of his memories. Fresh breezes gusted up from the cold, sparkling water of Naviglio canals, and small birds lifted from the reeds and wheeled into the morning air. As Rinaldo rode beneath the cool shadows of an old Roman gate, he laughed grimly over his fate.

After that last battle, he had tried to put behind him his soldiering life. But the old soldier's curse was powerful. Rinaldo could not relinquish his passion for the sword. In the uneasy truce that followed the Spanish victory, Rinaldo purchased three new rapiers, a handful of sharp poinards, and a set of parrying daggers, and opened a fencing school for the sons of noblemen.

Rinaldo's style lacked the grace and elegance of rival schools, but its blunt and brutal moves, born of battle experience, made it far more effective. Most duelists were content to wave their swords until a little blood was drawn and then retire. Rinaldo refused such gentilities. The sword, once engaged, must end in death. Many students who came to him determined to learn left in fear that they would not survive their education.

The duels began about a year after his school opened. Fencing masters, seeing their own skills challenged by an upstart from the wars, were forced to confront him for the honor of their schools. They came, they fought on the plains outside the city, and just as quickly they died.

As his reputation in the city as a rogue swordsman grew, so grew the interest of Milan's women. Rinaldo was good-looking, with a face as lean as a fox's, russet-colored hair, and startling blue eyes. He kept his mustache neatly trimmed over a soft full mouth and a set of perfect white teeth. Though his compact body was predatory even at rest, there was a weariness in the lines around his eyes that women interpreted as romantic vulnerability. On the heels of his many affairs had come the wronged husbands, like the man Rinaldo had dispatched that morning, seeking to restore their injured honor.

But for all his opponents' furious spouting about honor, Rinaldo believed there was no honor to be found in these engagements. Not since the battle with the old soldier had Rinaldo experienced a single contest worthy of being called honorable.

"Good morning, my captain," called a husky voice.

Rinaldo reined in the stallion. A tall, dark-haired woman was saun-

tering down the lane, crossing from the shadows into the narrow path
of bright sunlight. He smiled, watching her slow, unhurried approach.
She was thin, her pale throat gleaming like a dagger's shaft between the
ridge of her collarbones. Her arms were wiry and her fingers laced over
her forehead like the silver bands of a rapier's handguard to shield her
eyes from the sun's glare.

"Good morning, Simonetta. You're up early."

She shook her head. "I'm up late. I go only now to my own bed." She
stopped by Lapone's head and looked up at Rinaldo from beneath half-
closed eyes. A lazy smile parted her lips.

Something stirred in Rinaldo at the sight of her weary face. Her
muddied skirts were loosened around her waist and her bodice completely unlaced. The ribbon drawstring to her shift was untied, revealing the twin curves of her breasts.

"Will you dine with me, my captain?" Simonetta asked. The stallion
nuzzled her neck as though accepting her invitation. Laughing, she
grabbed Lapone. "Brute," she scolded gently, rubbing the stallion along
the curve of his cheek.

Rinaldo slid down from the saddle. Simonetta smelled of sweat and
smoke, like a soldier returning from the battlefield.

"I am hungry," he said.

"You've been hard at your trade again, my captain," Simonetta said,
lightly touching a smear of blood on his sleeve.

"So have you," he answered, and laid his finger over a purple bruise
on the side of her neck.

"Then we both deserve a meal. Come join me."

"My pleasure, Simonetta."

"Oh, I intend to make it mine," she answered tartly.

Rinaldo followed Simonetta up the narrow lane and turned into a
small courtyard nestled amid crumbling buildings. Beneath a sagging
balcony, the doors to a stable stood open and a huge man in a leather
apron sat on a barrel oiling a saddle. When Simonetta called out to him,
the man looked up from his work with a foolish, lopsided grin. He was
bald, his forehead grimy from the dirty rag he used to wipe away the
sweat. She fished up a coin from the depths of her bodice and tucked
it in the front pocket of his apron. He guffawed and held out a large
ham fist to take Lapone's reins. Rinaldo gave him the reins and followed Simonetta through a small wooden door.

As he stepped over the threshold and inhaled the scent of Simonetta's
kitchen, Rinaldo remembered the first time she had invited him to her
lodgings. They'd been friends for two years, meeting often at daybreak,
he on his way back from a duel, she from the inns and taverns where she

plied her trade. He knew she lived alone, though once, before the wars, there had been a husband and a family. While no great beauty, she had impressed Rinaldo with her wit, her independence, and her seeming immunity to his charm.

He had wanted her very much, but refused to ask her, knowing the moment he did, she would see him only as business and hide the frankness he admired most in her behind the whore's mask. He had resigned himself to friendship. So it had surprised him when she had asked him to dine with her and later had taken him to her bed.

"Control, more than power or wealth, is the greatest of all aphrodisiacs, my dear captain," Simonetta had told him in bed after they had played a game with silk ribbons. Rinaldo had taken the suggestion to heart and not pressed too firmly his demands on her, allowing her the privilege of choice. They met once or twice a month and always at her invitation.

Simonetta's lodgings were neat, the packed dirt floors swept clean. A geranium struggled to bloom on the window ledge of her kitchen. Scrubbed pots hung from the wall and a small hearth glowed with the remains of yesterday's ashes. Simonetta raked up the ashes into a new fire, adding more wood, swung two pots over the fire, and began to heat water in one of them. She took down a cured ham and sliced thin pink slices of the salted meat. Then she drew off a pitcher of wine from a small cask and set it on the table next to a bowl of yellow pears and blue-black grapes. In the second pot, she cooked rice and onions, adding broth and a white wine, stirring it constantly until it became a creamy porridge, then she folded in mushrooms and a crumbling yellow cheese. The room grew fragrant. Steam gathered on the glasses into which Rinaldo poured wine.

"Done," Simonetta announced, smacking her lips over a spoonful from the pot. She ladled out the risotto into big wooden bowls. "We eat!" she said, her tired face suddenly eager.

Rinaldo watched her sit, make a rapid sign of the cross over her bowl, and dig her spoon into the rice. She gave a small moan of pleasure as she swallowed and then took a huge sip of wine. "Good. So good." She sighed between bites. "My sweet thing," she crooned to a papery thin slice of ham just before she popped it into her mouth.

Rinaldo grinned. "Simonetta, is it the food or is it sex you're talking about?"

"Taste this!" she commanded, rolling another small slice of pink ham around a piece of pear. She slipped the morsel into Rinaldo's open mouth, her fingers staying on his lips. "You tell me, my captain."

Rinaldo closed his eyes. The sharp salty taste of the ham and the sweetness of the pear filled his mouth with a delicious flavor, and the musky scent of Simonetta's fingers brought a warm flush of blood to his thighs. He grabbed Simonetta's hand and held her fingers to his nose, inhaling the familiar scent as he chewed the pear and salted ham. When he had swallowed, he brought her fingers to his lips and bit them lightly. She snatched them back, laughing.

"Of course, why should it not be both?" he said with a shrug.

At the end of the meal, Simonetta took the pot of boiling water and carried it into her bedroom. The room was tiny and dark. There were no windows, only a worn tapestry of faded flowers that hung on the wall. Simonetta's bed was narrow, but the sheets were clean, with lace worked into the fringes of the pillows and an old cutwork bridal coverlet laid over all. The floor was strewn with fresh rushes. Outside it might have been day, but here, in Simonetta's room, was forested night.

Simonetta filled a tub with the boiling water and after adding some cold water and a few herbs, began to wash her body. Rinaldo undressed and lay stretched out on the narrow bed, watching her by the light of two candles. Her bath was both ritual and foreplay, stroking her skin with the cloth, throwing him sidelong glances to make sure he was watching and not sleeping. Carefully, she scrubbed her long legs, then the hollow of her belly. The points of her hipbones cast angled shadows on the wall. She twisted her body in the candlelight to wash her waist and back, moving the cloth up her shoulders. Like a sword, Rinaldo thought staring at the shining length of her slender frame, gold and sharp-edged in the candlelight. Finally, she bent over and washed her face, scrubbing her cheeks with the cloth and rinsing it clean in the last of the cold water.

When she had finished washing, she slid into bed next to him, slippery as a newly caught trout, smelling of herbs. They held each other close, the edges of the narrow bed perilously close. And in their shadowed forest, they made love.

The first time they had lain together, Rinaldo had wondered at Simonetta's complete silence. The women he had known had cried out during sex. Some had wept and one had called him by another man's name. Never had he met a woman so mute in bed as Simonetta. He thought that perhaps he had displeased her, although her willing body seemed to deny it.

Later, he had asked her about her silence. Laughing at his worried face, she had told him that silence was soothing after a night of false endearments and meaningless sighs. It was the greater joy to let the body speak its desires. So he had learned to listen to the wise motions of her hands, the press of her thighs. And later, no words could have driven him so powerfully as Simonetta's breath quickening and the sudden lengthening of her spine when she arched her back to receive him.

Later, the candles close to gutting, Rinaldo lay on his back, with Simonetta wrapped around him, her head on his chest and her thigh over his waist. He was almost asleep when she spoke, her drowsy voice rising like a dream in the dark room.

"Do you know of the city Labirinto? It gets its name from a great maze in the center of the city."

"I've heard of it," Rinaldo answered.

"I want to go there."

"Why?"

"To walk through the maze. It's said that when a pilgrim enters the maze in good faith, any curse that hounds him will be lost within the turns of the maze."

Rinaldo frowned and hugged her closer to his side, stroking the length of her smooth flank.

"Are you cursed, Simonetta?"

"Yes, my captain," she answered sadly.

"By what?"

"Old age."

"But you aren't old."

"Older than you, my pretty captain. And as the years pass, even you, my friend, will lose your love for me no matter how hard I may cling."

Rinaldo grunted. "Nonsense, Simonetta."

Simonetta went on as if he hadn't spoken. "There are wonders hidden inside the maze. Cities rise out of a mist in a single night and fade away in the morning. Forests grow there and an ocean whose waves lap upon a shore of diamond sand. It's peopled with the old gods, with devils and demons. Even dragons, Rinaldo, far more worthy of your sword than those outraged husbands." She laughed. "I have heard there is even a stream of water so pure that those who drink of it are returned to youth. I want to go there and drink. Oh, to have back my youth," she whispered passionately.

"Simonetta, this is a foolish dream," Rinaldo chided.

"Yes, but far more precious to me than the truth of growing old alone. Let me have it, Rinaldo, and don't scold."

"As you wish," he said. It startled him to hear her call him by name. She never did, nor did she ever mention the ten or more years' difference between them, the only weakness in the fabric of their otherwise comfortable relationship. Her rebuke made him wonder if she might be right.

"Tell me more about Labirinto," he asked, wanting to put away the disquieting thought. "Tell me about the maze."

She began to tell him stories of the maze she had heard in the markets, passed from mouth to ear around the countryside. Her voice was low, her tales full of fantastic visions. Unable to stay awake, Rinaldo felt himself drift into sleep, the creatures of Labirinto's maze briefly lighting up the corridors of his thoughts and then fading away into darkness.

3

With Lily in a basket on her arm, Mirabella pushed her way through the throngs crowding the Campo Santa Margherita as she searched for the vegetable stall belonging to Fillipo Cardillo. He was the only seller left who would extend her credit on Anna Forsetti's name alone. And even his trust, Mirabella fretted, was beginning to wear as thin as a Franciscan's habit. She fingered the few coins left in her pocket and worried. How else but credit? It was impossible to live on so few sequins. How did her mother expect her to purchase food and wine much less anything else they needed?

A young priest, his glance chastely lowered, passed close by, turning Mirabella's thoughts to more recent outrages. The girl fumed as she shouldered her way through the press of market goers. It was bad enough that her mother chose to ruin her own reputation with scandalous behavior. But what were Mirabella's chances of ever finding a respectable suitor if her mother insisted on sleeping with every eligible and not-so-eligible young man in Venice?

Sweat dripped from Mirabella's brow onto the gold rim of her spectacles, sliding down like a tear on the lens. She stopped to wipe the lenses clean and gazed around her, the world out of focus. Colors swirled, patterns of dark and light velvet, shimmering silk, and dull wool. On the carts, vegetables and fruit were daubs of bright colors with the hands of the sellers fluttering over them like bird wings. She listened to a man barking out the price of his fish, housemaids laughing, chickens cackling in their cages, and street children hurling insults like daggers at the velvet backs of the rich. She could smell the salt of the ocean mixed with the night soil tossed into the canals, the musk of a woman's perfume, the tang of cat urine.

Loneliness pressed like a stone on her chest. She knew no one in Venice as unhappy as herself. Not even her mother understood the terrible solitude of Mirabella's life.

"Hey, bella! Hey, Mirabella!" a familiar voice called. Mirabella quickly put on her spectacles. She wiped at the tear clouding her right eye and looked around.

"Good day, Roberto," she called, catching sight of him near a cheese seller's stall. She smiled at the sight of his comfortable pear-shaped paunch balanced on two slim legs. Behind him an old woman was entreating him to sample her cheese, holding the thin slice at the end of a knife. Roberto motioned to Mirabella to wait as he accepted it, closed his eyes while he chewed slowly, and indicated to the woman that he would take a piece. The woman gave a toothless smile of agreement, wrapped a huge piece of cheese in a cloth, weighed it, a sly fingertip resting on the scale, and waited eagerly as Roberto counted out the coins from a purse at his belt.

His purchase tucked under his arm, Roberto had started toward Mirabella when suddenly he was surrounded by a noisy flock of giggling girls. They were tossing a brightly colored ball back and forth between them while they wove in and out through the stalls. Bumping into a hip here, a backside there, Roberto had almost made it through them when the ball, tossed recklessly high in the air, hit him on the head. He winced. The girls broke into more hysterical giggles, and one girl, apologizing profusely, grabbed Roberto by the temples and kissed the offended spot on his head.

"Oh, it's nothing," Roberto said quickly, a blush staining his high forehead. "No, no, I'm fine."

Two more girls pressed themselves close to Roberto with a chorus of sweet apologies. One girl brushed down his doublet with a slim hand, disregarding his protestation that he was fine. Mirabella saw her hand slip beneath the hem of Roberto's doublet.

"Go, Lily!" she commanded the small dog. "Quick now, help Roberto!"

The little dog, her sharp ears pricking the air, leapt from the basket and flung herself onto the ground. Barking madly, she raced to the girl and snatched the hem of her dress in her jaws, growling and shaking her head. Attracted by Lily's fierce barking, Roberto glanced down and only just missed the sight of the slim white hand making a quick retreat.

"Go on, you naughty bitch. Get away!" the girl cried, tugging at her hem. But Lily pulled steadfastly, her weight set back on her haunches. Little barks escaped from the corners of her jaws.

Mirabella approached and quietly called to Lily who trotted back to Mirabella and leapt into her basket.

"Bitch like that should be drowned in the canal," the angry girl shouted, shaking a finger at Mirabella. "She's fevered."

A small crowd had gathered to watch the developing drama. The girl turned to them with a passionate face and showed her torn and saliva-stained hem to the crowd. "What if she'd taken my ankle instead?" she said hotly. "That bitch is dangerous!"

A liveried guard from the Ca' Foscari observed the angry girl's heaving bosom with interest. A matron hid her two small children behind her skirts to protect them from Lily's jaws and cocked her ear to hear Mirabella's reply.

"On the contrary, she's a good little bitch," Mirabella answered. "She dislikes pickpockets though. Won't stand for thievery of any kind. Even by another bitch."

There was a renewed mutter from the crowd and the faces shifted to the angry girl.

Outraged, she tossed back her head and opened her mouth to reply. But her friends quickly pulled her away, casting worried glances behind them. The crowd remained, hoping for one last slice of drama to season their morning.

Just before she disappeared around the corner with her friends the girl shrieked over her shoulder, "Your father took it up the ass!" The lingering crowd broke out into peals of laughter.

"Wretched pickpocket!" Mirabella muttered to Lily.

Roberto was mopping his bow. "Brava, Mirabella. Brava."

"But I lost, Roberto," Mirabella complained. "That girl had the last insult!"

"On the contrary, you won. I thought the girl was going to convince them to drown your Lily in the canal."

"Didn't you feel her hand in your purse?" Mirabella asked.

"Well, I suppose I did," Roberto answered a little sheepishly.

"Weren't you going to do anything about it?"

"Hmm. Yes. I suppose I would have, but only after that little hand had done a bit more exploring. Truth is, I don't keep my coins in that purse. But it's close to other jewels that do occasionally benefit from a polishing."

Mirabella frowned and pushed her glasses up higher onto her nose. "That's disgusting, Roberto."

"Hmm. Not really disgusting. Just diverting. Like a good piece of fruit, or . . . or a slice a cheese from the seller. Not a whole meal, to be sure. But a taste that is enjoyable none the less."

His reply made Mirabella feel worse than ever. Oh, why is my life so wretchedly dull? she moaned to herself.

"Well," Roberto said, shrugging, "each to his own pleasures, I suppose. And speaking of pleasures, how is Anna today? Better, I hope?"

At her mother's name, something inside Mirabella cracked, allowing her anger, her worry, and her loneliness to leak to the surface of her stony face. A small whimper crested into a sob and tears swamped her spectacles. She couldn't see Roberto's face, but she could feel his alarm as he took her by the arm and led her from the crowded campo to a quiet calle sheltered between two rows of tightly packed houses. Barcas hitched to rings in the canal wall bumped gently against the bricks in the shifting water.

"Bella Mirabella," he said softly and handed her his lace handkerchief. "What's wrong? Tell me."

Sniffling, Mirabella took off her spectacles and wiped them dry. She daubed at the corners of her eyes and then blew her nose. She started to hand the crumpled ball of lace back to him, but caught sight of his hesitant expression and thought better of it.

"Roberto, my life is ruined," she complained. "And it's all Mamma's fault."

"What are you saying?"

"You know how she is."

"A little excitable. But she would never hurt you."

"We've no money," Mirabella announced.

"Boh," Roberto puffed out his cheeks and shrugged his shoulders. "The life of every artist has its difficult moments. Surely things aren't that bad."

"I'm not a child, Roberto."

"No, of course not, Mirabella."

"You see, we're poor. There are only a few sequins left in the coffer besides the few I have in my purse. And furthermore," she continued as he started to protest, "I know how little they buy, since I've been doing all the marketing after Mamma turned out Prudensia—"

"The kitchen girl?" Roberto asked, surprised.

"And Florinda, the cook."

"But who cooks for you?"

"I do," Mirabella said flatly. And none too well, she thought dismally, thinking of the scorched frittata they had tried to eat last night.

"But why did she let them go?"

"She can't pay them," Mirabella said, exasperated. "I just told you, we have no money."

"O'Dio." Roberto sighed, a hand going to his forehead. "I didn't know. As her patron, I've asked her time and time again if she needed anything. But every time she has told me that it was all right, that she still had money to tide you over. I'm sorry," he said, and put a consoling arm around her. "You've been carrying this burden alone, haven't you?"

Mirabella's throat tightened. "Our life is awful, Roberto. It's been five years and still Mamma refuses to work. What's the matter with her?"

Roberto pulled at the strings of his doublet, worry clouding his brow. He shook his head. "I don't know."

"You must know. There is no one who knows her better than you."

Roberto shrugged, his whole body raised forward, his hands upturned. "Who can honestly say they know your mother's thoughts? I know she loves you and that she's the best maskmaker in Venice. But why she has stopped working?" He shook his head. "I don't know. I am certain, though," he added with a smile, "that she will sort it out and return to her studio. Artists rarely stray too far from the path God has chosen for them."

"Well she has," Mirabella said glumly. "She doesn't want to work any more. She's changed." Once more Mirabella's face crumpled. "I miss her so much, Roberto—the way she used to be. I used to sit in the studio just to be near her. She was always laughing then, telling jokes or funny stories. I loved to watch the mask being born between her hands. We had servants, food, the house was full of actors, friends, life." Mirabella threw her hands up in the air. "Now it's all dark and shadows. The servants are gone. She won't go into the studio. She won't talk about it. She'd rather drink and . . . all the rest." Mirabella clapped her hand on her chest. "I want to hate her. But I can't because I love her, even if she is pigheaded."

"In this you are not alone," he murmured, sadly. Then, patting her on the shoulders, he said: "Please, Mirabella, let your old friend Buffo help you. Tonight, the two of you will come to my house and dine. I promise I will talk to her. Maybe I can find out what is troubling her."

"Thank you, Buffo. Thank you for helping me," Mirabella said gratefully, and allowed him to lead her once more through the crowded campo. She wanted to believe that he could make a difference. But she knew her mother; Anna's pride was a jagged rock on which Roberto would cut his hands while trying to dig it out of the mire. Mirabella sighed and petted Lily in her basket. At least they would eat well tonight, she thought, watching Roberto carefully sniffing the hams and bundled sausages.

Anna opened the door to her studio, letting the afternoon sun chase into the room before her. She waited on the threshold. The room was cool and dry, the dust swirling up from the unswept floor in the slanted sunlight. Her awls and gougers were scattered over the workbench as if thrown. A mold lay upturned like a beetle on its back and in its depths was the tattered paper remains of a mask.

Nervously, Anna fingered the strings of her cap and stepped into the room beneath the masks hanging from the rafters. She inhaled the earthy fragrance of clay and wood shavings, the pungent fumes of old liniments and paints and closed her eyes, dizzily. This was where she belonged—heart and soul and belly. Anna pressed her hands over her middle. A low pain woke with a gentle throb.

"Please," she whispered. "Not now. I must work. I need to work."

The coils of cursed thorns slowly turned within her. Anna dropped her hands and moved with determination toward the windows. As she threw open the first shutter with a loud bang, sunlight filled the hollowed backs of three Gorgon masks hanging over the lintel. The twisting snakes over their brows hissed to life, their green scales brightened by the touch of day. They opened their heavily lidded eyes and the sun shot gold tongues through their parted lips.

"Anna, you are here," they whispered.

"Good day my beauties." Anna saluted them.

The eyes of the Gorgons followed Anna as she crossed the room to the other window. She threw back the second shutter and the sun woke the sleeping faces of a satyr and his nymph, hanging side by side. The satyr's face was painted a silky black. His hair and brows were flecked with gold and two gold horns coiled around his temples. He grinned at Anna, a tongue pressed between his sharp teeth while, beside him, his nymph woke more slowly. Her drowsy face was wreathed with dried flowers and leaves. Anna reached up and touched the faint blush on the mask's cheek. The nymph sighed and the leaves shivered in the new breezes.

All of Anna masks were waiting like old friends and she moved around the room, greeting each one. How could she be afraid to be here? she wondered, a finger smoothing the puffed leather cheeks of a fool's mask, the long nose of Il Capitano, the lace trimmed forehead of the ingenue.

Her fingers tingled with the memory of work. The slow task of sculpting an idea for a mask, watching a face emerge from the red clay, then meticulously translating it into carved wood. She loved the sharpness of the gougers, peeling back coiled strips of wood from the planes of a new face. She loved stretching leather over the wooden form and gently tooling it into the carved features.

On her work bench she saw the sleeping image of her own face molded out of plaster.

Even though the eyes of the mold were closed, there was a liveliness to her expression, a boldness, as though at any moment the eyes would spring open, the mouth part with a laugh or a curse. Anna laid her palms against her cheeks. Where had that woman gone?

She sat down by an unfinished clay head swaddled in linen cloth, peeled back the cloth, and studied it. It was a Commedia mask: the comic face of Arlecchino with his snub nose and carbuncle over his left eye. She smiled at the sly expression and started to work the clay.

Bent over her work, she could sense the hush of the masks above her. Had she returned to them? Anna tried not to think as she laid her hands on the face of Arlecchino. Her fingers warmed over the clay and the face changed expressions under her hands: one moment stupid and dull-witted, the next cat-eyed and hungry. She knew the joy of creation that she had known before her world had soured.

Before.

The word stung her like a wasp. Before her life grew barren. Before she was cursed. Her hands faltered over the mask; the foolish grin turned cruel. How could love make your life so hateful? The fool's face beneath her hands opened wide its eyes and then died, suffocated by the rough twisting of her hands on the clay.

Cupping the cool clay cheeks Anna leaned down close to the mask, her lips nearly touching it. "Breathe, my love, and I will give you the prettiest of actresses to kiss before the world," she promised. She laid her own lips against the mask to seal the bargain.

When she pulled away, she saw that the clay lips were flat and lifeless. The skill she had once possessed was scattered like the dust on the studio floor. In her belly, the thorns twisted and gouged at her flesh.

"Cursed," Anna whispered to the masks above her. "Do you see how he cursed me that day? He so poisoned my heart with black bile that nothing grows, and nothing here"—her hands gripped her belly— "will ever flourish again."

Anna pushed away from her workbench and stood, swaying. She could feel the heat of the sun, the gold light spilling over the studio floor, and then the past returning to her in a sudden gust of chilling fog.

She dug her fingernails into her palms with the effort to stay in the warm present. But the swirling mist came between her and the bright sunlight of the afternoon.

She was trapped in the darkness of painful memory.

She had been foolish to love him at all. She had vowed when her husband had died that she would remain independent and alone. She had a daughter to raise and an art to learn. It was Carnevale and a noble, masked as the young Bacchus, appeared at her shop with his friends. Without meaning to, she had fallen deeply in love with the sensual face of the god. For a year their affair had been full of passion and many promises.

But the promises had all been lies, his love a mask.

When Carnevale had ended the following year, he came to her studio, a cold Lenten fog cascading around his shoulders. He told her that he was to be married after Easter to a much younger and, in his opinion, more suitable bride, not a widow like Anna. Out of loyalty to their former romance, he would continue to share her bed, though not as frequently. With each word he spoke, Anna grew more furious at being set so callously aside. They fought in words and then her temper exploded. She attacked him with a gouger, opening a small gash on the side of his cheek before he hit her hard with the back of his hand and sent her reeling to the floor.

He touched the wound on his cheek. "You wear the mask of the rose," he snarled down at her, "but beneath the facade, the bloom has long since withered. In you, there remains only thorns. Wretched whore, may you choke on those thorns. May they tear your flesh into shreds."

Lying on the floor, Anna had wept into her palms, while above her in the rafters the masks witnessed her humiliation.

In the months that followed, her tears and rages fed the thorns that, even now, tore at her. And everything that once bloomed within her— every spark of life, every creative desire—died, torn apart by the bitter thorns her lover planted with his curse.

"Why didn't you save me!" she cried to the Gorgons.

"His heart was already stone," the Gorgons answered sadly.

"And you, my beloved satyr. Where were you?"

The satyr grinned and rolled his eyes to one side. Next to him the nymph sighed, dewlike tears in her eyes.

"Of course," Anna said. "You were caught in your own snare. I should have put Il Capitano over my door! A sword to fall on the bastard's neck when he cursed me and left me lying there like a fool." Anna spit angrily, the blood surging in her veins, the old anger returning. "Pezzo di merda. That miserable piece of shit! I hope his ass is covered with boils, that he shits piles, that he vomits blood, that his whey-faced bitch of a wife chokes on his poisoned seed."

The thorns in her belly unfurled their sharp points. Anna cried out, and, with a swipe of her arm, shoved all the tools off the workbench. She dashed jars of old paint against the walls and tore stacked paper into tatters. High on the wall an Arlecchino mask barked with laughter.

"Hey! S'iora!" a voice called from the door. Anna, still shouting obscenities, stopped and turned slowly, the plaster mold of her face in one hand. A small boy with a runny nose hovered at the threshold, his dark eyes watching Anna warily. In his hands he was holding a rolled piece of vellum, sealed with red wax.

"What do you want?" Anna snapped, her pulse racing.

The boy hesitated.

"What do you want, boy?" she demanded again, waving the plaster mold in the air.

"Man give this to me. To give to you," the boy said.

"What is it?"

"Don't know. Just give me a coin to give it to S'iora Anna Forsetti, the maskmaker. That's you isn't it?" He peered at the masks with a fearful wonder.

"Yes. That's me. Come here, boy." Suddenly realizing it was heavy, Anna carefully lowered the plaster mold to the workbench and brushed stray locks of her hair out of her face. "Don't be afraid. I won't bite."

"I'm not afraid," he answered quickly, but his dark eyes were lit with caution. "Just in a hurry." He held out the vellum. As soon as Anna touched it, he scampered off.

Anna caught sight of the tools lying scattered on the floor. "Madonna, what a madwoman I've become." She sat on her stool and woefully surveyed the mess she had made of her studio. Overwhelmed, she stared down at the rolled vellum in her hands instead.

It was a smooth and milky skin that she recognized as the kind of parchment used by monasteries in their illuminated books. Small hairs adhered to the outer surface of the calfskin. She studied the red wax, but there was no seal impressed on its surface. With mild curiosity, she cracked the wax and unrolled the vellum to lay it on the workbench, where she studied it with growing interest.

On the vellum was a drawing of a maze, the black lines spiraling in patterns to create an impenetrable knot of paths. The artist had painted small figures, dragons, and a mermaid in some of the dead-end alleys of the maze. In one corner a weary-looking minotaur rested his chin on an axe handle, while around the spiral, Theseus waited. In the heart of the maze the artist had painted a huge tree whose leafy branches spread out over the top of the maze.

Anna stared at the drawing, puzzled. Why would anyone send this to her? What did it mean? At the bottom of the vellum was a small Latin verse. Anna read it, stopping to contemplate one line in particular:

"He who is ensnared by the woes of this world and burdened by its vices can regain the doctrine of life only with difficulty."

"Hah!" Anna exclaimed. "What does a Latin scholar know about my difficulties? Or my vices?"

There was a title inscribed at the top of the drawing.

"Labirinto, the maze of the cursed."

Anna gazed out at the sunshine beyond the door of the studio, an idea forming in her head. She had heard of Labirinto, but she had always thought it a tall tale. There were two churches in Venice with mazes etched in black on their stone walls, designed to be traveled by the fingertip, to trace the difficult journey of the faithful through the many paths of sin.

Labirinto was different. Stories said it was huge and stood alone outside of any church. Come to Labirinto, the drawing told her, struggle through the maze, and your curse will be lifted.

"To regain the doctrine of life," she whispered.

The life was gone from her art; her masks were stillborn, killed by the thorns tearing her belly. If she was ever to work again as before, she needed to journey the maze and purge herself of these cursed thorns.

Anna looked down again at the map of Labirinto.

"Madonna Santissima," she breathed. It didn't matter who was responsible for sending her the map. It was a gift; but more than that, it was sign of what she must do to regain her life. She must walk the maze of the cursed, free herself from this living death and remember what it was to work, to love without pain.

"Mamma! Mamma!" Mirabella called from the door. "I met Roberto in the Campo di Santa Margherita and he bought us a wonderful feast." The girl bustled into the room, her arms laden with packages, Lily prancing at her feet, and stopped, seeing the disaster of the studio. "Mamma, what happened? Who has done this to your studio?"

Anna looked around her at the mess and shrugged. "I did. A tempest, is all." She waved it away with one hand. "Mirabella, I have much better news! We are going to Labirinto."

"Where?"

"Labirinto, the maze of the cursed."

"Why would we go there?"

"Because I know I am cursed. Don't you see? If I can find my way through the maze, I will lose this curse. Then I will be able to return to my studio. Life will be as it was before." Anna looked at her daughter's solemn face. "Of course, you'll come with me." Mirabella's eyes were unreadable behind the protection of her spectacles, and her mouth was tight with disapproval. "You will come, won't you?" Anna repeated anxiously.

Mirabella's lips softened. "Of course, Mamma, I'll come with you," she answered. "When?"

"Now. Tonight!" Anna exclaimed.

"No!" Mirabella protested. "Roberto is expecting us."

"Send him a note. He'll understand."

"We have no money."

"I'll pawn my jewelry. It'll be enough. We have no servants to worry about. There's nothing here to hold us back."

"Not even the masks? What will become of them?"

Anna looked up at her masks and smiled. "I'll bring them. They'll bring us luck on the journey. And if not, we can always sell them."

The masks hissed, barked, and spat. Even the leaves of the nymph's wreath rustled angrily.

Anna held up her hands in supplication. "I'm teasing, my beauties. I'd sooner sell my soul."

"Can I bring the dogs?" Mirabella asked.

"Lily, yes. Bobo, no. He's too old to make the journey. Send him to Roberto. He won't mind."

Mirabella looked skeptical but Anna laughed and pinched the girl's cheek. When had her daughter grown so tall?

"Amore mio, it will be a wonderful journey," Anna promised. "You and I together. We will leave behind all this sadness. Come, help me pack."

"Yes," Mirabella agreed, her cheeks coloring. "Let's go away from here. Away from the shadows."

Laughing, Anna clasped her daughter in her arms. Around their ankles, Lily barked and pranced on the dusty floor, while above them, the masks watched, silent and aprehensive.

Roberto could not remember when the twilight had been so luminescent. The dark blue of the night sky hovered over the last threads of sunlight, and a sliver of moon appeared above the edge of the darkening sea. Along the balcony of his house, trailing vines wrapped their leaves around the railings and bees stumbled through pots of flowering

rosemary. Below, the sea splashed against the hulls of barcas and gon-
dolas.

Roberto had the table set outside on the balcony so Anna and
Mirabella could eat their meal alfresco. He was humming to himself as
he set out candles. He had planned everything. A small starting dish of
squid in a steaming ink sauce, followed by a fish risotto, then beef with
saffron, finocchio with oil and lemon, and a grape crostata to end. It
would be perfect. He had sent his young nephew, Domenico, to bring
Anna and Mirabella back to his house. Domenico was a decent boy, a
bit dull perhaps but certainly easy company for a young girl of delicate
sensibilities. Roberto had spoken with Domenico about taking
Mirabella off for a stroll after the meal so that Roberto could talk pri-
vately with Anna.

Roberto smoothed down the wispy locks of greying hair over the top
of his head. He took stock of himself, as he knew he must before
proposing marriage to the temperamental Anna Forsetti. He was not
young, but then neither was she, though he would never suggest that to
her. Touching his privates lightly, he was confident that he could perform
the duties of a husband. Perhaps the eagle was more of an ucellino now,
but it was clever enough to make women happy. Furthermore, he had a
good business in trade and enough money to keep them all comfortable.
Anna had been a widow too long, and though he had been a coward
in the past, the time had come to ask Anna to marry him. She needed
him. They both needed him, he thought, remembering Mirabella's tears.

"Zio Roberto," Domenico called as he came out onto the balcony. "I
have some strange news for you."

Roberto turned and saw the perplexed young man holding Bobo's
leash. The old hound barked when he saw Roberto and stumbled over
to him.

"What's happened? Where's Anna and Mirabella?"

"There was no one there when I arrived, Zio. Only this note and the
dog waiting for me." Domenico handed Roberto a folded piece of paper.

Roberto took the note and his eyes raced across scrawled words.

Dear Roberto,

   Mother and I have gone to the city of Labirinto. We intend to journey the maze of the cursed and free ourselves
from all this terrible bad luck. Please don't be angry with us.
And please take care of Bobo, as he is too old to travel.
   I send you kisses,

Mirabella.

Roberto stared down at the letter, stunned.

"Merda!" he swore, and crumpled the letter. All his carefully laid plans had been put to the storm by Anna's impulsive flight. Why was he always a half step behind her?

"Zio, are you all right?" Domenico asked.

"No. I'm an idioto. Stupido. Un cazzone cafone. I have lost her by being too slow."

Bobo whined and sat next to Roberto, his old haunches shaking. Roberto puffed his cheeks in resignation and bent to caress the dog's head.

"They have left us behind, Bobo. What does that say about us?"

The dog gave a long, noisy sigh and slid to the ground, his snout tucked miserably between his front paws.

"I agree," Roberto answered. He sat down at the table, pushed away the food, grabbed a bottle of wine, and poured out a large glass. Then he saluted Bobo and took a long draught.

4

$\int$ imonetta closed her eyes and tried to forget her body, tried to forget the man mounting her from behind, slamming his weight into her hips and pulling her hair as though he held the reins of a horse. She tried to forget the pain radiating up from her knees, her thighs, lancing the very center of her sex. She imagined herself a hundred years away, just bones settled into dust, the late glow of the afternoon sun lighting the grass over her grave, the sound of birds. It was easier to imagine being dead than pretending to be alive to this cretino.

Her instinct had warned her he was trouble when she met him in the tavern. His small eyes held violence. His mouth was hard, his words veiled threats. But his uniform and armor showed high rank, and his boots were of fine leather. A condottiere, perhaps, come from Naples. He wasn't used to being denied. So she had said yes, she would go with him. She could handle him.

Now, listening to the man's groans as he climaxed above her, she wished she had refused him. Beneath the shining armor, the man was coarse as dung. His breath stank of a rotten tooth when he forced his mouth over hers in a kiss that sucked the air from her chest. He slapped and pinched her buttocks painfully as he mounted her. The man finished his climax and Simonetta gave a quiet sigh of relief. Panting from his labors, he collapsed over her back. It was hard for her to breathe but she waited for him to pull himself away.

Finally, he roused himself and rolled to the side of the bed. One massive hand resting on the damp matted hair of his chest, he gave her a wolfish grin. Simonetta lowered her eyes to keep her disgust from showing. She rose slowly from the bed and began to search for her shift and skirts lying on the floor. A red pinch mark was throbbing on her breast.

"So soon?" the man asked.

She frowned at the floor, but turned and gave him a half smile. "You're done, my lord. It's time I was on my way."

"I paid for the night," he said.

"And indeed, my lord, the night is nearly over. I can hear the carts making their way to the market now." Simonetta tried to stay calm but her nerves were taut, her instincts screaming, "Get out, get out." She glanced at the door of the tavern room. It was barred. She was going to have to talk her way out.

"There is more that I wish," he demanded.

"It will cost more."

He stood abruptly, anger igniting a new flame of passion. He grabbed for a small leather pouch filled with coins resting on the table beside the bed, opened it roughly, and reached in. Simonetta barely had time to raise her arms over her face before he hurled a handful of coins at her.

The coins pelted her arms and head and fell to the floor with a bright clinking. Simonetta looked up; the man was sneering at her, his hands curled into fists.

"I'm not done with you."

Simonetta stumbled back as he lunged for her, grabbing her once more by the hair. He twisted a handful around his fist, drawing her close to him, forcing her to her knees. Tears of pain started in her eyes.

"My lord, this is not necessary. I will stay with you." Simonetta laid her palms against his thighs and stroked them gently, praying her submission would change his mind.

"You will stay until I am done with you," he snapped. He dragged her up and threw her on the bed, slapping her hard across the face as he released his hold on her. Simonetta struggled to turn away, but he hit her again, harder.

"Bitch. Whore," he shouted, branding each word on her face with a slap of his hand. Simonetta's ears rang, the pain scalded her cheeks, while purple and gold flashes of light blinded her eyes.

"Get up," he ordered.

She stayed where she was, curled on the bed. One of her eyes was beginning to swell shut. "I said get up, whore!" he roared and jerked her to her feet.

She didn't dare look at him. She didn't dare raise her eyes to him. That would provoke him further. Get this over with this, she thought. She was preparing herself for the next onslaught when she heard the sound of a sword being drawn from its scabbard.

"I have more than one sword to fuck an old whore with," the man grunted.

Simonetta's head jerked up. Sweat beaded his forehead and glistened on the scar-etched shoulders. He was breathing hard, and in his hand he clasped the hilt of his sword.

"A cut here, a cut there. Like a lover's bite."

She stared at him, and for one heartbeat, a hundred terrifying memories pierced her mind. Her house burned, her husband impaled, with the hard tongue of a lance between his teeth. Her two sons mutilated by so many stab wounds it was impossible to tell their corpses apart. Her mother, her sister, their skirts wrapped over their bloody heads, their legs splayed to the sky. All her family gutted like the livestock and left for the crows.

She had fled, too afraid to stay and bury the corpses. Visions of their mangled bodies had pursued her in nightmares, a terrible penance for having avoided their death. And now the nightmare of soldiers and swords took flesh, and death, it seemed, had found her at last. Fear trembled in Simonetta's thighs, sent a cold hand to paralyze her heart.

From beneath half-closed lids, Simonetta appraised the skill of the man. He was heavy-bodied, with a big torso balanced unevenly over his legs. She guessed he would use the sword like a cudgel, driving it down over his head in a two-handed grip: crude but effective on a battlefield. But this was a small space, with little room to wield a sword. She thought of her own blade, a sharp stiletto inside a pocket of her petticoat laying near the bed. If she could reach it, she could use it.

As the man raised his sword, Simonetta flung herself on the bed, rolled to the other side, and ducked down in the narrow space between the bed and the wall. The man snarled a curse and Simonetta felt the thump of the blade landing on the bed. Feathers from the torn quilt exploded in the air. Simonetta crouched beside the bed and rifled quickly through her heaped clothing until her fingers found the cool handle of the stiletto. She slid it out quickly just as the man came around, capturing her between the wall and the bed.

Get in close, she thought. There was no room for a sword to maneuver inside an embrace. But a stiletto was an intimate dagger, made for a rapid thrust under the ribs or in the throat. Though it terrified her, she launched herself at the man as he raised his sword. She shoved her shoulder hard into his armpit, pushing his sword hand upward so that the blade scraped the low ceiling. Then she grabbed his ear and twisted it savagely. The man roared with anger as she tore his ear. He reached across with his free hand and snatched a handful of her hair.

In that instant, both of his hands full, Simonetta stabbed him in the throat, plunging in the stiletto all the way to its delicate curved handles. The man stumbled back, shocked, blood spurting from his throat. She stabbed him again. His arms dropped and closed around her, elbows and forearms locking her arms tight against his chest. Blood poured over his teeth and he growled at her, trying to sound the words bubbling in his throat. Simonetta and the man staggered around the room, a drunken couple in a frenzied dance, the sword gouging the wooden floor.

"To the devil, you fucking bastard," she hissed. Her chin was forced up by his grip on her hair. He leaned down and made to kiss her, blood filling his mouth, blackening his teeth. She reared back, and with a desperate tug of her arm, freed her hand. The wet stiletto flashed red in the candlelight as she stabbed him again and again.

Eyes rolling upward, he stumbled and crashed to the floor with Simonetta on top of him. With a cry, she tore her hair free of his clawed fingers and dragged herself away on all fours to lean against the bed, gulping for air. Blood was on her hands and on her face, clotting in her hair. It was smeared over her shoulders and between her breasts. She looked at the pool of blood forming beneath the dead man's head and shoulders. His skin was white, the old scars on his body livid.

"Cazzo!" she swore, fury replacing fear. Simonetta pulled herself up slowly, feeling every bruise sing out in her ravaged body. She needed to get out of the tavern without being seen.

Simonetta used the sheets to wipe herself clean, then wiped her blade, her stomach turning at the cloying stench of blood. She dressed quickly and looked around. The door was still bolted from the inside. And so it might remain for a long time if she could find another way out.

There was a small window near the eaves of the sloping roof. She stood on a chair and peered out. A balcony jutted from the window on the floor below. She might be able to slip through the window and drop down to this balcony, near which two oak trees stretched their branches over the courtyard to the roof of the house opposite.

Feet first, Simonetta wriggled her way through the tiny window. For a moment her hips stuck, refusing to budge, while her legs scissored outside. Frustrated, she stared blankly at the dead man sprawled on the floor until a cart rattling in the street below reminded her that soon it would be day. She pushed harder, biting back a cry when the window latch carved a gash in her hip. After her hips came her waist, then one shoulder at a time. Now she was holding on to the window ledge by her hands, her knees scraping the stone walls. She chanced one look down at the balcony. It seemed farther away than she remembered, maybe too far to land on without breaking an ankle or a leg. She hesitated, her arms aching and her palms burning.

What difference did it make? she thought angrily. It was the only way down. She would have to let go and hope she landed on her feet. She took in a breath, held it as she muttered a prayer to the Virgin. Then, trusting in the generosity of the Madonna, she let go.

The day was breaking with far too much noise for Rinaldo. The rattle of cart wheels battered his skull and the squeal of a pig sent a bolt of pain through his temple. He imagined he was falling out of his saddle and lurched sideways on Lapone's back. The stallion stopped in the road, confused by Rinaldo's heels signaling left while his arms pulled right. Rinaldo squinted around him. The street was a blur, every scene strangely doubled. Two cats sat on two barrels and surveyed him with interest. Two pennants fluttered above the street. He shook his head and closed his eyes.

"Go on, Lapone," he mumbled drunkenly. "Home. You know the way." The stallion started up again, walking slowly while Rinaldo half dozed, his ear catching the distant sound of his own snores.

Disgusting. That's what a part of him was thinking, looking down at his wretched state from some far sober corner of his mind. He had let this happen. He had let his guard down and, with the aid of two well-meaning friends, drunk himself into a stupor. But why?

The boy. That's who had started this—Carlo di Brunellesco, a boy not more than thirteen years old and one of his students. Rinaldo could see the boy, the bloody tip of his sword, the look of astonished horror on his young face.

For two years, Carlo had been one of his best students, perhaps the best. Studious and willing. A curious mixture of pride and humility, with none of the bluff and swagger of his older students who tried to mask their myriad faults with aggression. Carlo had a purity of intention. He never held back. He pushed the older students by his example, able to parry their attacks and reply with his own.

And yesterday, Rinaldo had learned, Carlo was beginning to push the master. They had sparred, Rinaldo assuming as always the superior role. But in one moment, a slip of concentration, a moment of underestimation, the boy had parried an attack and countered with a thrust that caught Rinaldo under the chin. A few inches closer and the blade might have penetrated his throat. As it was, it nicked him so that he bled. Carlo threw down his weapon, his cheeks flushed with the heat of battle, then white with the horror of what he had done.

"Good, good," Rinaldo said evenly, daubing at the stubborn drip of blood beneath his chin. "Well done," he said, picking up the student's sword and handing it to him. "Never be ashamed of a good attack."

Rinaldo had left the sparring round in apparent good humor. But as he arrived in his own quarters, he realized that a small demon had perched itself on his shoulders and was whispering into his ear.

"Old. I am growing old and slow," he said to his friends Adolfo and Lucio later as they shared a meal in a nearby tavern. "My students begin to pass me."

"Boh. You're not old. It's merely the sign of a good teacher, Rinaldo." Lucio laughed and helped himself to a platter of risotto with saffron. "Why are you so dour?"

"He thinks to live forever," retorted Adolfo, tearing the wing off a roasted pigeon.

"Can't be done," Lucio said. "Unless we pickle you in balsamic vinegar. You'll turn black and weathered as an old saddle but at least then your upstart students won't be able to carve their initials in your throat."

Rinaldo grunted and reached for the wine, leaving the food untouched. "I don't care that the student is good. I care that I am not as good."

"Cockshit, Rinaldo. You're the best swordsman in Milan. Even the Spanish dogs don't argue that." Aldolfo swallowed his mouthful of pigeon and licked his lips. "How many more dead husbands do you need to prove that?"

"I'm sick of dead husbands. I'm sick of limp-pricked fencing masters, sick of opponents who want to cut off my balls to replace their missing ones. At least that boy back there cut me in a clean fight. And yet I can't seem to enjoy it."

"Ah," said Lucio, pushing aside the risotto to load stewed rabbit and polenta on his plate. "I see the problem." He swirled the polenta into the thick brown sauce.

"What?" Rinaldo asked, warm with the wine and his annoyance.

"Time you were married, Rinaldo. To a broad-hipped girl that you can fuck forever. Or at least until she gives you sons."

"Ridiculous. I don't want a wife."

"It's not the wife, my friend. It's the sons. A man's only hope of immortality. And that's what's eating you. Not encroaching age, but missing a little bastard coming up to challenge you. In the end, Rinaldo, a man's fight to shape his son is the most noble fight of all, because when you lose—and this is one you hope you lose—it means you have won. The boy does you better and you have given him something to carry into the future."

Rinaldo groaned and poured another glass of wine. "But the business of marriage. The priest, the contracts, a woman tying me to one bed—"

"Pretty thought, that," Adolfo said with a crooked smile. "Don't disparage it until you've had the pleasure."

"I have had the pleasure—" Rinaldo answered hotly, and the two men hooted and stamped their feet, shutting off anything else he might say.

"Look, Rinaldo," Adolfo said, "if you feel completely unsuited to marriage, there must be one or two of your bastards kept in a quiet corner in Milan? I mean, there are more than enough women who have welcomed you. Surely one of them has born fruit?"

"If they have, none has told me."

Lucio shrugged. "That's what comes from sleeping with other men's wives, Rinaldo. There may be a dozen, and the saints know I've seen more than one babe with a fluff of red hair peeking from under its cap. But what woman would tell you without risking her own reputation?"

"I'm telling you, Rinaldo, get married," Adolfo repeated as he carved slabs of cheese from a wheel. "Retire to a villa and be a gentleman farmer. I'll talk to my cousin. He has a young daughter, almost fifteen. A beauty with black hair and white skin. She'll give you what you want, Rinaldo. And then, mio Dio," he said crossing himself, "our own wives will be safe at last."

He had let his friends chatter and eat at his expense while he drank only wine—a lot of it, followed by a bottle of throat-stinging grappa. When Adolfo mentioned his cousin's daughter with black hair and white skin, Rinaldo could not help but think of Simonetta as she might have been in her youth. And a troubling thought rose to join the other troubling thoughts.

He realized that he did want sons, sons like his student, Carlo di Brunellesco: battle-ready and eager to take the sword from his hands when the time came. But Simonetta was the only woman he would even consider marrying and Simonetta would never agree. Perhaps, he thought, she was too old. Desires warred in him. To marry a young woman who would give him sons, or to marry Simonetta whom he had learned to love. And if he married another, what would Simonetta think of him? Would it change between them?

He knew it would. Though she would never say it, she would be hurt. She might fuck him, but for money. And when his own sons were born, could she see him without feeling the sorrow of having lost her own?

Rather than think about it, Rinaldo chose to drink himself into oblivion. And that was why he was drunk and drowsy in the early-morning traffic of Milan's streets, astride Lapone and leaning against the gate.

A hand emptied a night pot out into the street, and the splash followed by the stink roused him from his torpor. He blinked and saw two pale figures of Simonetta running down the shadowed edge of the lane. "You're up early, Simonetta," he greeted her thickly.

She stopped running and stared at him. Her face was white, the black eyebrows crossed like swords over her eyes. But her eye, or was it eyes?— Rinaldo stared hard, trying to keep the two images of her face in focus—was red and blooming like a flower. The black lashes had nearly disappeared in the thick folds of her swollen lid.

"I am up late, my captain," she said in a low, husky voice. She glanced nervously over her shoulder and back at Rinaldo. She touched a hand to the corner of her mouth and smiled thinly at him. "It is you who are early."

He shook his head to disagree and then wished he hadn't. The contents of his brain banged against his skull and pain scorched his eyes. "I am late to my bed and . . . and very drunk."

Simonetta grabbed hold of the stallion's bridle. By closing one eye and squinting with the other, Rinaldo could see her more clearly. She'd been battered, beaten about the face, he realized suddenly.

"Who has done this to you? I shall gut them for it," he slurred, trying in vain to reach for his sword.

"Too late," she whispered. "Come with me, Rinaldo. Dine with me and tell me of your adventures," she said softly.

Rinaldo stared at her, confused. Too late? What did she mean by that? But he let the thought slip, seduced by the invitation. To dine with Simonetta. To touch her gently and take away the sorrow of those bruises. Mayhap, he thought with a dart of happiness, to make a child between them, a son to carry the bright steel of his father.

"Take me home, Simonetta. I am lost without you."

She nodded, and taking the stallion by his halter, she led them to the alley behind her house.

Simonetta turned the horse into the stable, mumbling a word or two to the stable hand who helped Rinaldo to dismount. Rinaldo was shocked to discover that the ground reared upward with every step he took and then fell away behind him. With Simonetta at his side, he worked hard to cross the lane and enter her small house. Simonetta sat him down at her table and quickly untied his cape and doublet.

"Simonetta, I love you," he burbled as she undressed him like a child.

"Of course you do, my captain." She unbuckled his sword and laid it across the table, then started to pull off his boots.

"Simonetta, marry me."

Her fingers stopped pulling. Her black hair hung like a veil, hiding her face from him.

"Oh, my captain, would that it were possible," she said quietly to the fire.

"It is, Simonetta. Be my bride, my love, the mother of my sons . . ." Once started, Rinaldo couldn't stop pleading with her.

"Tomorrow, my captain," she said, and held a finger to his lips. He kissed it with a grin. "Tomorrow. I shall give you my answer tomorrow."

They went into the bedroom, and as Rinaldo lay weary and drunk on the bed, he watched Simonetta at the ritual of bathing, though she moved stiffly and cast no warm glances his way. She peeled off the dirty shift, and he saw dried blood caked over her breasts. She began to wash, scrubbing her skin hard with a little brush. A long cut bled over her hip and bruises were beginning to appear across the insides of her thighs.

When she was done, she brought Rinaldo a small glass, the bottom filled with a golden syrup of olive oil and betony. "Drink, Rinaldo. It'll rid your head of the pain you will most certainly have when you wake up again."

He drank it quickly, anticipating her arrival into their bed. It was thick and fragrant with olives, but carried a bitter aftertaste. Simonetta doused the candles and shimmied under the covers next to him. He wrapped his arms around her, stroked the length of her back, and inhaled the herbed perfume of her skin. She was trembling, her breathing ragged.

"Are you crying, Simonetta?" he asked.

"No, my captain," she replied, her face buried in his shoulder. "I am only cold."

"Then I will warm you," he answered, throwing his thigh over her waist and drawing her body into the enclosure of his legs.

"Sleep, Rinaldo," she said. "I must sleep. But hold me all the same."

Rinaldo sighed, a little disappointed. But exhaustion caught him like a wave and he drifted, his limbs relaxed. Between his arms and legs Simonetta stretched out, a blade held secure in the scabbard of his embrace. Tomorrow, he thought, she would tell him yes tomorrow.

He slept then, troubled only by the vague flitting of dreams, a battle long finished, a bloodied sword. There was a road and he began to walk its long straight path only to find that he was surrounded by tall cypress. The road narrowed, twisting into blind alleys. He turned in his sleep, the sheets winding between his legs. A dragon appeared, smoke issuing from its nostrils, steam rising in a wreath about its scaled head. It started lumbering toward him and he saw himself flee down the turnings of the cypress corridors. He could hear the beast, the heavy tread of its feet, its muffled roar drawing closer.

A splintering crash threw him upright in the bed, sweating and breathing hard. He turned quickly and saw that he was alone.

He heard a heavy thudding and a crack as the wooden door to Simonetta's front rooms burst open followed by rude shouts and yells.

Rinaldo grabbed at the sheets and searched for his clothes. They must still be in the kitchen, he thought, where Simonetta had undressed him the night before. He stood up dizzily. He could taste the lingering bitterness of Simonetta's drink on his tongue. His legs wobbled like bending reeds. The small house shook, the walls echoing with the sounds of booted feet and furniture being broken. Rinaldo had made it to the door of the kitchen when the back door exploded inward.

At once the tiny room was filled with soldiers, their swords drawn, the metal of their breastplates shining in the afternoon sun. They stopped, surprised by the sight of Rinaldo standing naked, with an old lace sheet wrapped around his waist. A captain shoved his way between the waiting soldiers.

"What do you want?" Rinaldo demanded. "What is the meaning of this?" Where the hell is Simonetta, he thought, and as his eyes darted around the kitchen, he realized something else was missing. His sword. Where was his sword?

"Where is the whore known as Simonetta Morello?" the captain demanded.

"I've no idea," Rinaldo answered.

"Do you expect me to believe that?"

"Cazzone!" Rinaldo replied. "Look for yourself. The woman isn't here."

The captain motioned with one hand and two soldiers penetrated into the bedroom. Rinaldo could hear them turning over the mattress and emptying the cupboard. The captain kept his eyes on Rinaldo, a smug expression on his face.

The soldiers returned, shaking their heads. "The woman is gone."

"And what crime do you suspect her of?" demanded Rinaldo.

"I don't suspect her. It is known that she consorted last night with the condottiere of Naples, who was found this afternoon with his throat cut."

The memory of caked blood on Simonetta's breast and of her battered face flashed in Rinaldo's mind.

"It's not possible. Simonetta could not have done that. She was with me." Where were his clothes? Rinaldo was thinking. And where in the hell was his sword?

"All night?"

He hesitated before answering, his eyes still searching for the sight of his sword. "Almost all night," he amended.

"You'll come with me," the captain ordered. "For questioning."

"I've done nothing," Rinaldo retorted, clutching the sheet tighter around his body. If only he had his clothes and his sword.

"You know something. Maybe you were working together and it is you who was the killer. There are some in power who might have wished this man's death. Perhaps your whore has taken to her heels and left you to face the gallows," he said with a sneer. "I repeat. You will come with us for questioning."

"I've done nothing, you little turd. Give me my clothes at once."

The soldiers moved to the sides of the room as Rinaldo began to search for his clothes. They were gone, as was his sword. A nagging thought climbed his back. He didn't want to believe it, but he could feel it take shape. He could see the logic in her actions even as he felt the lash of betrayal.

"Lapone," he said between gritted teeth, and pushed his way through the line of soldiers out of Simonetta's house. He stood in the alley, a storm of rage gathering in his breast. The stable door was wide open, the stalls empty. "God damn her!" he swore. She had stolen everything: his clothes, his sword, and his horse. And she had robbed him not with a sword, which he could have fought, but with the gentleness of her hands and the seduction of her voice.

"She took your horse too?" the captain jeered. "Imbecile. Look, come on, you can lick your wounds in prison. I'm in a hurry. Get up behind one of them."

Stiffly, and still not believing that he could have been so easily unmanned, Rinaldo Gustiano, the best swordsman in Milan, clad only in a sheet, mounted up behind a young soldier. The slanting sunlight blazed in his eyes as he rode through the crowded streets, heading for the castello. He refused to look at the curious faces around him, but he could hear the buzz of whispers, the low taunts, and finally, the jeering laughter.

He glanced up once to the sky and saw a group of noblewomen on a balcony. Out of deference for his shame and their past love, they hid their faces behind their fans.

He should have married one of them, he thought sourly. Too stupid to fly the roost. But where could Simonetta have gone? he wondered. She had no family left. And as the horses threaded their way through Milan's narrow lanes, Rinaldo suddenly knew.

"Labirinto," he spat. To find her lost youth in the maze. Just as soon as he was free, Rinaldo vowed, he'd get a horse and go after her. And since marriage was now out of the question, when he found her, he'd kill her just as he would any man who'd robbed him.

5

Beneath a star-studded sky, the maestro of the Libertini Troupe studied his actors and pondered the next two weeks. Alberto Torelli was a tall, well-built man. Though in his forties, he carried himself like an athlete. His black hair, salted with grey at the temples, was thick and wavy. He had an expressive face, with arched eyebrows poised over intense, dark eyes. He wore a neatly trimmed mustache and goatee, which he stroked as he thought about their plans.

In a month the Libertini would perform in the wealthy palazzos of Milan's nobles. There they would find a much better reception than at this rude seaside camp where they were now. But Alberto knew that his company needed the journey along the coast to develop new plays. They needed more rehearsals and the opportunity to experiment in front of rougher audiences. If these villagers laughed, if they wept and applauded, then Alberto knew his troupe could proceed with confidence to the more daunting audiences of the nobility.

Alberto had high hopes for this company. It was a good mix of experienced hands and energetic newcomers. From Milan they would go west to Turin, and then across the border into France. There, with the right letters of introduction, they would be able to make a comfortable season for themselves.

Alberto glanced at his wife, Isabella, where she sat reading a book of poetry. She was radiant in the glow of firelight, her skin the color of ivory, her long golden hair rippling over her soft, rounded shoulders. Even in the crude camp of wagons and horses, she maintained an aura of elegance. She sat on rugs amid Turkish pillows, her tiny feet encased in embroidered slippers. Isabella was born a prima donna, an Innamorata who could seduce the audience simply by her feminine presence. Alberto had never been happier in his life than the day she had consented to marry him.

As if feeling the warmth of his stare, Isabella glanced up from her book and smiled. Alberto felt his knees go weak. She kissed a pearl-colored fingertip and blew the kiss to him before returning to her book.

Alberto caught the kiss and touched his fingers to his own lips. Beyond Isabella sat Fiammetta, who was nursing her baby daughter, Rosella. Fiammetta was married to Flavio Fiorillo, the actor working on the role of Il Dottore. Sitting next to her was Alberto's daughter, Silvia, practicing a singing duet with Fiammetta. At sixteen, Silvia was already a charming young woman. But where her mother, Isabella, was golden, Silvia was raven-haired, like Alberto. She had expressive dark eyes and a pouty red mouth.

"You piece of Spanish shit!"

"Italian sop!"

"Paella-breath!"

"Pasta-head!"

"Crab louse! You're getting on my tits!"

"Pus-plague sore!"

"I vomit your insults and throw them at your pox-covered face!"

"I'm going to kill you for that!"

Alberto smiled, watching the antics of Gianni Moretti and Bruno Pasquati rehearsing a scene between the blustering Il Capitano and the scrappy king of insults, Pulchinella. The upper halves of their faces were covered by black leather masks with huge black noses and rumpled foreheads. Bruno, playing Pulchinella, wore a tall dusty fez, while Gianni, as Il Capitano, had a sweeping mustache that puffed out with every word he spat. The two actors swaggered with huge pot bellies, their shoulders thrust back as they traded insults.

"Hold him while I run him through!" an enraged Il Capitano barked to the imaginary audience. Grunting and puffing, Il Capitano struggled to draw his absurdly long sword, squeaking when he nearly sliced himself up the middle in the process. With his sword liberated, Il Capitano tried to beat Pulchinella over the head.

"Wait! It's not right," Flavio interrupted them. Both actors turned to look at the speaker.

"What's wrong?" growled Il Capitano, pushing his mask up to his forehead. Gianni's square middle-aged face reappeared, bushy eyebrows knitted together over the bridge of his nose. His cheeks were ruddy, his skin flushed from the heat of the mask.

"Something's missing. It seems you're beating Pulchinella too soon."

"Flavio's right," offered Matteo Riccoboni, who was squatting close to the fire. A young man in his twenties, well suited to Arlecchino's pranks, he was slender and strong, like a rangy tomcat. Firelight left strands of gold in the curly brown hair and sparkled in the almond eyes. "I think you need more balance between the masks or Il Capitano will win over Pulchinella. Which wouldn't be right."

"Suggestions?" Pulchinella asked, pushing his mask up on his forehead to reveal Bruno's plump, boyish face. He coughed and adjusted the big padded belly in front of him. His long legs kicked out at the dust to keep the muscles limber.

"Ca-ca-ca . . ." stuttered Fabrizio, the newest member to the troupe.

"Castrate him!" crowed Bruno, snatching Il Capitano's long sword from Gianni's hand with a wicked grin. Bruno brandished it wildly about Il Capitano's potbelly.

"Cazzo!" Gianni cursed as he dodged the flailing sword, clamping his hands over his groin.

"No!" Fabrizio said, and an angry blush started on his fair cheeks. "Ca-ca-pita-"

"Corporal punishment! Whack him severely! That's what he needs!" shouted Antonio Balletti, who was carefully trimming his nails with a Venetian stiletto. Antonio played the role of the lover, Lelio. He was fastidious about his body; his hair was always washed and combed, his fingers clean, his armpits scented with rosewater and bay.

Matteo leapt up from his place by the fire and, with a bow, presented the sword-dodging Gianni with Arlecchino's bat. Armed and bellowing, Gianni swung the bat to counterattack Bruno's waving sword. The two men capered madly around the campfire, the loud whack of their weapons startling the picketed horses. Gianni and Bruno swung their weapons gleefully, knocking over piles of books and stepping into plates of leftover dinner. Bruno kicked a ham and sent it rolling under the wagon while Gianni tipped over a half-filled bottle of red wine.

"D-dio, che pe-pe-pezzi di m-m-erda," stuttered Fabrizio. "Il Capitano should kn-kn-"

"Knock him out!" shrieked Silvia as Bruno tripped over her feet trying to avoid a hard spank of Arlecchino's bat. The bat just missed smacking Fiammetta and Silvia on their heads. The baby Rosella at Fiammetta's breast stopped suckling to stare wide-eyed at the two shouting men. Her lips puckered and she began to wail.

"Basta! Stop it!" Fiammetta cried, and slapped the two men on their legs to move them away.

Bruno leaped into the air and did a forward somersault over the fire. He cursed as the long sword tangled in his legs, upsetting the balance of his forward roll. He landed hard on the far side of the fire, his padded belly flattening out like a squashed pancake around him. With a roar, Gianni followed after, Arlecchino's bat dragging on the ground and scattering ashes from the fire.

"I sa-sa-id to knight him!" Fabrizio shouted, trying to be heard over the din of a wailing baby, whinnying horses, and the shouting men.

"I am fighting him!" Gianni shouted back, slapping the bat repeatedly against the ground and raising a cloud of dust and ashes as Bruno rolled from side to side.

"Listen to him, you buffuni! Listen to Fabrizio," commanded a woman. The two men stopped their fighting, though Gianni got one last blow to Bruno's backside before they put their weapons down. Laughing and panting with their exertions, the men turned their attentions to the woman who had called them to a halt.

Giuliana was close in age to Isabella, maybe older, Alberto thought, though she refused to say. Her beauty cut a rougher figure, being solid and fleshy where Isabella was translucent as porcelain. Giuliana's skin was a pale sienna from the sun, her eyes earthen-brown, and her lips the stained color of red wine. Heavy tresses of auburn hair fell in loose curls around her broad shoulders. The laces of her bodice struggled to meet over her generous bosom and waist. She rested balled fists on her hips.

"Eh, finalmente," she said with a light toss of her head. "Fabrizio has a good idea. You need to listen," she said. Giuliana opened one fist and, turning her palm upward to Fabrizio, invited him to speak.

Fabrizio blushed furiously from his collarbone to the roots of his blond hair. His face grew pinched with concentration; his shoulders tightened and his chest lifted with the effort of speaking. The cords of his neck strained and Alberto imagined he could see the words knotting up in the young man's throat. Watching him struggle, Alberto silently berated himself for taking on Fabrizio in the first place. But he had come to them with an inheritance that amounted to a lot of money, money that Alberto had desperately needed to finance this trip. Fabrizio had bought the horses, many of their supplies, and the wagon that served as their trestle stage. Alberto couldn't refuse the young man's request to join them as an actor. But his stutter. That stutter was going to be impossible to hide.

"Il Ca-ca-pitano sh-sh-sh-ould m-m-ake Pulchinella a knight!"

"What?" said Bruno with a frown.

"It's a wonderful idea," said Isabella, looking up from her book. Her voice drifted like a song in the air. "Of course, Il Capitano can't fight Pulchinella, because they are not equals. Pulchinella is a street chicken. So, Il Capitano must knight him before he tries to kill him or he will lose his honor. Such as it is," she added with a smile.

"And Pulchinella can then get Il Capitano, now that they are equals and fellow knights, to buy him a meal, which is all Pulchinella wants anyway," finished Giuliana. "Thus Pulchinella may enjoy the pleasure of insulting and eating at Il Capitano's expense. What do you think?"

Bruno and Gianni looked at each other and gave a deep shrug of their shoulders before plumping up their sagging bellies and slipping their masks over their faces again.

A heartbeat later, Il Capitano and Pulchinella began the scene again. This time it worked. After the two masks had insulted and threatened each other with certain death, Il Capitano offered to make Pulchinella a knight so that they could fight a duel as equals. Pulchinella agreed and then suggested they eat to celebrate his new status, since it was a better fate to die on a full belly of minestrone than an empty one.

"Bravissimo," said Giuliana, clapping her hands gently when the two men had finished the scene. "What do you think, Alberto?"

"Va bene," he answered with a curt nod of his head. "It works. A good suggestion, Fabrizio,"

The young man smiled shyly and waved the compliment away. His face grew tense again as he struggled to speak. "Co-co-could I be-be-be gi-gi-ven a r-r-role? Perha-ha-haps a mask?" Fabrizio exhaled hard with the effort of his speech.

The other actors looked at Alberto curiously, waiting to see what he would say. Even Isabella crooked her eyebrow and glanced at him over the edge of her book. Alberto gave Fabrizio a wan smile.

"Of course you must practice until you can say the lines without, without"—he groped trying to find a tactful word—"without error," he finished. "Giuliana, perhaps you can give Fabrizio a hand with some of the lover's duets?" Giuliana pursed her lips with the faintest hint of annoyance, though she didn't let Fabrizio see her face. Distract him, Alberto said to her with his eyes, keep him from pressing too hard for a part.

Giuliana turned and gave Fabrizio a dazzling smile. "Allora, Fabrizio. Let's go to the shore where it's quiet, and I'll teach you the lover's duet."

"And, may-may-be Arlech-ch-ch-ino's scenes wi-wi-th Colombina?" Fabrizio asked, his face hopeful.

Giuliana looked back at Alberto, who shrugged his shoulders and opened his hands to the sky.

"Why not? Matteo, give him a mask."

Matteo handed Fabrizio an old leather mask of Arlecchino. It was frayed around the edges, and years of other actors' sweat had stained the inside of the cheeks black. Matteo gave it to Fabrizio reluctantly, as though he were tearing off a piece of his soul.

Fabrizio took it eagerly and hung it on his arm by its straps. He followed Giuliana through a path amid the scruffy gorse and twisted pine trees that led down a steep hill to the dark sea.

Alberto sat down beside Isabella. He rested his elbows on his knees, one hand cupping his cheek. "What am I going to do with Fabrizio and that stutter of his?"

Isabella raked her fingers gently through Alberto's thick hair. "Niente, amore mio. It will all work out somehow."

"If only we hadn't needed the money," he grumbled.

Isabella laughed, a silvery sound like a bell. "It will be all right, Alberto. Giuliana will see to Fabrizio. He may yet become something."

"Something other than a pain in the ass, I hope," Alberto said glumly. Then he closed his eyes, relaxing as Isabella's soothing hand continued to comb through his hair.

"Let's play the lovers, Fabrizio," Giuliana said. They sat on a huge slab of rock that hung out over the water. Giuliana had raised her skirts above her knees and let her feet dangle in the lapping waves. Moonlight spangled the water and bleached the skin of her knees the color of marble.

Fabrizio sat beside her, staring at the sea and bouncing the mask of Arlecchino from hand to hand. He inhaled the salt tang of the ocean, the smell of fish and dried kelp. Memories of his home far to the south seized him, pungent as the brittle spines of anchovy. He loved the sea, its whispering voice, and the cold caress of the waves. They reminded him of his mother and her sisters falling into the foaming surf, their shifts transparent where the fabric clung to their wet skin, the bright sunlight leaving a spattering of freckles across their breasts. Loneliness coiled around his heart.

"Here, take my hand," said Giuliana, and squeezed his hand.

He smiled in the dark as the strong fingers wrapped around his. Absently he brought her hand to his lips and licked the salt from the back. As a child he had kissed the hands of his aunts, savoring the dried lacy brine on their skin. They laughed at him, called him their gallant lover. Then they chucked him under the chin, placed kisses like butterfly wings on his closed eyelids, and ruffled his golden curls.

"Go away!" recited Giuliana.

"Disappear!" Fabrizio answered.

". . . from my eyes."

". . . from my sight."

"Demon with a mask of love."

"Fury with a heavenly face."

"How I curse . . ."

"How I detest . . ."

". . . the moment I adored you."

". . . the moment I set eyes on you."

"But, Fabrizio, I don't understand," Giuliana said, breaking the rhythmical spell of the lover's duet. "You aren't stuttering at all now."

"No, I'm not, am I?" he said.

"But what's different?"

"It's being out here, by the sea," he answered dreamily. "No one here but you. The words come easily."

Giuliana leaned closer to Fabrizio. Her breasts pressed into his arm as she rested her chin on his shoulder. "But not on stage?"

Fabrizio shook his head. "Something happens. I choke on the very words that burn in my veins. I can't get them out."

"How long has it been this way?" Giuliana asked, a sympathetic hand stroking the length of his arm.

"Ever since I left my mother's home in the south and ca-came to li-live with my fa-father in Rimini."

"It's back."

Fabrizio nodded.

"But we're alone."

"Except for the gh-ghost of my pa-pa-father," Fabrizio finished bitterly.

"Then send him away," Giuliana said gently.

"I'm tr-trying."

"Ah, I begin to understand. The stage isn't the problem; neither are women. Do you stutter in the company of men? Men in authority like Alberto and your father?"

"Alberto is a go-good man. My fa-fa-ther was a ba-ba-"

"Bastardo?"

"Ballbuster."

Giuliana laughed. "I was daughter to one of those wretched men too. And foolish girl that I was, when I was old enough to get away from him, what did I do but marry another one? Che stronzo," she spat. "King of shits, he was."

"But you didn't learn to stutter," Fabrizio said.

"I did worse. I disappeared a little more each day, feeding pieces of my heart to that monster."

"What happened?"

"I got lucky. My husband fell over dead, blasted by pestilence. His skin turned black, just like his soul. I was left a widow, young enough to remarry but much too smart to go back into harness." Giuliana laughed again and kicked a silvery spray of water into the air. "I went to join my sisters in Breschia. On the road there, I fell in with a troupe of Commedians and never made it to my sisters. That troupe was no where near as good as the Libertini," she said with a shake of her finger. "But good enough for me to learn the parts. The role of Colombina was made for me," Giuliana said passionately. "She speaks from her heart, but she rules with her mind. I adore her. And if I am ever lucky enough, perhaps I will find a worthy Arlecchino on whom to set my sights."

Fabrizio lifted the mask of Arlecchino to his eyes and grinned, his teeth shark-white beneath the black mask.

"I love you. I love you as much as sausages and pancetta!"

Giuliana leaned in and kissed his mouth beneath the mask. She wrapped her arms loosely around his neck and gazed lovingly into the dark hollows of the mask's eyes. "And I love you as much as men love lying!" she recited.

"And I love you as much as pickpockets love fairs."

"And I love you as much as playwrights love applause."

"And I love you as much as doctors love epidemics."

Giuliana released her hold on Fabrizio's neck and burst out laughing. Fabrizio lowered the mask and smiled at her. He liked the way she laughed, with her head thrown back so that the moon lit the roof of her mouth.

"O'Dio, what a wonderful actor you are, Fabrizio."

"If I can stop stuttering."

"Maybe all that is needed is tenderness to give you strength," she suggested. She put her hand on his thigh and squeezed the muscle. It tensed beneath her hand. "Are you a virgin?"

"I may not be able to speak as I wish, but I have never stalled when it came to women," he said circling her waist with one arm. He pulled her close, inhaling the damp fragrance that rose up from between her breasts: fish from the deep waters, dried roses, and sweat. He gave her small kisses on her upper lip and then nibbled lightly on her lower lip. She leaned her body into him, her back curved into an arc. Slowly, he kissed her behind her ears, and tasting the salt of her sweat, he licked her neck.

"O'Dio." She sighed as his tongue lapped at the edge of her collarbone. His head slipped lower. He took the fabric of her bodice between his teeth and pulled it opened. She shivered as a gust of wind cooled her heated skin, puckering her exposed nipples. "Oh, mio Dio." She sighed again, her breath quickening as Fabrizio's warm mouth fastened on her nipples.

Fabrizio lay Giuliana down on the damp slab, covering her with his eager body. A small wave splashed up the sides of the rock and spattered its cold spray on their faces. His eyes were blinded by mirrors of moonlight reflected in water droplets on his lashes. Fabrizio snuggled his face in the warm cleft between Giuliana's full breasts. With a free hand he raised the hem of her skirts and bared her shapely legs.

"Come to me now!" she cried breathlessly. Her hands grabbed at the strings that held his hose and violently tugged them free of his doublet. She snaked her hands under his shirt and wrenched it over his back and then pulled down his hose over his hips.

Dimly Fabrizio heard something splash, falling into the sea. But he forgot it almost instantly as Giuliana's strong hands began to knead his bare buttocks. Her legs circled his waist and pulled him into the heated shelter of her thighs. If only he could learn to speak like he fucked, he thought, hearing the woman moan with delight beneath his driving body.

6

Erminia picked her way carefully between the rocks and gnarled tree roots of the path as she made her way down a steep slope to the sea. Behind her, the hills rose into pleated crests, lined with cedar, oak, and pine. In the faint dawn light, the gorse was blooming a bright yellow amid the deep green leaves. The sky was streaked pink, striped with scudding clouds that were chased by an ocean breeze. The last fingers of the night's mist clung to the trees.

Erminia smiled, breathing in the fresh taste of the sea. She was a tall woman, big-boned at the wrists and heavyset across the shoulders. Her face was long and square, her black hair a matted tangle of curls and snagged twigs. Beneath dark eyebrows her eyes were surprisingly light in color, shifting from grey to sapphire blue. She moved confidently down the switchback trail, unafraid of the steep slope or the hazards it presented. Long muscles in her thighs bunched as each calloused heel dug into the path for balance.

She reached a rocky coastline where boulders worn into smooth slabs tumbled into the water. Erminia noted the sea was rough this morning, the white waves churning against the rocks. She stared hungrily at the waves breaking over the rocks, sending high plumes of foam into the air.

Erminia inhaled deeply through her parted lips and then held her breath. In that mouthful of sea-damp air, she tasted every shore that the sea had touched. And from the taste of it, she created a vision of what had dipped into the water: the bitter oil of olives, their pits tossed into the sea farther up the coast; the peppery trail of spices carried on a ship into Genoa; the fear-sweat of horses confined in the hold of another ship. With each breath Erminia took, something else materialized in the air above her head: a canvas sail, torn and mended; a sailor's wool sweater rank with lanolin from the sheep; old wine bottles; the cast-off beak of an octopus; a basil-seasoned mussel shell.

Her dark brow wrinkled as she tasted linseed oil and saw a brown leather mask with a red carbuncle over one eye. She touched her own face, following the line of her brow and nose to mirror the roughly shaped mask. It was different from the masks she had once known, being smaller and somehow more energetic. Curiously, she reached out a finger. The mask dissolved at her touch into a puff of mist, the hollow eyes holding her gaze for a moment longer.

Erminia laughed soundlessly and swept the sky clean of all the clutter of images. No more calling on the sea for stories. She was in a hurry today. The goats were impatient to reach their fields and graze. Erminia quickly undressed, pulling the coarse wool over her head and slipping her dirty shift down to her feet. She bunched the clothes together between the cleft of two rocks where they were hidden from view.

Naked, she scrambled over the rocks, taking care to avoid stepping on the crusted patches of tiny, sharp, black mussels. The sea spray jetted between two boulders, sending a lace of white foam over her thighs. The cold thrilled her. Shivering, Erminia reached out her hands to catch the next wave. When it hit, crashing over the rocks, she grabbed the falling water in her arms and rubbed the white spume over her shoulders.

Though she was chilled to the bone, the brisk seawater woke something warm in her. She tossed her hair out of her face and peered over the edge to where the rocks offered a small open space for a diver not afraid of the lashing waves. Her hands holding down her hair, Erminia jumped into the narrow corridor between the rocks, feet first.

The shock of cold water stung, and then blazed over the surface of her skin, ripping the air from her lungs. Beneath the waves, she opened her mouth in a soundless scream of delight. White bubbles cascaded from her lips. The current twirled her in a whirlpool and in its funnel she surged upward to the surface.

She burst through the boiling crest of a wave and inhaled misted air. She forced her arms to stroke against the waves, and, like a knife slashing the water, drove her body out into the open sea, away from the intense pull of the tide.

Shoals of anchovies joined her, their tiny silver bodies lighting a shimmering path beneath her. They nipped at her black hair that fanned out over the surface of the water. She turned suddenly on her back and floated, staring up at the pale dawn sky. Her breasts bobbed like two small islands. She shivered with pleasure as the anchovies slithered over her belly.

She stretched herself out across the surface of the water and waited. It happened slowly at first, a slight tug and then a hard tear at the skin of her groin as an outer shell of skin dissolved along a hidden seam, splitting apart down the center like the worn carapace of a crayfish. Her chest lifted in the water and her arms dangled beneath her. The dark skin parted from her breasts and fell away into the sea. Erminia put her hands to either side of her face and gently pushed away spent skin to drift on the current.

Now Erminia's skin was as luminescent as the interior of an abalone. Her rough calloused heels were a shell pink, her toes translucent. Beneath the weather-beaten brown mask was a woman's face, still long and square in shape, but an alabaster white. She held up her hands out of the water, luminous as the phosphorescent waves. She stroked her hair free of twigs and dirt, and it glistened, slick as the kelp.

Erminia looked up at the pink clouds, growing ruddy with the rising sun, and sighed. The end of her exile was nearing. She had endured it for nearly ten years. Ten years of silence. Ten years of landlegged ugliness. At the beginning, it hadn't seemed such a terrible challenge. The Sirens had suffered far worse humiliations. To think that they had lost their songs and their island in a contest of musical skill to that wretched Orpheus. And for what? So that cafone Jason and his argonauts could go and plunder a woman of her birthright and her power. Che stronzino, Erminia thought angrily, smacking the water with the flat of her palm. The anchovies scattered in terror. The Sirens should have won against Orpheus. They should have sent the argonauts crashing into the shores.

Erminia shrugged and turned over on her stomach, stroking her arms lazily through the sea. Well, it was true that Orpheus had finally got his comeuppance when the maenads ripped him apart for being such a joy-less prick. Now all that was left of him was a head that wouldn't shut up. That galled her the most. She, who could sing the harmony of the spheres, mute before a head that chattered nonsense! But she had swal-lowed her pride and gone to see him on behalf of herself and her sis-ters, who in their misery had vanished off the coast of Naples. She had tried to reason with the head of Orpheus, plead for the return of their singing voices and their island. They had been banished long enough. But he was as much of an arrogant piece of shit as ever.

Erminia submerged her head in the cold water. She had almost con-vinced him it was time to relent, but then he told her that he might be willing to give back their voices because their voices were worthless. Sirens were remembered now as no more than flute-playing whores who had killed and robbed strangers on the road. It had made her furious to think that this donkey's ass had probably spread the disgusting rumor himself. She couldn't stop herself from returning the insult, from telling him that he was remembered as the man who raised his wife from one death only to murder her himself the second time. And then instead of grieving his loss, he had taken up with boys!

She had been stupid to say it, even if she did think it fair. They had fought until, foaming at the mouth, Orpheus had cast down a chal-lenge. Let the siren try to turn her back on what she loved best and walk blindly out of hell. Let her test her own willpower.

"Ten years of silence on land," he said. "I will give you back your voice but you may not use it. You may not speak, above all you may not sing. Not one note but that I shall know of it. If you can last the term of exile, then will I restore to you and to your sisters the island of An-themoessa and your voices."

Erminia had pounced on the challenge, convinced that after centuries of silence on the sea, ten years would be a blink of an eye.

Erminia was ageless, known among her sisters as Leucosia, the white-skinned. But on taking up Orpheus's challenge, she changed her form into that of a very young girl and allowed the sea to cast her on the rocks below the church in the village of Camogli. A family had taken her in and, believing that she was mute and ignorant, set her to work as a servant.

On land she grew as any human girl must, though she was taller and more raw-boned than the other village women. She hid her dazzling white skin from them by casting an enchantment over herself that created a mask of weathered brown skin. She could not change the brilliance of her sapphire eyes, so she darkened her brows and covered her head with black matted hair that hid the better part of her face.

The first years on land were dry and hard. She ate poorly, slept in the straw near the animals, and thirsted for the freedom of the ocean. But her foster family had kept her from the sea, fearing she would drown. Not until she was old enough to wander across the hills herding the goats did Erminia find a way to return to the sea for a respite. Just before dawn when the village still slept, she would lead the goats out, stopping briefly along the rocky coast. Slipping into the cold salty water, she would shed the dry, weathered skin and drift again in the sea.

For a few years, the morning visits to the sea had been enough to soothe her. As a mute and ugly goat girl, she had nothing to fear. No one had looked twice at her as she scampered through the hills. But lately, that had changed. Though still ugly, she had grown into womanhood and had drawn the unwanted attentions of her foster brothers. She could disguise her face, but it was harder to hide the allure of her body. It rose from her body like an undefined scent, filled the air with a thick attar that attracted them even as the sight of her face repulsed them. Their confusion made them hostile.

"Thick, ain't she?" Pietro said, rapping his knuckles on her forehead. "Nothing there."

"Leave her alone," Mamma Donatello hissed. "The girl's addled, but she works hard."

"Imbecile," Pietro said, pinching her cheek hard.

Erminia said nothing because she didn't feel the pain. Pietro's fingers had folded around the browned skin of her mask. Only her eyes, half-hidden beneath her brow, turned a livid blue.

"How can you trust the goats to her, Mamma? What if she loses them?" Pietro complained.

"The goats trust her. And she hasn't lost any of them, Pietro. What picks at your liver?" insisted his mother.

"Nothing. Yes, something. It's her silence I don't like. Not normal. She's no better than a dumb beast."

"She stinks of fish guts," complained Nicolo, sniffing her hair. "How can I bring a bride into this house with this mackerel of a woman?"

"Boh," answered his father, Teodoro. "Leave her be. To marry one needs a dowry and this one has none."

"Besides, she'll make a better servant if she stays unwed," Mamma answered. "No man would want her as she is."

But Erminia knew differently. She looked at Nicolo, his eyes refusing to meet hers, and remembered the way he cornered her in the shed and rubbed himself against her. She didn't cry out when he ground his hips against her with a furious urgency. She watched him with distant amazement as he clutched at her breasts and then tried to kiss her. The urgent probing of his tongue failed to persuade her to part her teeth. He sucked the lobes of her ears but she refused to hear him.

Though he tried, he could find no entrance in her. When he lifted her skirts, she pulled them down, slapping away his hand. She was taller than he, solid as a block of stone, and no matter how hard he tried, he could not hoist himself into the closed valley of her thighs. In desperation, red-faced and panting, he grabbed her by the shoulders and tried to throw her down. But she wouldn't budge and remained where she stood, feet rooted to the ground.

In the end he contented himself with rubbing his crotch fiercely against the wooden length of her leg while she stared down at him from cold blue eyes. He clawed at her shoulders when he climaxed, small barks issuing from his mouth. When he finally released her, sweat under his arms, the front of his hose stained, he wagged a finger at her.

"Next time," he panted. "Next time, you'll take it up the ass, god-damn it!"

Erminia sighed to the sea and it gently carried her into a shallow groove between two rocks. Her exile was almost done. Stay firm only a little longer. And then she could shed her skin a final time and return forever to the sea to find her lost sisters. They would sing again among the rocks. Fuck the head of Orpheus! What did he know of the songs that lingered in the hearts of men?

Erminia dragged herself out of the water and felt the morning's chilly wind dry her skin. A substance on the surface of her flesh hardened at the touch of the wind. Her features grew coarse again. Her hair lost its silken shine and became tangled with twigs. She shrugged into her clothing and slowly took the path up the steep slope to the village.

As the mask hardened around her features, Erminia turned to face the sea. She inhaled, tasting again the linseed tang of a leather mask. It appeared before her, the eyes round, the half mouth a full-lipped grin. She grinned back at it and screwed her features to match its expression. It was too hard to hold such a face for long, though. Reluctantly, she waved her hand and let the image dissolve. Far out on the sea, she could just make out the drifting skin, the arms flung wide, the outline fragile as foam.

High up on the hill, the goats bleated for her. They had waited long enough. Now it was their turn. The sun broke over the horizon, shafts of light piercing the scudding clouds. In the next valley the monastery bell tolled its sad voice of resignation. Erminia let the sound vibrate through her, strengthening her resolve to survive this silent exile. She turned away, her soft blue eyes hardening into a stone grey. The yellowed calluses of her heels dug into the dirt as she trudged up the slope.

7

The actors of the Libertini huddled beneath the archway of a narrow street leading into Camogli's triangular piazza. Slanting sheets of rain splashed down on its black and white patterned stones; a church built on the seaward side sheltered it from the worst of the storm. Next to the church, the fishing boats tied to the harbor wall bounced in the rough sea. All along the landward side of the piazza, a tall row of houses had closed their shutters against the wind and driving rain. There was no one abroad in the streets of Camogli, not even the usual stray cat.

In the archway, the Commedians stared glumly at the rain. The women held their skirts gathered in their hands to keep the hems from dragging in the water that sluiced down the shining black cobblestones. The baby, Rosella, fussed, her cheeks bright red in the chill. The men, leaning against the wall, wrapped their short capes around them, the feathers of their costume hats drooping with the damp. Alberto was alternately swearing at himself, swearing at God, and swearing at the bad luck that had brought this wretched storm on the day of their first performance.

They had entered Camogli in the early morning, when the sky was burning with red clouds to match the intensity of Alberto's temper. He was seething over the loss of the Arlecchino mask. Fabrizio had stammeringly confessed to having accidentally dropped the mask in the sea. Dropped it into the sea! It could portend disaster for the whole troupe. Silvia fingered her little gold cross nervously, Bruno and Gianni made secret gestures to ward off bad luck, Matteo sulked, Flavio chewed his nails, and Antonio tucked a blue Turkish bead on a string underneath his doublet to protect himself from evil. The damn fool, Fabrizio, just made it worse by stuttering worthless apologies to anyone with the patience to listen.

Once they had arrived in Camogli, Isabella urged Alberto to set up the show early and begin with some short pieces to advertise the evening performance. "Give them something to do so they don't fret," she advised. "Applause is the best cure!"

They set up the wagon and the trestle stage on top. From the trestle they had hung bright yellow drop cloths to form background walls. Fiammetta played her mandolin and Silvia danced a salterello to attract the villagers. As a crowd gathered, Arlecchino and Pulchinella made their appearance amid snickers and light applause. The two masks were arguing over a piece of cake that Arlecchino was happily eating but Pulchinella wanted. When Arlecchino refused to share even a morsel with his companion, Pulchinella decided to trick Arlecchino into believing he was very ill. Before long poor Arlechino was staggering and moaning while Pulchinella expounded on his pallor. When Pulchinella at last declared him dead, Arlecchino obediently lay down and surrendered the cake to his greedy tormenter. It was left to Colombina to labor to convince her beloved Arlecchino that he wasn't dead after all.

Everything was going well. The crowd was small but enthusiastic, standing attentively before the stage, their tasks temporarily forgotten as everyone watched the performance. Alberto knew that if the troupe could hook them now, the audience would return in the evening to see the full performance and pay out a few of their hard-sweated coins. The crowd had just begun to loosen up when a thick bank of dark grey clouds settled heavily above the piazza.

The wind shifted, gusting off the ocean and billowing the background cloth like an untrimmed sail. The villagers turned a worried eye toward the horizon, their attention divided between the players, the rising sea, and the dark clouds. A snarl-haired shepherdess came trotting through the piazza with her herd of bleating goats and, one by one, the villagers hurried from the piazza to secure the ties on their boats and the shutters on the windows, to pull barrels and other stray chairs and tables sitting out of doors into safety. In the end there was only the shepherdess, her weathered face staring at the actors in stupefied wonder.

She jerked Arlecchino's shoe, trying to get his attention. Arlecchino bent low and bawled out how miserable he had been when he was dead and unable to eat his cake. The hulking woman touched his masked face with dirty, chapped fingers. Without warning she grabbed Arlecchino by the nose and pulled hard against the headstraps. Arlecchino yelped and moved forward, arms waving frantically for help, while the shepherdess handled his masked face. Just in time, Pulchinella jumped forward, and, with a great deal of cape swishing, loud extemporaneous poetry, and artful hand waving, finally convinced the shepherdess to let go of Arlecchino's face.

As Arlecchino had scampered back to the safety of Colombina's skirts, the dark sky broke with a hard patter of rain. Gathering up props, instruments, and masks, the Commedians had made a run for the covered archway. Within moments, the stage was flooded with the downpour. Beneath a jacaranda tree, the horses bowed their heads under their soggy manes while thunder rumbled and lightning sizzled between thick clouds. The odd shepherdess, cowed by the fury above, ran out of the piazza after her scampered goats.

And in the archway they remained, Alberto thought miserably, while the day slipped away. Isabella leaned on his arm and sneezed daintily. Alberto pulled on the fine hairs of his beard. All because that stupid fool of a stuttering actor—no, Alberto refused even to entertain the notion of calling Fabrizio an actor—all because that stupid fool had witlessly lost an Arlecchino mask. Nothing but bad luck would follow them now. Unless of course they could find a way to toss the wretch into the ocean. Agitated, Alberto tugged harder.

"Look, I think it's stopping!" Flavio said through gritted teeth.

"Madonna Santa," Silvia trilled. She leaned her head out from beneath the protection of the archway and peered up at the sky. "I can see patches of blue sky beyond the tops of those hills."

"Ah, at last," said Isabella gently, patting her husband's arm. "Stop insulting your beard, Alberto. The road is always like this, amore mio. Good and bad together."

Alberto let go of his beard, but his anger remained. Someone banged open the shutters of a tall house across the piazza and stuck their head out the window: a man with a bald pate and a fringe of long grey hair. He clapped his hands as if surprised to discover them all standing like wet geese beneath the archway.

"Come, come," he called, and motioned to a tightly shut green door below him. "Come and warm yourselves! What are you doing in the rain? Hurry, come inside!"

The Commedians needed no further encouragement but crossed the piazza quickly, Alberto pausing for a moment to murmur an apologetic prayer at the wooden doors of the church for having cursed God for the rain. After all it wasn't His fault. It was that fool Fabrizio's fault.

The green doors creaked open to reveal the common room of a small inn with a huge hearth nestled in the corner. An orange tomcat sauntered out and sat on his haunches, the yellow eyes following them curiously. At the doorway, Matteo leaned down and gave the cat a quick rub under the chin. The cat stretched his forepaws on the actor's leg and purred.

Fabrizio came up behind Matteo and went to pet the cat as well. The creature hissed as he laid his hand across its back, twisted its spine, and struck out with its claws.

"Merda!" Fabrizio cried, and drew his bleeding hand back to the safety of his chest.

Matteo didn't say anything but cast Fabrizio a smug look. Fabrizio's shoulders slumped.

Once inside, the troupe found the room warm and deliciously fragrant with the scent of food and wood smoke. They stood near the hearth, peeling off wet capes and cloaks and hanging them to dry on pegs near the fire. Steam rose from the rain-soaked garments and sighs from the Commedians holding out their chilled fingers to the fire.

"I thought for certain you had gone into the church for shelter," the balding man was saying. His round black button eyes glistened beneath pale wisps of eyebrows. "I saw you just before the storm hit, when Erminia was giving Arlecchino a twist of the nose. But when the rain came and the lightning, I'm afraid I was distracted. If I had known . . ."

"Signore, you can not imagine how grateful we are for your hospitality at this moment," Alberto said. "Perhaps you would let us know the name of our rescuer?"

"I am Giovanni Arrighi. This is my inn. I'm not from here originally, though. I'm Florentine," he said with some pride. "But you know how the politics in that city go." His fingers scraped beneath his chin in a gesture of disgust. "Once I was a well-known wool trader, but I supported the wrong man in the Signoria and then, of course, there was the war. So, for now, I am here."

"Signor Arrighi, we cannot thank you enough. Please let us introduce ourselves," Alberto began.

"Oh, no need!" Giovanni said happily, wispy eyebrows lifting over his bright eyes. "You are the Libertini. I have seen your troupe perform before, at Carnevale in Venice." He bowed low to Isabella, a hand over his heart. "You are the exquisite Isabella. Signora, there is no finer Innamorata on stage than you. Your beauty and intelligence . . . che brava." He straightened and faced Alberto again. "And you, of course, are Libertini's Il Maestro, Alberto Torelli. Even without Pantelone's mask and black cape, I'd recognize that voice!"

"How fortunate to find a true patron of the arts here in Liguria," Giuliana said, shaking the water from her hair.

"Signora Giuliana di Brescia, it is I who am fortunate," Giovanni said, giving the surprised Giuliana a bow as well. "Indeed, I am familiar with your performances on stage too. The fame of your clever Colombina precedes you."

"You are too kind, Signor Arrighi," Giuliana murmured with a smile. Rain dripped off the hem of her soaked dress and puddled around her feet.

"Please, all of you sit and be my guests. Our fare is simple but I think you will find the ravioli excellent, the pesto full of garlic, and the zuppa di pesce quite fresh. Later, when everything has dried out, I will call a couple of boys to help set up your stage again. You can't imagine how it pleases me to have some real theater in this dreary village! But we must have some wine." Giovanni shouted to a boy leaning against the kitchen door. "Forget that Ligurian horse piss behind the bar, Marco. Bring up the Montalcinos and Albanas! This is a special occasion."

The boy snapped to attention and disappeared through a door, reappearing laden with dust-covered bottles of red and pale gold wine. Giovanni shouted to the serving girls, who began to bring bowls filled with steaming soup in which red-shelled scampi and chunks of white turbot competed for space. Then came platters full of warm flat bread, crusted with salt and shiny with olive oil. Giovanni uncorked the white wine and began pouring, talking as he poured. The Commedians listened respectfully but their eyes were fixed on the wine swirling into the glasses and the hot soup steaming beneath their noses.

"Buon appetito!" offered their host, and those actors not diving their spoons into the soup tore off pieces of the warm flat bread and stuffed them into their mouths.

For the next few hours, while it drizzled outside, the Commedians dined inside, growing warm and sated with food and wines. In the course of the meal, they conversed with their host on almost every subject, from the quality, or lack thereof, of Ligurian wines, to the perfection of Toscana pecorino cheese, Petrarch's poetry, the complex politics of Florence and the even more complex politics of Milan and France and Spain. They shared gossip about the great houses: the Sforza, the Medici, the Gonzagas, the Borgias.

Finally, they gossiped about the village of Camogli. For although the scandals of the village were not much beside the scandals of the noble houses, local gossip would provide the finishing details of their performance that night. The success of a performance lay in personalizing the drama, in taking the universal masks of Arlecchino and Pulchinella and placing them onto recognizable local characters: the farmer too cheap to pay a decent dowry for his daughter, the old randy widower chasing young girls, the beautiful and now rich widow receiving condolence calls from the men of the village. Even the village bully might see himself in the performance of Il Capitano, and become during the life of the performance not a person to be feared by the crowd, but mocked.

Giovanni told the Commedians much about the village: which wives were adulterous, which husbands sniffed around the skirts of the maids, who hid their gold under the straw, and who watered their wine before bringing it to market. He also spoke of the new married couple whose joyous cries woke the village every night for a month, and the golden-haired child who once prophesied a bumper harvest of fish. Each actor listened thoughtfully, turning over in his mind the subtle changes he would make to his performance to bring it alive to the audience.

"What about that shepherdess? The one who nearly pulled off Arlecchino's face?" Alberto asked.

"Ah, Erminia," Giovanni began, and belched quietly, his cheeks glowing a bright pink from heat and wine.

"She is a sad story, really. Like me, she doesn't belong to this village."

"Where does she come from?" asked Fiammetta, feeding a piece of flat bread to Rosella.

"No one knows. I've been told she appeared one day after a violent storm, washed up on the rocks. She was a little girl, maybe eight, but it's hard to say for certain since she was tall even then. That was almost ten years ago."

"But can't she remember her family, or where she came from?" Bruno asked, plucking a handful of red grapes.

"Even if she did know, she couldn't tell us. She's mute."

"Is she deaf?" Alberto frowned and loosened the ties of his doublet.

"No. She answers to her name and the call of the goats. But she's never spoken a word or even cried out that I've heard. She is an imbecile, just smart enough to herd the goats and stay out of the way of a beating."

"Poveretta. She's so ugly," Silvia said, twisting a black curl around her finger.

"Except for her eyes," Matteo said softly. "I saw them when she grabbed my mask. A man could get lost in their color—clear blue, like Venetian glass."

"A mermaid, cast up from the sea," Giuliana joked, and playfully kicked the young man under the table. He blushed and looked away with a shrug.

"But mermaids are supposed to be beautiful," Silvia said.

"Perhaps they don't look so inviting on land," Giuliana argued. "Like a silver mackerel that turns putrid two days later on the fishmonger's slab."

Giovanni laughed. "Erminia is a poor soul, but good to the goats. Be kind to her, my friends, if you use her in your show tonight. She has seen little enough kindness in her years here."

Isabella put one white hand over Giovanni's and gave him a radiant smile. "My dear Giovanni, we will treat her with the utmost respect. Her plight suggests an interesting little drama to me. Let us pretend that she is a mermaid, disguised as a shepherdess as she searches on land for the man she loves—"

"Lelio, of course," Antonio put in. "She has seen his face as he peered over the sides of his ship bound for Genoa."

"No doubt returning from France, where his father Il Dottore sent him to stay out of trouble!" Fiammetta added.

"Only one night they had," Giuliana said, her hands clasped over her heart. "Whispering the lover's duet—she floating on the foamy surface of the waves, he leaning over the railing to see her face and . . . well her breasts, of course, naked in the moonlight."

Flavio held up his finger. "But his father, Il Dottore, is planning to marry Lelio off to Isabella, who is in love with someone else."

"Who will play the shepherdess?" Alberto asked.

"I will, Papa," Silvia answered gamely.

"You don't mind being ugly for awhile?"

"It's a disguise. A mask, like the men wear. But when it is removed, the pearl beneath will be revealed," she answered. "Take off Arlecchino's mask and poof . . . he disappears completely."

"Va bene," Alberto said, with a proud nod of his head.

"C-can I h-h-have a r-role?" Fabrizio asked. "I c-could be a s-s-ervant or Isabella's o-o-ther lover?"

Alberto turned a cold eye on the young man. "You will stay out of sight."

In the tense silence that followed, Isabella's eyes and gentle smile quietly beseeched Alberto to be lenient.

"Boh." Alberto exhaled. "I'm angry today. Tomorrow it will be over. But for now, it would be best if you took yourself to the shore, stuffed your mouth with stones, and shouted your lines to the sea. Maybe it'll help get rid of that stutter. Then ask me tomorrow on the road and we will see."

Fabrizio's face flushed a wine red to the tips of his ears. He kept his mouth tightly closed and nodded stiffly.

"Ah look, the sun at last," Giovanni announced, pointing to the gold rectangle of sunlight creeping into the open doorway. "It will be a beautiful evening after all!"

The troupe left their places at the tables, groaning as they stood, their arms cradling their full stomachs. They crowded in the doorway smiling at the late afternoon sun beaming down on the wet stones of the piazza. The air was clean, salty, and pine-scented. The last of the storm clouds were a grey ridge on the far horizon. Birds called in the jacaranda tree. The loud bang of shutters being thrown open broke the quiet calm of the piazza.

"Allora," Alberto said, and clapped his hands together. "To work. We'll give them a great show tonight!"

The Commedians spilled out into the piazza and, with the help of two boys from Giovanni's inn, they went about resetting the soggy stage. Only Fabrizio hung back by the door of the inn, his hands balled into fists. He knew he should set aside his anger and go and help. But he just couldn't bring himself to join the actors. They were going to perform tonight and he was going to the sea to mumble lines with a mouthful of stones. Giuliana glanced up at him from the trunks where she was pulling out costumes. She gave him a wistful smile and a light shrug.

Fabrizio was angry at her, too. If she hadn't distracted him with her scent, her mouth, her body, he might have managed to keep his hands on the mask instead of dropping it into the sea to grapple with her. "Merda," he swore, and started walking across the piazza, past the church, and under the archway where the road led to the sea.

He could already taste the stones, their hard round shapes crowding into his mouth, and the words oozing between them like mortar. He had tried the trick before. It had helped his diction, which, when he could speak without stuttering, was flawless. But Alberto was wrong. A mouthful of stones would do nothing to correct the stutter. The solution to that curse lay somewhere else and Fabrizio was damned if he knew where to look for it. At least it wasn't to be found in Giuliana's arms.

8

Over the piazza, the twilight sky was a soft lavender. A scattering of oil lamps lit the small stage. The curtains had been rehung, and they shivered lightly in the ocean breeze. The white blossoms of the jacaranda tree glowed like stars. Young Lelio, dressed in green, white, and gold silk leaned over the imaginary railing of a ship and whispered loving words to the mermaid. Antonio's curled yellow hair cascaded over his broad shoulders like a flow of wild honey. His unmasked face was brightened by makeup that accentuated the brooding quality of his eyes and the sensuality of his mouth. In the audience women watched, awed, as the words lingered on his reddened lips.

Silvia sat on the bare stage nearby, a shimmering gown of blue silk eddying around her knees. It was cut low in the front to expose the plump curves of her breasts outlined by scallops of stiffened lace. She had loosed her black hair and the wind played through it with the swirling motions of the tide. She answered Lelio with a song, her clear soprano rising over the hush of the crowd. Men nudged each other, their hands making silent gestures of admiration at Silvia's figure and voice.

The rest of the actors waited for their cues offstage, half-hidden in the shadows of the jacaranda tree. Alberto watched the performance with a keen eye, studying it for weaknesses and strengths. They would improvise it all tonight, and tomorrow they would discuss what worked and what didn't. If the show was successful, it might prove an unusual offering for the Spanish court in Milan. Alberto watched nervously, listening to Silvia, pleased when her improvised phrases matched Antonio's intensity. She was learning quickly and he felt a puff of pride lift his chest.

Pantelone's long black cloak was heavy on Alberto's shoulders in the warm summer night, but he was used to it. He wore the wool cape, the red hose, and the stuffed codpiece like a second skin. Though his mask rested on his forehead, Alberto had already affected Pantelone's backward slouch and dangling arms. The wine of excitement bubbled in his veins as the scene drew to a close and he heard the uscite, the exit speech, of the two lovers.

On the other side of the stage, Isabella smiled, preparing to join him on stage in the role of Pantelone's daughter. Dressed in a gown of yellow silk, her golden hair twined with ropes of pearls, she shone like a small sun. Alberto let the calm of experience settle over his excitement as he smiled back at her. Then he lowered Pantelone's mask.

The audience howled with laughter at Pantelone's entrance: the slouching walk, the money bag hanging at his waist, which was indistinguishable from the pouch of his overstuffed codpiece. Protectively clutching first one pouch and then the other, Pantelone complained about the dowry he was to spend on his daughter's marriage in a scratchy whine. Isabella floated over the stage, stealing the audience's attention with her melodious voice and expressive white hands, holding them mesmerized until Arlecchino rolled onto the stage like a flurry of autumn leaves.

On the fringes of the audience Erminia watched the performance with silent fascination. Beneath her matted black hair her crystalline blue eyes absorbed the twilight's lavender hue turning them into living amethysts. She stared, mouth agape, at Lelio's handsome figure strutting back and forth, and frowned when his heart was captivated by the false mermaid's song. When Arlecchino somersaulted on and gobbled a chicken leg, she clapped her hands over her mouth to swallow the sound of her laughter.

Her foster brother Pietro guffawed at Arlecchino's antics while his young wife, panting under the burden of another pregnancy, stared enviously at Isabella's trim figure. In the tight press of the crowd, the younger brother, Nicolo, leaned his body against Erminia. When she refused to respond, he pinched her hard on the buttocks. She didn't cry out but stepped back onto his foot and ground her heel into his instep. He yelped and swore until two men wanting to hear Isabella shut him up. Erminia moved forward, parting the crowd with the crude points of her elbows until she stood close to the front.

Arlecchino was fishing off the end of the stage and every few seconds he brought up something unexpected: a weathered boot, a barrel stave, a woman's petticoat. He spoke to the audience, engaging them in a heart-to-heart talk about the rigors of a fishing life, how hungry it made him. He was grinning, his lips stretched wide when he happened to glance down and catch Erminia's gaze.

A sudden spark of light flashed in Erminia's eyes, crisp as summer lightning. She was entranced by Arlecchino's mask, shining black as polished ebony, the leather skin so slick it appeared to sweat. Its face spoke to her, rousing her emotions. The dark pupils of the mask widened as the man hidden beneath took fright at the blaze of her eyes. Arlecchino's words stumbled; he blinked slowly and managed to look away. He threw down his fishing rod and danced drunkenly across the stage.

A sharp thrill slid like quicksilver through Erminia's blood. The actor behind the mask would never have looked beyond her dirty hair and rough skin. He looked at the world with the limited vision of a mortal man. But the masks saw the world differently. And the mask of Arlecchino had dived below her ugly carapace and discovered the well of magic in her eyes.

Erminia had let the magic flare, let the man behind the mask feel it pierce him like an arrow. She should be more careful, she told herself. But it was irresistible after ten years of hiding what she was. Her heart beat fiercely, warnings clamoring in her head.

Erminia looked down at her dirty chapped hands and a silent sob caught her throat. To be unloved was punishment enough. But not to

blaze with the ether of desire and fill every corner of a man's thoughts
with her song was almost more than her nature could bear. Dry tears
salted her cheeks as she forced the light to dim behind her sea-blue
eyes.

Only when Fiammetta announced the second act did Erminia dare
lift her head again to the stage. Her face was a collection of roughly
sketched planes. But beneath the husk of her skin Erminia struggled
with the flame of her true self. She chafed at the prison of her mask and
the rank smell of sweat from the audience filled her nostrils. Even the
muck of the goats on the hem of her skirts offended her.

What was happening to her? Erminia wondered, swaying as though
pulled by the tides. For nearly ten years she had managed to keep quiet,
to trap her desires within her leathery husk. And now a fool's mask had
awakened all her longings. How was this possible?

Erminia watched Il Dottore quarreling with Pulchinella over the
dowry price. The two black masks glistened in the lamplight, the stiff
features seeming to dance with fleeting expressions. Garbled Latin
spewed from Il Dottore's mouth as his thick eyebrows quivered with
pomposity. Pulchinella lifted his huge nose into the air and wrinkled it
in derision. Beneath the masks, the actor's bodies grew fat or thin,
stooped-shouldered or nimble, obedient to the demands of the mask.

Erminia understood it now. The masks' unique magic was like a bon-
ing knife sliding the length of her spine, separating her flesh from the
thin film of her disguise. She knew she should leave, but remained where
she stood, entranced.

As they took the stage, each masked character wrapped her in a net
of silvery longing, whetted her parched lips, and released the songs
buried in her throat like bubbles breaking the surface of the sea. Under
the starry blossoms of the jacaranda tree, magic breathed in every word
the masked Commedians spoke. Erminia could see it rising in a band of
colors and shapes around their faces and their hands. Pulchinella's fingers gleamed gold from fingering his coins, Arlecchino curled and un-
curled his cat's claws, his long pink tongue licking his greasy chin. Il
Dottore's fingers, stained with ink, lengthened into quill points as he
pronounced his pedantries.

Erminia watched, her heart pounding faster as she inhaled the dusty
fragments of magic swirling in lamplight. Silvia's song made Erminia
ache, not because it reminded her of her own forced silence, but because
it could not touch the ravishing beauty of the true siren's cry. How far
from herself she was, Erminia grieved, how folded and withered she
had lived. Orpheus be damned! A bleak despair bloomed darkly in her
heart.

Agitated, Erminia tensed, hearing her foster brother sidle next to her in the crowd once more.

"Up the ass, goddamn it," Nicolo threatened savagely in her ear. "One of these days I'll give it to you up the ass." He pinched her hard again, his rough nails trying to pierce her skin.

Foam-flecked tears welled in her eyes and bled into the tiny space between her skin and the dirty surface of her mask, trickling down her cheeks and throat, weakening the carapace. Erminia turned to face him and he was leering at her as if glad to see her tears. How small he was, she thought, and pathetic, like a mangy cur. What chance had he to know the sublime ecstasy of love? How easy it would be for her to bestow that blessing and that curse upon him.

Erminia felt where her tears had dissolved the outer shell of her mask. She inhaled sharply and the skin tore in a jagged line from her breastbone to her cheek. She parted her lips and the skin tore over her mouth, her nose, and her forehead, the radiance of her white skin blistering through the dissolving husk. The wind blew her tangled hair out of her face, and her sapphire eyes ignited to capture Nicolo's gaze.

Terror leapt into his eyes. Like the mask of Arlecchino, he struggled to turn away, but she would not release him. The edges of his lips twitched. She grabbed him by the bosom of his shirt, her eyes boring into the shallow well of his heart. Now will I sing for you! she thought angrily, drunk with the dust of the masks' magic.

Sound boiled in her throat, filled the cavern of her mouth, pressed against her teeth. She tilted back her head and released one long note in a thin stream of blue light. Somewhere between the tines of her backbone she mourned her broken silence, her broken vow. But the flowing sound scraped the hard crust of loneliness from her skin like the sea tearing the mussels from the rocks.

Once freed, Erminia could no more swallow her voice into silence than she could stop the arms of the moon from pulling the sea every night to the shore. It had been wrong to hide it. Silence was a curse laid on a curse.

Dimly, Erminia heard other sounds swirling about the edges of her song. Human sounds. Swearing, terrified shouts, men roaring, women screaming. A child bawled for its mother and a man called out the name of Isabella. But those sounds meant nothing. They were only ordinary noises from the mouths of mortals.

But the siren's song was created from the foam that gave birth to Venus. It was a gift and a curse, the howl of the inferno and the sweet descant of paradisio. Her voice was so pure that all, even the masks, must bow before its authority and listen. Her song coiled in the ears, blinded the eyes, filled the nostrils. It crashed over mortals like sea spray, drowning them in their own tears.

Erminia felt the surge of panic around her as the crowd, unable to flee her song, huddled beneath its power. She took pity on their weakness and dampened its razored edges. The light of her voice changed, softening from a sapphire blaze into the muted green of the deep sea, as she gathered the terrified cries and transformed them into a hard shell, built of a thousand dead dreams. She let her song cover the villagers like a mask and shelter them from the madness brought on by hearing her voice.

Erminia closed her eyes as she sang. Her body stretched thin and high, swaying like the sea grass beneath the rising tide. She filled every corner of the village with her voice, flooded it with her passion, covered the cold, rumpled beds, the empty cradles, even the straw still warm from the couple who had stolen away. She laid her voice over the last shouted curses, the last pleas for mercy, the last cries for love until all was drowned in the depths of her watery song.

Fatigue touched her. The greening sound of her voice began to falter, the ribbon of music to fade. When she opened her eyes, she saw the last notes trapped in the flowers of the jacaranda tree. A wind freed them and carried them in a handful of leaves out to the sea. Her limbs felt heavy as sea-sodden wood. She gazed at her arms gleaming white in the moonlight and then she lifted her weary head to look around her. Slowly, she raised a hand to cover her mouth.

Her song had transformed the village into a world of brittle coral. The high-walled houses, even the dour face of the church, had been covered with the terraced bark of coral cliffs. Slender arms of coral reached out into the night from the lintels of the shops and branched from the covered archways of the street. The village stood in the moonlight as though the ocean had receded, revealing this strange configuration from its hidden floor.

The villagers too had been encased by coral. A mother, her features masked by the pocked surface of a grey coral, clutched coral children to the hardness of her coral skirts. Pietro's pregnant wife lay on the ground, her bone-white form curved around her belly, her hair a carpet of mussels over her back. Erminia moved among them silently, touching them in wonder. Bleached white faces with eyes of abalone stared back at her. A child's face was pink coral, an old woman's teeth were black coral.

Erminia went to the stage and looked up at the actors. Anguish pricked her at the sight of their coral faces, their arms held up to express themselves one last time before the hard shell encased them in silence.

Only the masks remained untouched by the transformation. They stood out in stark contrast, a black satiny skin against bleached whiteness. Liming the edge of the masks, a narrow band of gold light shimmered. Arlecchino stared out at Erminia, his coral lips parted to speak, his hand held up to her. The patched diamonds of his costume were mimicked in pink and green coral. But in the dark holes of the mask his eyes were a lifeless grey.

What have I done? Erminia asked herself as she turned slowly in the quiet village. No wind could rustle the coral leaves of the jacaranda tree. She touched her face and found the hard skin of the mask renewed over her skin. She looked at her hands, brown and chafed, the nails dirty. What have I done, she thought bitterly, but lay one curse against another?

As great as the joy she had felt in singing was the cyclone of despair that now claimed her. She sat down amid the coral statues, her knees drawn up to her chest, her arms wrapped around her legs. Orpheus had won again. That head of his was laughing and she could almost hear the mocking sound of it in the scraping of the waves. Laying her head on her knees, she wept silently.

Much farther up the beach, well beyond the village, Fabrizio had spent the evening casting pebbles into the ocean. What was the point of this stupid exercise? he wondered. It wouldn't help. He had been standing here all night, the sea sighing answers to his perfectly spoken lines. Why couldn't he speak in public? He remembered with frustration reciting pages of poetry for an audience of his adoring mother and aunts when he was only ten years old. How they had marveled at his skill, his maturity, his ability to memorize so many beautiful words! How he had made them weep!

Fabrizio had always known he was meant to be a great actor. He had known it from the moment he was born—a moment he could remember with clarity. It was just like the theater: the dark hushed quiet of the wings, waiting for the cue, the distant light of the stage, bright beyond the dark, folded curtains. And the faces, peering at him through the darkness, eagerly awaiting his first entrance on the stage. In his mother's womb he had prepared his voice, and the final squeeze through the narrow canal between her thighs had cleared his throat. He pushed hard through the dark curtains and blinked at the sudden wash of light as he slid headfirst onto the wooden table. Turning over in the stream of blood and water, he cried out his first lines to the women waiting to see him.

They clapped and wept and cried out "bravo, bravo, che bello!" when he waved his fists in the air. His mother lifted his slick body and praised him. His aunts had taken him to the sea and washed him, stroking his cheek every time he cried out new lines of poetry.

His mother had loved this first performance. She had praised him for it almost every day he had lived in her house by the sea. Fabrizio put a hand to his face, remembering the sound of their applause and the gentleness of their hands as they wrapped him in warm swaddling and then passed him from woman to woman, each planting a kiss on his round cheeks.

"Cazzo!" he swore, hurling a pebble into the sea. It had never again been that easy. He would probably spend the rest of his life trying to experience that one perfect moment between his arrival on the stage and an audience's adoring reception.

The sea tossed a wave up on the shore as if to protest the sting of so many pebbles. As Fabrizio danced back from the foaming water, he heard the first screams from the village. He stopped, frozen by the sound, and the water rushed over his boots. The cold shook him and he moved farther up the shore, listening with growing fear to the sounds of the village in despair. He ran up the beach toward the looming shadow of the church. A fire perhaps, he thought, a lamp knocked over by one of Arlecchino's pratfalls. But there was no smell of smoke and the voices were growing softer, not louder, as he neared.

Fabrizio scrambled up the steps to the church which crumbled under his pounding feet. Hadn't they been stone before? He found the covered alley that led to the piazza and was startled by the strange sight of coral branches reaching down from the curved roof. There were no sounds now, no voices to be heard.

As he stepped into what remained of the lamplight in the piazza, Fabrizio halted in amazement. Hoping to wake himself from a horrible dream, he slapped his hand to his forehead, then wandered dumbstruck, studying the frightened faces of the villagers, their bodies twisted into trunks of coral.

"Madonna," he whispered, and crossed himself feverishly. He edged cautiously toward the stage. Alberto was holding out one hand as if to ward off something, while his other arm clutched Isabella's waist. Their skin was grey in the moonlight, Isabella's skirts lined with the fragments of shells. Silvia was on the ground trying to raise herself on thin white arms of coral. Bruno and Matteo, still masked as Pulchinella and Arlecchino, were hunched over, as though their cloaks of black coral weighed them down.

"What has happened here?" Fabrizio asked to break the unnerving silence.

A finger tapped Fabrizio on the shoulder and he leapt into the air, his heart racing with terror. He twisted around, arms held out before him to grapple with whatever demon had done this deed. Instead, he found the shepherdess Erminia, her head bowed, her face hidden by her matted black hair.

"What?" he shouted, his heart slamming into his ribs. "What the fuck is it?"

Erminia was silent.

Fabrizio's tongue darted out to lick his dry lips. "What?" he demanded of the shepherdess again. "What has happened?"

The woman said nothing. She raised her sad, stupid face and her fingers touched her lips. She shook her head and then dropped her fingers.

"You can't talk, can you?" Fabrizio said, remembering Giovanni's gossip.

Erminia nodded again.

"Show me then. Show me what happened," he insisted.

Erminia raised her hand, pointed to her lips, and opened her mouth. Her fingers drifted in the air in front of her mouth suggesting singing.

Fabrizio frowned. "Someone sang a song?" he asked.

She nodded.

"That's it?" he demanded.

She nodded again.

"Who?"

Erminia touched her fingers to her own throat.

"You?" he asked. "But you don't even talk, much less sing."

Erminia's eyes flashed with anger, the eerie blue light brightening the darkness. She raised her hands again and there appeared between her fingers the twirling form of a woman, caught in a whirlpool.

Fabrizio gasped as he peered at the vision turning gracefully in the water. The woman had radiant white skin and kelp-black hair. Her head was thrown back and her mouth opened. Bubbles rose to the surface of the whirlpool. Suddenly a man dressed like a sailor tumbled into the whirlpool, arms held out. The woman embraced him, her hair swirling to hide his face, and pulled him deeper into the narrow funnel. Erminia brushed the air with her fingertips and the vision faded.

"Madonna di Christo, mamma mia," Fabrizio babbled, crossing himself rapidly. He stared up at Erminia's blazing eyes. "What are you? A demon of hell?"

Erminia shook her head quickly and stared out at the sea. She pointed to the waves crashing against the low seawall.

"Siren? Are you a siren?" Fabrizio whispered.

She nodded slowly.

"Washed up to shore? Just as Giuliana joked?" Fabrizio's voice squeaked with emotion.

She nodded again.

"Why are you here and not in the sea where you belong?"

She shrugged, her hands trying to find a way to explain.

"But why did you do this? And why attack the Libertini? They were nice people. They never gave you any reason!" Fabrizio spoke rapidly, trying to fill the dreadful silence with the sound of his voice.

Erminia gave a quiet sigh. Her fingers pulled together into the sign of the curse. Then she pointed to herself.

"You! You think you're cursed?" Fabrizio roared, anger replacing his fear. "What about me? I paid out the last of my inheritance from that shitfaced bastard of a fa-fa-ther of mine to join this troupe. No one else would take me as I am. Now everything's ruined. You've ruined my whole life, busted my balls, cut me across the throat. It's no fucking good. I can't go on. That's it, I'm going to kill myself."

Fabrizio grabbed for the nearest dagger he could find, which was conveniently attached to the belt of an old villager. As soon as he stabbed himself in the chest, the coral shattered into dust.

"Oh, merda, I can't even do that," he moaned, and sat down in the dirt, cradling his head between his hands.

Erminia tapped him on the shoulder with a finger. Furious, he ignored her. She hit him again, this time a little harder.

"Ow, damn it," he complained, and rubbed his shoulder. "What do you want? Can't you see I'm starving myself to death? Leave me alone."

Erminia waved an image into the air. It was a red-faced squalling infant.

"Go fuck yourself," Fabrizio snapped, and waved away the image with his hand.

Erminia caught his hand in her strong grip while she shaped a new image—a maze rising up out of the center of a large town. A name was carved into the huge wooden gates.

"Labirinto," Fabrizio read softly. He looked at Erminia, awed by the strange blue glimmer in her eyes. "The maze of the cursed?"

She nodded and released his hand.

"If we go there, can it undo this?" he asked, pointing to the village.

Erminia gave a small smile. Her eyes held a fragile hope.

"And my stutter?"

Erminia shrugged, palms turned upward.

"Why not?" Fabrizio said, putting words to her gesture. "Perhaps our curses are not so different. I can't speak my part on stage, you can't sing in the ocean where you belong. And every time we try and open our mouths, we make a mess of things."

Erminia nodded, casting a longing look at the quiet sea. Fabrizio looked up to the black masks shimmering with a golden light on the frozen faces of Arlecchino and Pulchinella. With a grunt, he hoisted himself off the ground and carefully stripped the masks from the coral faces. He tied the straps around the front of his doublet so that the two faces stared out at Erminia from his chest.

"Let's go," he said. "There's nothing to be gained by staying here."

He started walking up the narrow road leading away from the center of the village. Fabrizio thought he heard Erminia sigh, but when he turned around, he saw that it was only the waves crashing against the sea-wall. Erminia was following him, her face hidden by the tangle of her dark hair.

9

In the middle of the night, the young priest Don Gianlucca di Baptistta awoke from a disturbing dream. It was the same dream he had had every night since the night he made love to Anna Forsetti. The images of the dream scattered as his body jerked awake, but a sense of anguish lingered in his breast. He looked around, disoriented by the rustle of leaves and the cool night air blowing on his warm face. The whitewashed walls of his cell had disappeared.

He remembered that it had been three days since he had left his cell in San Pantelon. He was no longer in Venice, but somewhere on the road between Ferrara and Bologna, sleeping in a vineyard, with clusters of newly formed grapes hanging just above his head.

He groaned and closed his eyes so as not to see the grapes. They reminded him of her: their roundness, their sturdy scent, the tartness of the juice. He touched his face, almost imagining a mask lay there, but found only his sweating skin.

"Maledizione!" he swore. He sat up and wrapped his woolen robes around his legs. He hugged his knees close to his chest and stared out at the soft rolling hillside and the moonlight scattered over the broad leaves of the vineyard. He tried to match his agitated spirit to the calm of the night, slow his breathing until it was as easy as the wind shuddering the leaves. He relaxed his shoulders, rounding them into the shape of the rolling hills. Even his feet tried to sink into the earth to root him as simply as these vines, to be tended by others' hands.

But the anguish crept into his thoughts, and he tensed, hearing again the frail voice that called him by name. That was the tyranny of the dream. Someone was calling to him, begging to be found. But always in the dream the way was dark, the path beneath his feet twisted as the gnarled stems of the vine. He searched in vain, brushing aside the heavy boughs of trees, wading through a pile of bones. A small glimmer of light would bob before him. But no matter how hard he chased it, it wavered just beyond his reach. Only in dreams could he see the phantom light. But awake, he still felt its presence, its hushed plaintive voice as palpable as a beating heart.

"Anna, what have you cursed me with?" he asked the grapes, and touched them with a finger. They trembled but did not answer.

It had to be her fault. Until that night with Anna nothing had ever scratched beneath his skin, not even the faith he had assumed at his father's insistence. It was either that or be sent off to the army. He might never have been forced into such a choice if he had been a better son. But he had read somewhere that a family's wealth was only good for three generations: one to build it, one to sustain it, and the third generation to squander it all. Don Gianlucca shrugged to the vines. His grandfather and father had worked hard all their lives to amass the family fortune. But Don Gianlucca was of the third generation. Was it his fault then that money was easy to lose gambling? Was it not the natural order that he should spend his time with his friends and with women? Don Gianlucca truly believed that his father's stern attempts to make something of him were wasted. But his father was determined. Redeem thyself, he had commanded, be it in the armies of the duke or the pope. So Don Gianlucca had taken up the cloth, knowing the clergy had as many sins as their flocks and more opportunities to commit them without getting killed on a battlefield.

Venice was a reasonable place to be a priest. One could be pious and decadent all in the same breath. The gold ceilings of the Basilica gleamed no less bright than the gold hair of the Venetian beauties who came to him for confession. And there was Carnevale. Though the church condemned the paganism of the masks, every year the carnival flourished like a last hot lick of fire before all cooled into the somber ashes of Lent.

"Anna, what have you done to me?" Don Gianlucca wondered again, and held his head. The wind rustled with his name. He was certain he heard the faint sounds of someone weeping. He felt a touch on his shoulder, but when he turned, it was only a stray vine brushing his cowl.

He had enjoyed their night together. Savored it, in fact. He'd even enjoyed the morning, sick with wine as he was. He had wondered whether Anna's attempts to convince him that he'd had a religious vision were for his benefit or that of the older man and girl in the room. He had wanted to laugh out loud. The dog licking his feet had been hilarious. He had thought to join her in her little Commedia just in case the man staring at him open-mouthed might decide to defend Anna's honor, or his own for that matter.

But something had happened. When Don Gianlucca glanced down at her while she tied on his robe, he had seen something in her face that had not been there the day before. Then her eyes had been hard and bright, reflecting the brilliant gleam of his own lust. Her mouth had been as red as blood, her teeth white. Everything about her had exuded confidence and strength. From behind Pantelone's mask she had bullied him in bed and he had enjoyed it.

But seeing the woman's mask he'd worn lying on the sheets, he experienced an unexpected epiphany. The mask was a parody of Anna's face, beautiful but rigid, without any doubt or sadness. That was not the Anna he saw kneeling by his side. Anna's face was soft with age, her mouth bruised, and her eyes, when she looked up at him, haunted by pain.

What else could it have been but grace that had enlightened him? Grace stabbing him with its spiritual lance to make him aware of her hidden sorrow, of her need. Pain had welled up in Don Gianlucca's chest, seized his heart, captured his breath. The sunlight had blazed into the room, but an even brighter light blazed throughout his body. He thought he would break into tears. His own vows rang in his head: "whose sins you shall forgive, they are forgiven them." So he had put his hand on her head and absolved her to free her of her nameless sorrow.

For the first time in his life, Don Gianlucca had given something precious to someone else instead of squandering it. And she had spurned him, not recognizing the value of the gift. Well, why should she? he thought, and plucked one of the grapes. It was underripe, sour and bitter on his tongue. He spit it out with a grimace. He had been, until that moment, just what she had called him, a whoring, drunken priest. But that fierce moment of grace in Anna's bedroom had been real. He had seen the pain in her eyes, seen it in the distance between the mask and her own true face.

Don Gianlucca rolled over on his stomach and laid his head in the cradle of his arms. He had tried to help her. She had refused the gesture and had given him this nightmare, this aching dream of someone hovering, whispering, beseeching.

What was it? A demon? A soul? Was it even Anna's, he wondered, or had she unleashed something in his own soul? He had sent a map of Labirinto to her as a parting gift. Even if she never left Venice, he wanted her to know that he understood that she was plagued by misery. Perhaps in the map she might find the courage to return to the source of her sorrow and arrive at forgiveness for herself.

Don Gianlucca himself was making the pilgrimage to Labirinto because the dreams seemed to propel him into the dark turns of a maze so vast and full of mystery that he was certain it was Labirinto—Labirinto with its reputation for magic, where curses flapped like crows down the dark corridors. Perhaps, he thought, within its walls and twisting paths, he would catch the circle of light that called to him.

Anna lay on her back staring angrily at the black beams crossing the low ceiling of their room. What kind of an idiota was she? she asked herself. What sort of stupidly romantic, ridiculously impulsive, and absurdly foolish woman? Hadn't she learned her lesson already? She had let her blind romantic heart lead her into despair over that cruel man. And now it was leading her on a goose chase to a place she'd never seen, in search of a cure she didn't dare hope to find.

The trip from Venice to the mainland had been horrendous. Anna could only afford passage for herself and Mirabella on a sea-battered barca da pesca. The little fishing boat sat unsteadily in the water, catching every swell of the lagoon and bouncing from island to island. The fisherman who poled them along was a craggy, dour old man with precious few teeth and a nasty temper. It started to rain before they reached the mainland, and even though it was summer, on the sea, it felt like autumn.

Lily, they discovered, didn't take well to water. As soon as they approached the lagoon, she began vomiting. She flooded the basin of the boat with the leavings of her stomach. Anna wondered that such a small dog could contain so much. Finally, against Mirabella's protestations, Anna held the quaking creature over the side of the boat so she could puke in the sea. The old fisherman swore savagely at them in a thick lisping dialect.

On the mainland they had purchased a small cart and a mangy-looking donkey to pull it. The road was rough, the donkey slow and plodding. Any romantic notions Anna had of traveling to Labirinto had rapidly soured. After an exhausting day of travel, they had finally found lodgings for the night in a ramshackle inn. The cheese at dinner had been a hard rind, the bread stale, the wine like vinegar. Even Lily wouldn't touch the mutton stew. Men stared at them in the common room; and when the drink had loosened their tongues as well as their doublet strings, Anna decided it was wiser if they got out of sight.

They found their room, a mean affair under the eaves, and bolted the door. Wearily, they had shed their clothes and gotten into the lumpy bed, first pulling back the covers and brushing off the black dots of fleas. Mirabella had been quietly seething since the lagoon ride, giving all her attention to Lily. But the sagging bed forced them into intimacy as they rolled into the soft valley of its center.

Now it was impossible for Anna to sleep. She could hear the men carousing loudly downstairs, slamming their tankards on the table, and crying out for more drink. Anna licked her lips. She wanted a bottle of wine in which to drown her misery. Why not just go home and admit it had all been a foolish mistake? And then she shuddered thinking of her ravaged studio and the twisting thorns in her belly. She must go. At home there was only sadness and pain.

"Mamma, are you awake?" Mirabella asked softly.

"Yes, amore," Anna answered.

"Can't you sleep?"

"No."

They lay quiet a moment longer and then Mirabella sat up. Anna looked at her daughter's round face, free of the glint of her spectacles. She's like a cherub, Anna thought fondly.

"What is it?" Mirabella asked. "Is it Lily? I know she's a pest. I probably should have left her at home."

"No, no, it's all right. Lily's annoying, but she isn't the problem," Anna replied, and touched her daughter on the cheek. "The problem is me. I'm wondering if I've made a good decision dragging us on this pilgrimage."

"Ah." Mirabella sighed and lay back down. The crease in the bed drew them closer together. "It doesn't matter right now whether it was a good decision or a bad one," Mirabella said slowly. "It matters that you made a decision to do something."

"Instead of doing nothing, you mean?" Anna asked.

"Yes."

"Have I done so much nothing?"

"It seems that way."

"I have been . . . distracted," Anna said. "I didn't think you noticed."

"Not notice? How could I not notice? Oh, Mamma, if you only knew how much I miss—" Mirabella stopped.

Anna listened to her daughter choke as though it was hard for her to speak.

"What do you miss?" Anna whispered.

"Everything," the girl replied sadly. "Everything about our life before—before you changed."

"Before. How I have learned to hate that word," Anna said harshly.

"But it's true. There were better times before. Even after Papa died, we could still be happy. I had you, and you had the masks."

"Do you think I've abandoned you, Mirabella?" Anna asked.

"Have your masks abandoned you, Mamma?" she returned. "You never work on them."

Anna sighed deeply and pulled her daughter into the well of her shoulder. She had forgotten how comforting Mirabella's soft shape could feel. "No, amore mio. The masks, like you, wait for me. But I can't work. Something happens to me when I try. It's like a hedge of thorns in my womb and it tears at me. I've tried drowning it in wine, but the roots only grow stronger. I've tried ignoring it in the distractions of love affairs, but it yields new thorns to torture me."

Anna wanted to explain to Mirabella about the man who had cursed her, planting the hateful thorns in her womb. But a loud banging at the door prevented her.

"Open up! Open up!" a man's voice called drunkenly. The bolt rattled in its slot as he hammered at the door.

"Bestiale!" Anna hissed.

"Mamma what do we do?" Mirabella whispered. She had pulled the sheets up to her chin. Lily burrowed under a blanket.

"Open up. I'm here to fuck you! I saw you whores making eyes at me. Open up and give me what I want!" he roared. "Or I'll break the door down!"

"Madonna Santa! Dio!" Mirabella clutched the sheets tighter. "Do you think he means it?"

Anna heaved herself out of the sagging bed. She quickly crossed the tiny room to stand before the quaking door. She bent down by a knothole in the wood and called out in as deep a man's voice as she could muster.

"Fuck off, you shitty, bed-pissing hangman's knot! Or I'll shove my Catalan lance up her arsehole."

There was a heartbeat of silence. Then the man on the other side of the door resumed his bellowing. "Who's in there?"

"Il Capitano Matamoros, Killer of Moors, you slimy snot-nosed, prickless son of a bitch! I'll beat you to a pulp if you don't shove off! The women are mine!"

In the bed Mirabella clapped her hand over her mouth to keep from laughing. Anna just prayed that the man was too drunk to recognize the voice of Commedia's Il Capitano, king of cowards. On stage, how quickly his bluff vanished under the stinging lash of Colombina's insults. But for now, she needed the Spanish braggart's speeches to protect them.

There was another hushed silence on the other side of the door, then a low conversation which she couldn't quite make out. Anna realized a second man was there too. One drunk fool was bad enough. But two! Her palms were sweating, though her body was cold.

"When are you gonna be done with the women?" the second man demanded in a slurred country accent.

Anna shouted into the knothole, "Get lost, you pestilent blobs of phlegm. A man like me likes to load the cannon at least five times before he's spent. Take your limp pricks out to the barn and play with yourselves, you fuckless wonders."

Anna tucked her ear to the knothole and bit her knuckle.

"I'm too drunk to fight," one muttered to the other. "Let him keep the whores. Maybe they'll give him the pox."

"I hate those fucking Spaniards."

"Yeah. But he swears like an Italian."

"Learned it from us."

"Too bad he didn't learn how to die. C'mon, let's drink. We'll get the bastard back in the morning."

Anna heard them stumble off, their footsteps clumping down the stairs. She slipped back into bed and put her arms around Mirabella. It was only then that she realized she was trembling.

"Mamma, are you scared?" Mirabella asked. "You're shaking."

"No, just cold," Anna lied. "Go on now, go to sleep. We have a long way to go tomorrow."

"Mamma, you're so brave," the girl said.

"It's only a mask and words. Just an act," she answered lightly, trying to brush away the danger as no more than a harmless scene in a drama she had watched a hundred times at Carnevale. She didn't want to think of how close she had come to ruining her daughter's life with her impetuous decision to seek a cure in the maze.

Later, as the inn settled again into peaceful quiet, Anna heard a complaining voice coming from the bag of masks. Half-asleep, she listened awhile and recognized the Castilian accent of Il Capitano, annoyed with her for having made so free with his reputation.

"Hey," she grumbled to the mask, "five times in one night is good enough for any man's reputation."

"Should have been six," he groused. "Next time, make it six!"

"Boh!" Anna groaned, and turned over in the bed, drawing the musty pillows over her head to muffle his voice.

Roberto sat at the table, his chin resting in his hand, and gazed blankly into the soft glow of the beeswax candles. The candlelight folded over the rounded tops of pears gathered in a bowl near his elbow. Crumbs of cheese and bread were scattered over the white linen cloth. A bottle of wine waited, half-empty. The quiet night was broken now and again by a gondolier singing himself home in the canal below the window. Normally, Roberto loved the melancholy sound of their voices, the love songs sweet as marzipan. But not tonight.

In fact, in the last two days, it seemed as if everything about Venice had changed. It was as though when Anna had left, she took the light with her, muting the golden glitter of San Marco's mosaics, stripping the canals of their greens and robbing the tiles of the ducal palace of their shell pink, turning them grey and ugly. Even Roberto's taste buds had dulled in her absence. One piece of fruit was as much like another. Cheese was like gruel, and the best of his wines was flat and tasteless. Could one woman do all that? Rob him of his pleasure in his city? In food and wine? And all this time, he had thought it was Venice he loved. But then, he had never thought, not for one moment, that Anna would ever leave.

They had been friends for ten years. It was her masks that had brought them together. When she had started making her own masks after her husband's death, they had appeared almost at once everywhere in Venice. He had seen them on the faces of actors performing on the small stages lining the grand Piazza San Marco. He had met them at private parties held in the palazzos of Venice's wealthier merchants. At Carnevale one could pick out a Forsetti mask from the sea of masked faces flowing through the narrow calli and filling the campos. Only Forsetti masks boasted expressions of humor and tragedy at the same time. They were full of rapture one moment, scorn the next. They could leer and they could weep. They could cough out obscenities and they could sing poetry. They bristled with arrogance.

Roberto had gone to visit Anna's studio to buy a mask of Pantelone for himself. He blinked at the candles, remembering the first time he had seen her. It had been like a dunking in a canal in April. Her beauty had nearly frozen him to the threshold of her studio. He stared, mesmerized by the pale olive sheen of her skin, the ruddy hue of her cheeks. She was simply dressed, her sleeves rolled back while she worked, a dirty muslin apron covering her plain blue dress. Heavy blond hair lay coiled at the nape of her neck. Her dark brown eyes sparkled when she looked up at him, her full mouth lifted in a questioning smile. She had laughed when he grew flustered and mangled the words to his request.

Mirabella had been a little girl then, six years old, but the solemn blue eyes that blinked at him seemed too wise for her child's face. Her father was recently dead. And her mother had found solace for her grief by working in the studio, feverishly producing masks to tame the beasts of her loneliness. Roberto had chatted with Mirabella that day. She, too, was lonely and nowhere near as good as her mother at hiding her sadness. Moved by her plight, Roberto had brought Mirabella Bobo as a gift the following week. In those days, the hound was a rowdy young dog, as in need of affection as Mirabella herself.

Roberto had decided shortly after that first visit that he would offer Anna protection. There was nothing romantic involved of course. No, no, that would have been unseemly. She was only recently widowed, after all. He would be her patron, see to it that her masks fetched the highest prices and found themselves in the noblest hands, not only in Venice but throughout Italy and Europe. Later, when Anna's period of mourning was past, Roberto had convinced himself that Anna would never be interested in marrying him. He had thought himself wise because he refrained from making any overtures that she might regard as romantic. He had wanted her friendship, her trust more than her heart.

"What a collection of shit," he muttered now, slapping his palm against his forehead. The candlelight fluttered at his breath and the shadows danced over the walls. "What I really wanted was her. All of her, in my arms, in my bed, in my house, instead of just in my imagination. Why couldn't I have told her that? Why did I have to be such a coward and wait until it was too late?" At Roberto's feet, Bobo lay asleep. He whimpered and his legs twitched.

"Uffa! I'm like you, Bobo," Roberto said. "Only dreaming of chasing rabbits."

I am a cautious man, he thought. A careful man. I think before I do anything. I look before I enter a barca, pay my taxes before they are due, walk the same way every day to the piazza even though I couldn't possibly get lost in this damn city if I tried.

"Perhaps, Roberto, it's time you did the unexpected. Go after her."

Roberto's eyebrows rose in surprise at his own suggestion. Maybe he should go after her. His eyebrows dropped into a frown. He wasn't prepared for a journey. He'd need to pack. He'd need to make sure his business was secured before he left. That would take, oh, say a week.

"Vaffanculo, Roberto," he said aloud, and again his eyebrows went up. "Why not just stay home and fuck yourself? A week you say? A week and you'll die from the dullness of this place without her. Go, Roberto. Go now! Some things don't wait for your careful plans."

Hearing Roberto speak, Bobo roused himself, rested his greying snout on Roberto's knee, and wagged his tail.

"So you agree with this buffune, eh, Bobo?" Roberto asked, rubbing the dog behind his ears. "You think I should go after them?" The dog huffed a bark and then licked Roberto's hand.

"Va bene. I'll leave tomorrow. First light." Roberto looked back at the flickering candle flame. "Is that soon enough for you?" he asked. And getting no dissenting answer he decided it was.

Simonetta was riding hard on the road to Parma. Her hands, too tired to clutch the reins, lay pressed against the stallion's sweat-damp neck. She was so weary that she could hardly think. The urge to flee didn't need much thought. It was purely instinctual, and running as fast as any set of legs would carry her far outweighed fatigue and hunger. She and the stallion were alone on the road, the night cloaking them in darkness. What moon there was lay hidden behind a bank of clouds.

Simonetta glanced behind her. She knew he would come for her. Well, not her exactly—but the belted sword that lay heavy on her waist and the horse between her thighs that galloped even though he must be exhausted. For two nights she had ridden Lapone, stopping only briefly to let him rest. In the daylight hours, she curled up to sleep, hidden in a copse of trees one day, an abandoned farm on another.

The moon escaped from behind the bank of clouds and a shaft of silver light caught them on the dark road. The brilliant light startled the weary stallion. His head reeled back, and his swift stride broke as he danced away from the sudden spill of light. He raised up on his haunches, raked the band of eerie light with his hooves. Then he fell forward again with Simonetta clinging to his neck, her legs pressed tightly to his sides. Finally, he stood stood perfectly still, his head bowed between his forelocks, his great chest heaving and his haunches trembling.

"Come, Lapone," Simonetta urged, giving the reins a light tap. The stallion flattened his ears against his skull and stepped away from the glowing band of moonlight. "Don't be afraid," Simonetta whispered. "It's only the moon. Come, we must go," she tried again. But the stallion shook his head, the tangled mane whipping in Simonetta's face.

"Basta," she sighed. "I won't press. You have your reasons. And perhaps they are wiser than mine," she said. She lowered herself from the stallion's back, groaning as her feet touched the ground. She rubbed her backside with her palms and winced. "Too long away from the farm," she said to the stallion with a half smile. "Time was, I could ride the back of a plow horse for a week and never get sore. But not now. Not enough flesh to pad these old bones."

Simonetta stroked the horse along his neck, the muscles quivering at her touch. He turned his head into her chest and exhaled heavily into her palms.

"Che brutto," she teased, and rubbed the stallion along his velvety lips. Bristles of stiff hair tickled her palms. "Come on then. I'll find a place for us to rest a while. You deserve it, my captain cavallo, for bringing us this far so swiftly."

Simonetta led the stallion off the main road. They wandered up the slope of a hill, staying to a small path that ran between fields of abandoned olive trees. The wind hissed through the skeletal branches, fluttering the leaves as she passed. At the top of the hill, the olive grove gave way to a small forest of oaks and umbrella pines. Simonetta could just make out the remains of an old shepherd's hut. She went to it, brushing aside the choking vines of belladonna and fox grapes. A tiny garden flourished with weeds and herbs near the gap where a door had once opened.

Simonetta took off the stallion's tack and laid the saddle and bridle over the crumbling stones of a low wall. She rubbed the sweating horse down with the coarse sack containing Rinaldo's clothing. Then she sat down wearily amid the ancient garden and fingered the tangled herbs.

The names leapt into her mouth like the names of lost children: borragine, galega, malva, borsa di pastore, luppolo. Once she had known them all. In that life before. She plucked the furred leaves of a borage plant and sniffed it. Memories flooded back: a young wife, a farm, two children, a husband. Then she could heal anything.

"Don't go," her husband had said. "The road is dangerous. There are mercenaries."

"I must go. A woman needs me and I am the only one who can help. I'll be careful."

"You'd be safer at home." He had scowled.

"She will die without me."

Reluctantly, he had let her go. Then, as now, she had traveled at night, keeping to the shadows to avoid the armies marching up from the south. She had stayed almost a month with the woman, treating her fevers. And when she was finally well, Simonetta had returned home.

Home. Simonetta bit down on the borage. The taste was bitter. The Spanish and their mercenaries had sacked the village. They had looted the churches of what little gold they had, stole from the farms, and raped as many women as they could find hidden in cellars. When Simonetta had arrived home, there was nothing left but smoldering ruins and the desecrated bodies of the dead.

Her life should have ended then, Simonetta thought. Inside it had. All she had left were the nightmares that plagued her, the horsemen riding to cut her down as they had cut down the others. She had become a whore so that she might eat and so that she might not have to sleep at night and dream. She brushed her hand over the blossoms of a yarrow plant. Why hadn't she simply killed herself? Perhaps because she feared God and because she had once spent her time saving lives. And perhaps, she thought darkly, because being a whore was her punishment for having survived. She would change that in the maze.

Simonetta stood brusquely and walked to where an old trough was filled with rainwater. She gazed down at its moonlit surface, at the reflection of her narrow face and long black hair hanging in matted locks on her shoulders. She dipped her hand in the water and discovered it was still reasonably warm from the day's heat. She stripped off her clothes. She cupped her hands together, and filling them with water, poured it over her body.

An old ritual. Washing away sorrow, washing away sin. Simonetta used her petticoat to scrub the grime collected on her neck, beneath her arms, and on her belly. She used the rough hem of her wool skirts to scrub the mud from her legs and her feet. Last, she plunged her face into the water, letting its coolness settle behind her ears. Her hair floated in the water around her face and she used her fingers to ease the collected sand and dirt of the road from her hair. Slowly she lifted her head, her wet hair heavy. She dried her face with her shift before she put it on again, then wrapped her hair in Rinaldo's shirt to keep her shoulders dry. Last, she shrugged into Rinaldo's cloak and sat down again.

There was one small loaf of bread in the bottom of her sack. She held it between her fingers and thought about eating. Fatigue warred with hunger. She tried taking a bite, but the bread was hard and resisted. She sighed and shook her head.

"In the morning, Lapone," she said to the stallion. "In the morning we go into the nearest town and have a plate of something good. Maybe some tortellini, maybe a pasta fagioli. And wine too. And for you, my captain, a decent bag of oats. I may be a whore and a thief, but I won't eat like a beggar."

Simonetta tossed the bread back into the sack with a weary sigh. She unwrapped Rinaldo's shirt from her head and spread her wet hair out across her back to dry, then brought the damp garment close to her nose. It smelled like him: the peppery odor of a man's sweat, the musk of horses, and the faint perfume of saffron. She closed her eyes, shame overwhelming her. How she missed him. And how foolish and how sweet his last protestation of love had been. "Forgive me, Rinaldo," she whispered. "I only did what I had to." Holding the shirt close to her chest, she curled into a ball amid the borage and chamomile, placed her cheek on her folded hands, and closed her eyes. The pointed bones of her hip settled into the earth. She would sleep now, but as soon as she could, she would take to the road again. Rinaldo might be following her, but she was determined that he would not catch her before she reached Labirinto.

Below the castello, the prisoner's cell was cold, damp, and black as ebony. No light shone through the bars of the tiny window in the door, not even the stray beam of firelight from the turnkey's torch. Rinaldo stared into the blackness and cursed. He cursed the dying soldier who had set him on the path of the sword. He cursed the men stupid enough to die for their blighted honor. He cursed the woman bold enough to rob him of his own. It was hard to speak the curses out loud, but he did anyway. His lips were swollen and cut where the soldiers had beat him with their gloved fists. His breath came in sharp painful gasps where their boots had kicked him in the ribs. Yet cursing aloud was all that let him endure his agony.

"May you be seized with paralysis, Simonetta. May you grow plague boils in your armpits, hair on your tongue. May your breasts shrivel like dried figs and your cunt—"

"Rinaldo is that you?" a man's voice called out.

"Who calls?" he croaked.

"It's me, Lucio. I'm here to free you."

An orange light flickered on the wall outside the cell. Rinaldo could see it, like the promise of sunrise after a long night.

"I'm here," he answered weakly.

"I'm coming."

The key clanged in the rusted lock and the door slowly swung open. Rinaldo, lying on his back, squinted into the sudden brightness of a flaming torch. Cold air swept into the cell from the hallways beyond.

"What have they done to you, Rinaldo?" Lucio cried. "You look half-dead."

"Come and help the half that's still alive to stand," Rinaldo answered, and held out his hand.

Lucio rushed into the cell and pulled his friend upright. Rinaldo barked with pain, stood wobbling, a fierce pain gripping his injured ribs. He felt the shock of cold stone against the soles of his bare feet.

"Come quickly, before anyone sees us," Lucio said nervously. He tucked one arm around Rinaldo's waist and started out of the cell.

Rinaldo grimaced as pain shot up and down his body. His legs were on fire. "Who'd you bribe?" he asked through gritted teeth.

"Just about everybody, but only to look the other way. It was the laundry maid who brought me the keys when she found out it was you. And all for nothing! Not one soldi di piccolo! Can you believe that!"

"Sometimes it helps to have a reputation," Rinaldo said. He was hunched over, his arm held across his waist trying to ease the ache in his ribs. His feet dragged over the stones.

"It's your reputation that's landed you here," Lucio said brusquely. "For every woman who sighs your name, there's a dozen men only too delighted to see you rot down here."

They were climbing up the stairs, Rinaldo groaning with the effort of lifting his legs. At the top of the stairs, Lucio let go of Rinaldo to shove open a door braced with iron bands. Rinaldo leaned against the clammy wall, his breath coming in sharp gasps.

The door didn't budge even though Lucio pushed with both hands. Lucio gathered his strength and with a muttered curse, shouldered it open a small crack.

"It's enough," Rinaldo said. He squeezed himself through the narrow opening and into the courtyard beyond.

"This way," Lucio directed him, and hoisted Rinaldo once more, with one arm around his waist. They moved as quickly as Rinaldo could manage, slipping through the courtyards, staying to the shadows and avoiding the torches. Every guard they passed made a pretense of not seeing them, and it occurred to Rinaldo that his friend had indeed paid a small fortune to secure his release.

Above them, the night sky was quiet, the stars wheeling over the turrets of the castello. Firelight flickered behind the amber panes of glass in the windows of the turrets. Doves fluttered restlessly in the cotes.

"How long?" Rinaldo asked.

"Three days," Lucio answered grimly.

"Seemed like one. Or maybe eternity," Rinaldo answered. "I wondered if I was dead." He tried to laugh, but it hurt too much.

They arrived in the outer courtyard where a hay cart stood waiting. A farmer sat on the bench, anxiously fiddling with the reins of a team of horses. When he saw them, he scrambled down from his perch and came to help Lucio. Together they loaded Rinaldo onto the back of the hay wagon. Nestled in the soft straw, Rinaldo mumbled his thanks.

"This is Beppe," Lucio said, introducing the old farmer. "He's a servant of my uncle in Modena. He'll take you there, hidden in the straw, so stay quiet. And once you are well again, I want to know what you think of my uncle's daughter. She's the beauty I told you about with black hair and white skin."

"I'm through with women," Rinaldo spat.

"Yes, yes, my friend." Lucio sighed as he pulled the straw over Rinaldo's body. "But are they through with you?"

"Lend me your sword," Rinaldo asked from beneath the straw.

"You'll be safe with Beppe, I guarantee it."

"Please, Lucio. I am naked without one."

Lucio shrugged, unbuckled his sword, and pushed it into the straw next to Rinaldo.

"It's not a very good blade," he apologized.

"It's enough to skin the cat when I find her," Rinaldo muttered.

Wait!" Lucio called. He reached through the straw to find Rinaldo again, but Beppe slapped the reins over the back of his team and the cart lurched forward. "Remember," he said as he trotted after the cart, "go to my uncle in Modena!"

Buried in the straw, Rinaldo clutched the sword in his arms. He would go to Modena. But he wouldn't stay. There was only one woman with black hair that he wanted to see. Even if he had to crawl, he was going to Labirinto to find Simonetta.

Morning was just breaking the lip of the horizon when Fabrizio woke. He lay nestled in his cloak, his face near the sooty remains of the fire. The backbone of a fish curled in the ashes. He groaned, his eyes swollen with grit, and rolled onto his back. The sky was pale and luminous, with mackerel clouds swimming in its pink depths. He looked across the dead fire and saw that he was alone.

Fabrizio rose quickly and resettled his twisted clothing. He wiped his face clean with his sleeve and quickly walked down the steep slope of gorse and bent pines heading for the rocky coast. Just before the trees dropped away to reveal the sea-covered rocks, he stopped to relieve himself before hurrying to the sea. He hoped he had arrived in time.

Stepping out on a ledge of rocks, Fabrizio put a hand to his forehead and scanned the sea for Erminia. Waves tossed up white fans of foam, but he couldn't see her. A circle of gulls screeching overhead caught his attention. He turned, straining to see what they were bickering about.

Below the flapping birds, a long white shape floated indolently on the water. At first he thought it was her and cried out as the gulls attacked it, plucking out fragments in their beaks. A moment later, her head bobbed to the surface much closer to the shore, and he realized it was only her cast-off skin.

He watched Erminia swimming toward the shore, her slender arms as white as bleached shells. Fabrizio bit his lower lip at the sight of her rounded buttocks and long muscular thighs rippling beneath the surface of the water. As she emerged from the water his eyes darted over her dazzling body. Wet hair covered her white shoulders and chest, but Fabrizio could see taut pink nipples peeking arrogantly from the curtain of black hair. Below the smooth rounded belly, the dark valley of curling hair with its secret entrance intrigued him more than the maze of Labirinto. Oh for the chance to enter it, he thought hungrily. To get lost, hopelessly lost in it, and wind up, Fabrizio was convinced, in paradise.

Erminia neared his rock and Fabrizio scrambled to his feet to meet her. He wanted to touch her before the wind dried her skin and she was imprisoned again in her ugly husk. She smiled at him, her sapphire eyes full of secrets. Fabrizio held out his fingers and brushed them along her collarbone. Her lips parted with a sigh, echoed by the waves drawing away from the rocks. He ran his fingers down between her breasts, astonished at the cool, slick feel of her wet skin. He could feel the rapid pulse of her heart. As he moved his hand to cover her breast, the wind shifted.

"No," he cried as the skin beneath his fingers changed. The alabaster whiteness dulled into dirt, the cool damp smoothness roughened and dried. On her arms the change was slower, and he quickly grabbed her clean fingers. He kissed them, licking the salt from her palms just before they, too, were transformed into the chapped hands of a shepherdess.

Fabrizio released her and slapped himself on the forehead in frustration. "Why don't you wake me! Let me come into the sea with you! Please, please," he begged. "I swear I love you!"

Erminia shook her homely face and laughed soundlessly. She twirled her brown fingers in the air and Fabrizio saw again the image of the siren floating in a funnel of water. A man fell into the tunnel and was carried down into her arms. As Fabrizio watched, he saw the man struggle in the deep water, while the siren held him tightly in her embrace. A tiny stream of bubbles escaped the man's lips and then he struggled no more.

"Are you saying you would drown me?" he asked.

Erminia waved away the image. She rolled her eyes to the sky as if thinking. Smiling, she grabbed Fabrizio and pulled him closer to the sea.

Fabrizio panicked, believing she meant to drag him into the water, but she only picked up a dried oak leaf and set it in the water between some rocks, where the current would not worry it. She glanced back at Fabrizio to see that he was watching her.

The leaf floated, twirling gently in the water. Erminia picked up a handful of pebbles. One by one she loaded them onto the fragile leaf. With the third pebble, the leaf sank. Erminia looked back at Fabrizio triumphantly. Fabrizio shook his head, bewildered.

"I don't understand."

Erminia held up one stone, and with her other hand she tapped him on the chest.

"The stone has something to do with my heart?" he asked.

She nodded.

"Are you the leaf?"

She nodded again.

"And too many stones make you sink."

She beamed at him.

"Too much of my heart makes us both sink."

She clapped her hands.

Fabrizio scratched his head. "It's not my heart, is it? But what my heart carries. Desire? A man drowns himself with the weight of his own desire."

Erminia smiled at him and began to put on her clothes. Fabrizio sat down again and watched the sea as he thought about what she had revealed to him. What man could not see the siren without desiring her? And what man traveled through life without stones of longing and desire in his pockets, small weights collected from his history? Those stones were what crowded his mouth and kept him from being an actor. Could he lose them in the maze, he wondered, spit them out one by one as he penetrated its twists and turns?

Fabrizio followed Erminia up the slope of the hill, realizing that traveling with such a rare creature was hard on a mortal. He didn't mind dreaming about her, but it was strange when the dream ate with you by the fire, slept like any woman, and then turned into a goddess in the sea.

Erminia stopped at the top of the hill. She was staring out at the sea, her expression doleful. Her sapphire eyes had faded to grey.

"We leave the coast today," Fabrizio said, "to travel inland, away from the sea. Will you be all right?"

She didn't answer, but he saw her eyes gather in the last sight of the sea just before she turned away.

GLI ZANNI,
THE BUFFOONS

Let us amuse ourselves today. You will never guess
my name and I won't ask you to try. I am a mad
spirit or goblin. I come from the other world and
one of those spirits, Actius or Plautus, orders me to
tell you that a comedy will be played this evening.

—*Angelo Beolco as Ruzzante, circa sixteenth century*

10

On the rim of Labirinto's Piazza del Mercato, Giano squatted on his haunches and gazed with annoyance at the withered vegetables laid out on an old sack before him. He coughed noisily and, turning his head, spat on the black paving stones.

"Greens!' he called hoarsely. "Fresh greens!" An ass tethered to the wheelbarrow beside Giano brayed. "Traitor!" Giano muttered. "All day I've waited for you to produce. And all you can do is hee-haw! We'd have been away before now if you'd done your part of the act!"

The ass's ears twitched nervously and his hooves clattered as they shifted over the paving stones.

"No good will come of holding on to my coins, old man," Giano scolded.

The shabby cloth cape was rough on his back and Giano scratched his arms, wishing he could remove it. But it was an important part of his costume, like his formless cap and patched breeches. His ancient knitted hose were a dirty red and holes gaped at the heels of his cracked wooden clogs. To complete the disguise, he had on a large fake nose, veined and bulbous like a rose-stained truffle. When he coughed the goat hairs of a scraggly mustache puffed out over his mouth.

Giano was especially fond of the nose. It was a simple mask signed a long time ago by its maker, Anna Forsetti. It was one of two Forsetti masks he owned and they were among his most prized possessions. Giano had won the masks in a game of dice with an actor too stupid to know he was being cheated. He could have taken the actor's money, but when he saw the masks, he had changed his mind. Almost at once, the masks had suggested far more lucrative possibilities than a few thin coins.

Most of the time the masks had proven themselves worthy. Giano frowned at the withered vegetables. But not today. His stomach growled and he patted it sympathetically. Up and down market street the stalls were preparing to close. It was late afternoon, and farmers momentarily wealthy from having sold their livestock would be heading home with pouches of money clutched in their grimy hands. Giano swore. Soon. It had to happen soon, while there was still light.

"Greens! Fresh greens!" he bawled again to the street.

The ass kicked out his back hooves and strained at the tether.

"You'll go home to your oats when I get my coins!" Giano whispered savagely, and struck the ass across the back with a poplar switch.

A group of half-drunk farmers passed him and, looking over the withered produce, laughed derisively.

"Why beat your ass when even he knows better?" one called.

"Come closer and I'll beat yours instead!" Giano retorted.

The other farmers roared with laughter but the insulted man angrily kicked at the withered vegetables.

"Look at these rotted weeds. And this! What's this?" The farmer held up a soggy carrot. It waggled back and forth as the farmer shook it at Giano.

"Look familiar to you does it?" Giano growled, and snatched it back. "Go shake your own!"

"You old nun's fart. How can a decent farmer stand by and watch you sell yesterday's garbage?"

"Garbage, is it?" Giano demanded.

"Garbage," they all agreed, crowding angrily around Giano's wheelbarrow.

Beneath the fake nose, Giano smiled. This was exactly where he wanted them. A little drunk and a little angry, but close enough to see the show. Now if only the stubborn ass did his job. The sun was fading fast, and if the creature waited much longer, these farmers would probably beat Giano with his own rotten vegetables. The clods were quite right: these withered specimens were indeed street gleanings of yesterday's market he had gathered up the night before. But he had concocted a brilliant use for them.

Earlier that morning, Giano had borrowed the ass for the day from the blacksmith, Zusto. In the shadow of a dark lane, he had stuffed a handful of gold coins into the beast's asshole. Together they had made their way to the market, a disguised Giano leading the ass by a rope and pushing his wheelbarrow of withered vegetables. They had found a place in the busy Piazza del Mercato conveniently located near the taverns and then waited. Waited for a willing crowd of fools exhaling wine and a bit of fading sunlight.

"Let me tell you about these greens," Giano said in a low, rumbling voice. He placed a finger by his nose to suggest that he was imparting to them a secret of great importance. "These vegetables may look limp. But it's because they have within them a hidden secret."

"A secret?" one of the farmers asked, frowning.

"The secret is buried in my soil and can only be revealed through the juice of my crops."

"The old fart is selling love potions!" a second farmer guffawed.

"There's no doubt you're in need of one!" Giano snapped. "Too used to your partners bleating their woolly sighs."

The farmer made a lunge for Giano, who nimbly backed away out of range.

"Fools," Giano spat. "Go away then. I have nothing to sell you."

As they started to leave, Giano slapped the ass over its rump in desperation. And for once, as if responding to the command, the ass defecated. The hard sound of coins hitting the paving stones stopped one of the farmers. As his companions continued on their way, the farmer stared puzzled at the bright glint of gold nestled in the steaming turds.

Giano leaned down swiftly and plucked a gold coin out of a turd and, before the famer's amazed eyes, wiped it clean on his cape and bit it.

"That ass shits gold," the farmer exclaimed.

"Ssh," Giano said. "Do you want the others to hear?" He beckoned the curious man closer. "Indeed I see that you, unlike your friends, are a smart tool." Giano continued to hold the gold coin out and watched the way its reflection glittered in the man's eyes. "The secret is in these here vegetables. I grow them on an abandoned lot that lies alongside the ruins of an ancient fort. Some say it once belonged to an alchemist condemned by the church. No one but me has ever dared to plant near its old walls. The greens may grow sick and weakly looking, but, my friend, these same withered greens are all I've ever fed the beast and look, he shits gold. I ate them once myself, but I only got silver coins and they were painful to pass. So now I give it all to the beast here and get enough to tide me over the winter."

"You're lying," the farmer protested, staring at the gold coin.

"See for yourself," Giano offered.

The farmer kicked at the turds with the tip of his boot and two more coins rolled out. He knelt, picked one up between his fingertips, and held it up to the light.

"See how preciously it gleams? The saint's face stamped there for all to see!" Giano said softly.

"How much?" the farmer demanded.

"For all of it?"

"All of it! How much do you want for all of these . . . vegetables?"

Giano stroked his fake mustache thoughtfully.

"Name your price," the farmer said more desperately.

"Because I think you are a shrewd buyer, I will give you a good price, as it is the end of the day and you alone of your loutish companions believed me," Giano answered. "Twenty gold saints takes it all."

The farmer paled. "But that's everything I've made today. I'll go home with nothing."

"But there are enough vegetables here to help you recover double your money and more in a short time. Your family can even help in the endeavor," Giano suggested, chewing on a carrot.

"Agreed!" the man said thickly and, with a slow reluctance, took his purse from his doublet. Smiling beneath the bulbous nose, Giano began to gather up the withered vegetables into a sack, which he tied with a rope. There was a moment of jostling as the farmer and Giano nervously traded the sack for the purse, each afraid to relinquish the one until firmly holding on to the other. When the exchange was at last concluded, Giano quickly bid the dazed farmer farewell, and leading the ass, he hurried away from the market pushing the empty wheelbarrow.

"Quick, old man, before he comes to his senses," Giano urged the ass.

Giano rattled the wheelbarrow over the paving stones of a dozen small streets, turning here and there down even smaller lanes. Finally, he entered a dark alley that reeked of coal and smoke from a blacksmith's forge. The forge's doors were open, and from the top of the alley, Giano could see the blacksmith Zusto bent over his anvil. Swiftly checking over his shoulder to be certain he had not been followed, Giano halted the ass and proceeded to remove his disguise.

First, he removed his mask and carefully wrapped it in a bit of dirty white silk. Then he threw off the scratchy sackcloth cape, kicked off the cracked clogs, and slipped down the patched trousers. He was standing just in his shirt, pulling his better clothes out of a second sack, when a young whore passed him and flashed him a dazzling smile.

"That's quite a nice ass you have," she said, stopping to stroke the animal's long grey ears. She had red hair braided with fluttering ribbons and a comely face.

Giano, who was bending over to thrust his legs into his hose, grinned back at her. "He works well, but only if roundly slapped. His cousin here takes far less effort to get into the harness." Giano turned to face her and slowly lifted his shirt above his waist as if to tuck it into his hose. The young whore gave a little gasp. Between the recently acquired bag of money and the red-haired girl's smile, Giano's body felt a certain urge to celebrate. He struggled to straighten his hose over his hips. "Still, you know," Giano added as he pulled up his boots, "it's nice to have a hand with them from time to time."

"Oh if you please, kind sir, I could assist you," the whore answered, her eyes bright with amusement. She held up a small hand. "I do have experience in slapping asses."

"Brava carina," Giano murmured and, taking her hand, kissed it wetly on the palm. "Tonight then, for I have business now. Come to the Via Stradella, and beneath the sign of the quill you will find my master's quarters. Use the bell over the little blue door at the side and I'll let you in."

"Hmm. Sounds promising," the girl replied. "Perhaps a coin or two to marry the deal between us."

Giano pulled out a gold coin from his pocket and passed it to the girl. She examined it and slipped it inside her bodice.

"Later," Giano whispered, and gave the girl a quick squeeze around her narrow waist.

"As you will, amore mio," she replied, and wriggled away from his grasp.

Giano watched her swaying hips as she sauntered down the lane. He kissed his fingers. "Bellissima!" he said to her retreating figure. The ass brayed and Giano quickly straightened his doublet over his shirt and resumed his journey to the blacksmith shop.

Zusto was outside the door, smoke rising above his powerful shoulders as he hammered a horseshoe over the anvil.

"I expected you back hours ago," Zusto grumbled. He was a short but stoutly built man, with a thick mat of black hair covering his head, his chest, and his forearms. He grunted as he worked, giving the impression of an angry bear wielding a hammer. Though his mouth was a cherry red, there was little humor in it. Giano approached him cautiously, knowing Zusto to be famous not only for his skill at the anvil but his raging temper.

"Your pardon, Master smith," Giano said, respectfully eyeing the smith's powerful forearms. "I was detained, though your ass was quite a help in my endeavor. I shall pay you extra."

"I don't care about the money," the smith replied, and Giano's heart skipped a beat at the treasonous words. "It's the state of my ass I'm worried about."

Giano suppressed a dozen quick retorts, choosing the prudence of caution over the risk of cleverness.

"I can assure you, I've treated your ass with the utmost care," he answered diplomatically. "Why he's eaten only the best today and so well have I cared for him that it may well be he shits gold at the memory of my tenderness," Giano concluded, trying to remember how many coins he had stuffed up the beast and how many had he retrieved. It occurred to him that one or two were still missing. What a pity he thought, looking over the sloping back of the ass.

Zusto ran his fire-scarred hands over the ass's scrubby hide as if to reassure himself that the creature was indeed the picture of health. "All right. I'll take him back at the usual rate. I see you've done him no injury. And his belly feels full enough." Zusto held out a muscular hand to Giano for his payment.

Giano gave him the few coins he'd agreed on in advance, though it pained him. Every coin paid out seemed like a lost opportunity for some wonderful fulfillment: a woman, a bottle of good wine, a blood-rare piece of meat. He sighed, hating the cold, empty feeling of money leaving his palm.

But soon it was done and Zusto took the ass by the halter and led him away to the stable beside the forge. As Giano reached the top of the alley he heard the ass's loud braying, followed by the smith's incredulous shouts of "Bravo! Bravo!"

The missing coins, Giano guessed, half-tempted to return and find some way to reclaim them. His stomach growled, reminding him that he was very hungry and it was time to turn his attention to other needs.

Giano continued walking, a new plan forming in his head. He had gotten money and set up a pretty whore for his evening's delight, and now he needed food to sustain him through the night's activities. And of course, there was his master, Lorenzo Falcomatta. He, too, would need some looking after.

Giano made a sour face. Lorenzo Falcomatta was a cold fish without a hint of humor or cunning. He never lied, never schemed, never slept with women or anyone else that Giano knew about. And for all his pinched way of living, he had the balls to call himself a poet and a playwright. Giano snorted and shook his head. A poet indeed! Well once maybe, long ago when there was sap in his veins. But now this dry stick of a man, forced by some inner compulsion always to tell the truth, hadn't managed to write a line of poetry in the six months that Giano had been his manservant.

All poetry was composed of lies, Giano reasoned, beautiful words strung together like a strand of pearls on a woman's neck. To say a woman's face was like a flower was a lie. But any fool knew that it meant the woman was beautiful, sweet-smelling, fresh as petals. And any fool ought to be able to make one image describe another. But not Lorenzo. He'd have none of it. It was as though the man saw metaphor as a venial sin.

It wasn't that Lorenzo wasn't talented in his own way. He could write very well. In fact, he could describe the physical state of his morning's phlegm with appalling accuracy. But who wanted to read that? Giano shuddered. Only some nephew awaiting this dry uncle's approaching death by catarrh. No, no, it was impossible for Lorenzo to think or write anything that wasn't absolutely true. Which was why he had gone from being a poet to being a scribe, copying out reports and claims for the guild of Doctors of Law. Giano guffawed. If Lorenzo knew how much fiction there was in those law accounts, his hand would wither at the mere touch of the quill.

But then, it was Lorenzo's black-and-white vision of the world that had led him to hire Giano as his servant. Giano was a clever man, with features that shifted as easily as the afternoon shadows over the piazza. He was never without a disguise, a dissembling face, a costume or a trick hidden in the folds of his cloak. Others saw in him only what Giano wished them to see. It was how he had survived the long journey of his life from a boy in Bergamo, to a thief and servant in the city of Labirinto.

Another man might find his servant's shifting face troubling over time. Doubts would rise as the silver plate disappeared. But not Lorenzo. Unless he caught someone in an act of deception, Lorenzo would accept all that was said as truth, because he himself could not possibly lie. As long as Giano was careful, he knew that Lorenzo would never recognize him for the thimblerigger and bawd he truly was, but think of him as the humble manservant who managed to bring a meal out of a near-empty larder and keep enough candles trimmed to allow the master to continue copying his dry manuscripts. And if a few extra coins and objects out of Lorenzo's coffers found their way into Giano's pockets as payment for such services, who was Lorenzo to complain as long as his modest needs were met?

On the other side of the Piazza del Mercato, Giano stopped and put down his bag. He reached into it and pulled up the second Forsetti mask. Giano grinned at the mask. This was the face of a Doctor of Law: a long, prominent nose from poking into too many people's business, eyes squinted together under heavy lamb's wool eyebrows. Across the brow, the tanned leather was creased to give the wearer the look of permanent consternation.

Giano slipped the mask over the front of his face and tied it securely onto his head. Touching the leather cheeks, he sighed as he felt the persona of the mask fuse onto his face. His throat swelled with a new stentorian voice. His shoulders sloped downward into a lawyer's stoop and his hands groped the air, searching for lost phrases of Latin. Quickly Giano turned the bag inside out and undid a row of tiny buttons along one side seam. In an instant the bag became a dusty black velvet cape, which he clasped with a chain he had borrowed from an unsuspecting Lorenzo. Turning his own bright red cap inside out, he slapped the resulting black, shapeless pancake on his head and fluffed out a fringe of fake grey hair. A cane completed his disguise.

"A man who is ill can say that he is unwell," Giano muttered, trying out his new voice. He bent his body a little over the cane and thought about his second journey of the day to the piazza, where he would find a sausage vendor named Rosaria, a toothless hag of a countrywoman despite her delicate name. He had begun terrorizing her a month ago with the news that a client was prepared to sue her for filling her sausages with dog entrails, which had made him violently and chronically ill. This client was willing to be carried on a litter before Labirinto's tribunal and have her denounced. But through his, Giano's, intervention as a Doctor of the Law, perhaps their disagreements might be settled in a mutually beneficial way and the client might be persuaded to forgo his suit. Rosaria had rolled her eyes and blinked in ignorant terror as Giano had rattled off threats in words and laws she had never heard of before—or probably ever would—Giano thought gleefully, as he had invented most of them on the spur of the moment. Rosaria had glared, she had trembled, she had shaken her hands in outrage that her sausages should have been so maligned. Giano pressed his claim, drowning her in legal terms, until at last, Rosaria succumbed meekly.

Now, at every market day, there was a packet waiting for Il Dottore, a haunch of veal, a country rabbit, or a dozen excellent sausages all tied up in paper. Soon, Giano knew sadly from past experience, Rosaria would lose her fear of him and maybe even grow wise to his ruse. Life would get complicated, Il Dottore would have to retire from the stage and Giano would have to find a suitable replacement and a new game would begin. But for now, Rosaria's little packet was the perfect answer to his hunger. Giano didn't want to miss the appointment with his future dinner, so he stowed his remaining possessions in hidden pockets in his cape and the front of his shirt, giving his disguise a professional paunch. Taking a last glance at himself in a puddle, Giano glared beneath the furred brow. Hunch-shouldered, stooped by the weight of too much education, the Doctor of Law minced into the Piazza del Mercato.

11

Zizola struggled under the shifting weight of the waking baby, who was thrashing her arms against the restraints of the shawl holding her captive on Zizola's aching back.

"Shush, shush, quiet, Nina," Zizola murmured soothingly. "We're almost there."

Zizola hurried through the twisting turns of Labirinto's narrow streets, now growing dark in the fading daylight. Above her, the shuttered windows were still opened to the streets, some casting faint squares of candlelight to brighten her way. She could smell food being prepared for the evening meal, and her stomach growled a complaint against its emptiness.

From an open window a child called to his mother for bread. Spoons chimed against bowls and knives scraped over plates. A man demanded more wine and pasta. A woman laughed shrilly from another candlelit window and tossed out a handful of orange peels into the gutter below. Zizola dodged the falling debris and glanced up in annoyance. To eat like that, she sighed, her nose dissecting the collected aromas: the sharpness of garlic, the sweetness of risotto with pumpkin, and the tartness of gorgonzola. To eat at all!

Above the leaning balconies and lizard-faced drain spouts, the first evening star competed with the last of the sun's rays. Zizola forced her tired legs to go faster, wanting more than anything to get Nina to her mother, Stelladonna, before she woke completely. Since morning, Zizola had walked the streets and piazzas of Labirinto begging for coins with the baby tied onto her back. Nina had slept like the dead because Stelladonna had given her something black to drink, something that always made the baby sleep and wake in the evening with a howling cry. It was the prospect of that howling that made Zizola hurry despite her fatigue.

Zizola didn't like the way Stelladonna drugged her baby, but she understood the reason for it. Undrugged, Nina would want food, she would want her mother, she would whine all day. It was much easier and certainly more effective to look desolate and forlorn with Nina peacefully asleep on her back rather than wriggling or crying for someone to play with her. Still, Zizola thought, she hated to be around Nina when she woke with what Zizola figured to be a wretched hangover.

At least the begging had gone well today, Zizola smiled to herself. The stash of coins weighed nicely in her deep pockets and made a sweet clinking sound as she jogged over the paving stones. Zizola imagined the bread it would buy, maybe a plate of capelletti. Later, if there were enough left over, she would buy a pasty from Nonna Michela, who never stinted on the cheese or salted ham.

Nina was waking, her cries forcing away all pleasant thoughts of food.

"Saint's hell!" Zizola swore. At the brow of a steep hill, she turned down a lane almost hidden between two sagging buildings. The lane smelled of dank stone and urine. Zizola couldn't see her way in the dark, but knew exactly when steps began to tumble sharply downward. Unexpectedly, her foot nudged a sleeping man sprawled across the steps and she nearly fell down the uneven stairs. Zizola grabbed at the wall for support and regained her balance.

"Bastardo!" she hissed, and turning quickly, kicked at the man in the dark.

"Oh, Lauretta," he moaned. "My sweet dove. Why do you spurn me, when I would have given you everything I own?" The man's voice was slurred and to Zizola's practiced ear, sounded very drunk. "Your breasts, your mouth . . ."

She hesitated a moment. Making a swift decision, she reached down to where the drunk man lay stretched across the stairs. "Amore, my sweet," she crooned. "How could I have been so cruel?" She patted her experienced hands over his doublet, feeling for his purse. "And is this what you would give your Lauretta?" She pulled his purse free from his belt.

"Money means nothing," the man sobbed, and grabbed her hand. She frowned but didn't move, feeling the wide band of a ring on one of his fingers.

"Yes, yes, caro," she said softly, working her fingers around the ring, slipping it gently over his knuckles.

"Take my heart, cruel vixen. Take it! For already you have broken it!" The man pulled her down violently onto his chest. Zizola swore, and struggled to free herself from his ardent embrace, gagging at the stench of his filthy clothes and wine-soaked sighs. Nina's quiet whimpering erupted into wails.

At once the man released his hold on Zizola. "Our child?" he croaked.

With a vigorous twist, Zizola pulled off the huge ring and righted herself.

"Your heart is mine. Farewell!" she called, and pelted down the stairs, Nina's wails and the man's piteous cries sounding in her ears.

As she ran, Zizola smiled. What a stroke of luck! It meant a hot meal and decent wine. Her mouth beginning to water, Zizola could taste savory rabbit stew poured over a warm plate of polenta. She could feel a bench beneath her buttocks, her toes stretched out to the warmth of some inn's hearth fire. She had to get Nina back to Stelladonna at the Arch of Dreams quickly. At the bottom of the stairs, the dark lane spilled the rushing Zizola and Nina out between the colonnades of the curved row of buildings that edged the Piazza del Labirinto.

The final rays of sunset broke through a flank of low-lying clouds and settled over the open piazza, turning its black paving stones into a sea of gold. Zizola stopped and caught her breath, astonished as always by the sight of the Great Maze on the other side of the piazza, haloed in sunset. Even Nina quieted in the sudden shower of gold light. She found her thumb and, sucking noisily, curled her fingers around Zizola's braid for comfort.

"How beautiful," Zizola said softly.

Though she had been in a hurry a moment before, Zizola strolled across the piazza, her gaze trained on the carved wooden gates of the Great Maze. The living green walls of the maze rose serenely out of the city's stones and undulated away as far as the eye could see. Small finches flitted out between the dense lower branches of the maze wall; higher up, black-winged martins arrowed through the evening sky catching insects in the open air. On the top of the wall, mist snaked up through the foliage and exhaled into the evening air. A falcon circled over the maze and, then shrieking, folded his wings and plummeted behind the green walls.

Zizola knew from experience that to look directly at the maze was to see only the high green hedges. But if she looked away, the maze shivered with a second life at the corner of her vision. A face had once peered out at her from an opening and stuck out its tongue. Another time, she had held her breath as a manticore wedged through the thickets, its head wreathed in fire, and then was pulled inside again. She had seen the spires of a marble tower rising over the green walls in the time it took to sigh, and then as quickly vanished into the mist. She had seen winged angels armed with silver bows fighting serpents that breathed fire and smoke.

Stelladonna told Zizola that she was imagining it all. That the clouds, the sun, the mist all conspired to make her see what she wanted. But Zizola didn't believe her. No one knew what lay behind the gates.

Opposite the Great Maze, the piazza opened into a huge half circle. On the far side a curved wall of buildings had been built, their many windows facing the maze. On the ground floors beneath the colonnades were artisans' workshops. Above the arched colonnades were the private residences of Labirinto's wealthy. Zizola wondered if the rich could glimpse the secrets of the maze from their high windows. And in the piazza, huddled about fires in singles or in small groups, were the pilgrims waiting for the gates of the maze to open and let them in.

Zizola made her way through the clusters of pilgrims with a smug smile. These sheep were the easiest to fleece. They came from all over the country, believing in the old story. They came with the curse of bad luck riding hard on their heels, looking to the maze to offer them an escape from their miserable lives. On the streets all her life, Zizola at fourteen had become a master at wheedling a coin, a cast-off shawl, or a meal out of the pilgrims as they tried to prepare themselves to be accepted by the maze.

The maze was as fickle as a nobleman's heart. The gates opened of their own will from inside and at unpredictable intervals. Zizola had been there when the piazza had been crowded with pilgrims because more than two months had passed since the gates had opened. Those were good times for her. Desperate pilgrims, grown frantic with the waiting, often gave away everything they had hoping that by acts of generosity they might appease the gates into opening. Zizola owed her shawl and red bodice to a woman cursed by barrenness. She owed her boots, a size too large but still serviceable, to a merchant whose ships sank at every voyage. Her dirty linen shift with the bit of lace came from a country girl with a big belly and no husband. An actress who had lost her voice had given her a handful of red and yellow ribbons, which Zizola had tied into her bodice and braided into her blond hair. Colored scraps of old velvet from cloaks and cast-off doublets had been cut into diamonds and sewn to cover the holes in her old skirt, a final offering from a rake-thin girl who coughed constantly. Zizola had taken it all without hesitation.

But the gates had a will of their own, for at other times Zizola had seen them open for a solitary traveler. Once it had been a woman in a black dress and bare feet who sang to the gates, which opened just wide enough for her to slip inside. And once, while the city was still sleeping behind shutters, Zizola had seen the gates open to no one. A stag with a rack of ivory-colored horns bounded out from the maze, ran across the empty piazza, and disappeared down a lane.

Nina was beginning to whimper again, reminding Zizola to hurry. By the time she had crossed the piazza to the small side street known as the Arch of Dreams, Nina had taken her thumb out of her mouth and begun to cry more loudly.

"Saint's hell!" Zizola muttered, seeing Stelladonna standing by the crumbling remains of a Roman arch with her fists on her hips and a wooden spoon in one hand. With a quick furtive movement, Zizola hid the gold ring in her cheek, against her teeth. "Quiet, Nina, or you'll be the death of me!" she urged the baby. But as soon as Nina had seen her mother, she started wailing.

"You're late, you stupid slut," Stelladonna screeched, and swung the wooden spoon hard across Zizola's legs.

"I had a good day," Zizola shouted back, trying to dodge the spoon.

"Give it here!" demanded Stelladonna. She held up the spoon as a threat and thrust out her other hand while the baby wriggled and screamed in Zizola's ear.

"Help me get Nina off first," Zizola said. "The shawl's coming loose and she's falling."

Roughly Stelladonna grabbed Nina from the tangles of Zizola's shawl and sat her hard on the street. "Be quiet brat or you'll get the spoon too!" she spat, brandishing the spoon over her daughter's head. Nina's wails rose higher and she held out her trembling arms to be picked up.

But Stelladonna ignored her and turned savagely back to Zizola. "Give me the take," she commanded. By the dimming light Zizola could see the purple bruise on her gaunt cheek. Her eye was puffy, and a cut over her eyebrow was crusted with dried blood. Slender bruises like the shadows of long fingers were joined over her thin neck. She was breathing hard, as though a stitch in her ribs prevented her from taking in a full breath.

Zizola's glance darted to the alley. A man waited beneath the lit torch, leaning against the wall as he carefully pared his nails with a dagger. He wore an old battered hat pulled low on his brow, shading his features. Long black hair hung down over his forehead and shoulders. A mustache hid his mouth. When he looked up at Zizola, she flinched at the malice in his black eyes. Zizola gave Stelladonna the purse she had taken off the drunk man, then reached into her pocket and pulled up the bag of coins she and Nina had managed to earn begging during the day.

Though the day had been good, Zizola's heart sank. It didn't matter how well fortune had smiled on her that day. Ruggerio was back. He had already beaten Stelladonna and now she would be cruel and hard.

"That's all?" Stelladonna demanded, weighing the bags in her palm.

"It's a fair sum," Zizola retorted.

"You're holding out, slut. There's more!" Fear haunted Stelladonna's eyes. How much money did Ruggerio need this time? Zizola wondered. How much would be enough to make him leave them alone?

"There is no more," Zizola insisted. Her heart was pounding in her chest. She was lying. Besides the ring in her cheek, she had two coins hidden in her boot, burning circles on the bottom of her left heel. They were hers, she thought angrily, protection against Stelladonna's unpredictable cruelty. She would not surrender them. No matter what.

Ruggerio pushed off the wall and came to face Zizola. Stelladonna winced and shrank away. Zizola tensed. He swung a punch at her and she ducked instinctively. As her head came up again, the return swing caught her on her cheek and slammed her back into the street. She tasted a warm burst of blood in her mouth and stars jangled in her eyes. He reached down and hauled her upright. She held her hands up but a second blow caught her on the other side of her face. He released her and she crumpled to the ground in pain. She squeezed her eyes shut, wishing for the blackness that hovered at the edges of her sight to claim her completely.

"Strip her," Ruggerio ordered in his raspy voice, kicking her with the toe of his boot. "She's hiding something. They all do, the cunning bitches."

Now Zizola struggled to stay conscious. The ring. Her coins. They mustn't find her coins. She curled her body into a tight knot, clinging to her clothes and fighting Stelladonna's hands, which tore at her garments.

"No, no," she cried out. "There's no more!"

Nina wailed from the gutter.

Stelladonna slapped Zizola hard and Zizola slapped her back, the two women gasping with the sharpness of their mutual pain. Then Stelladonna grabbed one of Zizola's boots and gave a savage twist. Zizola curled her toes, trying to keep the boot on her foot, but the boot was too large. It slid off and the coins rolled out on to the street.

"Aha!" Stelladonna crowed, and snatched up the coins.

Ruggerio grabbed them from Stelladonna and leaned down to where Zizola lay clutching at her clothes. Sneering, he placed his knife alongside her neck.

"I could finish it here," Ruggio whispered. Zizola lay still, imprisoned by the thin edge of the knife's blade. Ruggerio gave a smile full of rotten teeth. "Lucky you're better 'un most at the fleece, ragazza. I'll let you off this time. But next time . . ." He dug the blade a little deeper. Zizola was afraid even to swallow. "Understand?" He moved the knife away so she could talk. "Understand?"

"Yes," she answered, rubbing the thin cut on her throat. She inhaled deeply, so relieved that she was still alive that she didn't see his fist until it was too late to dodge it. It caught her beneath the ear and she heard her jaw crack. Something hard caught in her throat and she choked, swallowing heavily until it was forced down. Nina's wails were not half as loud as the roaring pain in her ears.

"That's a reminder. You be here tomorrow."

Zizola lay motionless, watching as Stelladonna picked Nina up from the gutter. All she could see of the brutal pair was their muddy boots walking quickly down a side lane, leaving her alone.

Zizola could feel the faint trickle of blood coming from one ear. The cooling night air made her shiver and in a sudden fit of anger, she hoisted herself up.

"Saint's hell," she moaned, and touched her injured cheek gingerly. "I swallowed the ring."

She forced herself to her feet, her body stiff and cold. Stars woke in the sky above the balconies as she made her way back to the Piazza del Labirinto. Over a few cook fires hung pots whose fragrant steam mingled with the acrid scent of burning wood. She appeared at every camp, trying to ask for a bit of broth. But her battered face produced terror rather than sympathy. The pilgrims waved her off as if she were a demon from hell come to taunt them for their misfortune. She touched her stomach, aware of the cold hardness of the ring. It made for a very poor meal, she thought angrily.

As she limped toward the walls of the maze she saw a crust of old bread on the ground. She picked it up and tried to eat it. Her jaw opened and closed with a horrible popping sound and new pain shot through her cheek. She finally contented herself with sucking on it, though it tasted more of the dirty street than the wheat that had gone into it.

Zizola sat down close to the thicket wall of the maze. She sighed and leaned her head back into a nest of branches. She ripped a piece off her hem and tied it around her face from her chin to the top of her head to support her injured jaw. She hadn't wanted to cry, but the tears came anyway. She was in pain, and worse, she was hungry. It would take a while for this injury to heal. And what about the next injury? she thought, remembering the sharp blade against her throat. Stelladonna was not bad on her own and together she and Zizola had managed to keep themselves in bread and sausages. But when Ruggerio turned up like a hangman's curse, it was a different story. Zizola was an orphan and Stelladonna, who could mistreat her own child, had even less reason to protect Zizola from Ruggerio's cruelty.

"Curse them all," Zizola muttered. "Curse the whole fucking line of hard-luck bastards who brought me here to this wretched place. I wish they'd all been put to the flame, every fucking one of them. And I wish myself, just cold ash!"

Zizola pulled her knees up close to her chest and, laying her injured cheek in the cradle of her hands, wept miserably.

A wind rustled the leaves of the hedges, a worried sound that faded into silence. Beneath her haunches, the cobblestones trembled as though shaken by the intensity of Zizola's angry words. The words sank deeper and the ground rumbled, sending a message, a spell, a curse rippling through the crust of the earth.

The angry murmur of Zizola's words traveled slowly beneath the surface of the earth like a wave through a river of lava until it settled in a crucible far to the south in Calabria, where volcanic mountains gripped the shoreline with rocky knuckles. Some of the peaks, newly born, emitted sulphurous vapors from tiny fissures between the boulders while larger fissures erupted, sending narrow streams of crimson lava down to a boiling sea. Overhead, the night sky shone black as obsidian, with bright flecks of stars.

Goats wandered through the heated stones, pulling at the long grass that dared to grow in the meager soil. They had no fear of this place, no fear of the cracks that split the earth with a sudden exhalation of yellow steam nor of the ground that shifted restlessly beneath their hooves. The clanking of the lead goat's bell directed them higher up the mountain and they followed it without concern.

In the quiet of the night, a new crevice opened suddenly in the earth near the ruby-throated cone of a narrow peak. From a fiery gash in the earth, molten rock scorched the grass as it formed an oblong pool. The sea winds cooled it quickly and its color changed from brilliant red to charred black, pulsing with a network of bright red veins. The pool of lava stirred, forcing itself into a momentary shape, then fell formless again. The veins glowed, and again the pool took on form: a head, a torso, arms, and legs. A hand of cooling lava lifted from the pool and clutched at the stars. Eyes of flaming white flared in a black face and a mouth opened.

Hunger. Raw unquenchable hunger. It was a feeling, not a word, a pain thundering in the fierce heat of the form's near-liquid body. Hunger. A hollowness to be filled. The form didn't understand this yet.

It sank back into the pool. A new breeze drifted over Its surface and It was charged with salt, with the minutiae of particles that in the sea held life. The face surfaced from the black ooze like a man breaching a wave. Again the wave of pain. Of hunger. The mouth opened and shut. Damp air filled It, and the shape of a chest rose out of the blackness, swelling with air. Black lids peeled back and white eyes found the sky.

It saw the hard flint of the stars high above It and wondered. It felt the earth beneath It and recognized the husk of Its own womb. It knew itself to be like these things and yet more. The stars, the earth, and the salt tang of the air that touched Its lips were fixed points, solid as It was not, enduring and permanent as It could never be. It had but a single purpose, like an arrow let loose in search of a target.

Beneath the raw hunger came a word to the newly formed lips.

"Curse," the lips said, and awareness of self crackled in the hollow chambers of Its rapidly forming thoughts.

Red veins snaked over the face, and the fragile features were consumed in a corona of radiant white heat. The creature turned from the sky and knelt on four limbs, curling around the pain of Its raging hunger. The clanking of a bell sounded in the wind and cunning spiraled into the chamber of Its ear. The creature resettled into a pool of cooling black lava as the lead billy goat came over the top of the hillside and began to graze nearby.

The creature could sense the presence of the goat, hear the rough tearing of dry grass. It lay still and listened to the steady pulse of the goat's heart, a tapping vibration carried through the tremors of the earth between them. It felt for such a thing in Itself, but couldn't find it. As the breeze carried the gamey scent of the goat, hunger shrieked in Its hollow core. It could not wait. But the wind whistled over Its cooling surface: Wait.

The goat approached the pool with head down and nostrils flared. One step and then another, curiosity carrying it closer. At the fringe of the shining black pool, the goat leaned forward, head cocked to one side. Distant starlight showed the goat the wavering reflection of its face.

Now! the roaring hunger demanded. The pool yawned a mouth of fire. A tongue lapped at the air and circled the head of the startled goat, which struggled, its legs kicking wildly against the loose stones. The bell clanked a frenzied warning as the mouth lengthened into a long tunnel of fire and took the goat whole into Itself. It closed around the body of the goat, hesitating as It examined what It held in Its maw. Knowledge snapped through Its perceptions. Teeth, produced in imitation of the goat's own flat worn molars, began to crush the goat with slow grinding motions.

Bones cracked, crushed into tiny fragments. The creature shuddered at the unexpected softness of flesh seared by the heat. Out of evaporating blood, the taste of salt lingered in Its senses. It learned from the scattering last thoughts of the goat: the feathery touch of grass, the look of the green earth at the mountain's foot where there waited an up-right, two-legged figure holding a stick in its hand.

It opened Its gleaming eyes to the night sky. The pain of Its gnaw-ing hunger had abated. It could digest these images. Use them. Out of the pool a hand reached out to the stars. The hand was followed by the length of an arm, a head, and a chest. It rose, baffled by the marvel of trembling legs supported on feet blazing with soles of fire. There were no features on Its radiant face save an open mouth and the smoky shad-ows of Its eyes. The hunger lay quiet in Its belly. It knew from the knowledge gleaned from the goat that when the pain returned, It must feed again. But a stronger urge moved It now.

"Curse," the mouth said, and Zizola's curse began to walk north to fulfill Its purpose and the reason for Its existence.

12

Lorenzo pursed his lips and dutifully copied the dry sentences from one page onto another. His stylus scratched like an insect desper-ately attempting to cross a desert of heavily starched paper. He stopped and stared at the words, the black lines wavering. He rubbed his right hand where it ached along the edge. Ink smudges stained his fin-gers black.

"Meaningless," he muttered aloud. "All meaningless. Surely the law was meant to illuminate the truth, not drown it in ink."

He laid down his stylus and ran his fingers through his hair. It was as black as the ink, except for a white streak near his forehead that split the black waves like a bolt of lightning. Absently he fingered the white lock, easily found because its texture was coarser than the rest of his hair.

"Where you were kissed by the angels," his mother had crooned.

"Where you were cursed by the devil," his wife, Cecilia, had hissed, her bloodstained fingers grasping it just before she died in his arms.

White and black, Lorenzo thought, a lock of truth surrounded by a black sea of lies. "Boh." Lorenzo exhaled, not wanting his mind to run against that old argument again. He pushed his chair away from his desk and stood, stretching his arms over his head. The blood tingled in his fingertips. He glanced around the dreary shop and wondered how his life had been reduced to such a narrow plane: a suit of black, a gouged wooden desk, dust filtering through the tiny window, the scent of mold on the leather book covers. And the dullness of the law.

"At least it's honest," he said morosely. Not like that other life he had once led. That life might have been brighter, full of loud, arrogant poetry and the rich beauty of a woman. But in the end, he had discovered that the poet's words were lies, that the woman's love had been a mask. Imagining the horns of a cuckold, Lorenzo raised his hands again to his forehead, and promptly dropped them. Men do not wear horns on their heads. Horns are a poet's conceit. No, Lorenzo thought, remembering his wife sleeping in the arms of another man. Honest men take a sword and make the way straight for the truth again. Even if the way lies through your beloved's heart.

A shadow darkened the tiny window and the door to Lorenzo's shop flew open. The little bells, which should have jingled gaily at the arrival of a client, were muted by the shouting of two men crowding together through the doorway.

"I won't be turned away from this path, Girolamo. That lying scum of a pig's arsehole will be made to pay for his slander with my sword." The speaker was a tall, powerfully built man with a huge nose, broad at the bridge and hooked over heavy lips. He wore a livid blue-and-green striped doublet. His trunk hose was of the same brilliant blue, while his lower legs were covered with green, crisscrossed at the knees with purple garters. His black hair was crammed under a wide purple hat, fluted at the edges with an extra drape of gold-dyed wool hanging decoratively from the back. He clutched at the hilt of a sword buckled around his hips.

"But, Massimo, it's illegal to duel," Girolamo argued. The second man was smaller, ferret-faced, and pale. He wore a drab olive-green doublet over bright yellow hose. His hair was long and hung in greasy locks around his narrow, pointed face. "Let the family do it. We'll dump the shithead's corpse into the Po!"

"No, damn the pox carrier to hell. I, at least, am a courtier. I demand a duel to prove it!" Massimo's forehead was sweating under the purple and gold hat, his black brows drawn together in fury. His wide nostrils flared like a bull as he inhaled the steam of his rage.

Lorenzo blinked, as unused to the screaming colors of their bright clothing as he was to the volume of their arguments.

"Signori," he interrupted them. "Perhaps I may be of assistance to you."

They turned and gaped at Lorenzo, as if surprised to suddenly discover him there. Massimo shuddered off his bad humor and assumed a noble posture. Girolamo ground his teeth.

Lorenzo refrained from laughing outright. The deliberate pose of the offended man was something out of Castiglione's book of rules for the well-behaved courtier. Practiced in front of the glass, Lorenzo guessed. A true courtier's demeanor must always be calm; he must eschew excess in any emotion as a sign of poor breeding and bad taste. Such a calm was a mask, worn better by some, more poorly by others. Massimo for example was almost weeping with frustrated emotion, his knuckles white on the sword, and the long sinews in his neck strained with the rigor of his pose.

"How may I serve you?" Lorenzo asked, and sat down at his desk.

"I wish to send a challenge to a lying son of a bitch," Massimo declared.

"Ah, the signore wishes to prepare the challenge for a duel?" Lorenzo asked.

"No. I wish *you* to prepare the challenge for the duel. And write it in good Tuscan so that crab louse, prickless lover of boys will know which one of us is more cultured," Massimo answered hotly.

"Perhaps the signore could give me the details. I must know whether I am to prepare a rogito, a manifesto, or a cartello."

"Which is the cheapest?" Massimo demanded.

"Signore, money is not the issue here. Correctness is. Now perhaps you will be so kind as to tell me who gave the lie?"

"Well, he did!" Massimo stammered. "Marzio Colloredo insulted my family by claiming that the Savorgnans of Mantua had attacked his family and left them to be eaten by dogs."

"Is that true?" asked Lorenzo.

"Yes, we did attack the family," Girolamo said, and slashed his hand through the air. "Magnificently in fact. But we didn't leave them for the dogs. The jackals were too cowardly to come and pick up their dead, so the corpses stayed where they were in the streets and were eaten."

"I see," Lorenzo said, and picked up his stylus. "And why did the Savorgnan family attack the Colloredos?"

"Does it matter?" Massimo snapped. "We were insulted first."

"Yes, it does matter," Lorenzo answered firmly. "A duel must be concerned with a man's personal honor only. The law states that a duel may not be fought for reasons of vendetta or revenge. Revenge, after all, has nothing to do with honor and can be acquired in other ways."

"There, as I told you, Massimo," Girolamo hissed. "Let the family handle it. We'll send them an exploding letter. Kill the lot of them."

"I want the duel!" Massimo roared. "I'm a courtier, damn it. I must uphold honor. Without it, I am nothing."

"True," Lorenzo agreed. "Though dueling is usually illegal, the law has graciously allowed for single combats so that entire families do not engage in destructive feuds. However, Signore, I must warn you that the duel may not be fought to acquire honor."

"Then what is it for?" demanded Massimo, who was becoming confused.

"A duel may be fought to retain one's honor, or to regain it when it has been falsely attacked. The honor must be yours to begin with. For instance, I call you a bastard—"

Massimo stiffened.

"Calm yourself, it is only an example," Lorenzo soothed him. "But if it were true, and you were illegitimate, then you could not engage me in a duel, for no lie would be given."

"Under what circumstances is a duel allowable?" Massimo asked through gritted teeth.

"Ah. Perhaps you have been falsely called a traitor to your prince, or perhaps you have been falsely accused of insulting another man. These are matters that impinge on your honor as a courtier and demand action for the restoration of that honor."

"Colloredo falsely insulted me," Massimo said gravely, lifting his chin. "And I announced to several witnesses that the man lied in his throat."

"That is the first step. Now we must decide into which category this particular lie falls so we know how to proceed. Wait, I must find my manuals." Lorenzo rose and went to the bookshelves, returning to his desk with two books. He began to thumb through them, aware that his clients were growing impatient.

"Now, here we have seven different classifications of lies that may be used for the first challenge in the cartello. This text also gives us an additional thirty-two classifications of lies. Let us go through them together and perhaps you can identify which is the most precise in this case."

Lorenzo looked up at Massimo and saw the man's composure was beginning to crumble beneath twitching cheek muscles. Girolamo slapped his hand to his forehead.

"Madonna mio, Massimo, by the time this scholar has figured out which end of the spear Colloredo tried to screw you with, we'll be dead from old age. Away now, and let's do this thing the right way. Alla Macchia! A field, any field, and a pair of swords."

"But it's not honorable. I want the return of my honor," Massimo complained, "or I can't seek the hand of the Widow Battiferri with any hope of success. And I want those lands."

"Then you will need to tell me the truth, so I can determine into what category of lie the insult must fall," Lorenzo explained patiently.

The little bells above the door jingled merrily as Giano entered the shop, whistling. Seeing the two brightly dressed lords, he stopped short, took off his felt hat, and gave a wobbly bow. He belched quietly and the room was immediately filled with the odor of wine.

"Ah, there you are, at last, you scoundrel," Lorenzo said with a touch of annoyance. "You're late. I expected you at least two hours ago."

"The past is done, and as it is now the present, I am here, on time for the time it is now," Giano said, and straightened himself slowly.

"You've been drinking," Lorenzo stated.

"True enough, I've been drinking," Giano said with a silly grin. "But be calm, good master. I don't drink from the sin of dissolution! On the contrary, it's my habit to drink and as it's natural to have habits, and nature is the product of divine inspiration, why then, my drinking is good."

"Sot," grumbled Massimo.

"Peacock," retorted Giano, riffling the trailing flaps of Massimo's bright hat. "That's quite a beak you've got there," he added, tweaking a surprised Massimo by his prominent nose. "Mantuan no doubt."

"Riffraff," sniffed Girolamo, and reached for his sword.

"Ah, the peahen," Giano bubbled, squinting into Girolamo's pinched face. "Not as brightly colored as her mate, but easily riled."

"How dare you insult us!" Massimo rumbled angrily. His hand twisted the hilt of his sword.

"And how like a virgin is your sword, Signor Peacock—afraid to be seen naked the first time."

"You lie," Massimo yelled, slapping Giano hard across the face with a leather glove. Giano fell back against the bookcases, and three volumes, precariously perched on top, fell over onto his head. "I want another challenge drawn up right now," Massimo ordered. "I shall kill this fool for insulting me."

"I am afraid you can't," Lorenzo answered, holding up his hands in a placating gesture. "You're not the same rank. This is my servant. A foolish man perhaps, but a simple one. No match for your nobility, sirs."

Giano groaned, his head covered by books. Feebly, he raised his hands and sketched the curving outline of a woman in the air. "Angelica, you kiss like a wet fish," he moaned. "Come take the worm, my pretty mackerel."

Girolamo kicked him and turned a weasel eye to Massimo. "For the sake of Christ's blood, what are we doing here, Massimo? How can you let this puff of a lawyer, with a drunken imbecile for a servant, instruct you about lies and honor? He'll have your balls in a net of legal blather and that bastardo Colloredo will make you a laughing stock. You can forget about the widow! Come on. I know an alchemist who learned the secret of the Borgia poisons."

Massimo hesitated, his eyes wavering between Lorenzo's hands resting on the pages of his law book, and Giano sprawled on the floor, moaning into the pages of the dusty tomes.

"Bah," he said at last, and, with an angry gesture, stormed out of the door. Girolamo followed close behind him, slamming the door so hard that the bells were knocked off the wall.

The room was suddenly quiet. Lorenzo pursed his lips and pressed his fingertips together, pulsing them irritably.

"Have they left?" Giano asked, lifting a book from his head.

"Yes," Lorenzo snapped.

"Look, sir, you're better off without those two," Giano said, springing to his feet with surprising agility. "I'm telling you, they're bad business. I know them. Heard all about their bloody feud in the market. They're Mantuan all right but I'd say their blood is running a little thin. It's made them mad."

"What do you mean their blood is thin?"

"Well, take that nose."

"What about it?"

"Everyone in that family has that nose."

"Impossible."

"No, sir, it's true. Even the women. It's a known fact that few of them marry outside a veeeery close circle." Giano pinched his fingers together.

Lorenzo stared a moment longer at Giano, his fingertips pulsing faster. It was true that the man Massimo had a very pronounced nose. It was true that he came from Mantua. It was also true that he appeared temperamental. Lorenzo folded his fingers into a two-handed clasp. "Still, it would have meant a fee of a hundred ducats."

"He never would have paid, sir. Gossips say that the fool's already deep in debt. He hopes to wed a rich widow. Long before you even saw one coin, he would have settled his duel on a road somewhere in the dark with a band of hired mercenaries."

"So you lied about being drunk?" Lorenzo said, suddenly changing the subject.

Giano smiled. "I spoke the truth that I had followed my habit of refreshing myself with wine. But it was the signore who decided I must be drunk."

Lorenzo shrugged, knowing that to argue with his servant was useless. The man was a fool, a halfwit who told the truth because he was too simple to lie. But he paused none the less, studying Giano's smiling face. It occurred to Lorenzo that had he been asked to give a precise and truthful description of the man, he could not. His eyes, Lorenzo decided, were a medium blue, but in the next instant the light shifted, and he had to claim they were brown. Or were they green? He had a large nose, Lorenzo thought firmly, and then watched as it seem to shrink into a button mushroom as Giano idly picked it. Nothing on the man's face held its contours for very long. But that was impossible. His inability to describe his servant must be because Giano had such an ordinary face. One does not need to describe a glass of water after all, or the color of dirt.

Lorenzo glanced down at Giano's boots as he always did when disturbed by his servant's physical vagueness. The boots, at least, were always the same: dirty black leather, a size too large, and curled up at the toes. A pattern of red and gold diamonds was painted into the leather tops.

Satisfied that he had found one invariable truth about his servant, Lorenzo handed him a sheaf of papers tied with a red ribbon and sealed with wax.

"Here, take these manifestos to the home of Gasparo Colonna on the Via Apuleuis. He has ships leaving the port of Genoa in three days, but they cannot leave without these documents. Go there immediately. When you have completed your task, you are to come this evening to the tavern near the Arch of Dreams where I am meeting a client. See that you bring the third and fourth copies signed. Do you understand?"

"A woman client, perhaps?" Giano said hopefully. "A young widow in need of legal assistance?"

"Don't be impertinent," Lorenzo snapped. "It's an elderly ironmonger with a belly like a—"

Giano's eyebrows lifted expectantly. Lorenzo hesitated. The promise of a poetic simile hovered for an instant and then withered as his mind drew a blank.

"He has a huge belly and gout in one leg," he said precisely. "He's missing three teeth and has hair in his ears."

Giano's eyebrows fell. "Tonight then, Master. At the Arch of Dreams," Giano repeated. He turned gracefully and swung his long body through the doorway.

Lorenzo grunted, turning his attention back to the words written in black ink spelling out an endless stream of legal arguments. He picked up his stylus and sighed at its dreary insect scratchings.

Giano smiled at the busy street. This was the sort of day he cherished. That morning he had taken a few of the master's coins and procured for himself a very fine lunch. There had been a plate of tagliatelle with fresh porcini mushrooms, a meat pie filled with rabbit, chicken, and slivers of ham, a little soup to cleanse the palate, and a crostata di ricotta with green grapes to finish. He had washed it all down with two bottles of very good Tuscan red wine. His stomach was full and his lips were still savoring the wine's oaken taste. There was not much in the way of work before him, and he felt the day would be well spent either napping along the river or, if he was feeling frisky, strolling through the Piazza del Labirinto in search of opportunities.

Giano patted his chest, he cupped his groin, he tweaked his cheek, and decided he was feeling frisky. Humming lightly to himself, he set his feet in the direction of the Great Maze. The streets were very narrow, some alleys no more than creases between grey-black walls. The sun blazed on top floors and shimmered in windows, but couldn't penetrate the lower portions of the street. Ropes crisscrossed near the rooftops, hung with linen sheets that quietly dripped water onto the heads of the passersby. Pigeons settled on the ropes, scrabbling their claws over the linens and streaking them with grey droppings. An angry maid raked a broom out of an open window to shoo the birds away. A stray white spotted feather drifted down in front of Giano's face.

After pawing the air a few times, he succeeded in catching the feather. Examining it thoroughly, Giano decided it was an omen of good luck. He tucked it into his cap and continued ambling toward the piazza, around a corner and past a bakery, whose open door allowed the smell of warm bread to waft into the street. Giano's feet slowed. He lingered, indecisive. Despite a full stomach, Giano believed there was always room for a little something else. He pulled up a few soldi di piccolo and bought three flat breads, one studded with green olives, the other two smothered in rosemary and oil.

Oppressed by the dark winding streets of the city, Giano beamed as he stepped onto the paving stones of the piazza. A few stray clouds puffed over the high cedar walls of the maze. There was a good crowd gathered around the wooden gates. They hadn't opened in a while and the feverish hope of the collected pilgrims permeated the air.

Giano watched a wealthy woman in a veil that revealed only her injured eyes dig into her pockets and drop a few coins into an old woman's begging bowl. Nearby, a family huddled around a two-wheeled cart, the mother suckling her infant while the father and two other children played with a little dog. Giano wondered what would have brought this seemingly content family to the maze until he saw a fourth child, a boy, lying on a filthy litter of straw in the cart. This child's wrists and feet were bound but still he writhed, foam bubbling at the corners of his mouth. He began shouting curses and howling as he rolled his body from side to side. Hearing the curses, the father wiped the spittle from his son's face, taking care not to let his hand stray too close to the snapping teeth.

Not too far from this domestic scene, two elderly men were sitting side by side comparing their ailments. One had sores on his leg, the other a withered arm. One was missing teeth, the other his hair. Each time a young female pilgrim passed them, lost in her private misery, the men forgot their own, and kissed their fingertips.

Giano circled the outer rim of the piazza slowly, studying the pilgrims for hopeful prospects; people with money they were willing to lose. Giano patted his chest, feeling the maps rolled in his doublet alongside the legal papers destined for Signor Colonna. They were secret maps of the maze, showing the way through the terrible traps filled with monsters and how to avoid the dead ends. They were very good maps, Giano thought. After all, he had made them himself, borrowing a few of Lorenzo's starched papers and inks. He wasn't greedy. He was willing to sell them at a reasonable price and found that some pilgrims were desperate enough to purchase them.

Giano's eyes lighted on a priest looking very pensive as he read a small book. An old beggar woman bounced her begging bowl, jingling her coins to get his attention. Without glancing up from his book, the priest took a coin from the recesses of his habit. It flashed with a spark of gold as it fell from his fingers into the begging bowl. The old woman snatched the coin and quickly tucked it into the folds of her ragged black dress. Giano grinned and made his way across the piazza toward the priest.

"My blackbird, pretty ucellino," he crooned softly to himself, his eyes on the priest. "Save another gold coin for this lost soul."

Giano sidled up next to the priest and peeked at the title of the book the man was reading so intently. *The Confessions of St. Augustine* was tooled in gold into the leather binding. Ah, thought Giano, the priest must be feeling guilty as well as desperate.

"Excuse me, good Father," Giano said in a hushed voice. "Perhaps I can give you better guidance in your hour of need than this devoted church father. Though of course I respect him very much," he added obsequiously.

The priest looked up. Giano stumbled back, not expecting the handsome young face he saw. Even the tonsure had not humbled the man's fine white brow, nor the faded black robes dulled the clarity of his large dark eyes.

"Are you familiar with St. Augustine?" the priest asked with an amused smile.

"Of course," Giano babbled. "An excellent treatise on . . . on . . . confession, of course. A useful guide on the path of spiritual perfection," he improvised. "If I may be so bold, Father, it's not spirituality that has brought you to Labirinto, eh? Looking at your sturdy youth, I'd say some other reason drives you here, haunts you like the fresh breast of a girl while she confesses. Believe me, I know. These are powerful temptations, even for my humble self. For a holy man such as yourself, it can only be a curse to suffer." Giano gave a knowing wink.

The priest laughed and shook his head. "Those were not temptations my good man. They were, alas, my habits."

"Even in your habit?" Giano asked, tugging on the black robes.

"More often out of the habit, though there is little enough room in a confessional to shed the habit of clothing. Once I disguised two Venetian courtesans, hiding their golden hair under friar's cowls, and led them past the other priests of San Pantelon into my cell. What limbs they had, their skin whiter than the alabaster, their lips red as the wine! We stayed awake all night finding new ways to celebrate the hours. Signore, you are drooling on my book."

"Ah, Dio, you priests know how to pray," Giano said breathlessly. "Listen, why would a man like you with such an excellent calling come to the maze?"

"Because I have only just heard my calling, and it keeps me awake at night," the priest answered softly.

"I have a map—" Giano began.

The priest shook his head. "I don't need it."

"But surely you will want to visit those courtesans again one day? I know I wouldn't give up such a pretty flock of sinners."

"Anyone can service them. It only takes money."

"Then help me achieve such divine service, my good priest, and buy my map," Giano urged. He couldn't stop thinking about the courtesans, their firm white legs flashing beneath the brown folds of a friar's garb.

The priest shook his head. "I have no money left. I gave my last sequin to a beggar woman. Farewell, my friend, and may God keep you well." The priest edged away from Giano, heading for the gates of the maze.

"Cazzo," Giano muttered as he watched the priest disappear amid the waiting pilgrims. His gaze lifted over the piazza, searching for another possible customer.

"Sant' Anna, my blessings to you," he exclaimed, seeing a strange pair leave the shelter of the curved colonnades and enter the piazza. A tall, hulking woman, her face nearly hidden by her matted black hair, walked beside a young and very dirty-looking man. Her dress was a ragged wool, and beneath the torn hem her feet splayed over the paving stones. The man beside her pushed back a fringe of blond hair from a tired, petulant face. It was the two masks, hanging from his neck, their silent stares peering out at the crowds from the man's chest that caught Giano's eye and made his heart jump.

Had the grubby pair walked past him, he would not have paid the slightest attention to them. But the masks cried out to him, trumpeted their superiority over the slovenly youth who hauled them around his neck like a stupid donkey. Recognizing their glistening black faces and stern eyes from across the piazza, Giano gave them a little bow of respect. Even from so far away, he knew they were the work of Anna Forsetti. And if he played the game right, the masks could be his, falling into his hands like a gift from God.

Giano sprinted across the piazza, annoyed to see the old beggar woman reaching the pair before him. She was an irritating sort of crone. Hunched over, swaddled in black rags, her hand holding the begging bowl under the noses of the pilgrims, she shook the bowl to make the few coins dance. With a certain amount of professional superiority, Giano watched the man brush her off. The woman stopped and stared into the old face. It almost made Giano laugh, for the tall woman had her own veil of black hair, while the beggar hid her face in a thick wrapping of dirty black cloth. The women eyed each other before the beggar woman moved off, rather more quickly than Giano might have guessed, looking at her swaddled legs and bandaged feet.

"You there," Giano called out to the man. "You're an actor, aren't you? I swear to Christ I've seen you perform before. Where was it? Bergamo with the Uniti? Or could it have been Padua with the Gelosi? There is something about you that is so familiar," he lied.

The man stopped abruptly and scowled at Giano.

"F-f-fuck yourself," he spluttered.

"Ah now I recognize you," Giano answered, refusing to be deterred.

"It was at Venice. Carnevale last year. The Infiniti. You performed the stammering servant! You were brilliant. I laughed until tears rolled down my cheeks."

"Sh-sh-sh—"

"Oh, of course, I won't let anyone know you are here," Giano said confidentially.

"Sh-shut up, you ad-ad—"

"Admirer. Well, yes, I am," Giano said gaily.

"Addled old fart."

"No, really. Your secret is safe with me. My lips are shut, my good sir." He mimed the locking of his mouth.

The man's face grew ruddy beneath its grime. His stomach growled, a noise that delighted Giano's ears. A hungry actor, with a stammer like an idiot. The masks were as good as his.

"I say, let me help you out, my good man, seeing how we are fellow theater lovers—you a sublime actor, and me, a devoted patron of the arts. Please share my simple repast with me." Giano unwrapped the two loaves of rosemary bread he had brought and handed them to the man.

The man hesitated, his scowl deepening, his lips pressed around an unspoken fury. The woman nudged him hard in the side. The man took the breads, giving one to the woman. He tore off a huge bite and chewed like a ravenous dog.

"Th-thank you," he said glumly.

"I am Giano of Labirinto. Please remind me of your name, that I may etch it forever in my memory."

The young man rolled his eyes and shook his head. "Y-y-you don't know me."

"But I must!" Giano insisted. "The stammer so perfectly executed, the slouch in your walk, the narrow eyes in your dissipated face . . ."

"Not dis-dis-sipated. J-j-just hungry," the man said angrily. "And I-I don't slouch!"

"Ah, I begin to see the problem now," Giano said, a finger laid against his nose. "You don't stutter by choice, but by curse. And you hope like so many pilgrims to lose your afflictions among the mysterious corridors of the maze, eh?"

The man nodded, eating the last bite of bread. He licked the grease from his lips and wiped his mouth on his sleeve. The woman beside him sucked the oil off her fingers with a smacking noise.

"But, I have the very thing for you, my friend," Giano said, stepping up closer to the man. He put his arm around the hunched shoulders and whispered into his ear. "I have a map of the maze."

"A m-m-map?"

"Shush, or the others will hear."

"I had intended to enter the maze myself, stricken with the curse of love that is not returned. But seeing you here, and remembering my greater love for the theater that has never deserted me, I feel I must assist you in some way. I would gladly sacrifice my own journey to see that you, a promising young actor, should be able to complete yours. I will sell you this map, which I bought for a hundred florins from a Florentine sorcerer who has traveled the maze many times to learn its secrets." Giano saw the light of hope flare in the man's eyes and then just as quickly extinguish.

"B-b-but I have n-no money to pay you."

"No money? Well, perhaps a trade then. You could give me those masks, say, in exchange. I will hold them for you here in Labirinto. And when you have successfully journeyed the maze, you may return the map to me and I will give you back your masks."

The man scowled uncertainly and glanced up at the woman, a silent question on his face.

"The stage calls to you," Giano urged. "You must not disappoint it. Even now the audience is ready to applaud your courage. Come, take the map and I will keep your masks safe." Giano held out a rolled copy of the map.

It was the woman who took the map roughly from Giano's hand. When he tried to protest, she held him off with one strong hand, while the other let the map unroll before her eyes. Beneath her matted black hair, Giano saw her sapphire eyes dart across the painted lines.

Abruptly, she released her hold on Giano's doublet and her finger pointed to a figure in the maze. She grinned, showing teeth flecked with rosemary. She opened her mouth as though to laugh, but no sound came from her lips. The man's gaze followed her finger and he snickered, seeing the clumsy figure of a siren spouting water from a hidden lake in the maze. Two round circles defined her breasts, her nipples were black spots of ink. Her eyes were crossed beneath the plume of spraying water.

The man rolled the map back up and handed it Giano.

"N-no thank you," he said. "It-it's a fake."

"Eh! So the painting is rough, surely we can't all be masters. But it's real I tell you! It will get you through the maze!"

"My fr-fr-friend here thinks it will not."

"Your friend. And what sort of expert is she?" Giano squeaked. "Excuse me, Signorina, but you don't look the type to study the science of black magic. Nor art, for that matter," Giano said angrily. The masks were slipping from his grasp. Arlecchino's lips were curled into a sneer. Pantelone's creased eyebrows rebuked him for being too slow.

"The Signorina knows what she is talking about—"

"She hasn't said a word!" protested Giano.

"Nevertheless, I understand. I won't give you my masks. Now, please leave us alone."

"But you can't be serious," Giano said, growing desperate. He clutched the man's arm tightly. The woman thumped Giano hard across the back of his head with an open hand and he gasped in shocked surprise and let go. The pair hurried away, melting into the crowd of pilgrims.

Giano stood there, rubbing the back of his head. "Cazzo," he spat. "Stupid ass. Even a pig speaks better than you."

Angry, Giano tried to assess why his promising afternoon had crumbled into failure. As he thought his eyes found the bent-over figure of the begging woman. He watched her with a growing malice. He hated her corpulent body wrapped like a dumpy sack in black cloth. He hated her bandaged feet, her hidden face. It was all her fault, he decided. The old strega. She was a curse, a black cat crossing in front of every one of his prospects.

She was doing rather well for herself, he thought, appraising her skill as a beggar. She kept her head abjectly down, not to offend the eyes of the pilgrims, but the dancing coins, bouncing noisily in the begging bowl, made it impossible to ignore her. A strolling pair of young noblemen passed close to her and, at the sound of her jingling coins, casually dropped a good silver coin into her bowl. Giano's eyes slitted in envy and then widened as he saw a slim white hand appear from the folds of black rags, quickly pick up the coin, and carry it to her mouth to bite. For a brief instant, Giano saw the face of a girl and not a crone at all.

He smiled. "Brava ragazza!" he muttered. Not a bad little actress. She had almost had him fooled. He decided to stroll a while and watch her work the crowds. He had time yet before he had to deliver the manifestos. He took out his remaining loaf, plucked out an olive, and sucked on it, enjoying its salty bitterness. Sometimes, he decided, it was as good as any theater to watch these clever thieves at play. Oh, how they could perform for the crowd! Wasn't it a pity that the audience never knew enough to appreciate it?

Two hours later, the sun was slanting through the afternoon clouds, burnishing the black paving stones once more into a field of golden nuggets. Giano was growing bored. The crone had done reasonably well, though once it had surprised him when, just as she was about to score a large piece of jewelry from a distraught-looking courtesan, she scuttled out of the piazza and into a side street. Giano had frowned, perplexed, then shrugged when she had returned to the piazza a moment later. She continued to work and had even managed to collect the jewelry from the courtesan after all. And now here she was in front of a burly countryman who was sobbing as he sliced off shavings of cured ham into her bowl. "Mamma, Mamma," he was crying, and there were tears in his eyes.

Giano licked his lips, thinking of the sweet taste of the ham. The old crone seemed eager, too. But, as before, she clutched her stomach and ran out of the piazza, leaving a trail of sliced ham. A little dog followed after her, pausing to gobble up the fallen slices. Too curious to ignore it this time, Giano followed the crone quickly, noting where she disappeared down a narrow alley.

A few moments later Giano entered the alley, moving slowly and quietly. Wooden crates and wheelbarrows cluttered the alley. A door opened and an apprentice in a leather apron tossed wood shavings into the street. Giano couldn't see any sign of the crone but he kept going, making his way carefully around the debris of the alley.

He heard her before he saw her. Quiet grunts were coming from behind a stack of crates. A piebald cat on top of the crate was staring intently behind the crate. Giano held his finger to his lips as the cat raised its head and lifted its tail into a question mark. Giano petted the cat's scrawny head and peered over the top of the crates.

The crone had pulled up her huge black skirts and was squatting down to defecate. Her straining thighs were slender beneath the bunched skirts, the skin pale and very young.

"O'Dio." She sighed and grunted a little harder. "Come on. You've been in there long enough," she whispered.

She sighed more heavily and the odor of shit rose to assault Giano's nostrils. He was about to retreat when the crone turned around and began to examine her feces.

She'd pushed back the heavy wrappings around her face and Giano was charmed by her girlish features. A vixen, with a narrow chin, a sharp pointed nose, and a bad bruise coloring one cheek. She reached down to the pile of excrement and pulled out a soiled gold ring set with a good stone. She smiled in triumph and wiped it clean with a rag.

"I usually do that trick with an ass," Giano remarked.

She looked up startled, palmed the ring, and pulled her skirts securely around her.

"Most people shit from their ass," she snapped.

"No. I mean I get another ass to shit the gold."

"What are you, crazy?" she asked angrily.

"No, it's a great trick and far less painful than shitting your own gold. But really it works best if you have an audience."

"I do have an audience. You, you perverted old man. Do you like to watch little girls crapping? Schifo! Get the hell away from me."

The cat twitched its tail, the knobby head swiveling back and forth between Giano and the angry girl.

"Come, come," Giano said, his hands raised to show he meant no harm. "I was only speaking professionally. I've been watching you—"

"See! You admit it. You are a dirty old man. Now bugger off."

"Signorina, be reasonable—"

"A maid can't have a private moment with her bowels, and you ask her to be reasonable."

"Most maids don't shit gold rings."

"No, you testa di merda, they shit flowers. Go sniff them, you goat."

Giano grinned even more widely. He liked this girl. She was sharp, like cut glass, and nasty. She was eyeing him warily, the narrow confines of the crowded alley not giving her too much room for escape.

"Are you hungry?" Giano asked, and saw the answer leap into her eyes.

"Who isn't?"

"So, come. Let's eat. I'm on an errand for my master," he said, tapping his chest where the manifestos lay hidden beneath his doublet. "But there is still time for a little something. I am curious to know the truth about your ability to shit rings."

"The ring belongs to me!" she answered defiantly.

"Of course, Signorina! Would one thief be so dishonorable as to give another thief an invitation to dine only to steal from her? Out of respect for our profession, I am only interested in your tale, not your ring," Giano said. The piebald cat sat back on its haunches and meowed loudly. "Hush, cat. Your opinion doesn't count here."

"All right," the girl said. "But no funny stuff, and keep your hands to yourself."

"Of course, Signorina."

In truth, Giano had not thought to steal the ring from the girl. But the moment she suggested it, he was taken with the idea. After all, the girl probably expected him to try, so who was he to let her down? But how? First a little food to soften the hard tilt of her arms, maybe some wine to blur the senses. Hmm, could be amusing, he thought as he watched her black skirts sweep the dirt of the alley before him.

The sun was setting when they returned to the piazza. Giano figured he had just enough time to bamboozle the little thief and still do his errand for Lorenzo. The fading light was beautiful, gold and serene as though sprinkled with dust from the goldsmith's shop. The pilgrims were drowsing like bees in the heat of summer. Even the green cedar trees of the Great Maze were changed, standing like sentries in the sunlight with fiery lances.

A loud creak sounded across the piazza. Heads looked up expectantly. A second creak followed, and the gates to the maze began to swing open. They didn't open completely, just enough to let one person at a time enter. All across the piazza, the pilgrims hurried to their feet. Some gathered their scattered belongings while others abandoned them to join the throng running toward the open gates. Giano saw the priest enter first, squeezing his body in sideways. Behind him, a crowd pressed, the pilgrims swearing and screaming at those in front to hurry. The gates groaned and slowly began to close. The crowd pushed even more urgently and cries of agony rose from those closest to the gates who were being crushed by the overeager crowd.

"O'Dio!" the girl at his side cried out, and leaned her body against Giano for support. "They're being killed!" she sobbed, and buried her head in his shoulder. Her arms circled his neck and clung to him tightly.

A hard clang thundered in the air. The metallic echo drifted over the shouts of angry pilgrims and the agonized wails of those wounded in the crush.

"There, there." Giano patted the girl's head, surprised by this sudden outburst of emotion. Well, she was young. Tender maybe, when it came to scenes of death. He had seen enough of wars and plagues to find it all too familiar. Wait a minute, he thought, startled to discover her hand roaming inside his doublet. What's she doing?

All at once the girl yanked out the rolled manifestos and jumped back, free of Giano's arms.

"Merda!" they cried out, simultaneously outraged. The girl glared at the rolled paper.

"Give those back to me!" Giano demanded.

"Pay me," she demanded.

"They're worthless."

"Then why do you want them?"

"Bitch!" Giano cried.

"Dirty old man! That's what you get for spying on me!"

Giano made a lunge for the girl, but she bolted away like a deer sprinting across the piazza. She snaked her body between the gathered knots of weeping pilgrims. Giano followed close behind her, snatching at her trailing clothes. As they zigzagged, she stayed one step ahead of him.

Close to the maze, he saw her glance back, her face pinched with the effort of running. He forced a spurt of speed into his legs, and she turned away in terror to run for all she was worth toward the wall of cedars and impenetrable hedges.

"Thief! Catch her!" Giano called, and a soldier leaning wearily against a pike straightened and looked about. He saw the girl approach and fanned his arms to catch her. She swerved to avoid him and the two elderly men opened their palsied arms to her, leers baring their toothless gums.

Giano had her cornered now: a soldier to her left, lechers to her right, and himself closing the distance between them. The girl turned wide-eyed with her back pressed against the leafy wall of the maze. Just as Giano was about to pounce on her, the maze behind her rustled. The branches parted, opening a tiny space no bigger than a rabbit hole. Two arms covered with brown patches of fur reached out and a pair of hands with black fingernails pulled the girl into the thick cover of the maze. She screamed and thrashed, and a host of tiny birds exploded out of the shrubbery, fluttering wildly into the air.

"No! Goddamn it, my papers!" Giano shouted as the girl's kicking feet disappeared through the leaves. He dove for her ankles, forcing his head and shoulders into the small opening. It was shrinking fast, but he gritted his teeth and pulled on the branches, breaking the woody stems of the shrubs in an effort to force a passage. Suddenly, a hand reached in between the thicket of leaves and grabbed his left hand. A second hand grabbed his right hand. These helpful hands were smooth and moist and felt decidedly feminine.

He was almost through the thick wall of the maze when he felt a hard jerk behind. Someone outside the maze was trying to pull him out again by his boots.

"Pull harder, sisters," a woman's voice ahead of him called, and Giano was dragged through the rough tangle of branches, sputtering as twigs and leaves forced their way into his mouth. Through the dense foliage he was certain he caught a glimpse of white skin, a leg, or an arm. A cloud of sweet perfume tickled his nose. He was almost there.

Another fierce tug on his boots from the other side of the maze slowed his progress. Impatient, he kicked his heels angrily. "Let go," he growled. "Let go!" Another tug, and he kicked against the invisible hands even harder. His boots suddenly slipped off, and he was hauled at last through the branches into the miraculous maze.

"Oh how pretty he is," said a melodious voice as Giano broke through the bushes and rolled onto the grass. "And he doesn't have hooves!"

Giano spit out a mouthful of leaves, looked up, and smiled blissfully. He was surrounded by women. All of them naked. In their long hair they wore garlands of flowers, their graceful necks were adorned with grapevines, and their wrists with bracelets of threaded acorns. Sunlight dappled their smooth shoulders and their haunches curved like white crescent moons.

"Che paradiso." Giano sighed.

The women laughed musically, and their naked skin blushed as pink as a handful of blooming roses.

13

The sun was dawning when Zizola's curse stumbled across the remains of a stone structure. It knew that the mountain had not made this shelter of stones and wood in the same manner that it had birthed Itself from the molten rock. It stopped, allowing the fingers of the wind to brush over Its heated surface. Hunger called to It again; It must feed. It raised Its head, devoid of features save for the white-streaked mouth and the hollow eyes. The wind eddied around Its curves and coaxed a nose from the oval head. It was long and pointed like a snout.

Sniffing, It found the ripe odors of the fields: the musk of sheep bedded down in the grass, the rich scent of hay-fed cattle. Stone jaws snapped in the air, tasting, remembering the goat. Flesh, blood. These were things It needed.

It walked toward the stone shelter, drawn by the solemn weight of the structure. The stones were stacked into walls, the low roof was curved like the peak of the mountain. It passed quietly through an opening and found Itself cradled in darkness. A center aisle split the shelter with rotting wood laid out to either side. It looked up and saw ribs of wooden beams struggling to keep the stone walls from falling inward. It walked forward, head turning from side to side as tiny windows bled light into the dark interior.

It stopped suddenly as shafts of sunlight arrowed into the figure of a man hanging silently on the outstretched branches of a leafless tree. It recognized the man's shape from the last thoughts of the goat It had consumed. It knew that man, like goats, could be eaten and consumed. It knew that man had power.

It moved cautiously, wary at the man's stillness, anticipating, though not fearing, a swift attack or flight. A mercury tongue flickered over the thin lips as It stood before the figure and gazed hungrily. The man seemed to be sleeping, his eyes heavily lidded, his body stretched thin and long down the tree's smooth trunk.

The sleeping man did not appear to see the iridescent form before him. He did not cry out when It turned Its body into a thick rope and coiled Itself around his ankles. There was a crackling noise and smoke hissed beneath the coils. Hunger hurried It to the man's head, which still slept.

It swallowed the head, sprouted the molars of the goat, and chewed, tasting only charred wood and then bitter ash as the man burned into a black powder. What was this thing? It asked the smoke. What was this man whom the goat feared, who had no blood to steam, no flesh?

The curse stretched Its arms along the crossbeam of wood, seeking an answer, taking the shape of the man It had just destroyed. The wood was mute, its only sense an infestation of tiny worms shriveling in their channels. Cold iron nails rusted in their sockets, changed into molten tears by Its heat.

It heard a noise at the entrance and lay still against the outstretched wood, Its eyes heavy lidded, Its head drooped against one shoulder. A small shadow darkened the entrance and another figure darted into the darkened shelter.

The curse heard a voice, chanting softly as the figure approached, breathing sweat, smoke, and the reek of animals. Its core began to pulse. This one was alive. Alive with flesh. Alive with the thing that beat, the thing It did not have.

The figure stopped before It and gazed upward. Eyes luminous in the gold shafts of light pleaded with It. The figure kneeled, hands clasped together before the rounded chest. Was this a man, It wondered, staring down from beneath Its half-closed lids. How different man seemed from what It had imagined from the vision of the goat: smaller, more vulnerable, lacking even the goat's instincts to flee.

But no matter that this man was not impressive. Hunger shrieked within Its core and the man was sustenance. It pulled Its arms away from the remains of the iron pegs and grabbed the kneeling figure into Its fiery embrace.

"O'Dio!" the parted lips cried.

It took longer to consume this feast than it had to consume the goat. For all its smallness, the flesh was rich, the blood thick. There were surprises: milk flowing in pouches and small eggs nestled in ruffled sacs. And still another surprise—yet a smaller man curled within the belly of the first. A man within a man, It thought, wondering at the complexity of this meal.

From Its meal's last thoughts, the curse learned that man was two: male and female. This larger man was female and the tiny man she carried within her the male. She and He. It asked Itself why such distinctions must be made. Wasn't it enough to be alive, to feel the pulse of the earth, to hunger and then to eat? To have a purpose for existence? What else must life contain?

It walked slowly out of the structure that It now knew was called a church. It knew also that the man of wood had once lived and died and lived again. This too It had learned from the woman. The man had not eaten as It did, but was eaten by the woman.

"Dio," It said. It let Its body relax into the woman's form, testing the shape. Smoky tendrils of hair curled over Its shoulders. Its hands questioned the weight of breasts, the cleft hidden between Its legs. It found pleasure in this shape. The wide hips gave It balance and It walked with a smooth rolling gait down the steep slopes of the hills. The tiny feet found their way easily between the rough path of stones.

"Curse," It said to the rising sun, letting the brilliant red-gold rays illuminate the way to Its unalterable destiny.

14

Mirabella was selecting onions from a cart in the market when she felt the first assault on her buttocks. A hard pinch through the fabric of her skirts made her cry out and whirl around. She glowered angrily, but could not identify the attacker among the pilgrims shopping in the open-air market that surrounded the Piazza del Labirinto. Two elderly men wheezing into their palms and leaning on each other for support appeared to be deep in conversation. A guard mused over a cart filled with ribbons and combs while the ribbon seller, a solid girl with plump arms, fussed over his selection. Three beggar boys threw dice. A scruffy young man talked to a tall, black-haired woman as they studied a cart loaded with tomatoes, radicchio, and eggplants. An orange seller and a fishmonger sang a clashing duet to the crowd shoving its way through the narrow aisles between the carts and stalls.

"Who was it, Lily?" Mirabella whispered to the little dog in her basket. "Pray God it's not those dirty old men." Maybe it was the guard, her inner voice said hopefully. Take another peek.

Mirabella glanced over her shoulder at the ribbon cart, but the guard had been replaced by two chattering serving girls. Mirabella shrugged and turned her attention back to the onions. She decided it had been the guard. At least he was handsome.

A second pinch on her buttock made her cry out and twirl on her heel, her hand ready for a slap. But the offender had once again slipped into the crowd, unless her tormenter was the solitary man in a black doublet walking past her. He appeared to be searching for someone. His face was somber, but it could be an act. Maybe he was just pretending to look for someone, when all the while he was just looking for innocent maids to pinch.

"Hey, Signore, who do you think you are?" Mirabella said loudly as he passed her a second time, looking distractedly over the heads of the crowd. She pushed up her spectacles and assumed a haughty air.

"I am Lorenzo Falcomatta," he answered, startled.

"And what do you mean, Signore, by abusing my maidenly honor in the market?" Mirabella demanded.

"I have no idea what you are talking about, Signorina. I am searching for my servant who disappeared in the piazza yesterday."

"Do you deny that you pinched my backside?"

"I am not interested in your backside, Signorina."

"Liar! I felt you! Twice you touched me."

"Signorina." The man drew himself up very straight. "I do not lie."

"It's the nature of every man to lie!" announced the ribbon seller belligerently.

"It was women who invented the lie," the onion seller scoffed. "After all, it was Eve who first seduced man into evil with her tongue."

"Imbecile!" snapped the ribbon seller. She brushed back her ringlets and shook her finger at the onion seller. "Eve ate the apple for the love of knowledge. Adam gobbled it up without a thought, just like any hungry pig."

"Eh, you've spiderwebs for brains. Everyone knows God loves man more," the orange seller broke in. "The Lord made man first!" he said, pointing his finger in the air. "He made a woman as an afterthought. And she's been trying to get back at Adam ever since, any way she knows how."

"Eh, Madonna mio," the fishmonger groaned, pinching her wet fingers together in a sign of disgust. "Everyone knows the Lord was practicing when he made Adam. He came from a fist of mud, out of which men have never climbed! But when it came to making a woman, the Lord knew better, so he formed her from a rib, not the mud. And Adam, that clod has been trying to drag her down ever since."

"You're all wrong," Lorenzo announced. "You should read Aristotle to learn the truth."

"I have, Signore," Mirabella said, lifting her chin. "And Saint Tomaso Aquino as well. With all respect to their intellects, they remain men, and their opinions are not to be trusted. I don't regard myself as an imperfect male, formed by the lack of heat in my father's sperm or the overwhelming cold wetness of my mother's blood. Furthermore, if such a theory of imperfection were true, why then would someone like yourself, a perfect male, be so interested in molesting my imperfect backside?"

"I told you I didn't molest your backside."

"Then who did?" Mirabella demanded.

The two elderly men snickered behind their hands and tried to hurry out from the growing crowd of onlookers.

"Oh no, not them! They're so disgusting," Mirabella moaned.

"Aren't they all?" chimed in one of the serving girls, her hands full of brightly colored ribbons.

"Hey you! Wait!" Lorenzo shouted as the old men were scuttling away. "Those boots you have on. I want to see them!"

The tall woman with black hair grabbed the old lechers by their moth-eaten capes and marched them back through the interested crowd to where Lorenzo was waiting.

"We've done nothing," they wheezed. "Pity us, sir, for we are ailing and blind. We never touched the girl! We couldn't, our hands shake too much." One held up a wrinkled hand and fluttered it at Mirabella, who leaned back against the onion cart. The old mottled pair reeked of garlic and dusty clothes. She rolled her eyes and tried to edge away from them.

"You can see very well," Lorenzo corrected. "Now. Where did you get those boots?"

"What boots?"

"The ones on your feet! They belonged to the servant I am searching for."

The crowd peered down over one anothers' shoulders to examine the old man's feet. No doubt about it—his boots were out of concert with the rest of his battered garb. Their black leather toes curled up expressively, and bright orange and gold leather diamonds circled his shriveled calves. The old man shuffled his feet back and forth as if trying to hide them.

"They're mine, I tell you," he whined.

"You, sir, lie."

"There, what did I tell you?" the ribbon seller threw a triumphant look at the onion seller. "From the cradle to the grave, men lie!"

"They learn it suckling the breast!" the onion seller retorted.

"Where did you get my servant's boots?" Lorenzo shouted, trying to be heard over the argument.

"They were dangling off his feet," the old man said angrily.

"And where were his feet?"

"Sticking out of the wall of the maze."

"And how did my servant's legs wind up there?"

Mirabella was leaning forward to catch the old man's reply when a hard pinch on her flank made her scream. This time she knew with certainty who had pinched her, and without another thought she turned to the second old man wheezing beside her and smacked him hard over the head with her basket. He howled and pitched forward, his hands scrabbling to hold on to something to keep from falling. His hands found her breasts and he squeezed them, coughing and spluttering with excitement. Mirabella screamed again and hit the man harder. A serving girl standing near assisted Mirabella by pelting the old man with onions from the onion seller's cart.

The onion seller roared in fury and the ribbon seller, not to be left out, raised her shrill voice in a battle cry against all men and threw a half-rotten orange at the onion seller's head. The orange vendor swore violently and was answered by the fishmonger, who emptied a bucket of fish guts over his feet, screaming all the while that men were not to be trusted. Ever.

In a matter of moments, the narrow street was filled with jostling couples, shouting insults and hurling rotting fruit and vegetables and a few loose paving stones. The gambling street boys took advantage of the confusion to pocket a few tomatoes, a handful of eggplants, and a couple of oranges. A serving maid palmed a velvet ribbon. Lily leapt from her basket, danced upright on her back paws, and barked wildly. Mirabella had just pulled herself free of the old man's grip when she was hit by a flying onion that knocked her spectacles right off her face.

The world suddenly went out of focus. A blur of colored shapes whirled and shouted around her, bumping into her and screeching in her ear. She touched her hair, then her ears, praying to find her spectacles still clinging there, perhaps by one stem. But they were gone. Ignoring the crowd around her, Mirabella dropped to her knees and began feeling about with her hands for the fallen spectacles.

"O'Dio," she groaned, patting the ground. "Lily, help me!"

But the little dog was twirling in circles, barking at the tall figures arguing over her head. Through the noise, Mirabella could hear Lorenzo demanding that the old man tell him where his servant had gone. She could hear the ribbon seller and the onion seller hurling insults at each other, each attack becoming increasingly more personal and passionate, until the tide turned entirely and the onion seller was admitting that women made him weak and the ribbon seller was offering happily to shore up his strength.

Through all this, Mirabella continued to search for her spectacles behind the wheels of the onion cart. She didn't want to think of how foolish she must look, down on all fours rooting among the vegetables like a pig.

"Are these what you're looking for?" a man's voice asked.

Mirabella looked up from the cobblestones and found herself squinting into the face of the scruffy young man. He, too, was down on all fours and he was holding out a pair of spectacles.

"Thank you," she whispered with sudden shyness. Gratefully she took her spectacles from him and wrapped the curling stems around her ears.

"Oh no," she groaned. One lens was shattered, fracturing the world into triangular images. The young man stared back at her with a hundred eyes and fifty noses. She closed one eye and looked at him through her remaining whole lens. He was smiling at her, a suggestion of humor lighting his eyes. And why shouldn't he find her predicament funny? Mirabella thought. How many times did she have to make a fool of herself in public before the whole world had learned to laugh at her? She lowered her eyes to hide the dismay on her face and saw the masks of Pantelone and Arlecchino hanging around his neck.

"Eh, perfetto!" She moaned and sat back on her haunches. "Hey, my old friends, what are you doing here?" The young man looked confused, turning his head to see who she was talking to.

Arlecchino rolled his eyes upward and gave his barking laugh. Pantelone snorted.

"Are you talking to the masks?" the young man asked, astonished.

"Of course I am," Mirabella replied. "I'm a fool just like them, aren't I? Idiota. Simpleton! Down on my knees in the street, waving my backside in the air! And stop your laughing, Arlecchino, or I'll get Mamma to take away your face!" she snapped at the mask, which was still barking with laughter. Arlecchino's mouth turned down and wailed while Pantelone began to protest. "Oh, do be quiet, both of you," Mirabella said testily. "You know I wouldn't hurt you."

"Amazing. Simply amazing," the young man said, and helped Mirabella to her feet.

"What? That I can make such a fool of myself in public? Not really. It seems as if I have rehearsed this scene every day of my life," Mirabella complained, throwing her arms up in the air. "Never the Innamorata! Always the zanni!"

"Signorina, I don't know how you conduct yourself in public. Though, if this is the usual, I'd say that your life will always be interesting. But what I want to know is, how can you talk to the masks? Do they talk to you?"

"Why not?" Mirabella shrugged. "After all, we're as good as siblings. My mother, Anna Forsetti, made them. She used to joke that their faces came right from her womb. Maybe it's all her fault, in that case. She was thinking of one of these when she slipped up and made me." She suddenly thought of Lorenzo, his somber eyes, the dramatic white streak in his dark wavy hair. He had seemed so poised in the midst of all that chaos. The memory made her sigh. She picked up Lily and petted her to quiet the agitated creature. "If only he had been the one who had pinched me, instead of that dirty old man." She looked up, squinting from one eye, at the young man who had found her spectacles. He was still standing in front of her looking perplexed.

"Thank you again for finding my spectacles. Such as they are," she said politely.

"Your eyes are very pretty behind those spectacles," he said. "Are you sure you need them?"

"I'd make a worse fool of myself without them. I can't see very well in front of me. I walk into things and sometimes off of things. For a Venetian, that's dangerous. More than once, I've plunked myself into a canal when I allowed vanity to keep me from wearing my spectacles."

"You speak well, Signorina. Are you educated?"

"Better than most," she answered with a shrug. "I like to read." What else was there to do? Men like that Lorenzo weren't knocking at the door of her house. Or if they were, it wasn't to see her!

"Let me present myself," the young man said. "I am Fabrizio Tarbotti. I'm an actor." Fabrizio flourished his hands and gave a slight bow.

"And your companion?" Mirabella asked, turning toward the silent dark-haired woman.

"Ah. This is Erminia," Fabrizio explained.

Erminia stood still as stone, her hands at her sides, her eyes on the rooftops above the narrow street.

"An actress?" Mirabella asked, her eyebrows raised over the gold-rimmed spectacles. The woman was baffling. Her skin was weathered, her hands rough and chapped. But her eyes, glancing through the thicket of hair, were a pure blue.

"No. A siren."

"A siren?"

"Yes a siren. I met her in Liguria."

Mirabella pursed her lips. What next? she asked herself. First he tells me he's an actor. Impossible! She had grown up knowing some of the best actors in Italy: the Gelosi, the Infiniti, the Fedeli. They had come to Anna's studio, tried on masks, eaten at her table. And not one of them had looked as scruffy as this vagabond. And now he was spinning an even wilder tale. Did he think she was an imbecile? Mirabella shoved her damaged spectacles up on her nose.

"I said I was a fool, not stupid. Whoever heard of a siren on land?"

"A strange remark indeed coming from a girl who converses with masks!" Fabrizio sniffed.

"I doubt very much whether you really are an actor. You probably stole those masks! For shame, ruining another man's livelihood by stealing his tools."

Fabrizio colored, the flush starting at his collarbone and working its way up his neck. With passionate fury, he untied one of the masks from around his neck. Pantelone coughed ostentatiously at Mirabella, wiggling his eyebrows as the mask was fitted over the young man's face.

Mirabella stepped back, watching for the subtle signs of transformation as the mask took over the actor's body. Fabrizio aged before her eyes, his body leaning back into Pantelone's slouch, his knees bending, his heels snapping together and his toes apart. Suddenly he looked very much like the grasping old man who had pinched her. The mask spluttered and the voice quavered and gathered strength as Pantelone began to strut.

"Ah love!" Pantelone exclaimed. "It is like a plague from whose fevers only a few escape. I myself have caught it not once but several times. When I was a boy, love seized me, turning me into a pigeon that flitted around women, pecking at crumbs. I was just happy to get my little beak in here and there. As a young man I was a lusty tomcat, forever on the prowl. When I married, love turned me into a messenger horse that rode hard for an hour and then rested for a day. Now I am like a little dog at a woman's ankles. Just a sniff and I'm off."

In spite of her anger, Mirabella found herself smiling. The man had a certain flair for Pantelone and he used Venetian dialect with good effect. His eyes behind the mask held hers as though she were the only person in the world. Suddenly he grabbed her hand and pulled her close to him.

"Good morning, Daughter."

"Good morning, Father," Mirabella answered, trying not to laugh. She felt her cheeks go hot, her fingers sweat in the young man's grasp.

"And what is it that you are doing there?"

Mirabella plucked a scene from her memory, hoping the young man could follow her lead. "I am making a coverlet, Father. Though I think it much too small to cover two people."

"And I pray that you are not sharing your little bed with anyone, Daughter. Or can it be that you are thinking of marriage?"

"Oh, if only I were so fortunate," Mirabella said, and batted her eyelashes. They brushed against the lenses, so she took off her spectacles and tucked them in her pocket. She didn't need to see to speak the lines from this scene. How many times had she watched the Innamorata's performance at Carnevale? How easily the words came to her.

"Hah! Think I don't know your game, you vixen! You don't always need a needle and cloth to do fancy work. Listen, Daughter, marriage is as old as the world."

"So I've been told many times, Father."

"And better left for those of us old enough to appreciate it! Fact is, I've been thinking about it myself."

"Oh, Father!"

"Oh, Daughter! Don't look so surprised." Pantelone struck a manly pose, one leg out thrust. "Am I not f-f-f—"

"Fucked already, I'd say," a boy shouted out.

"Feeble, I think," said another one.

"A fine figure of a ma-ma-ma—"

"Somebody quick, get him his mother!"

"Figure of a man!" Pantelone said through clenched teeth.

Mirabella frowned at Pantelone's unexpected stutter and tried to recover the momentum of the scene. Even without her spectacles she was aware that they had attracted a small crowd. And why not? Pantelone's mask was powerful enough to wake the dead in a cemetery if it chose. What was happening to the actor?

"Oh, Father! Married to a woman?"

There was no answer. The audience cat-called, demanded an answer, but Pantelone kept his mouth firmly shut. Mirabella put on her spectacles and the young man slid the mask of Pantelone off his face and wiped his sweating brow. Mirabella could see the knot of words bob up and down in his throat as he swallowed. Even the discarded mask of Pantelone looked miserable.

"Is that why you are here in Labirinto?" Mirabella asked.

"An actor who stutters isn't worth much, no matter how many lines he speaks correctly. But I am an actor," Fabrizio said vehemently. "Even if I do stutter."

"I believe you," Mirabella said with a faint smile. "For a while there, your performance was very good."

"As long as no one but yourself was watching."

The crowd was berating Fabrizio for his broken performance. When the young man bit his thumb at them, the insults grew uglier. Erminia pulled on Fabrizio's shirt, her eyes haunted by the sight of the sagging balconies overhead.

"Come on, let's get back to the piazza. People aren't too friendly here," Fabrizio said. He took Mirabella by the elbow and led her through the boisterous crowd.

Mirabella glanced sideways at Fabrizio. A stuttering actor. She felt sorry for the poor man, but she was also delighted that for the first time in her life, it hadn't been she who had appeared foolish. And he had found her spectacles. She owed him something for that alone.

"Would you like to dine with my mother and me?" she asked.

"I couldn't trouble you," Fabrizio mumbled.

"No trouble, really. Not for a fellow pilgrim. We don't have much, but you're welcome to share what there is."

"All right," Fabrizio answered. "It would be nice to have some speaking company for a while. Erminia doesn't speak."

"Nor even sing?" Mirabella asked.

"No. She must not. Some curse or other. I don't really understand it. But I have seen the disaster she can make with her voice."

Mirabella looked at the tall woman with pity. "A siren who must not sing. Che peccato."

Erminia looked down at Mirabella and gave an odd smile. She reached out her grubby fingers and touched Mirabella's spectacles. With a slight tug, she pulled them off and settled them on her own face.

Mirabella squinted and laughed to see the half-shattered spectacles on the siren's dirty face. The lenses made her bright blue eyes seem to swim like shining hot bubbles of Murano glass. Erminia fingered the broken lens curiously and then fluttered her hand excitedly in the air.

"Your spectacles must make her think she is home under the water," Fabrizio said. "Look where she has shaped the vision of her thoughts for you to see."

Mirabella gasped. Beneath the grubby fingers she saw an image of the sea with sunlight glancing off the surface. The water was cresting into waves that broke into opal shards of blue and green light. Erminia turned suddenly to Mirabella and held her firmly by the shoulders. She tapped one finger against the lenses. The odd eyes were beseeching her.

"I think she wants to know if she can have your spectacles," Fabrizio says. "She's been miserable lately. It started when we journeyed away from the sea through the mountains. I think she's missing the sea. Your spectacles seem to offer some comfort."

"But I can hardly see without them," Mirabella protested.

"If you will allow me, Signorina," Fabrizio said warmly, "I would be willing to escort you."

Mirabella turned sharply to peer at Fabrizio's face. She wanted to see that he wasn't mocking her or making a fool of her. She squinted but could only see the edge of his smile and his soft blond hair. He leaned in closer, as if sensing her uncertainty.

"Do you really mean that?" she asked.

"Absolutely," he replied.

Erminia linked her arm through Mirabella's, squeezing the girl happily. She stared out at the piazza, a huge grin spreading over her long face.

"You've made her really happy," Fabrizio said as he took her other arm.

"Really?" Mirabella asked, feeling dazed.

"Absolutely," Fabrizio repeated.

"I guess it's settled then," Mirabella said. "Lily, find Mamma! Take us to Anna!" Lily jumped out of the basket and began briskly trotting across the piazza. "Just follow Lily, she'll lead us back to my mother. Without my spectacles, I have no hope of finding her!"

"Wait for us, Lily," Fabrizio called, and Mirabella felt herself being pulled through the blurred crowds of pilgrims.

15

$\int$ o, Lapone," Simonetta whispered, clutching the restive stallion by the nose. "You don't like this place too much, do you?"

The stallion stamped his hooves nervously over the paving stones of the piazza.

"Too many crazy people here," Simonetta continued, watching the other pilgrims out of the corner of her eye. "Not much longer," she consoled the horse. "Either we go into the maze soon, or I sell you because I can't afford to buy food to keep us both alive."

The stallion's coat was dirty. His belly had shrunk and his ribs were just beginning to show.

"You're used to the clash of battle, my brave one, but not this dreadful waiting for the gates of fate to open." Simonetta reached into her skirt pocket and pulled up a shriveled apple. "Here, my brute, to sweeten your unhappy mood."

The stallion gobbled the apple from her palm, the juice dribbling over the grey hairs of his muzzle. Then he huffed his chest, exhaling into Simonetta's now-empty palm in a sigh of resignation.

Simonetta returned to the small fire she was tending. She turned a rabbit on a spit, the juices from the fat hissing as they landed on the coals. Rosemary and garlic burned in tendrils of grey smoke over the fire. Next to her an eggplant, sliced and smeared with oil and basil, waited its turn on the fire. Simonetta was cooking the last of her provisions bought with the last of her money. Tomorrow she would sell the stallion and Rinaldo's sword. And then what? she asked herself. How long will you wait? How long before Rinaldo arrives? The gates had to open soon, she thought with a worried frown. They had to.

It didn't matter any more to her if she went empty-handed into the maze. In the two days that Simonetta had camped in the piazza she had learned from other pilgrims that many went into the maze with nothing, trusting in God to lead them. There were rumors that the maze provided for the pilgrims. She had met a few people in the piazza who boasted of knowing the way, which they'd describe to her for a large fee.

One man had tried to sell her a golden topaz that he guaranteed would light a path through the maze. Simonetta ignored them all.

Simonetta turned the spit, cooking her rabbit on all sides. She took a swig of mediocre wine from a bottle, noticing as she did a woman watching her intently. Normally, women avoided her in public. Even though Simonetta wore Rinaldo's doublet over her dress, they knew she belonged to the street. Her profession declared itself in the cut of her skirts, the depth of her neckline, the way she wore her hair. But this woman had watched her moving around in camp. Simonetta found it unnerving.

The woman had arrived a short time after Simonetta had set up her own camp. She had come with her awkward daughter and an annoying little dog that barked feverishly at Lapone. The stallion had merely flicked its tail, whisking the bitch away as though it were a biting fly. A strange pair, as unsuited to travel as any she had seen. Venetian by their dress. The woman was well-clothed in a gown of intricately patterned red velvet. Starched lace and gold threads decorated the square neckline of her stiff farthingale, and her wide undersleeves were of fine linen. She wore a traveling cape of good wool and shoes with high wooden soles.

By comparison, the daughter was dressed like a servant. Her dress was old and a faded green that did nothing for her olive complexion, and she wore gold-rimmed spectacles that gave her the look of an owl. But it was the daughter who took care of them. She had sold their mangy-looking donkey and cart. She had shopped for the food they ate, prepared the sleeping blankets, and combed out the woman's long hair while ignoring her own.

And now the woman was sitting alone on one of her traveling boxes, staring at Simonetta. The daughter was gone, perhaps to find food for the evening meal. Simonetta turned her back, hoping to avoid a conversation.

"Excuse me, Signora," the woman called out.

"Damn," Simonetta muttered. She turned slowly and found the woman standing before her. "Yes?"

"I wonder if I might impose upon your gentle nature to ask a favor?"

"What makes you think I'm gentle?" Simonetta asked.

"I'm good at guessing. After all, beneath our clothes, we are both women living in troubled times."

"What do you want?" Simonetta asked, bristling.

"You have a rabbit, Signora. And the smell of it is driving me insane. Perhaps my daughter and I could contribute something of equal value to your meal in exchange for a few bites?"

Simonetta, in spite of her wariness, smiled. To be complimented on her cooking was fair coin. She relented.

"Signora, please sit. I'm willing to share the rabbit."

"Grazie," the woman said eagerly, and sat down on Lapone's saddle. She gathered her skirts around her and leaned her tired face on her palm. "You can't imagine how we have suffered on the road here. The food was intolerable, the wine dreadful. But this rabbit of yours, all I can think of is my nonna in Friuli. The scent makes me nostalgic as well as desperately hungry."

"Your grandmother was a good cook?" Simonetta said absently. She was thinking of her own grandmother, her arms covered to the elbows in flour, her fingers always plucking something sweet or savory out of a bowl to pop into Simonetta's mouth.

"Madonna, the angels used to beg for mortality so they could partake of her meals." The woman laughed. "Many lost their wings to the sin of gluttony at her table."

"So it is with good food." Simonetta shrugged. "What doesn't kill you, makes you fat."

"Nonna was very plump, an accomplishment during the wars."

"Hard years indeed," Simonetta said softly.

The fat crackled in the fire and the woman rubbed her hands at its promising sound.

"I am Anna Forsetti of Friuli, though when I was married I lived in Venice."

"I am—" Simonetta hesitated. "Simonetta. Just Simonetta. And are you still married?"

"Widowed," Anna answered.

"Was he a soldier, then?"

"Oh no. He was Carlo Mansoni, master maskmaker to the ducal palace at Venice. He was older than I, but a wonderful man." Anna shrugged her shoulders. "He died of a plague that swept the city one winter."

"You didn't return to your family in Friuli?" Simonetta asked, skewering a slice of eggplant on a stick and setting it over the fire.

"No. I wanted to stay in Venice. I got used to living on islands and to the sound of the sea lapping in the canals. There was nothing for me but the convent to look forward to if I went home. So I sued my husband's family for the return of my dowry. They returned it, but disowned me shortly after."

"Ah, but, Signora, the law does not allow you to live unprotected. You must have a man to watch over your accounts," Simonetta said, trying to hide the sarcasm in her voice. The law had not protected her, widowed and abandoned after the mercenaries had ravaged their village. There had been no dowry returned to her, no widow's fee that might have kept her from shame.

"My family was furious that I chose not to return," Anna was saying. "They thought a year or two and my money would run out and I would come home and retire to the convent."

"But you didn't?"

"No, I didn't. My husband had taught me the skill of maskmaking. I often worked with him in the studio. After his death I continued to work and was able to sell my masks to many of his former customers. I've been fortunate enough to supply masks to some of the best Commedia troupes in Venice. Eventually, I did meet a man who agreed to be my patron and, in so doing, quieted any of the misgivings the council might have had about my status."

"You were lucky," Simonetta said.

"If I were lucky I wouldn't be here," Anna retorted, "but that is another story."

"The same one told all over this piazza, I think."

Simonetta handed Anna the slice of eggplant, its purple skin blackened by the fire. Anna took it delicately between her fingers and blew on it.

"Speaking of stories," Anna said, "surely you must have one. You travel alone on a stallion with an extraordinary sword dangling from the saddle. But there is no man?" she asked, raising her eyebrows.

"No man."

"And no traveling bags, no clothes?"

"I took only what was handy at the time of my flight."

"Ah, flight. From a husband?"

Simonetta shook her head.

"Then the man who owned the sword," Anna whispered, her face brightening with amazement. "And maybe the horse as well. Did you even take his horse?"

"You don't want to know more."

"Che brava! What courage. What balls!" Anna gave a deep-throated chuckle. Then, she slipped the cooled eggplant into her mouth and closed her eyes while she chewed. "Delicious!"

"Isn't that your daughter? It looks as though she's made some friends in the market," Simonetta said.

Anna turned quickly and Simonetta saw her frown. Mirabella's arms were linked with a dirty-looking woman in a ragged skirt and a scruffy young man. Simonetta stared at the girl. She looked different somehow.

Ah, the spectacles were gone, well not gone, but winking in the sunlight over the nose of the tall woman. On Mirabella's young face, Simonetta thought she detected a happy flush. How pretty it made her seem. Simonetta glanced at Anna and saw a ripple of emotions cloud the woman's face: concern, curiosity, and, for a moment, a green spark of jealousy. Simonetta turned back to study the trio. Well, the man was young, maybe only a few years older than Mirabella herself. And while not exactly possessed of manly features, he had a certain charm.

"Mirabella, are you all right?" Anna asked, rising to her feet. "What happened to your spectacles?"

"They were knocked off my face by an onion. But Fabrizio here found them for me in the street again. Only Erminia likes to wear them because they remind her of her life in the sea."

"Amore, I don't understand a word you've said." Anna replied, shaking her head. She took Mirabella by the arm, drawing her away from Fabrizio and Erminia. "Who are these people?"

"They rescued me in the market from a disgusting old man who was pinching my backside."

"And then an argument began over who was better, women or men," Fabrizio put in earnestly. "A couple of women lost their tempers, and, of course, so did some of the men. Within moments the air was thick with curses and rotten vegetables."

Simonetta started laughing. "That's one battle that is never over."

"But wait," Mirabella interrupted. "They didn't start really fighting until the old man tried to hide his boots from Signor Falcomatta."

"What old man? And who is Signor Falcomatta?" Anna demanded. "Mirabella, I sent you to do a simple task and you return with some fantasy and . . . and . . . who are these people?"

"Mamma, I'm all right," Mirabella said calmly. "A man named Lorenzo Falcomatta was searching for his servant, who disappeared yesterday. The old man who pinched me had on the servant's boots. As for the ribbon seller and onion seller, I don't know, perhaps they have been looking for an excuse to fall into each other's arms and we provided it." Mirabella sat back, her hands neatly folded in her lap, and beamed.

"Those masks you wear," Anna said, turning to Fabrizio, "where did you get them?"

"Fabrizio is an actor, Mamma," Mirabella announced.

Simonetta watched Anna's eyes narrow as she stared first at her daughter's blushing cheeks and then at Fabrizio's grimy face.

"And this is Erminia," Mirabella said, turning to the woman. "She's a siren. She has come to the maze because she can't speak. Or she must not speak. We are not sure which."

Simonetta looked at the odd woman and pursed her lips. The boy she could accept as being a fledgling actor. Never mind that he was not very impressive-looking, his charm won over his dirty clothes. But the woman, mute as a stone, her eyes fractured by Mirabella's broken spectacles—that was one too many, even for Simonetta.

"Mirabella, amore mio," Anna was whispering. "What story have these people told you? How can you believe such nonsense?"

Mirabella turned to Erminia. "Can you show them? Please, for me?"

Erminia gave a nod. She lowered the gold-rimmed spectacles and placed them gently in her lap. She looked at Anna, who gasped, and then at Simonetta, who bit her tongue at the bright blue eyes, shimmering like opals. Erminia held up her chapped hands and shaped a vision of the sea—not its surface, but far below, where a crystalline palace surrounded by banks of coral lifted out of the ocean floor. Other sirens swam smoothly down corridors of green glistening stone. Shoals of fish followed them or circled like tiaras in their flowing hair.

"But how did this happen?" Anna asked.

Erminia raised her hands and shaped a tiny stage on which the actors played their roles. Simonetta saw the troupe of actors, Pantelone and Arlecchino on stage with Lelio and an Innamorata disguised as a mermaid. She saw a man harassing Erminia and Erminia's mouth open. She saw the village turn into coral. Last she saw Fabrizio, wandering terrified amid the coral statues that had once been the villagers."

"No, no," Fabrizio protested. "That's not right. I wasn't scared! Show them how I really looked!"

Wordlessly, Erminia changed the scene and Fabrizio reappeared, this time sitting on the ground and threatening to starve himself.

In spite of her awe, Simonetta laughed. Fabrizio uttered an obscenity and scattered the vision with his hand.

"I'm not that bad," he grumbled.

"No, of course not," Anna replied more warmly. "But it does prove that you are an actor! How melodramatic to starve yourself amid so much wonder."

"Mamma, don't tease. Fabrizio is a good actor. He just has a little problem with stuttering. The maze will cure him of that," she announced.

"But only food will cure us of this hunger," Simonetta said, looking sadly at the roasting rabbit. With five of them, it had suddenly gotten a good deal smaller.

Erminia immediately began unloading zucchinis from inside her loose bodice. She pulled out another eggplant from her apron pocket and after a quick glance around, she freed a slab of dried cod from between her thighs.

Fabrizio too began to unload his doublet of tomatoes, oranges, onions, and a stray ribbon, which he gave to Mirabella.

"What else could we do?" he said with a shrug. "The food was flying in the air. I figured it was there for anyone standing close enough to catch it."

Mirabella's basket produced two salamis, three loaves of bread, a bottle of wine, and a soup bone for Lily to gnaw on.

"It's a feast," Simonetta said, suddenly happy. She had been right to come here to Labirinto, where everyone's fortunes hung so delicately in the balance that it was easy to be kind, even to strangers. She peeled, chopped, and slathered oil over the vegetables while Fabrizio, Anna, and Mirabella argued about the theater. Erminia soaked the dried cod in a wooden bowl Mirabella had fetched up from the traveling boxes. She squeezed the fish gently in her hands as though remembering the slippery scales and the wriggling body it once had. When it had finally absorbed enough water to resemble a fish again, she handed it to Simonetta, who poured oil over it and cut it into pieces that they stuck onto Anna's silver-tined forks and cooked over the fire.

Much later, when the stars had hoisted themselves out of the dark recesses of the maze, they spread their blankets and slept. Simonetta watched the moon lift out of the unseen belly of the maze, following the path of the stars. The night was soft and the wind blew the scent of the cedars through the thin trails of smoke drifting over the piazza. She closed her eyes and let her weary body sleep.

It seemed that she had hardly slept when Lapone roused her from an old nightmare. She was running terrified from the drumming of hooves behind her. She knew she must outrun them. Her body was tense, her breath ragged. The sudden shock of Lapone's bony nose nudging her startled her awake. She clutched at the horse in confused terror, expecting to be trampled. Lapone continued to snort worriedly in her face.

"I'm awake. I'm awake," she said at last, brusquely pushing the horse away. "What has you riled, my brute?" Lapone paced in a tight circle, his hooves clapping on the paving stones.

Simonetta looked around the quiet piazza. It was still night and the pilgrims were huddled in their camps, looking more like a field of boulders than weary sleepers. Iron hinges creaked and the gates to the maze opened. A sliver of gold light flowed over the paving stones and stopped near Simonetta's feet.

"Madonna, it's time!" she said softly.

She turned quickly to Anna and Mirabella. She roused them, then moved on to Fabrizio and Erminia. "Wake up!" she said in a harsh whisper. "The gates have opened. Now is the time! Wake up."

Anna and Mirabella turned to each other with a small groan.

"It's still dark," Anna mumbled.

"Look at the light through the door of the maze. Come on! Don't delay, or the gates will close again!"

Erminia woke quickly and, grabbing Fabrizio by the scruff of his shirt, hauled him upright. The masks around his neck yawned noisily. Arlecchino yipped at the golden spear of light coming from the gates of the maze and Fabrizio shook his sleepy head awake.

"I'm coming," he complained as Erminia continued to drag at him. "Hold on, I'll get there."

Anna and Mirabella were standing, rubbing the grit from their eyes.

"Come on," Simonetta said. The stallion, who was walking toward the narrow band of light, began to trot as if instinct warned him this might be their only chance. "Hurry," Simonetta begged. "The gates may close before we can enter. Leave everything behind."

"I can't leave the masks." Anna reached inside one of her traveling boxes and pulled out a white cloth bag. Clutching it in one hand, she grabbed Mirabella with the other hand and they started running after Simonetta and the stallion. Fabrizio and Erminia hurried behind them, the masks on Fabrizio's neck chattering with glee.

At the entrance to the maze, Simonetta stopped suddenly. Lapone had already slipped inside. The gates beckoned, but the gold light beyond dazed and frightened her. What was she doing?

"Come on," Fabrizio said.

Simonetta tore her gaze away from the blazing light and looked at her companions. At least she was not alone. She took Fabrizio's hand and Erminia's, and with them walked into the liquid gold entrance of the maze.

Simonetta shuddered in the sudden heat and blazing light. Even with her eyes shut tightly, the afterimage of the gates burned against her closed lids in thin black outline. The sea of gold confused her senses. Touch failed her and the comforting hands were gone. She grasped at the air and cried out to Erminia and Fabrizio, but there was no answer. Desperately she called out to Lapone. The stallion whinnied loudly and Simonetta felt a rush of air and smelled his animal sweat as he pushed past her. She reached out to stop him, but the stallion disappeared as swiftly as a shadow bleached by light. Deep within the blinding gold, a chorus of horses neighed shrilly. Simonetta raised her head to the sound and heard the hard clink of bridles and the scrape of swords freed from their scabbards. She crouched, tensed. Soldiers! Soldiers were galloping toward her! Terrified and alone, Simonetta turned in the glare and began to run.

16

Roberto's head nodded to his chest, his eyes closed, his jaw slack, as his horse plodded on its way to Labirinto. The last three nights on the road had been very disagreeable. At the first inn the bed had been full of vermin. At the second, dogs had howled in the courtyards below. At the third, Roberto had been alarmed by the late-night appearance of three coarse-looking men. Their hair was long and unkempt, their faces unshaven; their dark eyes roved hungrily over the room. They had ensconced themselves in the darkest corner of the inn and demanded to be served. They carved their meat and their fingernails with the same short-handled knives and drank heavily, throwing back tankard after tankard of wine. They regarded Roberto with hostility, whispered a few words among themselves, and then ignored him. Nevertheless, Roberto had slept with one eye open, glad for the dawn when he could slip away unnoticed from the inn.

It was now midmorning and the warm sun and quiet buzzing of insects in the ditch beside the road had lulled Roberto into a drowsy state. His backside ached and his thighs were sore. There was grit in his eyes and dirt under his nails. Anna, he wondered bleakly as he dozed, why have you done this to us? We could be home in bed in sheets of fine damask from Florence, pillows edged with lace from Murano, wool blankets from Flanders, and perfumes from Arabia scenting the mattress. The sun would be coming up over the canals, the tide bringing a fresh breeze from the ocean. I could be touching you. Roberto groaned softly, his head nodding deeper on his chest. He slumped to one side, expecting his shoulder to settle into the softness of Anna's flesh.

"Hold there!" a voice shouted.

Roberto's head snapped up. He discovered he was sliding over the horse's right shoulder. He lurched violently, grabbing at the reins to straighten himself. The horse, startled by the man scrabbling on its back, jogged faster, making it impossible for Roberto to regain his balance. One moment his buttocks were slapping against the saddle, the next he was clawing at thin air.

His first thought was how ridiculous he must look, arms and legs waving as he toppled off the horse. His second was the realization that any moment now, he would hit the ground, hard. Just then, a pair of hands caught him neatly beneath the shoulders and controlled his fall, bringing his head and shoulders to rest gently on the ground while his foot was still caught in the stirrup of his saddle. The hands released his shoulders and snatched the bridle of the prancing horse. The horse, relieved by the recognizable command to hold, settled down, and Roberto was able to free his foot from the stirrup. He gave a small grunt as the rest of his body landed on the ground.

The sun was bright behind the shoulders of his rescuer, so it was difficult for Roberto to see him. He looked tall and well built, and the sun formed a golden corona around a head of red hair, but his features, eclipsed by shadow, remained dark. He wore the clothes of a farmer, a dirty homespun shirt and brown woolen hose tied together with leather strings. But the skin of his neck was white where the shirt lay open at the collar and around his waist he had buckled a sword. The man reached down a helping hand and Roberto took it gratefully.

"I am sorry, Signore, to have startled your horse. You looked asleep and I had only hoped to awaken you before you fell out of the saddle."

"Ah, thank you, Signore. I'm afraid you were right. I was napping. As you can tell, I'm not the most accomplished of riders."

"More accustomed to a gondola?" the man asked.

"Yes. How did you know?" Roberto asked. He brushed the dirt from the shoulders of his black doublet and resettled the belted sword at his side, ignoring the twinge of pain in his right shoulder.

"Your clothing, Signore. A little too fine for this rude countryside, and certainly more stylish than a Florentine's. Also, I recognize the unusual shape of your sabre and its decorative scabbard. Like many things in Venice, it began its life somewhere else in the world. A pretty piece, though not too practical in battle, I'd wager."

"Bene," Roberto said with a smile. "Molto bene. And now it is my turn. You, Signore," Roberto said, studying the man, "are Milanese and, despite your clothes, certainly not a peasant."

"Ah. And what gives me away?" When the man smiled, Roberto noticed that his blue eyes were wary beneath his red-gold eyebrows and there were bruises around his jaw. A recent gash at his hairline still showed signs of healing.

"Your accent is too flat to come from these parts," Roberto continued. "And your neck too white to be a man of the fields. And that sword you carry is not a peasant's weapon. Judging from the thickness of the steel and the bluntness of its shape, it was forged in Milan for practicality, not beauty. You're right, Signore, about my sabre's origin; it once belonged to an Estradiot from Armenia. But I can assure you, it has seen more battles in the Venetian wars than that pigsticker of yours from Milan."

The taut skin around the man's eyes softened. His features relaxed as he laughed and he clapped Roberto on the shoulder. "You've a good eye, Venetian. Now take care to keep it open when you ride. There are pilgrims on this road and there are thieves who know them to be easy targets. I think you will find more trouble than your beautiful sabre can handle if you don't keep a watch out."

"Perhaps you are right. I still marvel that I find myself on this road at all," Roberto said with a wry smile. He smoothed down the strands of greying hair that wafted from his forehead. "Labirinto is as far as the moon to a settled Venetian such as myself."

"Don't tell me you are a pilgrim?" the man scoffed, stroking the cheek of Roberto's horse.

"Not really. I'm looking for someone who came this way some days earlier. She intends to journey the maze. I only hope that I may dissuade her." Roberto saw the man's expression change as a cruel look contracted the pleasant features.

"I, too, am looking for a woman," he said coldly.

Roberto grew nervous as the darkness clouded the man's face. "I think, Signore, I shall continue my journey, but I do thank you again," he said politely.

As he moved to take the reins of his horse, the man stopped him. "No, Signore, I think it would be best if you went quickly into the ditch. And keep your head down." The man pulled his sword from his makeshift belt.

"How dare you!" Roberto exclaimed. "Give me my horse!"

"Quick, to the ditch, before those men riding down on us see you." The man tilted his head toward the road and hid his sword behind his back. Roberto glanced over his horse's shoulder and saw the three coarse men from the inn riding hard down the dirt road in a little cloud of dust. "I can handle them on my own," the red-haired man was saying. "But you they will kill before you open your mouth. Get down before they see you."

Roberto obeyed, ducking behind his horse and rolling his body down the steep slope of the ditch. Tall grass and flowering weeds shielded him from sight. He felt the thundering hooves of the approaching horses through the dry earth and heard the riders shouting for the red-haired man to hold fast where he stood.

"Well, well, what have we here?" one sneered.

"That's a fine-looking nag for a piece of scum like you." The second thief hawked and spat. "Didn't we see this nag just yesterday, Mario?"

"Indeed we did. But it was being ridden by an old rooster with a purse of gold. What have you done with him, scum? Have you plucked our rooster, you miserable piece of pig's shit?"

"Signore, peace I pray you. Don't hurt me," the red-haired man begged. "I only found the beast out this morning. There weren't no one around."

"You expect us to believe that?" roared the first man.

"But it's the truth," the red-haired man whined.

"Check the saddlebags, Mario. I want the old rooster's gold," the man with the sneering voice commanded.

Roberto crawled to the crest of the ditch. He watched as Mario dismounted and gruffly pushed the red-haired man out of the way to claim the saddlebags. With frightening speed, the sword hidden behind the red-haired man's back swung forward and bit deep into Mario's left armpit as he reached up for the saddlebag. The man gagged and turned slowly, his eyes white with pain and shock. Blood streamed from the wound in his side.

The red-haired man yanked his sword free and shoved the dying man out of his way. He came quickly around Roberto's horse to where the other two thieves waited, still mounted on their horses. With the sword held over his head, the red-haired man hacked at the legs of the second thief. The horses shied from the bright flash of the swinging blade, rearing and crashing into each other. The second thief bellowed in surprise as his horse, goaded by the red-haired man's blade, pawed the air and threw him, stunned, to the dirt road. The red-haired man stood over the thief and with a two-handed grip, brought the sword down, driving the point like a spear into his chest. The thief screamed and folded his hands around the blade, his legs kicking wildly.

By this time, the last thief had finally succeeded in regaining control of his terrified horse. Shouting, the thief kicked his horse hard, driving it into the red-haired man, who was pinned between the other riled horses. The thief jerked the reins and his horse reared back, front hooves sawing the air above the red-haired man's shoulders. Roberto cried out as the third thief's horse kicked the red-haired man in the chest and knocked him to the ground. Still gripping the long sword, the red-haired man struggled to get back to his feet and meet the thief's attack but he was obviously too dazed to stand. The thief urged his horse forward again, leaning over the saddle to strike the red-haired man dead.

Without another thought, Roberto pulled his own sabre from its scabbard and, lunging over the brow of the hill with a furious shout, shoved himself between the horses. He stood over the red-haired man's prone body, the polished length of the sabre rising to meet the thief's sword. The two blades slid against each other with a ringing chime. Roberto pushed harder and drove the sabre up along the shaft of the thief's sword. The curved blade skittered past the cross-handled hilt of the thief's sword and nicked the thief's hand. Swearing, the thief wheeled his horse around to avoid Roberto's second attack.

Flinging himself against the thief's side, Roberto struck out again with his sword. He made a slashing cut across the thief's right leg. The man shouted with renewed rage as a thin river of blood spilled across his thigh. Roberto twisted on the balls of his feet and, with a two-handed grip, slashed the sabre sideways, cutting a seam across the man's middle. The heavy velvet doublet split apart and the torn shirt beneath grew scarlet with fresh blood. Roberto leapt back as the wounded thief tried desperately to drive his sword downward into Roberto's head while the terrified horse pranced back and forth.

Roberto ducked beneath the frantic horse's neck, feeling for an instant its hot labored breath before he bounced up on the other side and attacked the thief once more. As the thief raised his sword to strike, Roberto darted forward with the sabre and sliced upward, cutting a neat incision into the man's throat with the curved tip of his blade. The thief dropped his weapon to clutch the gaping wound in his throat. Blood gurgled in his mouth, and he pitched forward over the neck of the agitated horse. The horse bucked, kicking out its back legs to free itself. The thief rolled out of his saddle and fell under the stamping hooves. Roberto waited, crouched, his sword primed for another attack. But the last thief lay silent on the ground.

Slowly, Roberto straightened, wiped the bloody sabre on the skirt of his doublet, and returned the sword to its scabbard. He calmed the horses with a soothing hand and dropped their reins over the branches of a bush to hold them. Then he attended to the red-haired man.

The red-haired man was rising from the ground, rubbing his chest where the horse had kicked him. The thieves' blood stained his shirt and the white skin of his throat seemed even paler. His eyes burned, his red hair bristled like the pelt of a fox. He was smiling through gritted teeth.

Nodding to Roberto, he replaced his sword in his belt and staggered to sit on a boulder beside the road.

Seeing that his rescuer was reasonably whole, Roberto went to the other two thieves. Mario was already dead, his eyes staring upward in utter astonishment. Roberto bent and shut them, flinching at the coolness of the body. The second man was barely alive, his pierced chest rising and falling with shallow rattling breaths. Roberto knelt by the dying man and lifted his head. The man stared at him belligerently.

"Do you wish to confess before you die?" Roberto asked.

The man gave a barking laugh that ended in a groan. Blood gouted from his chest wound and dripped slowly into the dirt. The pupils of his eyes widened, blotting the fading color of the iris. The man was silent, the eyes opaque. Thinking the thief dead, Roberto laid his head down again when a last sigh caught his ear.

"I repent," the man exhaled.

"Then you are forgiven and the kingdom of heaven shall be yours to enter." Roberto sketched the sign of the cross and closed the dead man's eyes before coming to sit on the boulder beside the red-haired man. It was then he realized he was exhausted. His sword arm ached, the muscles of his thighs trembled. Too sedentary a life, he thought wistfully. But looking at the corpses around him, he decided that a sedentary life had something to recommend it.

"You fight better than I would have guessed, Venetian," said the red-haired man.

"And you fight like the devil. Without warning or mercy."

"What archangel taught you to kill?"

Roberto gave a dry laugh. He combed the drifting wisps of his grey hair down across his sweating forehead again and blotted the sweat from his upper lip with the sleeve of his doublet. "When I was a young man I served as a personal valet to an Armenian Estradiot who fought for Venice in the Venetian wars. Toward the end of his life, this soldier decided to make a pilgrimage to the Holy Lands and asked me to accompany him. I was eager for adventure, and traveling the ocean is the desire of most Venetian boys. My master was a skilled mercenary and a fine swordsman. It was he who taught me to use the sabre on our journey east. After our arrival in the Holy Lands he gave me the sabre as a gift. He said he didn't need it any more."

"What happened to him?"

"Ah. The last I saw of him, he was stripped naked in a courtyard, putting on a brown robe while the sun beat down on his clean-shaven head. His ferocity had been gentled into the meekness of a lamb. He told me he had had enough of killing and war. He was renouncing the worldly life and joining one of the desert orders that seal themselves in caves to pray for the sinful likes of you and me. I was, of course, unhappy to lose his company so far from all that I knew, but I did finally make my way home alone."

"And did you have occasion to put your training to the test on the journey?"

"Too often, I'm afraid," Roberto answered grimly. "It was enough to convince me of the wisdom of remaining content and well off at home."

"Until now," the red-haired man pointed out.

"Yes, until now." Roberto shrugged lightly. "One cannot play the Innamorato sitting at home gnawing one's thumbs."

"I think you make a better Pantelone," the red-haired man said dryly. "Older, but not wiser, a wealthy Venetian with a hard-on chasing the skirts of a young girl."

"And who are you, my friend?" Roberto answered gruffly. "Il Capitano, the liar with a scabbard full of cobwebs, who goes limp before a woman's scorn?"

"That hurt worse than the horse's kick," the red-haired man complained.

"Forgive me," Roberto said, "I'm not myself right now. I don't enjoy all this killing."

The red-haired man eyed Roberto pensively. Then he shrugged. "And I do, I'm afraid. It comes easily to me."

"Who are you?" Roberto asked. "You speak like a courtier, but you fight like a paid mercenary."

"Il Capitano Rinaldo Gustiano," the red-haired man said, bowing slightly. "I am a soldier turned fencing master and noted duelist, recently living in Milan."

"And now?" Roberto asked, intrigued.

"And now, I am nothing. I hunt the woman who robbed me of my horse, my sword, and my good name, the whore who left me naked in her room to face charges for a murder I did not commit. I know she planned to escape into the maze of Labirinto. I intend to find her, get my possessions back, and have my revenge. And you, Signore, what is your story?"

Roberto paused before answering, regarding the red-haired man in a new light. Given the crime, he wasn't surprised by the man's vehemence. But the man's cold rage dismayed him nonetheless. His own search for Anna was so different.

"I am Roberto Farachi, a merchant and a trader of Venice. I am in love with the most beautiful and intelligent woman in Italy."

Rinaldo groaned. "You're a dead man, then. There's nothing I can do, Signore, to save you. Had I known your plight in advance, it would have been kinder for me to let these thieves kill you quickly. That beautiful woman will be your undoing. Look at me and take a warning."

Roberto laughed. "For the love of Anna Forsetti, I am willing to risk even my life."

Rinaldo thumped Roberto on the back. "Spoken like a true Innamorato!"

"Come, Il Capitano," Roberto said. "Let me assist you in your journey to Labirinto. It's the least I can do to repay you for all the trouble I've brought you."

"It's women who have brought us together on this road, Signore. And it's women who continue to cause us trouble."

With Rinaldo's help, Roberto lifted the bodies of the dead thieves and tied them over the backs of two of the horses. Rinaldo hoisted himself into the saddle of the third horse. Roberto mounted his own horse again, gathered up the reins of the thieves' horses, and led them down the road.

"Why not leave them for the crows?" Rinaldo asked.

"Because once they were men. And this one repented of his sins. They belong in the ground, not rotting in a ditch."

"And you believed that bastard's dying words?"

"The sincerity of his confession will be judged by one greater than me," Roberto said simply. "It's only for me to send them on their way. I wouldn't want their ghosts haunting me because I failed in my duty to see them buried."

Rinaldo laughed and then grimaced at the pain in his chest. "Signor Farachi, I have left more men than I can count rotting in fields and waysides, and not one of them has returned to haunt me."

Roberto shrugged. "Perhaps I have more delicate sensibilities than you, Captain Gustiano. I am certain I would not be able to eat as well or sleep as peacefully at night if I did not lay these three to rest. They would hover over my minestrone, dance in their rotting clothes around my roasted capons, and leave a moldy taste in the wine with their decaying lips."

"You don't really believe that," Rinaldo scoffed.

"But why would I chance it? Have you any wish to see again the men you have slain?"

Rinaldo was quiet for a moment. "Only one man," he said at last. "And that would be to kill him again before he could lay his curse on me."

Before long, they came to a small village composed mostly of yellow-brick farmhouses, a mill on a stream, and a smithy. They stopped at an ancient stone-walled church and Roberto went inside, where he found the priest busily setting out candles around the nave. He was a stooped elderly man in frayed black robes, with a round wrinkled face and pudgy, childish fingers. Roberto gave him a handful of coins to pay for the coffins and a mass for the repose of the dead thieves. Then Roberto remounted his horse and with a sigh for his aching backside and stiff sword arm, left the village with Rinaldo. The priest had told Roberto that they might reach Labirinto by late afternoon if they did not delay. Would that that love give him wings, he prayed, and speed him to Anna before she entered the maze.

17

The Piazza del Labirinto was bathed in amber light as the setting sun balanced briefly over the spiked tips of the maze's cedar walls. Lorenzo pounded his fist against the sealed wooden gates. He had been at it for almost an hour, enraged that his servant Giano had disappeared into the maze with the manifestos. Unfortunately, Signor Colonna was also enraged, since without the missing manifestos, his trading ships were now stuck in Genoa's harbor. He had given Lorenzo two days in which to recover the paperwork before he extracted his own painful form of compensation from the legal scribe.

Lorenzo was convinced that recovering the manifestos was a simple matter of getting into the maze, finding his wayward servant, and getting out again. But the getting in was proving more difficult than he'd imagined. His fist was raw from repeatedly hitting it against the gates and his voice was hoarse from shouting. The gates remained bolted shut, the sound of his fist echoing in some unseen hollow on the other side. Frustrated, he leaned back his head and shouted up at the high wall of cedars.

"I demand to see my servant!" he ordered. "I demand to be let in! Anyone who can hear me, I insist on being allowed to enter!"

"Chuido il becco! Shut your beak!" bawled a man with a withered leg. He hobbled toward Lorenzo, leaning his misshapen torso on a wooden crutch and shaking his fist. "You can't just shout to be let in. The gates open when the spirits of the maze think you are ready."

"Nonsense. There are no spirits of the maze."

"Silensio!" whispered a woman huddled in a dark cloak. She came close to Lorenzo, who backed away from the rank smell of her clothing. "They will hear you and then none of us will be allowed in." She reached out a trembling hand to the cedar walls. "Please, good spirits, do not let this cretino insult you. Those of us who are truly cursed know that only you have the power to open these gates and free us. Please," she sobbed quietly, "show us mercy where no one else has."

"You're being ridiculous," Lorenzo said angrily. "My servant disappeared into the maze with a set of important papers. Someone pulled him in and I want him back. Someone on the other side is sure to hear and respond."

"You think you're so important that the spirits stop their work and listen to you, eh, Signore?" a man dressed like a shepherd called out. Behind him, a small crowd of pilgrims, which had been attracted by the sounds of the argument, grumbled among themselves and glared at Lorenzo.

"No," Lorenzo answered sharply. "I think you are all foolish to believe that this maze will magically lift the curses from your back. The truth is, you have made miserable lives for yourselves. You would be better served by going home."

"What do you know of my misery?" the woman hissed from the depths of her cloak. She pulled back the hood to reveal a narrow face blotched with bruises and eyes ringed with dark circles. "My curse was sent to me on black wings. It shattered my windows and entered my house. It smothered my little child sleeping in his cradle. It drove my husband to the river where he fell in and drowned. It beat a fiery wind over my head and turned me into a hag. Even now it sits upon my shoulder, the talons driving me mad with pain. Can you pluck this curse from me?"

"No one can, because it doesn't exist," Lorenzo said gravely. The gathered crowd scoffed loudly. "Perhaps you suffer from an illness borne by bad wheat, rotted fruit, or spoiled meat," he shouted over the heckling. "Though your pain is real, this illness makes you see what is not there. The maze will not change that."

"Monster! Unbeliever!" the woman cried out.

"Devil! Let's hang him before he angers the spirits of the maze," the man with the withered leg demanded. "He will ruin it for all of us!"

The crowd of angry pilgrims encircled Lorenzo. One pilgrim picked up a paving stone, another brandished a walking stick. Lorenzo stepped back, his shoulders pressed against the hard wood of the gates. He stared at the glaring eyes, the haunted faces of people more willing to vent their frustrations on him than to confront the darkness in their own souls. They would kill him, he thought calmly, but their misery would not abate.

"Stop," he commanded. "I am not the cause of your problems. You gain nothing by my death."

"The signore has a point." An older man with greying hair pushed his way through the hostile crowd and raised his hands soothingly. He was well-dressed in a good black doublet and sensible hose. With his comfortable belly and thinnish legs, he was an odd sort to confront a hostile crowd. Yet, his reasonable voice and calm demeanor seemed to penetrate the inflamed passions of the crowd.

"Peace now, and hold your weapons," the man was saying. "Surely, good pilgrims, the spirits of the maze will not be appeased by an act of murder. It is to generosity that they respond. Leave the unbeliever to his own frustrations. A man deaf to the call of faith is already doomed."

"It's not faith, but a siren's song, giving voice to comforting lies," Lorenzo complained in a low voice.

"That may be, Signore," the man muttered back. "But these people are ready to kill you for your honesty. I urge you to keep quiet."

"I agree with the signore here," said another man breaking through the line of the hesitant crowd. The newcomer was dressed in a peasant's garb, with red hair catching the last rays of the late sunlight. Despite the poverty of his dress, he had a commanding presence. There was dried blood on his shirt and he held his naked sword in readiness by his side. "Leave the madman to his own visions of truth. It may be that he is no less cursed than you, good people, but has yet to admit it."

"That's taking license with my honor," Lorenzo said sourly.

"Less painful than taking license with your neck at the end of a rope," the red-haired man retorted.

Slowly the crowd dispersed, more moved by the sight of the red-haired man and his sword, Lorenzo thought, than by any real change of heart. Then again, they had misery enough of their own. Where was the profit in inflicting more? Only the woman remained, weeping noisily against the cedar walls. Lorenzo stared at her with pity, hearing in her sobs the depths of her despair. Memory sunk teeth into his heart as he recalled the last time he had heard that sound: Cecilia, his wife, crying alone in her chambers. He felt his throat constrict as if a noose had been place around his neck.

"Are you well, Signore?" the older man asked, eyeing him with alarm.

Lorenzo pulled his gaze away from the woman. "Thank you," he said brusquely.

"I am curious, Signore," the older man said.

"About what?" Lorenzo turned his full attention on the man. A Venetian, no doubt. The accent was lilting, the consonants softened into a throaty sound.

"I, too, am searching for someone, as is my companion. We are strangers here—"

"So are most in this piazza," Lorenzo said.

"Yes, but we have little knowledge of the maze other than what we have gleaned from these simple pilgrims. It all sounds very . . . very fantastical. Is there truly no set time when the gates might be opened? No one who could show us the way quickly through the maze?"

Lorenzo shook his head and waved his hands in the air. "Signori, I can't answer your questions. In all the years I have lived here, I have never been interested in the tales surrounding this maze. I am a scribe for the law—"

"A maze unto itself," the red-haired man put in.

"But with a logic I understand," Lorenzo said, "intricate and complex, but knowable. The maze of Labirinto is as great a mystery to me as it must appear to you."

"Are there no other ways inside that you know of, Signore?" the older man asked. "From the outside it does not seem as if the maze were so large as to take as much as a day for a pilgrim to enter and come out again. And yet from what I am told, none have been seen again once they have entered it."

"Again, Signore, I am ignorant and have no ready answer. On one occasion I attempted to walk the full perimeter of the maze. Halfway around I was distracted by a smaller street that led to the river. I stayed there a while and, on my return, could not find the streets that bordered the far side of the maze again. Until now, I have had little interest in the maze. But I have spent the last two days in this piazza questioning these pilgrims and have learned nothing more of its secrets. Or I should say, I've learned much of the fables and nothing of the truth."

"Perhaps you have seen the woman I seek," the older man asked. "A Venetian woman, traveling with her daughter?"

"And a little dog?" Lorenzo asked, remembering the melee in the market the day before.

"Yes. The girl has spectacles."

"I met with the girl. She accused me of pinching her backside."

"And did you?" the red-haired man asked with a glimmer of a smile.

"No. It was the work of two old lechers, one of whom had stolen my servant's boots and then told me that the man had been carried into the maze."

"Do you know where the woman and her daughter are now?" the older man asked.

"In the maze, I expect. The gates opened briefly in the night, I was told. Three small parties made their way into the maze before the gates sealed themselves shut again."

"Simonetta," the red-haired man said, his head lowered in thought. Then he raised his face, the eyes hard. "Did you see a thin woman, black-haired and dressed like a whore? She would have been riding a grey Arab stallion and carrying a good sword."

Lorenzo stared at the man, incredulous. "A whore? What man looks at a whore's face, much less remembers it?"

The man clamped his jaws and his fist twisted over the handle of his sword. Lorenzo thought for a brief instant that he might strike him dead for his callous reply. Did the red-haired man hate the whore or love her? How closely wedded were the two passions. How easy to hate the woman you once loved. Cecilia, golden-haired and sweet-tongued. Cecilia, deceitful as a serpent, saliva bitter as gall.

"Perhaps, Signore," the older man was saying, "we would do well to combine our interests. We are only recently come into the city and we are as anxious to find our missing companions as are you to find your servant. It may be of greater benefit to us all if we work together. I am Roberto Farachi of Venice and my companion is Il Capitano Rinaldo Gustiano of Milan."

"I am Lorenzo Falcomatta, originally of Bologna and for the last five years an inhabitant of Labirinto," Lorenzo answered with a slight tilt of his head. "I know very little but you are welcome to share what knowledge I have. It would be a refreshing change to examine the maze with men who confront its oddities with logic and are not blinded by the stupid superstition that surrounds these ignorant pilgrims."

"Ah yes, logic," Roberto said with a smile. He scratched the side of his nose sheepishly. "When a man leaves his comfortable home for the rigors of the road, all in search of a woman who may or may not return his love, logic, I am afraid plays little part in his decisions. Still, I hope I can be of some practical assistance in our mutual endeavors."

"I may not be much better," Rinaldo added. "I am here for a taste of revenge, as cold and biting as Roberto's love is hot and sweet. But by recognizing our weaknesses, we may well be able to judge between us what is useful knowledge and what speaks only to our desires."

"Fair enough, Signori. I have no such passions to distract me, I assure you." Lorenzo lifted his chin, his jaw stiff and his shoulders pulled back. "Let us proceed to the Arch of Dreams. It's there that I first lost the turning of the maze and found myself walking toward the river."

The three men walked along the high cedar walls of the maze, following the slow curve of the piazza. Birds rustled in the leaves and
Lorenzo could hear the soft snorting of animals hidden behind its walls.
The pungent scent of the cedars mingled with the musty smell of earth
and wet paving stones. From the pilgrims' fires, narrow strands of grey
smoke were spun into the clean air like slender arms raised in supplication to the night sky. Once they stopped and Rinaldo experimentally
shoved his sword up to the hilt into the green wall of the cedars to test
its thickness. When he withdrew the blade, there was blood on the tip.
A putrid odor rose from the blade, and though Rinaldo tried to wipe it
clean, the stench stayed with him as he belted the sword at his side.

They passed through a second smaller piazza and Robert stopped,
entranced by a marble ruin hunkered near the wall of the maze.

"What is that?" he asked Lorenzo.

"They call it the Arch of Dreams," Lorenzo answered. "It's an old
gate, and all that is left of a Roman fortification."

The marble arch was stained yellow and grey from rain and the city's
soot. Its broken crown stretched over two remaining columns like the
severed arms of a broad-shouldered warrior. Along the sides of the
crown were the remnants of an eroding bas-relief. Roberto studied the
arch, beginning at one end of the sculpted relief and moving slowly
along its length until the broken span ended near the cedar walls of the
maze.

"Look, do you recognize them?" he asked. Rinaldo was still trying to
wipe his blade clean, furious that he could not rid himself of the powerful stench. But Lorenzo glanced up at the old relief, squinting in the
flickering torchlight to make out the carved figures.

"It's a depiction of two different things," Roberto explained. "There,
you see a man like Hercules—the big figure standing among the other
two smaller ones."

"But what is he holding?" Lorenzo asked.

"Ah, a plate of food for the god Hermes. But this is not really a part
of Hercules's story. See how foolish Hercules gets greedy and eats the
offering? This is Pappas, the early Roman comic actor, portraying Hercules about to eat the sacrifice he'd intended to give the god. This is
where our masks were conceived. Arlecchino, Pantelone, and Pulchinella.
Once they wore the faces of gods. Now they wear the masks of our ap-
petites."

A beggar passed the trio staring up at the remains of the Arch of
Dreams. He grunted and pinched his nose between his fingers as he
passed Rinaldo.

"Che schifo," he croaked, and then, standing before one of the ancient columns, he undid his hose and urinated forcefully against the yellow marble. Roberto backed up quickly as the stream splashed everywhere. At last, sighing with relief, the beggar hitched up his hose and ambled away.

"A theater critic, no doubt," Roberto said with a shrug.

"A vagrant," Lorenzo corrected.

Roberto looked at him with a puzzled frown. "You don't have much imagination, do you, Signore?"

"I prefer the truth."

"Whist!" somebody hissed at them from up above.

Lorenzo looked up at the top of the Arch of Dreams. He couldn't see anyone.

"Over here, up here, look this way," the voice entreated in a harsh whisper.

The three men craned their heads, turning and twisting their necks to discover the source of the voice. At last Rinaldo pointed to the top of the cedar trees.

"Up there. I think I see someone."

Lorenzo followed Rinaldo's finger and saw in the dim twilight a boy with thick bushy eyebrows and long hair peering at them. His nose was flat against his face, his lips thick. He reached out his hand.

"Climb up, and I'll help you over. I heard you knocking at the gates. Come on quick, before he comes back and finds me."

"Who's he?" Rinaldo asked. "The keeper of the maze?"

The thick eyebrows pulled together into a single dark furrow. "No. The one you stuck with your sword. He's angry enough. You caught him up the arse. Me, I thought it a good game. Come on, quick. This is your only chance, while he's gone to fetch his sword."

"Can we trust this boy?" Lorenzo demanded.

"I can trust the stench on my sword to know I cut into something," Rinaldo answered. "I'm going up."

He reached up into the trees and gave a huff of air as his foot found a purchase in the trees, which swayed under his weight as he pulled himself upward, climbing the branches like a leafy ladder.

"It's not so bad," he called down to Lorenzo and Roberto.

"Hurry," the boy above him urged when Rinaldo had almost reached the crest of the trees. "Take my hand."

Rinaldo braced himself against a fork in the branches and struck out his hand. The boy grabbed it and, with one pull, lifted Rinaldo through the tops of the trees.

Below, Lorenzo heard a stifled curse and a shout, as though Rinaldo had fallen on the other side.

Roberto stood close to the wall of trees and called softly. "Rinaldo!" There was no answer.

"Rinaldo, are you all right?" he tried again.

The face of a second man appeared over the wall of trees. This one was a collection of big bones, slanted cheeks, and a huge lantern chin. A mouth picketed with teeth hawed in laughter.

"He made it over!" the second face shouted. "He made it. He's waiting fer you. Now, who's next! Come on! We ain't got all night."

Roberto looked uncertainly at Lorenzo and back to the strange face peering down at them.

"Shake it, old man, or he'll be back and who knows the frigging hot soup we'll be in for helping you over!"

"Madonna Santa," Roberto muttered. "Only for you, Anna." And he stepped into the branches of the cedars.

Lorenzo watched with growing concern as the older man struggled to climb up through the tangled branches of the cedars. He nearly fell once when a bird hurtled out of the trees near his face and gave him a fright. Lorenzo heard him swear and steady himself before he continued. At the top of the cedars, the second man reached out his hand, and as before, Lorenzo saw Roberto pulled briskly and effortlessly through the treetops before he gave a muffled yell. The cedars shuddered from top to bottom.

Lorenzo cupped his hands over his mouth and called, "Roberto! Rinaldo!" The sky had darkened into a deep midnight blue streaked with the last russet fingers of sunlight. Lorenzo heard a snigger behind him and he turned sharply. There was no one there. His eyes struggled to see someone hiding behind the columns, but he was alone in the street, except for the statues carved on the wall of the arch. The fading sunlight brightened their weathered grey faces and they gleamed for an instant. Pappas, his nose a rounded bulb, his lips pulled back in a sly toothless grin, seemed to be staring at Lorenzo.

"Hey you! Sourpuss! Are you coming? I can't wait much longer! Your friends are already on their way!"

Lorenzo turned back to the maze, where a third face was beckoning to him. This one had feminine features, like a boy's perhaps before the beard begins to darken his cheeks. The eyes appeared large and startled, the nose long and thin. The firm lips pouted like a flower over his narrow chin. It seemed to Lorenzo that the boy's features kept changing, almost like the face of his servant. Nonsense he told himself firmly. It was a trick of the twilight.

"Last chance!" the youthful face told him, and reached out a slender arm.

Lorenzo plunged his body into the trees, seeking the branches the other two men had used before him. His foot found a fork in the lower branch of one of the cedars, his hand found a sturdy twig. Easily, as if the trees themselves placed their willing arms in his grasp, Lorenzo climbed the wall of trees. Halfway up, he glanced over at the Arch of Dreams. Pappas's face was still laughing but the eyes were gazing at something on the top of the maze wall. Lorenzo looked up and saw a proffered hand. He grabbed it and gasped as he was pulled effortlessly through the treetops. His feet scrambled to find a foothold amid the branches.

"Stop squirming," the young man scolded. He reached down and, seizing the lock of white hair in Lorenzo's crown, pulled him through the feathery branches at the top of the cedars. Lorenzo spluttered, his eyes tearing and his mouth suddenly full of leaves and the muddied remnant of an old bird's nest. He reached out, trying desperately to seize the hand that held him fast by the hair. But no sooner did he feel his body break through the wall of the maze, than he was released.

Lorenzo fell headfirst down inside the tree wall, fighting to bring his arms up in a protective cradle around his head as he crashed through the trees. His body banged against the same branches that had accommodated his upward climb. He cried out, but his voice was buried in the lively snapping of branches and thrashing leaves. Finally, he slowed as the heavier lower branches of the cedars snagged him and he came to a stop, pressed between the dense branches. He struggled to free himself from the prison of the branches, but he was wedged tightly in their embrace, trapped deep within the maze wall. He coughed weakly and spit out splinters of bark. His skin prickled with dozens of tiny scratches on his cheeks and neck.

The same strong hands that had pulled him over and then shoved him down the wall of trees reached into the thickets and grabbed him by the shoulders. With a rough twist, they jerked him through a narrow gap between the branches and laid him flat on a stony pathway on the inside of the maze.

"Welcome, Lorenzo Falcomatta! We've been waiting a long time for you."

Lorenzo brushed away the chaff from his eyes and stared angrily at a pair of sandaled feet. The boy deserved a lecture and a thrashing, Lorenzo thought, just as soon as he was able to stand. But when Lorenzo caught sight of the boy's face, all thoughts of punishment and lectures evaporated. He stared hard, trying to comprehend the face—no, the collection of faces—that was staring back down at him.

There were three faces to be exact, wrapped around a single head. One side was the older youth with the heavy black eyebrows who had called down to Rinaldo. A side was Roberto's fool with the bony cheeks and picket teeth. In the middle, staring down with haughty amusement, was the feminine youth Lorenzo had seen peering down at him. Three faces, each with a set of eyes to study him, each with a mouth set in an individual humorous twist.

The three-faced man cackled with three different sounding laughs. Then he reached down one slender arm to Lorenzo and pulled him upright. Gently, he brushed the twigs and leaves from Lorenzo's black doublet. The eyes of the youthful face stared coyly at Lorenzo as he raked his fingers through the white patch of hair, smoothing it flat again. Lorenzo stared back, speechless.

"The journey begins, good poet," said the youth. The fool's face gave a lopsided grin, while the dark-browed boy sniggered. "Too long we have languished in your constipated silence."

"My servant—" Lorenzo began weakly.

"I am your servant now," the three faces said in unison. "Come, Lorenzo. I'll take you where you really want to go—where you need to go, to find your voice again." With one hand pointing out to indicate their direction, the three-faced man lightly shoved Lorenzo in the small of his back with the other hand to start him walking down the stony path through the maze.

IL LABIRINTO,
THE MAZE

This is what happens when you hurry through a
maze: the faster you go, the worse you are entangled.

—*Seneca, Epistulae, Morals #44*

18

Don Gianlucca di Baptistta sat down to rest on a stone bench nestled in the shelter of the trees. How long had he been walking? Was it three hours? Or had it been longer? The sun overhead barely penetrated to the narrow pathway. It seemed as if time had halted to keep the sun hovering permanently with the same lazy slant of amber light. But the fatigue of his legs, the ache in his calf muscles, told him he had walked far into the maze.

Don Gianlucca groaned softly as he eased his tired body down onto the moss-flecked bench. He'd been thinking about sitting. He had been thinking about how pleasant it would be if just such a bench existed on the pathway for the weary pilgrim. No sooner had the thought shaped itself in his mind than there, around the next corner, such a bench had appeared. A chance occurrence, or an answered prayer?

He gazed up at the cedar trees, their frondlike leaves intertwined into an impenetrable wall of deep green. They stood silent and upright. And yet his eye caught the subtle movements of small creatures rustling through the dense foliage. Looking back the way he had come, he could only see a short distance before the tree-lined corridor angled around a sharp corner. The path forward was equally obscured.

He remembered the maze etched on the wall of San Pantelon with its looping pathways, ambrages that meandered back and forth—its revocatis—the dead ends and its errores—the wrong turnings that led a man astray. At San Pantelon, he could trace the path with his finger, seeing the whole intricate plan of the maze laid out beneath his hand. Walking a planted maze of this size had proved far more frustrating. Lost within the confining walls of the cedars, the pattern of the maze seemed chaotic. So many turns had left him disoriented. Which way was north? Which way was south? He stared up at the sky, annoyed at the lazy sun. He couldn't even tell where it might set, which would offer him a sense of a westerly direction. Even the trees grew upright, neither bending to the western winds, nor turning their leaves to the southern sun. There was no moss clinging to the cool northern side of their trunks.

Don Gianlucca scratched at the light beard that itched his cheek. And where were all the pilgrims? He had expected to see other people journeying through the maze. Yet in the hours that he had walked, he had not seen another soul. He had entered the maze with three other people and within moments, they had scattered, each lost within the folded confines of the maze.

With a deep sigh, Don Gianlucca rose to his feet and decided he'd best continue walking. Perhaps a meal might appear with the same invisible hospitality as the bench.

The path appeared to turn again. Don Gianlucca scowled, wondering if he were looping back parallel to the way he had come. No sooner had he turned the corner of trees, than he heard a woman's screeching cries piercing the thick wall of trees. An animal howled and was answered by a chorus of shrill ululations that was joined by beating drums and the jangling of rattles. Don Gianlucca hitched his habit up around his knees and ran down the path toward the clamor.

The path curved, turning first one way and then another. The howling beast and the trilling cries of womens' voices echoed everywhere amid the trees. The path sloped upward beneath his feet, and Don Gianlucca began to pant, his breathing labored as he ran up the steep incline. But the shrill voices, the pounding drums, and the clash of the rattles exhorted his legs to move faster.

The path narrowed and then disappeared as the wall of cedars disintegrated into a broad forest of pines, larches, and oaks with small fluttering brown leaves. The light faded rapidly in the forest as though the sun were weary at last of holding its unnatural position in the sky. In the deepening shadows of the encroaching twilight, Don Gianlucca scrambled up a mud-covered incline, grabbing at roots and branches to keep his balance. At the crest of the incline, Don Gianlucca stopped, amazed as the trees fell away before him and he saw that he was standing on the brow of a grassy hill.

The narrow, sunlit walls of the maze were gone. Here it was night and above him the midnight blue sky was wide and dotted with unexpected stars. A haunted face was sketched across the surface of a full moon lifting out of a canopy of trees at the foot of the hill. The hill itself was softly sloping, covered with long grass and studded with ancient olive trees whose quaking leaves turned their silvery undersides to the moonlight. The wind rustled the dry bladed grass and brought the peppery scent of smoke to Don Gianlucca's nose.

The shrill ululations of women's voices continued to reverberate across the hillside, sending a chill up his spine. Don Gianlucca caught sight of bobbing globes of firelight cast from torches carried aloft at the bottom of the hill. By their harsh orange light he could see a pack of women running wildly through the olive grove. They had tied deer and lion skins across their backs. Beneath the wavering torchlight their faces were stark and contorted, their eyes dark hollows. Some held spears, two were banging drums, and one had a bone-and-metal rattle that she shook furiously. Their hair was tangled with vines and their arms were smeared with thick white clay.

Running before them, Don Gianlucca caught sight of a young lion streaking through the trees. The women fanned out in the grove, running hard in all directions, and quickly succeeded in entrapping the lion in the glare of their torches. With victorious cries they closed the circle, threatening him with their spears and drums. The lion, crouched, snarled in rage, and sprang at the nearest woman, the torchlight revealing the bronze flash of his extended claws.

Don Gianlucca clutched the trunk of the nearest olive tree, his eyes trained on the lion's body soaring in a golden arc toward the waiting woman. All noise had ceased. The cries that only seconds before had filled the hillside were silent; the drumming abruptly stopped. Even the wind held its breath as the woman lifted her spear and impaled the attacking lion. The moment the spear passed through his body, the hillside erupted once more with sound. The lion squalled, the drums beat savagely, the women threw back their heads to the ghostly face of the moon and trilled their piercing cries. Then the lion's writhing body disappeared under women's tearing hands.

Don Gianlucca leaned, shaking, against the olive tree as he watched the woman who had flung her spear first tear the head of the lion free from his mangled body. Blood dyed her white clay arms a livid red. She raised the head with an exalted cry and carried it aloft among the women. One by one her companions pulled off pieces of the slain lion, cradling the torn flesh in their arms. They took the skin and draped it over the shoulders of one of the drummers. Then they gathered together in a troop and began to sing and drum through the olive grove, moving slowly up the hill to where Don Gianlucca waited, half-hidden behind the tree.

The priest swallowed hard at the knot of fear in his throat. He knew who they were. Even though he had never seen their like before, only read their histories in books forbidden by the church, he knew these women. He knew that it was death for him to see their midnight revels. They were the maenads, followers of Bacchus, and their rituals were forbidden to men. He crouched low as they neared him, feverishly hoping that his black robes would blend into the dark shadows beneath the tree.

The retinue of women passed near his tree, and absorbed by the passions of their hunt, they did not notice him. He saw them clearly, however, their strangely adorned bodies illuminated by the burning torches. The upper halves of their faces were covered with stiff white masks, the eyes lined in black to make them appear more fierce. They swayed drunkenly, some wrapping their bloody arms around each other's shoulders. The woman carrying the lion's head licked her bloody fingers, her mouth and chin bright red.

Don Gianlucca watched them pass with fearful fascination. The masks were stark, pagan faces. The drums' wooden rims were carved with animals. The spearheads were sharpened bronze. But beneath the animal skins, the women were dressed in stained and rotting damask skirts and molding velvet bodices lashed together by vines, their colors long faded into dirt. Their sleeves were shredded rags of bloodstained silk flapping like ghosts over their bony arms. Don Gianlucca shuddered, nausea gripping his belly as a vaporous stench of mud and sweat, blood and the tang of cat urine followed in their wake.

A hand settled on his shoulder and jerked him to his feet.

"Would you join them?" asked a seductive voice.

Don Gianlucca stared terrified into the shadows and saw a beautiful, pale face smiling coldly at him. It belonged to a man, clean-shaven and youthful, his white brow wreathed in an abundance of dark curling hair. His eyes were black pools that absorbed the glow of moonlight like pearls. He was naked to the waist, his chest a smooth white plain. He smacked his full lips and leaned forward almost as though to kiss Don Gianlucca.

"Put on a mask and join them," the man coaxed. He laid a cool soft hand against Don Gianlucca's cheek. "All sorrow will cease. All pain will be erased. This is the divine joy. The grapes, the night, the hunt."

"Bacchus, the god of Wine," Don Gianlucca whispered.

"Oh, of much more than that," the god replied with a coy smile. "The god of pleasure, of fertility, of lust. Come, join us. With a mask, the maenads will not know you are a man. You may join in our secret revels." Bacchus held out a mask and Don Gianlucca recognized it at once. It was the same one he had worn that night with Anna: a woman's mask made of peach-colored leather.

Don Gianlucca beheld the silent gaze of the mask and struggled with himself. Most of his life had been devoted to the pursuit of pleasure; once he had believed in the virtue of wine. And now here was the god of pleasure and wine holding out his hand to welcome him. Fatigue disappeared from Don Gianlucca's limbs. His heart pounded, twin lances of sweet pain contracting the muscles of his thighs. On his tongue, the heady taste of wine banished all other hungers.

Still, he hesitated, cupping his hand over his genitals, holding them close to his feverish body. He stared into the polished eyes of the god, uncertain of his promise. Though his body clamored for pleasure and the taste of wine, he could not shake off the vision of the maenads in their rotting clothes, with their graveyard stench and their lips covered in blood. He was in a maze where nothing was as it seemed. Above one corridor the sun hovered, while over another, the cloth of night was spread. There was a path, but it was twisted and misleading.

He looked down again at Anna's mask. This time, the pretty face with its pouting lips filled him with sorrow and he remembered why he was in the maze. Passion alone had hollowed him. Although it had brought pain and anguish, the grace of bestowing forgiveness to Anna had given him strength. Wordlessly, he shook his head.

"Ah." Bacchus held up Anna's mask and smiled at it. "I was not called for you. But there is something about you . . . I know you." Bacchus brought his cheek close to Don Gianlucca's face, his hand on the priest's shoulder. He sniffed delicately at the tracks of sweat on Don Gianlucca's neck. Shivers rode the length of Don Gianlucca's spine and he closed his eyes.

At last, Bacchus allowed his hand to slip from Don Gianlucca's shoulder. "Another time," Bacchus said softly. He removed his crown of grape leaves and set it on Don Gianlucca's head, then he placed a bunch of blue-black grapes in Don Gianlucca's trembling hands. Don Gianlucca glanced down at them, hunger erupting in his belly.

"Another time," Bacchus whispered.

When Don Gianlucca looked up again the god had already melted back into the darkness. Only the weight of the grapes in his hands, the leaves brushing his forehead, and the god's lingering, dusky perfume told Don Gianlucca that he had seen him and been touched by him.

The rough bark of the vining crown scratched Don Gianlucca's temples. He tore it from his head with a curse and pulled up the scratchy wool hood of his habit. But the grapes still tempted him. He ate one, biting through the tart skin, the flesh sweet as it burst in his dry mouth. The grapes were much too good to waste. Don Gianlucca shrugged and turned his confused face to the stars. Why not eat them? he thought. Christ himself had eaten to slake his hunger. Don Gianlucca ate the grapes slowly as he trudged down through the olive grove.

The moon showed him the faint markings of a path, no more than a goat trail, and he followed it to the bottom of the hill where the olive grove became another forest of oak and pine trees. Don Gianlucca walked along the narrow grassy path that skirted the edge of the forest and then abruptly swerved into the wood's dark flank.

Don Gianlucca peered into the dark wall of trees, then looked back along the path curving away into the olive grove. How would he know if he had made the right decision? How would he know if this path through the forest would bring him through the maze? He looked up hopefully to the stars for a celestial sign, an omen from God that might direct him. But there was none. Just the quiet night awaiting his decision.

There was no way of knowing, he decided at last, tucking his hands into the folds of his sleeves. Faith would not assist him in choosing a direction, but only in surviving the consequences of that choice. He crossed himself and then stepped into the dark flank of the woods.

19

Basta! Stop! Let go of me, you . . . you . . . you spawn of goats!" Zizola shouted as she kicked the shins of the galloping creature that held her. She pinched the furred arms clamped around her waist and the creature roared and pitched her high into the air. She screamed, twirled, and was caught by another galloping creature, who flung her over one muscled shoulder as a peddler his sack of wares and continued running down the corridors of the maze.

"Saint's hell," she swore. Her head was bouncing up and down, but she couldn't help noticing that her abductor was only partially a man, naked to the waist and flocked with patches of light brown hair. Below the small of his back, the smooth skin became a pelt of shaggy brown fur. A short, scraggly tail flicked with excitement and two long spindly legs terminating in black hooves cut deep grooves in the dirt as he ran.

She glanced up through the curtain of her tangled blond hair. Following close behind her captor were three other creatures, prepared, Zizola thought, to relieve this one if she should prove too heavy. Their faces were squat and ugly, with protruding wide brows that hung like balconies over their deep-set yellow eyes. Horns burst through the ruddy skin of their foreheads and curled back over short manes of thick hair. Their noses were lumpy and their lips were thick and red. Below their furred navels, stiff erections bobbed furiously with each stride.

Satyrs! Zizola spat. What a curse to be rescued by them! Most of her life she had managed to avoid the lecherous gropes of dirty old men in the market, the nasty offers of soldiers twirling coins between their fingers, and the taunts of gambling street boys. And now it had come to this: a band of goatmen carting her off into the coils of a maze, their shameless pricks wagging at her as they licked their red lips.

Zizola hammered her fists against the satyr's back. "Let me down, you hairy-assed, shit-covered goat! Let me go!"

With a grunt, the satyr turned deftly on his cloven feet and tossed her to one of his companions. Zizola screamed and arched her back like a cat. She clawed the face of the satyr as he reached out to catch her. The satyr brayed and stumbled, his hands to his injuries, and the two satyrs galloping behind collided with him. Zizola landed on her feet in a tight crouch and sprinted down a corridor of green trees.

She could hear the satyrs behind her bleating and grunting. A dull clash of horns and the renewed drumming of their hooves told her they'd recovered and were after her again.

Zizola pumped her arms, stretched out her legs, and ran madly down the corridor, swearing at the maze and her own miserable luck.

Ah, Zizola, what the hell are you doing? Running for your life, as always. Stupid ragazza, what makes you think you can outrun anything, eh? Those men in the piazza, Ruggerio, Stelladonna and her wooden spoon, and now, as if God wasn't punishing her enough, He had sent satyrs after her. Why was she cursed to run like the hare? She ducked her head and urged more speed into her weary legs.

She didn't see the green wall of bushes blocking the path until she had slammed into it. Her head banged into the crossed arms of the branches and stars exploded in her eyes. She screeched as the branches repulsed her, staggered back, dazed and hurt, and fell on the path. Groaning, she curled in a tight ball, exhausted. Basta! It was over. There was nowhere to go.

She was breathing hard, pain riding her body. She inhaled the scent of grass and damp earth. Wet leaves and the tiny broken husks of acorns pressed into her cheek. Still gasping, she rolled onto her back and squinted up at the sunlight spearing through the branches.

What was this place? she wondered. Here it was midday, while outside the maze, the sun had already begun to set. Her legs ached from running, the back of her throat was parched, her lungs burned. To hell with it! Let them come. She closed her eyes, feeling as bruised and broken as an acorn fallen from the heights of its tree.

Hmm, she thought. Acorns were delicious, especially when cooked with game. How magnificent was the taste of a boar's crackling skin and how succulent the long pink slabs of wild meat on her tongue. Zizola inhaled dreamily, imagining the steaming platters of bread stuffings studded with acorns and chestnuts and yellow raisins. Lying on the dirt path, Zizola licked her lips and her stomach rumbled.

A snuffling noise made her open one eye. She shut it again and wrinkled her nose against the pungent scent of their shaggy hair. The satyrs were standing all around her, staring down quizzically. Someone tapped her on the shoulder. She opened her eyes and stared up at their curious faces.

"Madonna mia, what do you want with me? You must be pretty hard up in here to start chasing skinny maids like me. Look!" she shouted. "There's nothing here!" Roughly, she pulled open her ragged black bodice and revealed the small frame under the padded fabric. Her skin was a dirty olive, her small, flat breasts like pressed flowers over the narrow cage of her ribs. A satyr leaned down, ran his blackened nail over the taut skin, and shook his head sadly.

"What did I tell you?" Zizola barked, and pulled her bodice together, ashamed of her scrawniness. The satyrs began to confer with each other in guttural voices. She watched them fascinated and uncomprehending. She noticed now that they were different from each other: two were smaller, maybe younger, with pale blond and brown patches of fur on their torsos. The one she had scratched was still rubbing his cheek and flicking his dark auburn tail. He, at least, didn't look too happy with her. But they both listened respectfully to the largest one, the satyr that had first carried her in his arms. His horns curled twice around his temples and his black pelt was thick and long over his haunches. They argued, their hands raking the air for emphasis. At last they turned to her, having reached a decision.

"What?" Zizola asked. "Tell me." One of the smaller satyrs reached a hand to her and helped her stand. Their erections had subsided and their squat faces showed concern, even tenderness. They gathered around her, their bodies close and pressing. She felt the warm breath of one on the nape of her neck, the touch of another on her hair. Even the one she had scratched caressed her shoulder. The largest satyr took her hand and, turning it over, delicately kissed the palm. He looked down, his yellow eyes gazing deeply at her from beneath heavy brows.

As much as she disliked being touched by strangers, Zizola permitted the attentions of the satyrs. For all their wildness, their hands were soft. She was captivated by the ivory sheen of their curling horns and the pomegranate redness of their lips. Even their musky scent had a certain forest charm to it that she found more tolerable than the sour breath of drunks in the street.

The largest of the satyrs picked her up in his arms and cradled her carefully. Gingerly, she put her arms around his neck and he began to trot down a smaller, almost hidden path through the trees. As Zizola watched, the sky overhead shifted from day to night and from night to day again in a single heartbeat. The sun shot like a flaming arrow over the trees only to be followed by a glittering moon catapulted across the sky. The satyr began to run faster. Wind brought tears to her eyes, and the sun and moon chased each other across the sky, flickering in turn over the spires of the cedars. She ducked her head beneath the satyr's chin and closed her eyes.

When he stopped running finally, Zizola was happy to discover that the sun had settled firmly onto its throne over the cedars. The moon was taking a well-deserved rest. The satyr set Zizola on her feet and she looked around her with curiosity.

They were standing in a small sunlit boschetto shaded by cypress and citron trees. In the center of the grotto stood the Arch of Dreams. Here in the maze the arch was very different from the crumbling, desolate ruin that Zizola used to lean her back against. Here in the maze the Arch of Dreams was a pristine, alabaster white. Its frieze was whole, the once-eroded faces of Pappas and the other fools grinning down at her with cleanly chiseled smiles. And the broken arms of the arch now sloped down to either side of the columns into twin stairways. Best of all, there were no pigeons splattering droppings everywhere and no beggars sleeping among the dirty columns but only children waiting on the stairways with bright, eager faces. They waved their arms at Zizola's bewildered approach and shouted out a welcome.

As they scrambled down from the Arch of Dreams, Zizola was hardly surprised to see that these children weren't all human. The boys were obviously very young satyrs, their pelts a soft down on their plump hindquarters, their new horns budding from their foreheads like thorns, their little pink phalluses springing from their furry loins. The girls were naked except for their round bellies, wreathed by green vines whose clusters of leaves covered their shy sex.

"Why is the Arch of Dreams here?" she asked the largest satyr.

He grinned at her, his pink tongue held between his teeth. "It is the place you know best," he said in a thick unfamiliar accent. "It is the place that pleases you most. We have only to put our ear to the columns and we hear your dreams."

"It looks new," she said.

"Over there, it is old. Here it has been reborn from your thoughts. We are here to serve you, Maestra."

"Maestra? That's a good one. Don't you know who I am?" Zizola asked.

"There is no one in the maze who does not know the child of Gaetano," the satyr replied.

"Gaetano?"

"Il Maestro. The father of the maze. He has been waiting for your return."

By now the children were jostling the satyrs in a noisy confusion of laughter and pleading, shoving them aside to crowd around Zizola. They grabbed her by the hands and began leading her toward the Arch of Dreams, their moist hands pushing and pulling at her skirts, tugging at her elbow.

"Piantala! Stop now!" Zizola cried out, feigning annoyance. "What do you want?"

"Wash, Maestra. Wash yourself," they shouted.

"But why?"

"You smell bad," said one little girl in a serious voice. She wore a wreath of delicate flowers woven into her dark hair.

Zizola sniffed her armpits and clutched her throat, pretending to gag. The children laughed delightedly, but resumed pulling her toward the Arch of Dreams. Behind the arch, Zizola saw a low marble pool with flower petals and steam drifting lazily across its surface.

"I'll drown in there!" she complained.

"No, it's not deep," a young satyr proclaimed, his stubby tail twitching.

"I'll get sick! Dirt is healthy," Zizola argued, holding on to her clothes as the children yanked on her sleeves and tugged on her skirts.

"No, you will get clean!" a girl said, her face nearly hidden beneath a cloud of pale red hair. "It won't hurt!"

"Madonna mia," Zizola muttered. When they had removed her clothes, she stood embarrassed on the edge of the pool, her thin arms crossed over her naked chest. The wind caressed her flanks and she wondered if there was still time to flee.

The little girl with dark hair looked up at Zizola out of huge brown eyes. "Take my hand, Maestra, and don't be afraid."

With a sigh of resignation, Zizola gave the girl her hand and surrendered herself to the water. Three other girls joined them and they scrubbed Zizola with rough cloths. Two took her arms; the third did her legs, one at a time. They washed her hair and dug out the black dirt beneath her nails, even carefully cleaned the wax from her ears with long silver spoons. Afterwards, Zizola floated on the warm water, sighing blissfully. The only baths she'd ever managed was spit rubbed into her palms and over her ears in the winter and cold river water on her neck and between her legs in the summer.

After a while, the girls guided Zizola out of the water and dried her off while she stared down in wonder at her own skin, pink as a boiled squid. Her lank yellow hair was drying into a pale golden floss. Even the faint strands of hair on her arms and legs gleamed. With glad cries, the little girls presented a clean and dried Zizola to the largest satyr, who held out a billowing robe of purple silk.

Shy at her nakedness, Zizola dove quickly into the fabric, fumbled her arms into the loose sleeves, and wrapped it tight, laughing at its generous size. Three of her could fit inside that robe and not be crowded. The little dark-haired girl gave her a silver belt, which Zizola wrapped around her waist twice.

"Come, Maestra, now you shall eat!" the largest satyr said.

Zizola's golden eyebrows lifted joyfully and her stomach rumbled as the satyr led her to a low couch beneath the Arch of Dreams. She sat down amid its pillows and bolsters, feeling like nobility. The satyr clapped his hands and the children fell into line in front of him. Then the older satyrs began pulling platters of food out of the air and handing them to the waiting children, who brought them to the wide-eyed Zizola.

"Che paradiso," Zizola exclaimed. Where to begin? she wondered, rubbing her hands together. She took a plate from a young satyr whose hands were beginning to wobble. It was a tall tortello d'erbette, a savory mixture of cheese and herbs enclosed in a thick pastry crust. Zizola took the whole pie in her hands, broke it open, and shoved big pieces into her mouth, chewing as fast as she could. When crumbs fell over her lap, she scooped them up in her hand and stuffed them back into her mouth. She whimpered as she chewed and moaned as she licked away the buttery crumbs sticking to the corners of her mouth. Before she knew it, the entire pie had disappeared.

Zizola touched her stomach, happy to note that the pie had barely touched the perpetual emptiness of her belly. Two other children presented her with two more dishes: a plate of tagliatelle topped with caramelized oranges and almonds and a plate of roasted chicken with rosemary and black olives. A satyr handed her a fork and knife, and Zizola dug into a mouthful of pasta followed by a mouthful of chicken.

Glancing at the long line of platters still awaiting her attention, she determined to eat slowly, but continuously. And just as easily as the tortello, the roasted chicken and the side dish of pasta disappeared down her throat. She groaned when she was done, but her stomach felt hollow. When the next child brought forth a platter of risotto carciofi e piselli she couldn't resist the tiny artichokes and green peas hidden like emeralds among the mounds of creamed rice. She raised her fork again and began to eat.

After a while, her stomach started to expand. She could feel it growing like a gourd as she shoveled in a lifetime of missed food. Every time she finished another plate of food, the children shouted "Brava" and brought forth another enticing dish. Pregnant with delicacies, Zizola found it impossible to stop.

"Madonna, I'm so full, I think I shall burst," Zizola moaned when she'd polished off an entire almond tart. She undid the silver belt at her waist and let her bulging stomach distend over her lap. She belched uncomfortably. "But I don't want to stop!" she wailed.

A young satyr came forward with a goose feather in his hand and motioned for Zizola to open her mouth. As she did, he tickled the back of her throat until she felt all the food rising in her gorge. She gagged and the satyrs held her head over a marble basin as she vomited. Prodigious amounts of food in a riotous mixture of colors poured out of her, most of it undigested. Tears streamed from her eyes, but once she had started vomiting, she couldn't stop until she was empty again. Then she leaned back on her couch and let the satyrs wipe her face with a cool cloth.

"All my life I've dreamed of eating until I puked. What a feat, what a treasure, what an accomplishment!" She lay grinning with untold happiness, the taste of all those dishes still on her lips until she felt lighter. She was hungry again and the children still waited with steaming platters of food. "Now," she said smiling, "more food if you please."

Zizola ate diligently, praising each dish, but showing no signs of putting down her fork and knife. Even the older satyrs watched her with concern as platter after platter disappeared into her small frame. Night had fallen by the time she lay down her fork and exhaled. "Basta, enough." She lay down on her couch and tucked her hands beneath her cheek. Never before had she felt so full, so content. The satyrs pulled a thin linen blanket around her shoulders and sat at the bottom of the bed to watch over her.

In the middle of the night, Zizola turned on her couch. Her body felt swollen and squishy. She rubbed her face and her jaw quivered. Half-awake, she touched her chin and discovered she had more than one. When she turned on her back, she felt as if she'd been weighted down by sacks of grain. Sleepily she patted her chest. Her breasts fell in large pendulous handfuls on either side of her body.

"I'm dreaming," she muttered to herself and, grunting with the effort, managed to turn over on her other side. She tucked her hands beneath her cheek and giggled. Her fingers felt like sausages. She licked her lips and her stomach rumbled. When she woke in the morning, she wanted sausages. And she was certain they would be there, steaming in a plate of lentils, waiting for her beneath the Arch of Dreams.

"I'm dreaming," said Giano, to the woman straddled over his hips. "Or else I am truly in paradise," he said. The woman was well built and strong, her muscular thighs lifting and lowering her body over the upright spear of Giano's very hard sex. She kneaded his thighs, her fingers digging into his skin. Between the pleasure and the pain, Giano could hardly think. His head meanwhile, rested in the lap of another woman, whose naked breasts were dangling above him. He stretched up his neck and fastened his lips on one of her sun-browned nipples. She squealed happily and pinched him hard on the chest until he released her.

"Hurry up," the woman cradling his head urged the woman riding Giano's hips. "It's my turn!"

"Wait, wait." The other woman sighed breathlessly, her face flushed with heat, her eyes half-closed. Her black hair was damp with sweat at the temples. "Almost there," she gasped, and bit her lower lip. She began to ride Giano vigorously, slapping him on the flank like a jockey galloping toward the finish line. Thus admonished by her hands, her thighs, and the secret clamping of her body, there was nothing Giano could do but comply. His blood boiled over like a charger let loose in battle. He arched his back to give her a better seat in the saddle and she shouted out praises to the god that had brought them such a gift.

"My sweet sausage!" she cried, as she shuddered.

"My mound of polenta!" he answered, groaning as his climax overtook him. He grabbed her breasts in his hands.

"My veal bone!"

"My plate of split figs!"

"Culattelo!"

"My torta!" he groaned, his body trembling like a bird in the grip of the woman above him. Then he softened, feeling the wet release of her thighs as she collapsed over him with a small moan. She slid off his body and lay panting on her back next to him on the grass.

"O'Dio," he moaned. "I'm dying." His sweat-damp body rested in a shallow well in the soft earth beneath his buttocks.

"No, no, tesoro! You mustn't die yet," exclaimed the woman cradling his head. "It's my turn now!" She covered his fevered brow with kisses.

"You know, I'm a little tired," Giano said, opening one eye. He turned over on his belly and pulled himself up on his elbows. "And for some reason, a little hungry." All that shouting about sausages and veal had reminded him that somewhere on the other side of the maze he had missed the evening meal.

"Good, good," said the woman with a clap of her hands. "I'll give you something to eat while you rest up for later. Buon appetito!" she cried, and pulled Giano's head down between her thighs. "Eat, eat, my savior," she entreated, and folded her thighs about his neck.

Despite his fatigue, despite the awareness that for the last few hours all he had done was make love to one beautiful, voluptuous woman after another, Giano found it hard, no impossible, to resist the offer. In the dark center of her thighs, his mind reeled with the strong odor of the woman's skin. She smelled tart, like brandied apricots, and musky, like prugnoli mushrooms gathered in the fall. She offered herself to him, a loving feast, and he couldn't refuse. He pressed his face into the damp thatch of dark curls and used his tongue. Somewhere far above him, he could hear her cries, muffled by her thighs clamped over his ears.

Someone else began to stroke his bare buttocks with a soft, urgent hand. "My turn next," he thought he heard before the hand slipped between his thighs and began to fondle him.

Hours later, the sun long set and the glow of moonlight filtering through the trees, Giano lay on his back, exhausted in all of his limbs save one. He sat up with a tired groan and stared at his rigid penis, which stood upright like a tree, mocking the rest of Giano's weary body.

"Eh, fratellino, little brother," Giano called down to the swollen column of moonlit flesh. "Can't you sleep? You'll wear the rest of me out! Look, look at this hand. It's done groping for the night. Look, look at these lips." He pointed to his chapped lips. "They will not kiss or suck anything else tonight. And these hips," he said, giving his buttocks a shake, "they are at rest! So why not you? Eh? Go to sleep!"

But his penis resisted, deaf to his pleas. He tried to bat it down, but it sprang up again, throbbing. His testicles ached, feeling full and tender. It was almost as bad as when he was a boy, not yet old enough to sport with women, but old enough to long for them painfully. He gazed at the bodies of the women sleeping around him. The moon cast an icing of white sugar over their rounded haunches, splayed legs, and full breasts. He touched one woman on the belly with a wondering finger. Her flesh was warm, her skin silky soft.

"Eh, well then, il mio fratellino," he murmured to his erect penis.

"Perhaps you do know better than the rest of me. I should be grateful. I may well die of hunger, but at least you and I will be happily fucking when it happens!"

Giano lay down and closed his eyes. He knew his fratellino would not sleep, but remain on guard for the rest of the night. For the first time in his life, he wished for a nice, cold dousing of water to dampen its ardor. He tried to distract himself by thinking of his other passion, food. He decided to list all the exotic ingredients he knew went into a lasagna di Ferrara: golden raisins, a pinch of cinnamon, rosemary, saffron, veal, and pork. An egg pasta, rolled into thick sheets.

He had almost succeeded in forgetting his attentive little brother when one of the women, turning in her sleep, reached out and clapped a hand around his swollen member. Tethered to the ground by her tight grip, Giano woke fully. Now he could only pray for morning, when they would begin their sport again and he might find a few seconds of exhausted peace between one woman and the next.

20

I n the morning, two young satyrs helped Zizola up from her couch into a sitting position. She stared down at her changed body in mute amazement. The sleeves of the voluminous purple robe had grown tight under her arms. She pulled at the sides, but there was not enough fabric to cover her enormous girth. She was simply huge. Her pendulous breasts with nipples the size of chestnuts rested atop the gigantic mound of her swollen belly. She couldn't see her navel, her thighs were as broad as bolts of linen cloth, and her calves had grown to the thickness of Parma hams.

"Saint's hell," she muttered. "That didn't take long. Just a day of food and look at me. Che pancia!" She grabbed the draping folds of her gut and shook them. She scowled and her eyes were nearly buried in her cheeks.

A new line of children had appeared with a selection of morning meals. As Zizola worked her way through them, she thought it odd that no matter how much she ate, there was always room for more. She always felt an emptiness in her crying out for the consolation of a meat pie, a plate of pasta, a slice of a sweet tort. She couldn't stop eating.

The dark-haired girl dutifully wiped Zizola's face with a warm cloth in the moments between one platter and the next. She tried to adjust the purple robe over Zizola's enormous body but it was impossible. Her face clean, Zizola waved the little girl away and clapped her hands, eager for the next dish.

She was stuffing her face with handfuls of cream-filled tortelli when she noticed that the satyrs were not happy. Their golden eyes brooded beneath their heavy brows, and as they paced, their tails twitched angrily. Every now and then as they passed each other, they grunted warnings and then butted heads. The largest of the satyrs kept cracking his knuckles and then digging his fist into his palm.

"What's the matter with you all?" Zizola asked through a mouthful of tortelli. There was powdered sugar sprinkled over her lips and two of her three chins.

The largest satyr turned sharply on one hoof and faced her. His eyes flashed dangerously. "The nymphs have been taken from us."

"Nymphs?" Zizola asked, stretching a hand forward to start on a plate of fried eggplants. She couldn't reach over the folds of her belly so the girl with the cloud of red hair popped the slices into Zizola's mouth for her.

"Our consorts and the mothers of our children. We miss them. We . . . we need them," the satyr said urgently, indicating his sturdy erection.

"Why can't you get them back?" she asked.

"We are not permitted to leave your side. Unless, of course, you bid us go," he said. He stopped pacing and looked up at her, his yellow eyes glowing. Suddenly, Zizola smelled the sharp goaty stink of the satyrs' anger, a sour taste in the back of her throat. It almost spoiled her appetite for the plate of fritto misto; tiny fried fish, clams, and squid.

"Go, go," she said, waving them off. "Go get them if you want. I'll be here when you return." She squeezed a lemon over the plate of fried seafood, picked up a thin little fish, its entire body covered in batter, and crunched it between her teeth. The annoying stink of the angry satyrs dissipated almost as quickly as they did, galloping away through the grove of trees.

"Up! Get up and let's do it standing!" a woman called gaily to Giano.

"I can't," Giano moaned. Every muscle in his body was weary. His stomach had grown hollow, curving inward so that his navel met his spine. The skin of his cheeks was slack. His trembling fingers counted the corrugated ribs poking through the thin fabric of his chest. His thighs had withered into the flanks of an old man. Giano wanted to cry, but there wasn't enough juice left in him to produce even one tear. They had squeezed him dry, these insatiable women. Only his fratellino, that betraying son of a bitch, stood upright, hale and healthy while the rest of him shriveled into bone.

"Never mind, I'll come to you!" the woman carolled happily.

"O'Dio, don't you ever rest?" The woman lifted him under the arms and propped him against a tree trunk. Giano moaned again as he felt her weight claim him. He was bewildered by her vibrant energy, by her rosy skin and dimpled cheeks. His arms were too exhausted to raise his quaking hands to fondle her abundant breasts and his lips were too chapped to kiss.

He was dying. His body was dying, all except that crazy no-good fucker between his legs. And somehow he knew that even if he rattled out his last breath while the woman straddling his thighs continued taking pleasure from him, that fucker of his would stay hard as a nun's wooden toy for her.

Distantly, Giano heard loud, angry shouts and branches breaking. They were being attacked, he realized, almost grateful for the diversion. Horses, he thought, hearing the dull rapping thud in the dirt. But when he opened his weary eyes all he saw was a blur of hairy legs and black, cloven hooves. Goats? Marauding goats? He laughed.

All around him the women had risen to their feet and were screaming as they fled the grove. Slack-jawed, Giano watched a satyr run down a woman at the edge of the forest. Before she could reach the safety of the trees, the satyr had hoisted her up from the ground, one arm circling her waist. She thrashed wildly against his grasp, but it seemed to Giano that there was a shadow of a smile on her face.

The woman straddling his thighs was lifted away shouting and kicking up dirt, a lot of which landed on Giano. He was so exhausted he didn't even bother to brush the dirt away. A large satyr tossed the struggling woman easily to another satyr, who caught her with a triumphant cry and clasped her to his chest. Though they shouted angrily into each other's faces, the woman clung to his neck and locked her ample legs around his waist before the satyr galloped away with her, his fingers denting the flesh of her buttocks.

The large satyr looming over Giano stared down at him with contempt, muttered something in a low guttural voice, and spat.

Giano, assuming he'd been rescued, started to croak a thank-you, but the satyr raised a club and brought it down on his head. Pain flashed vibrant yellow before his eyes, his mouth turned up into a stupid grin, and he slid to the ground, his cheek resting in the damp mud. He prayed for blissful blackness, but remained awake enough to feel himself hoisted over the satyr's shoulder. The satyr started running and every step of his trotting hooves brought another painful flash of light to Giano's head.

How long they had run, Giano couldn't say. He only knew he was sick with the pain of his blow and the continued insult of the satyr's loping gait. His nostrils were assaulted by the satyr's gamey reek. He groaned, nausea combining with the pain in his head.

The satyr abruptly slowed to a bouncing walk, which shook fresh groans of pain from Giano. Slung over the back of the satyr, his eyes full of vibrating stars, Giano heard someone retching. Amazing, he thought. That should be me. How I wish it were me! He coughed and spluttered saliva down the satyr's back. The satyr brayed and rolled Giano off his shoulder to the ground.

Giano lay on his back, his knees curled up to his chest, his hands clutching his aching head, watching the dance of yellow stars, grateful for the stillness of the earth beneath him. The stars faded at last and he slowly sat up and looked around. When he saw the white columns of the Arch of Dreams, his eyebrows lifted.

Seated around the columns were the satyrs and the women who had so recently made a scarecrow of him. Each woman was lost in rapture, draped over the satyr of her choice. One woman squealed when her satyr companion stuck his ruby tongue into her ear. As for the satyrs, they held their willing Innamorati enclosed between their fur-tufted arms and the valley of their haunches, while they prodded, stroked, and squeezed them.

The satyrs and nymphs were not the only wonders beneath the Arch of Dreams. Seated on a sagging couch, Giano saw a gigantic, squat-bellied girl dressed in a purple robe. Two naked little girls held her long blond hair away from her face to keep it clean of the vomit she retched into a golden bowl. When she leaned back on the couch a very young satyr offered her a feather, but she waved him away with one hand. With the other, she signaled a line of children to serve her more food.

She caught sight of Giano as she was leaning over a plate of meat and game pie. The fork hovered uncertainly near her puffy face. She frowned at him, slowly put down the fork, and pushed away the plate. Her tiny eyes rolled upward and her fingers pinched together in a gesture of annoyance.

"This is your fault, you old shit! You did this to me!" she shouted.

Giano did his best to remember where he might have seen this enormous girl before. Her eyes were piggy, her mouth a tiny bud in the doughy folds of her cheeks. Her body was packed tightly into a purple robe like a stuffed eggplant.

"Signorina, do I know you?" he asked in a quavering voice. The smell of boiled beef and game pie was making him very hungry. Saliva he had thought long dried up flooded his teeth.

"You bastard, you chased me and they pulled me into the maze. And now look at me. I'm . . . I'm monstrous," she cried. "I've always dreamed of being fat, but I never thought it would be like this!" She started sobbing loudly, her jowls shaking.

"Here, let me help you out then," Giano said, and crawled on his hands and knees to Zizola's rejected plate. Giano broke off a crust of the pie and sucked on it, shuddering with delight at the warm taste of meat. While the girl bawled, he chewed slowly, studying her, trying to remember. He studied her hair, her hands, and her feet, still tiny beneath the huge body. He saw a ring set with a good stone hanging from a gold chain around her neck. And he remembered her. The thief from the market who shit gold rings. But that girl had been as skinny as a spoon handle.

"What happened to you?" he asked, waving a piece of pie. "You've changed!"

"Me?" she retorted, angrily wiping away the tears. She stopped crying and blew her nose on the hem of the purple robe. "What about you? Look at you. I've seen more meat on a corpse. And that thing between your legs! You're worse than the satyrs. Eh, have you no shame?"

Giano gave an irritated shrug. "It has nothing to do with me. It's all these women. They caught me, used me, taught my little brother a thing or two, and now it has a mind of its own."

"Can't you teach it who's in command?" Zizola sniffed.

"I tried, but look, it's no use." Giano pushed his defiant member down and tucked it between his clenched legs. They waited, Zizola's pale eyebrows raised in curiosity, Giano gobbling down the meat and game pie. After a few moments, he opened his thighs and his penis sprang up, as hard and as ready as before. "There, you see!" He took a plate of risotto and ate a spoonful. "It is its own master. And what about you, Signorina, eh? Have you no shame?"

Zizola frowned. "I can't help it. My stomach has a mind of its own."

"Can't you teach it who's in command?" Giano asked sarcastically, taking a sip of Zizola's wine to wash down the plate of risotto. The food was reviving his weakened spirits and he could see the slack hollow of his belly beginning to round out again. He was diving for a small roast of lamb covered with oil and rosemary when a hand slapped him hard across the back of the head.

Giano turned angrily and saw the large satyr glaring at him out of yellow eyes. "What's the matter with you?"

"You little turd of a man. You will speak with respect when you address La Maestra."

"But she's only a beggar," Giano complained. The satyr slapped him hard across the back of the head again. "Ow! I'm going to trim your tail if you don't leave me alone!" Giano struggled to his feet, disturbed at how wobbly his legs felt. He balled his hands into fists and tried to look menacing. The satyr's nostrils flared at the challenge. He held up a slingshot, armed with a stone pulled back in a stretched band of sinew. Giano realized where the satyr was aiming and immediately cupped his hands over his groin.

"Oh, stop it," Zizola said with a wave of her sausage fingers. "Leave the fool alone."

"You are the one we serve," the satyr protested. "I can't allow this dried turd to insult you."

"It's all right, he can't help himself. As you can see, his brains don't live in his head!" Zizola sighed heavily. "Listen, you have your nymphs back. Why don't you all go and enjoy the day somewhere else? The fool can keep me company."

The satyr hesitated, duty warring with desire. But it wasn't long until the sultry look of a nymph decided the matter for him. With a quick lick of his pomegranate lips, he turned back to Zizola.

"If you have need of anything, merely ask. It will be given."

"Where is Il Maestro Gaetano now?" Zizola asked.

"In the center of the maze where he has always been," the satyr replied politely, though his eyes had wandered to the ripe body of the nymph strolling toward the edge of the forest.

"Go," Zizola said with a nod of her head. "All of you, go and leave me. I'll be all right now."

The satyrs didn't wait for a further invitation. They trotted into the dark recesses of the trees after the nymphs. The children vanished, scattered into the forest. A woman laughed gaily and then all was quiet. Zizola and Giano were alone beneath the Arch of Dreams.

Giano continued to eat from abandoned plates of food. His strength was returning, heating his blood like the warm flush of wine. He crunched the little bones of a capon and then sucked out the thin veins of marrow.

"Madonna della Sante, what luck you have, Zizola!" Giano said enthusiastically. "You need never want for food again."

"Hmm," Zizola said pensively. "Wanting food nearly killed me. Another day like the last one, and I'd have exploded."

Giano grimaced at the thought of the white columns of the Arch of Dreams splattered with the remains of Zizola.

"And what about you, buffone—"

"Giano."

"Giano, then. Another day with the nymphs and you'd be a skeleton."

"But think what use they would have made of the stiffened body! What other man could boast of satisfying women from beyond the grave?" He picked up the carcass of the capon and began tearing off the remaining shreds of flesh.

"Listen, you graveyard asparagus, it wouldn't be much fun for you. They'd be enjoying themselves, but your soul would be off in purgetorio roasting away like one of these capons, with little devils cracking and sucking out your miserable marrow."

Giano sighed and put down the carcass of the capon. "You've made a good point, Signorina." He gazed around at the quiet grove, the flower-laden pool, and up at the white marble of the Arch of Dreams overhead. "It's a strange place, isn't it?" he said quietly. "Who would have known from the other side of the wall what wonders lay in here?"

"Wonders, yes. But dangers, too." Zizola shrugged. "Whatever we long for in our hearts, we will find in the maze, though that yearning may well kill us."

"Boh, you sound ungrateful."

"Look at you. Look at me. Our wants were simple: food and sex. One day in the maze, and our wants nearly ruined us."

"Who is Gaetano?"

Zizola rolled her eyes. "He rules the maze and I am supposedly his daughter. Beyond that, I know nothing." Her smile pushed back the folds of her cheeks. "What say we go find him?"

"How will we get there? I don't like the idea of wandering around in this maze dressed like Adam." Thoughtfully, Giano picked a ripe pear out of a bowl and bit into it.

Zizola pushed herself up from the couch and stood tottering on her tiny feet. She gazed up at the columns and smiled at the carved faces leering down at her from the bas-relief.

"I want to be as I was before. I am through with being fat. Give me back my old clothes, please. And some for my companion."

Giano stopped eating, the pear still in his hand, as clothing whispered out of the air and drifted down as though it had fallen from a laundry line. Invisible hands slipped a shirt of fine linen over his head and coaxed his legs into bright red hose tied with silver-tipped points. "My boots!" he exclaimed happily when he saw the familiar band of colored diamonds around his calves and the curled black toes. Last, he slid his arms into a doublet of red velvet and allowed the invisible hands to tie the cross laces. He looked up at Zizola and gave a wide grin.

Zizola was rapidly growing smaller again. She had a waist now, clothed in a bodice of colored patches of velvet. Her full skirts were a brilliant yellow silk with a pattern of green and red triangles stitched along the hem. Red ribbons fluttered at her shoulders. She smiled at him, the double chins receding like a tide to uncover a vixen's face.

"I'm changing back," she squeaked happily. She took a few steps and let her arms swing against her sides. Then she hugged herself. "Oh it feels good to be me again," she crowed. She raised her skirts and did a nimble salterello on the grass. "What about you?" she asked Giano.

Giano coughed, pulled on his shirt, adjusted the points of his hose, glanced below his waist, and sighed. "The rascal has finally gone to sleep."

"Let's go then," Zizola said, and walked toward the stony path.

"Where?"

"To the center, of course. I want to meet this papa of mine. And then kick him in the ass for having abandoned me to the shitheads in the world outside!"

Who knows, Giano thought as he fell in beside Zizola. Perhaps Gaetano could use another manservant, someone to watch out after his daughter's safety. Lord knows, Giano thought without disappointment, he was never going to see that dried-up stick Lorenzo again.

They left the grove of cypress trees and soon found the narrow path that threaded its way through the cedar corridors. Giano followed close beside Zizola as she walked confidently through the twisting of the maze. She never hesitated when the way split into a double path or turned unexpectedly. Once a stone wall appeared, painted over with faint markings. Giano thought they had landed in a dead end, but Zizola walked up to the wall and touched the painted markings. A tiny door sprung open in the wall and she passed through. Giano had to leap through the door behind her before it closed.

On the other side of the wall a small stream joined the path. Birds sang in the trees and the water splashed and gurgled over the stones. The grass was a succulent green, and willows spread veils of fluttering yellow leaves over the path. The path took them over a little wooden bridge and then split in two. One fork followed the lush, willow-lined stream, the second branched away into a forest of dying oaks. At the split, a man stood planted, clearly unable to make a decision.

He was a priest, dressed in a plain black habit. His hood lay against his back and Giano could see the pale circle of shaved scalp on the top of his head. The priest turned, startled by the loud rapping of their footsteps on the bridge, and Giano recognized him at once as the handsome priest from the piazza. Beneath the shadows of the willows, the priest's beauty seemed subdued. His eyes were haunted and the curling down of a new beard made him appear gaunt.

"Hey! It's you again," Giano called out.

"How do you know me?" the priest demanded.

"We met in the piazza!" Giano answered. "We spoke of the Venetian courtesans, though in truth, good Father, I have had my share of women for a while."

The priest's mouth curved into a faint smile and he nodded at Giano.

"I remember. How many days ago was that?"

Giano shook his head. "I don't know, Father. I've been rather busy since coming here. And, in any case, time is different on this side."

"Everything is different on this side," the priest replied softly.

"To the left, Father." Zizola pointed toward the dying oaks. "That's the path you seek."

"How do you know, Signorina?"

Zizola shrugged. "I just do."

"Yet you journey in the other direction."

"Everyone must arrive at the center if they are to find their way out of the maze again. But each arrives by his own path, Father. Yours lies through those dying trees. Mine is elsewhere."

The priest stared long at the forest of dying oaks. Then he nodded. "I had hoped for the more pleasant path: yet I believe you. Farewell to you both. If we don't die first—"

"We will meet again," Zizola said, finishing the proverb.

The priest turned up the hood of his habit, tucked his arms into the sleeves of his robe, and headed for the dying oaks. Giano watched him go and felt a shiver rise up his spine. Against the greying bark of the withered trees, the black-robed figure moved like the shadow of a demon hovering among the trees. He turned to Zizola but she was already moving ahead on the path.

Giano ran to catch up with her. "You know, you shouldn't give away such information," he groused.

"Why not?" Zizola demanded.

"We could make money selling advice like that."

"We?" Zizola's fists balled on her hips. "You know nothing."

"Hey, Signorina, remember if it weren't for me you'd still be trying to shit gold rings on the other side," Giano pointed out. "You owe me."

"Hah! If it weren't for me you'd be nothing but a sundial in the nymph's garden. That is, if the satyrs didn't cut you short."

"And if it weren't for me," Giano countered hotly, "you'd be as big as the Palazzo del Labirinto, crapping fields of shit, vomiting mountains of polenta—"

"Tool of another's lust!"

"Drawbridge mouth that's always open!"

"Stinking sardine!"

"Bowel builder!"

"Fine," Zizola shouted, slashing the air with her hand. She flicked her hair off her shoulder with a toss of her head. "You can be my servant. I've always wanted a servant to wait on me. I'll even pay you. Just don't tell me what to do!"

Giano grabbed her hand and gave it a little kiss before she snatched it back again. "As you wish, Signorina. I'm a good servant."

"So is a donkey," she answered sarcastically. "Just watch yourself."

Zizola stormed down the path, her mouth set in a hard frown. Giano capered after her, being careful to avoid the dagger points of her stabbing elbows.

21

T he Curse stood by the fountain in the moonlit piazza of the village, inhaling the multitude of scents that filled the air. It was hungry, Its appetite grown ravenous again as It made Its way down the slopes of the smoking mountains. It had not fed since It had encountered the woman and the man of wood named God. It snapped Its jaws wide to eat the scent of prey close by, but was confused by the emptiness of the piazza. It crouched by the ancient stone fountain and touched the ground for reassurance. Far below the black and white cobblestones of the piazza, It could sense a slow river of lava moving ponderously under the earth. It prowled around the fountain, wondering where the creatures called man were and why It could smell them but not see them?

Someone coughed and the door to a cottage banged open. The Curse hid behind the wall of the fountain to observe a man, who scratched his belly and yawned widely before stumbling around the corner of his cottage and disappearing. Quiet as a shadow, It slipped across the piazza to follow him, Its curiosity as aroused as Its hunger.

Peering around the wall of the cottage, It saw the old man, his head drooping to his chest, a hand braced against the wall of the cottage. There was a sound of water splashing against the grass. Standing so close to the inviting scent of prey, It no longer cared what he was doing or why. It moved swiftly toward the man, who looked up as if startled from a dream. It saw the reflection of Its diamond-bright eyes shining in the dark circles of the man's pupils, and then It lunged and embraced him. A burst of flame from Its molten skin ignited the man's clothing, exposing the skin. It gripped the man tighter, the intense heat penetrating beneath the thin veil of skin. It moved through the body of the man, absorbing flesh, swallowing the steam of blood, curling Its blistering tongue around the viscera. When It had passed through to the other side of the man, It turned around. Behind It balanced a fragile statue of thick black ash which a sudden gust of wind scattered.

It adjusted Its form to the last shape of the man and looked down at what the man had held in his hand. Its wrinkled face with grizzled cheeks frowned in confusion. Words taken from the man sparked in Its mind: il cazzo, a prick, a tool, a sword, a little brother. Each name was more puzzling than the last. How could this small bit of limp flesh be of such importance? It continued to examine the part, surprised when the flesh responded of its own will, growing tumescent and upright.

It remembered the woman It had taken, the child within her body and the hidden cleft between her legs. Ah, It nodded, this part was missing in the woman—perhaps on purpose, that these two parts might be joined together. It tried to recall the last images of the old man's thoughts and found the word *wife*. It could see a woman inside the cottage, lying in a lumpy bed and waiting for him. Smaller men—no, children—slept nearby, each in its own nest. This structure was called a house, It realized. People hid inside houses.

It hesitated at the cottage door, peering in.

"Vieni qui!" called a woman's voice from the dark interior. "Come to bed, amore mio."

It dimmed the starlight brilliance of Its eyes and entered. At once Its nostrils were assailed by unfamiliar odors: the remains of roasted meat, sharp cloves of garlic mingled with the sweat of sleeping children. Saliva filled the old man's mouth, and It ran Its tongue across Its teeth. The woman lay sprawled on the bed, a cloth pushed aside to reveal huge, pale thighs. Its nostrils flared, inhaling the ripe odor of the woman. It lay on the bed and took the woman in Its arms. The old man's prick throbbed as it touched the woman's thighs with a sensation almost as urgent as Its hunger.

"Amore mio, are you well?" the woman murmured as she stroked Its chest with a calloused hand. "Your skin is so hot. You're burning."

Hunger screamed and the light flared in Its eyes. The old man's face leaned forward as though to kiss her. But the face split apart as It opened wide Its jaws and swallowed her head. Her body shook violently, the hands tearing the hairs of the old man's chest. But It continued to consume her, the wide mouth swallowing her shoulders, her chest and torso, a thick tongue drawing her deeper into the cauldron of Its belly. Her skin peeled away and her bones cracked, squeezed by the grip of Its hunger. The damp sheets scorched and smoked. It slid off the bed and moved to another bed, filled with the smaller bodies of sleeping children. It flattened itself into a thick mantle of lava and flowed up over the headboard to cover the sleeping children with a blanket of flame. There was no time to cry out, no time even to experience pain. With a sigh of steam, they rendered up their flesh and their fleeting dreams to It.

It raised itself again into the form of an old man and stumbled out of the cottage. Outside, in the piazza, It discovered that Its hunger had not abated but changed. It scrabbled at the air as the thoughts of the family filled Its head, each one pricking Its interest, creating sensations It didn't understand. Visions marched across Its eyes, and Its hand opened and closed at the memories of hate, of greed, of love. It felt the pain of birth, the pleasures of infancy, and the fear of something mysterious called dying. Each thought erupted into another, producing a pang of hunger. It realized that it was not enough to fill Its burning hollow with the flesh of men. Their lives, captured in their last thoughts and fragments of dreams, had given It a hunger for human experience. It wanted to know more.

It abandoned the form of the old man and spread itself throughout the sleeping village in a flowing river of lava. Moving slowly and heavily, a thin black crust cracking over the fiery red underbelly, It poured into every home. It caught the villagers in the depths of their sleep, coiled in their beds, sprawled across mattresses, entangled in the arms of their beloveds. And It receded from the bodies, leaving behind in Its wake black ashen shapes. The night winds swept over the scorched thresholds into the open doors and swirled the ashes of the villagers into heaps of black dust.

Drunk and staggering, It dragged itself out of the last house, Its eyes dazed by the panorama of visions. It plucked an image from the treasure hoard and transformed Its shell of black crusted lava into the figure of an old man, hunchbacked and bowlegged. It didn't find this shape pleasing. It tried another—a woman, rake thin, with a squared jaw and too many teeth. This, too did not please It. It had learned that there were powers known as beauty and youth and that the forms It had chosen were old and ugly, a source of amusement and ridicule.

It panted as It tried to digest the wealth of Its new thoughts. These creatures had surprised him with the ferocity of their passions and their tenacious love of the earth. And though they were tiny beings beneath the vast sky, they regarded themselves as the gods and makers of their universe. They hoarded the gold of wheat, bottled the jeweled wine; they shot the birds from the skies and bent the wild animals to their yokes; and those they could not tame, they slaughtered in the woods and ate. They recreated themselves, naming themselves generation after generation, handing down land, knowledge, and power. It had only one purpose for Its existence, but they, it seemed, had many. It was stronger than they and yet not as powerful because it had no purpose of Its own devising, but followed the commands of Its maker.

Until now. Now, It knew better, and suddenly, Its hunger was not to consume flesh, but to be flesh, to be human and to choose Its own destiny.

It turned up the plain oval of Its featureless face to the sky. It howled at the night sky. It demanded humanity. It demanded the passions, the ambitions, and dreams that the human creatures It had eaten carried within them. The stars chimed with laughter and It felt anger. The moon hid her face, embarrassed by Its lust, and It felt shame. The rocks beneath It rumbled their disapproval, and It grew rebellious.

"Make me a man," It called to the night. "Give me a name that I may be as powerful as other men!"

The night fell quiet, the wind hushed. It felt a stirring in Its heated center and slowly Its body changed. It became a youth, a boy close to manhood with blond hair and dark eyes. Its face was long and narrow, the nose a sharp point over a feral grin. It stroked the length of Its body and found that Its waist was slender, Its thighs supple and strong.

It touched Its chest and discovered that the porous liquid of Its flesh had grown solid as molded clay. It had a pulse, quicker than the beat of the earth, quick as the pulse of a human being.

Still, there was something missing. The Curse sensed it briefly in the humans It had consumed, but it had slipped out of Its grasp, evading Its heat and Its grinding jaws. What was It lacking that those men had?

"A name. Give me a name!" It commanded.

"Zolfo," the wind hissed into his hears. "Zolfo di Labirinto."

"Zolfo," he repeated, hearing his voice pronounce his name with new pride.

Zolfo went quickly to the first cottage and took clothing, boots, and a small cap for his head. Dressed, he began walking down the dark road, aware that his purpose, like his body, had changed. He understood now that he had been created to travel to a place that humans called the maze of Labirinto and destroy its maker. But Zolfo was more than a curse now. He was a man, a maker of things and a creator of other men.

He would fulfill his duty as curse. That task he could not escape. But he would remain in the world as a man, and he would claim the maze of Labirinto as his own.

22

In the night, Don Gianlucca woke to the sound of his name being called. His body was chilled, his face damp with the heavy dew. He sat up slowly and leaned his back against the peeling bark of a blighted oak tree. The leaves rustled dryly, brittle twigs scratching against each other. Don Gianlucca looked around in the shadows of the forest, dappled with small patches of moonlight. There was no path here. He had lost it somehow in the twilight, his eyes searching in the growing dark, his feet wandering aimlessly through the brambles of the forest. He had given up finally and allowed himself to sleep.

"Don Gianlucca!" The whisper came again and suddenly the priest saw the faint white image of a ghost hovering in the shadows. It was hard to make out its features, though its glow brightened the gloom of the dying forest.

The longer Don Gianlucca stared it, the clearer he saw it. The orb of diamond light held the shape of a small body, tapered like a child swaddled in bands of light. Its arms were outspread, its tiny hands stretched to the edge of the soft halo. A baby, he thought, dazed by the ghostly light. It was a baby, like a Christ child floating in the air.

"Il Tago, il spirito dei bambini," his Sienese grandmother had once called such ghosts. "The Tago," she had explained, "is a spirit released from the earth to set right the sufferings of a child."

"Are you the Tago?" Don Gianlucca asked. "Did you bring me here?"

The ghost drifted closer to Don Gianlucca and he could see the rim of its face and the curve of one ear. Eyes opened into dark ovals and an azure tear streaked down its cheek.

"Don Gianlucca," it called. "Find me. She cannot hear my cries. The thorns hold me prisoner within her. Release me from this garden of grief."

"Who is it that imprisons you?" asked Don Gianlucca, though he was certain of the answer.

"Anna Forsetti."

"Where do I look?" Don Gianlucca asked.

"Follow," it called, and began to move away, drifting slowly between the trees.

Don Gianlucca rose to his feet, his hands reaching out to the silently moving light. It left a wake, a trail of sparkling dust that touched his face with the scent of almonds. He stumbled after it as twigs snagged his robes and plucked threads from the torn hem. Once he fell, and the Tago waited until he had risen again. Don Gianlucca wiped his face and found his cheeks were flooded with tears.

Throughout the night, he followed the Tago until its light began to fade with the dawn, and it rose high above the twisted trees where it glimmered faintly like the last spark of the evening star. Abruptly, the trees ended, and a pale, yellow sun cracked open its eye over the edge of a quiet sea. Don Gianlucca, his own eyes red and swollen with weeping, stared in silence at the strange shore where the Tago had led him.

The dying oaks sulked behind him and rattled their dry and barren acorns. Before him small waves lapped gently at the shore of a curved bay. He took a step toward the water and something cracked beneath his foot. Looking down, he saw bones littered among the rounded tide-washed pebbles: long, knobbed bones, broken teeth, the half shell of a skull, and the tiny doweled segments of a spine, scattered like beads across the sand. He stepped carefully, wincing as his feet ground the dry fragments into smaller pieces.

A sharp whistle brought his head up and he caught sight of a stoop-shouldered man, a sack over one shoulder, wandering down the beach. He was dressed in the rags of a beggar, the faded fabric blending into the dun of the dying oaks. On his head, he wore a drooping hat of bright red wool. He was whistling to himself as he poked the bones with a long stick. When he saw one that interested him, he picked it up and held it to the sky, turning it thoughtfully against the light. Some he tossed on the ground again with a snarl, but others he kissed reverently and then placed carefully into his sack. Then, taking another step forward, he'd whistle as he peered down at the bones again and turned them over with his stick.

"You there," Don Gianlucca called. The man's head jerked up and he crouched like an animal caught in the open. Don Gianlucca could see that the man was old, with a wizened face and a long pointed nose hooking down over thin lips. He pulled the red cap down tightly over his head and turned to run.

"Wait!"

But the man didn't wait. Turning quickly, he ran down the beach into the shelter of the dying oaks. Despite his age, he ran swiftly, barely making a sound as he trod lightly over the fragile bones. Don Gianlucca followed, trying not to hear the bones snapping beneath his running feet.

As the man entered the forest again, Don Gianlucca almost lost sight of him. The faded colors of his clothing hid him amid the weathered trunks of the old oaks. But his red cap, like a splash of blood, gave him away. Don Gianlucca followed the bright red hat back and forth between the blighted trees.

And then, amid a dense stand of yellowed larches and dying pines, Don Gianlucca lost sight of the red cap. Frantically, he searched through the pines for signs of the man's passing but saw only the dull bark of the trees. He looked down in frustrated disappointment and saw the remains of a path littered with bones. A wind gusted through the larches and a handful of yellow needles drifted down from the dying trees. As he watched, the trail widened and bones began to move.

It was the path from his dream. Skulls lined it, stacked two and three high, their gaping eyeholes staring as he passed. He came to a fence made of tibia and ulnas woven together like slats, beyond which a small cottage sat beneath the sweeping boughs of an old pine. Don Gianlucca raised the latch of finger bones from a gate and entered the yard.

The door was open and Don Gianlucca peered inside. The stoop-shouldered man was sitting at a bench, his bag of bones emptied over a long wooden table. His eyes were black seeds in his wizened face and his fierce glance darted over the offering of bones. He picked up a finger bone, sniffed it, and then delicately sucked on it, closing his eyes as if discerning its unique flavor. Then he pulled it out of his mouth with a grunt of approval and placed the bone in a separate pile. Don Gianlucca entered, and as his shadow fell on the table, the old man squinted sourly at him.

"Come in, come in," he said in a hoarse voice. A gnarled hand with distorted knuckles waved him inside. "What'll you have? A saint or a sinner?"

"I don't understand," Don Gianlucca said.

The old man laughed coldly and then spat at his heels. "I said, are you looking for a sinner or a saint? I've got 'em both here, you know." He held up the tiny finger bone. "Saint Olive of Palermo," he said with a smug grin. "Martyred in Tunis, but her bones drifted home to Italy. You don't look like one of those converted, though. How about the ribs of Saint Peter?" he asked, holding up a thick, curved bone. He shook his head. "Nah, you ain't the type to be looking for Saint Peter. Romans come looking for him, carrying their guilt like a rotten egg in their hands." The black eyes widened. "I know," he said, laying a finger along his nose, "you're looking for the whore, Vittorina Logetti of Venice."

"I knew such a woman, once," Don Gianlucca said in amazement. "She died, drinking poison."

"Turned her bones a shiny black, it did," the man answered.

"Where am I?" Don Gianlucca asked nervously.

"The shore of lost bones," the man said. "Where the unquiet dead are washed by a sea of tears and cast on this final shore where they may be found only by the truly penitent."

"I don't understand."

The old man shifted the woolen hat on his head and glared. "Confess, priest! Whose death is on your conscience?"

"No one's," snapped Don Gianlucca nervously.

"Not even the whore Vittorina Logetti?"

"I hardly knew the woman," Don Gianlucca protested. "I saw her twice—no three times. Paid well each time and that was it."

"Did you not promise her that you would leave the church and marry her?"

"If I did, I was drunk. And what man does not make such promises, even to a whore?"

"Still, she believed you," the old man said sourly. "And when she died? Did you not remember your words and turn in your sleep? Did you not feel the prick of shame?"

"No," Don Gianlucca insisted. But he knew he lied. He had seen her bloated body the day they fished her up from the canals. She was a suicide, so he knew they would refuse to let her be interred on the Isola di Morte. They would weight her ragged corpse with stones and drop her out in the sea beyond the lagoon. The thought of her alone in the sea troubled him more than he could say, and on gloomy days he found he could not forget her. It had been on such a day that Don Gianlucca, in his aimless wanderings, had met Anna Forsetti in the Campo Santa Margherita. The hot sparks of passion between them burned away his melancholy and he had buried his shame like ash beneath the fire of the woman's mask.

"She is here," the old man said scornfully. "And so are you."

"I am called by the Tago," Don Gianlucca said. At the corner of his vision he could see the translucent shapes of ghosts risen from the dirt floors. They crowded the room, some thickened in the sunlight like the swirl of dust, others draped in spiderwebs clinging to the rafters. Pale, hungry eyes watched him.

The old man hissed and hid his head in the deep valley of his hunched shoulders. He riffled through the bones, then he raised his head to Don Gianlucca. The ghosts hovered closer and a wave of dusted light settled around the table. "Ah. I know why the Tago brought you here. It's not for you, but one you know. It'll still cost you," the old man said with a sly grin.

"Name your price," Don Gianlucca said.

"All who come here must pay. I don't give anything away. You must pay to cleanse your hands of shame."

"What do you want?"

"Lay down your hand."

Without hesitation, Don Gianlucca laid his hand down on the table. The old man pulled up a knife belted at his waist and, with a sudden swift movement, chopped off Don Gianlucca's little finger. Don Gianlucca pulled back his hand with an agonized cry. Stunned, he cradled his mutilated hand as blood gouted from the wound and spiraled down his arm to his elbow. He wavered on his feet, sickened by the fierce pain that throbbed along his arm. The old man pulled out a rag from the bag and wrapped it around Don Gianlucca's hand while Don Gianlucca stared at his severed finger lying white and bloodied on the table amid the bleached bones. The hovering ghosts dipped their dusty fingers into the pool of blood and touched it gratefully to their lips.

"There. It is done," said the man, tying the rag tightly. He picked up the severed finger and tucked it underneath his cap.

"Who are you to take such a price?" Don Gianlucca asked.

"I have no name that you can say," the man answered. "But some speak of me as Il Folletto Colla Beretta, the spirit with the cap. I am a tree-knocker, a shape-changer, and a collector of little bones. And only I can rid you of the curses that come with the restless bones. Have you heard them call your name, felt their spirit close enough to suffocate you?"

"Yes." Then Don Gianlucca saw the wan face of Vittorina Logetti watching him from the other side of the table. He had forgotten how young she had been. Barely a woman. Her mother had been famous once, and had turned her daughter to the trade when she had grown too old to whore. Vittorina, with skin of milk and hair of honey. Now she was a shade, dipping a pale, slender finger into the pool of his blood.

The old man glanced at her and grunted. "He has not come for you. Go away!"

The eyes of the ghost widened and the sad mouth contorted into silent wails as she shivered and dissolved. Don Gianlucca raised his mutilated hand to call her back, but the old man stopped him.

"The Tago has a task for you," the man answered. He handed Don Gianlucca a rough cloth sack. "Come, we will search on the shore. For those bones are so small that even a mouse may find them hard to recover."

Don Gianlucca followed the man out of the cottage and back to the shore of bones.

"Here is the first," said the man, holding up a tiny fragment of a collarbone no bigger than the fragile arc of a sparrow's wing. "And here, another."

Don Gianlucca gazed at the bone with no idea what he was to do with it. The old man grunted and opened the rough sack and placed the bones in it.

Hour after hour they walked along the shore, the old man turning over washed pebbles and retrieving smaller and smaller fragments of bone from the sand beneath. Once he pulled out the curved cup of a pelvis caught between two dried pieces of driftwood. The vertebrae lay like pearls in a clump of withered grass. Near the water's edge, he found the two halves of the rib cage poking out of the sand like a mermaid's hair comb. As the sun descended into the dying treetops, the old man straightened up from his searching and shook his head.

"That's all there is," he said. "You must find the whole skeleton first. Only then can you ask for the forgiveness that will lay these bones to rest."

"But these bones are so small," Don Gianlucca said. "They belong to a child. How can it know enough to offer forgiveness?"

"That is why the Tago has called you," the old man said. "To speak for the infant silenced without a voice. But the spirit remains abroad. Are you the father?"

Don Gianlucca shook his head. "No, but I know the mother," he answered, beginning at last to understand the haunted look on Anna's face. This was her child. Her curse. He had offered her a man's forgiveness and God's forgiveness, but it had not been enough to make her remove the mask that hid her grief. So the Tago had come to him.

"Someone else has found the last piece," the old man was saying. "I can do no more."

Don Gianlucca glanced up in the faint twilight and saw the dull glow of the Tago hovering over the water. "Here comes the spirit. He will know where to find it," he said softly.

Don Gianlucca left the old man on the shore riffling through the bones, picking them up one at a time. He followed the pale luminescent glow of the Tago through the trees. It stopped near the trunk of an ancient oak with a few mud-colored leaves clinging to its twisted branches. A cluster of acorns dangled from the one living branch. Don Gianlucca plucked the acorns and sat down wearily at the base of the tree. He cracked the smooth dry husks of the nuts and ate them.

Then he emptied the sack of its bones and laid them out on the grass. The Tago drifted closer and gave him light. The old man had not told him what bone was missing. Throughout the night Don Gianlucca worked, fitting the bones together one by one until they made a tiny skeleton, complete but for the front of the skull. There was no face, no jaw or nose socket, no brow to shelter the eyes. In Don Gianlucca's palm there was only the hollowed bowl of the back of the child's head. It was a skeleton of an unborn child, Don Gianlucca realized, running his finger along the spine curved like the dolphin's back. Tiny arms, hands, and fingers were still furled.

Don Gianlucca rested his back against the tree trunk and thought of Anna. It was her baby, taken too soon from the womb. Had she killed it? Had she drunk a poison to shift the child out of her body? Or had it died after a night like the one he had spent with her? Either way, the shame of that death had eaten at her heart and the Tago had come, searching for freedom for the infant's soul. Carefully, he replaced the bones in the sack.

"What do I do now?" Don Gianlucca asked the Tago.

The small face flared brightly, a corona of light embracing Don Gianlucca's head with a shimmering crown.

"Anna is here. Find her," it beseeched. "Bring us together. Then we shall see what can be done. But first, you must sleep."

Don Gianlucca nodded, his eyes heavy with exhaustion, his wounded hand throbbing with a dull pain. The light of the Tago touched his face and he felt the warm peace of sleep overtake him. And for the first time in many days, he slept without dreams.

23

Simonetta ran blindly in the shower of golden light. Around her the sounds of fighting boomed and echoed: the hard grunting of horses, the clash of swords, and the shrill blast of war pipes drowning the moans of the wounded. The golden light lifted slowly like a gauzy curtain, and Simonetta found herself on a small grassy plain in the midst of a heated battle. Plumes of smoke billowed up from patches of burning grass over the ravaged remains of the dead and wounded, whose blood stained the earth. To one side of the field, Simonetta saw the redbrick towers of the city of Pavia and the leaning campanile of the church. She could just make out the thin sparkling line of the Ticino River bordering the city walls. She crouched low behind the fallen carcass of a horse, its rump studded with arrows, and glanced wildly about her.

In the drifting smoke the battle looked like an artist's rendering, a painted backdrop of the fields outside Pavia's walls when the forces of King Charles of Spain besieged the city. The field where she crouched, bordered on three sides by a dense pine forest, was like a stage on which the drama of war was being performed. Even the soldiers did not look quite real. There were no nobles with feathered hats, no Spanish soldiers firing Austrian cannons at Italian lancers.

The horse behind which she was crouching stirred and lifted a human head to gaze at her in bewildered pain. Simonetta fell back on the ground, her mouth open in wordless shock. It was not a horse, but a centaur. A stab wound gouted blood in the human torso that joined at the withers to the horse.

"Madonna, where am I?" Simonetta rose to her feet and began to run, seeking the shelter of the forest. At the thundering sound of galloping hooves, she glanced behind her and saw another centaur bearing down on her, his sword raised high. Simonetta screamed as she stumbled over a fallen soldier. She pitched forward and rolled on the ground, body clenched against the centaur's killing blow.

When none came, she lifted her head cautiously and saw the centaur fighting with another soldier. Compared to the towering figure of the centaur, the soldier was slight, clothed in leather armor and wearing a shining bronze mask. Long black hair streamed over the soldier's shoulders behind the mask's polished face.

The soldier Simonetta had tripped over moaned and turned a bronze-covered face upward to the smoke-filled skies. Simonetta realized that it was a woman, the fletch of an arrow rising and falling between her breasts. Simonetta sidled over to the groaning woman, lifted her head, and carefully removed the bronze mask, revealing a young face, grimacing in pain. The girl had a high forehead and wide-set eyes. Her cheeks were dotted with patterns of yellow ocher and her front teeth were sharpened into points. Her clothing was strange—tooled leather armor fitted over an old linen shift torn at the knees. Simonetta could still see the fading band of black Assisi embroidery stitched at the neck. Like everything here, it was at once familiar and foreign.

Simonetta touched the wound, gauging the depth of the arrow. The woman's hand shot out and seized Simonetta's wrist in a hard grasp. Simonetta stared down at the dirty hand graced by a golden ring set with a stone carved in the likeness of the Venetian lions. Farther up the woman's arm, a snake of greening copper twined around her bicep.

"The dagger," the woman said hoarsely, her eyes closed against the pain. She bit her lower lip to keep from crying out. Tiny beads of blood blistered beneath the points of her teeth. "Finish this with honor."

"I can save you," Simonetta said.

The woman opened her eyes, the dark pupils clouded. "Doomed am I, Sister. Poison on the arrow already makes me weak. The dagger! Quick! Let it be by your hand and not theirs!"

Simonetta stalled, frightened by the rank animal stench of the woman's body and the stream of blood that coursed between her breasts. The hand continued to grasp her about the wrist, wordlessly demanding action. Simonetta took the dagger from the woman's belt and held the point of the blade poised above the woman's heart. The clouded eyes followed the bright shaft of the blade, lips parted in the grim shadow of a smile.

Simonetta's hand trembled. "I can't," she whispered. "There is an herb, dittany, that may yet save you."

With a sudden burst of strength, the woman lifted her head from the muddy ground and called out a name. A slender lance whistled past Simonetta's ear and buried itself in the woman's throat, throwing her back to the ground. Blood splattered in a hot wave over Simonetta, the crimson rain scalding her cheeks and blinding her eyes. The hand released her wrist. Simonetta turned in terrified rage and struck out with the woman's dagger. A booted foot knocked it easily from Simonetta's hand and kicked it away. Strong hands forced Simonetta on her back.

"Be still, Sister," a second woman commanded. Her voice vibrated through the wide mouth of the bronze mask. She tore a cloth from the hem of her short garment and carefully wiped the blood from Simonetta's face. "The centaur's poison is strong enough to kill you should her blood enter your mouth."

"Where am I?" asked Simonetta weakly.

"You are among the Amazons and this is our battle with the Centaurs."

"Am I always to be in war?"

"Was it not your wish? To return to this moment and begin again?"

"No. I'm seeking a fountain of youth, not this well-worn battlefield."

The masked Amazon laughed, the sound cold in the bronze mouth. "Our youth is spent in battle, Sister. And in such a death we remain young forever!"

"No," Simonetta said, pulling away from the Amazon and standing. "No, there must be another way to find my youth again. It's not here, among this havoc!" She began to run back toward the pine forest. Behind her, she heard the Amazon urging her to return and fight, heard the hard twang of arrows, heard the deadly whisper of their fletches as they shot past her.

It had been like this before: the choking smoke of battle, the charred flesh and spilled blood, the churned mud and the burning fields. Tree branches snapped against her face and her eyes teared. Perhaps the Amazons were right. Returned to the vigor of her youth, she could fight back as a warrior. Perhaps she should join them and find freedom from her dreams in their powerful gleaming masks and fierce weapons. Perhaps such a death would cleanse her soul of the shame at having survived where others had died horribly.

Amid the quiet trees, Simonetta stopped running. Tears laid dirty tracks down her cheeks and her chest heaved with the effort of her flight. She closed her hands over her face. She could not choose an Amazon's life. She was not meant to be a soldier.

"There is another way, Simonetta," said a deep voice.

Simonetta dropped her hands quickly and saw the dim outline of a huge centaur waiting in the shadow of the pines. He stepped forward into a glowing patch of sunlight. He had a heavy face, solid as carved wood. His thick black hair and beard had been fashioned into heavy plaits that hung in fat coils around his shoulders. His stallion's body was sleek and black as the Duke of Milan's velvets. He carried no weapons, but a bag of woven grass was slung over his shoulder.

"Who are you that you know my name?" Simonetta asked, drawing back in the shelter of the trees.

"I am Cheiron, the wise. Don't fear me, Simonetta. I am not a warrior like my brothers, nor their enemies the Amazons. I am here to offer you another path. Come, let me show you." He beckoned with a smile.

"Show me what?" Simonetta asked, warily.

At once she could hear voices through the trees, shouting gaily and laughing. Two women were singing a duet. A child cried and was quickly comforted. In Simonetta's heart a spark of longing burst into brilliant flame.

"Do you hear them?" Cheiron asked.

She nodded.

"They wait for you on the other side of the river. Come, I'll take you to them." He held out his hand to her.

Simonetta drifted toward the centaur, the voices carrying her forward. She took his hand, her own dwarfed by the broad palm. Graceful as the night, he turned his massive body in the close press of the trees, his long tail switching away the tangling branches, and led her down a barely visible path through the pine trees. The sun's light trickled through the greening boughs, spangling her skin with bright golden sequins.

Faint traces of youth bloomed in Simonetta's face, suddenly made vulnerable by those voices. It was as though their death had robbed her of all sounds and she had lived deaf for many years. Now she heard them again, and they were more sweet than the chorus of birds, the bells of Santa Maria della Grazie, and the clink of spinning coins.

A gap between the trees parted to reveal a stream, coursing over rocks down tiny waterfalls. Simonetta gasped as she saw that beyond it stood her farmhouse, just as it had been before the war. Her family was gathered near the open doorway. Her mother sat a stool shelling peas into a bowl that rested in her lap. Her sister lifted and dropped a spindle down her thigh, twisting fat rolls of combed wool into thread. Her husband was lying on the ground, growling like a bear for the amusement of her two sons, who clambered over him. They were alive again, and though their faces carried a chalky paleness, her heart leapt to see them whole once more. The elder child, Marco, his pallid face smudged with dirt, looked up from the ground and cried out to her.

"Mamma! Mamma!" he called. "Nicco, it's Mamma!" he said, and grabbed his younger brother, who immediately broke out in tears.

"Simonetta, you've returned at last!" Her mother smiled and set aside her bowl of peas. She rose stiffly, reaching for her walking stick.

"Simonetta, I've missed you," cried her sister, dropping her spindle into a basket of wool.

"Simonetta, why has it taken you so long to find us?" her husband, Alfredo, demanded, standing up and brushing the dirt from his hose. "I've been waiting so long for your return."

"Oh, how I have missed you all," Simonetta said, her voice breaking with emotion. "I am coming to join you."

She put her foot to a rocky bank, but Cheiron stopped her with a hand. "There is something important you must know before you cross, Simonetta."

"Nothing else matters," she said, not taking her eyes from the sight of her family gathered at the river's edge.

"Hear me first," Cheiron said. "I was once immortal. But I was wounded by an arrow made poisonous by the venom of the Hydra. Even I, with all my knowledge, could not distill the poison from my blood. Since I could not die, I remained alive in agony. I decided at last to trade away my immortality for the painless peace of death. How great is your pain, Simonetta?"

Simonetta turned to the centaur, feeling the tremor of doubt. "What are you saying?"

"I am but a shade that inhabits the maze. A ghost. And so are they, Simonetta, kept alive here by your sorrowing memories. When you cross this river, your pain will end because you will die. You will find the youth you have sought by becoming the shade of a young wife, untroubled by memories of grief and war. Once you touch the waters of the Lethe, you will forget everything but the life you once had with them."

Simonetta looked out at the ghostly faces of her husband and her sons and felt doubt grow in her until she could hardly breathe. She had carried the pain of their death all these years as Cheiron had borne his poisonous wound. And yet, unlike Cheiron, she had found the strength to survive. Could she now disown that struggle? The water would make her forget. The water would make her young and reunite her with her family. But the water would make her a ghost like them and her life a pale reflection of an already-lived past.

Without warning, she remembered Rinaldo, and felt the sharp savage urge of sex. She remembered the deftness of his touch, his hands intimately aware of her body's needs. She inhaled the memory of his scent and felt the sting of his kisses on her mouth. The water would make her forget everything, even Rinaldo. But did she want such a gift?

"Damn," she muttered. "I need to talk to Alfredo," she said to Cheiron.

"Be careful of the water!" the centaur warned.

Simonetta balanced her way across rocks jutting out of the rushing stream, until she was almost halfway across, then stopped and called her husband's name. "Alfredo!"

"Hurry, Simonetta," he answered, pacing on the far bank. "I'm very hungry. And your mother is tired of doing all the cooking." The ghost leaned forward, a hand cupped around his mouth. "She's lousy at it too. Burns the damn risotto nearly every time!"

"Do you love me?" Simonetta asked.

"Don't be stupid."

"I've been a whore, Alfredo."

"Yes, yes, it doesn't matter what you did out there. You're back and we'll finally to get to eat like the old days."

"Why does a ghost need to eat?" Simonetta asked.

Alfredo scowled and waved his hands around in the air in frustrated circles, the dust following them. "Don't be difficult," he blustered. "You were always difficult, always wanting your own way. If you hadn't gone to that woman in the mountains, we'd have been together when they came. You'd be here now!"

"I'd be dead," she answered quietly.

"Does it matter?" he asked petulantly.

At once, Simonetta knew that it did matter. She had changed, matured in ways her mother, her sister, and Alfredo could never have imagined. Survival had been bitter as sour herbs. But there had been sweet moments too: her own house, the smell of lavender sheets, and Rinaldo in her bed with the curve of his hip pressed against hers. Those things were the precious gold not of her youth, but of her maturity. She glanced sadly at her children, then her mother and sister. Alfredo fumed on the far bank. She had loved them once. All of them. But they belonged to the past.

Simonetta retraced her steps to the riverbank, taking great care not to let the splashing droplets of water touch her. Behind her, the ghost of Alfredo called, beseeched, and finally, when she refused to reply, sent a flurry of insults after her retreating figure.

Cheiron lent her his hand to pull her up the riverbank into the trees. He had a weary smile on his ancient face.

"Will they be all right?" Simonetta asked, afraid to turn around and see them still waiting on the bank for her.

"They have already forgotten you were here."

"What do I do now?" she asked the centaur. "I came seeking youth and found the price too high. I don't want the glorious death of an Amazon in battle and I don't want to slip into the world of my ghosts."

"You must continue your journey in the maze. And for that, I offer you these gifts." First, Cheiron placed the string bag he wore over Simonetta's shoulder. Then he handed her a sword. "The bag contains healing herbs and a ball of twine. The sword I think you know already."

She took it with an amused smile, studying the rape of the pagan queen worked in silver on its guard. "Rinaldo's sword."

"He is in the maze," Cheiron said. "Go to him. Perhaps between the two of you, you will find your way together."

"If he doesn't kill me first," Simonetta said dryly, looking at the figure of the voluptuous queen surrendering to the violence of a soldier.

"He may not get the chance," said a young voice.

Simonetta looked up and saw a tow-headed girl approaching her on a path bordered by two rows of stalwart cypress trees. At her side walked a man dressed in bright red and yellow velvets. The centaur was gone. Even the pine forest had receded around her, leaving only the faint scent of pitch in the narrow corridors of the maze.

"How do you know about Rinaldo?" Simonetta asked.

The girl shrugged, her face pensive, as though she listened to a voice that only she could hear. "I just do," she said.

"Where is he?"

"Down the way we have come. You will find a cave. Enter it. But have a care. The way is dangerous."

"Zizola, I saw no cave as we came," the man argued beside her.

"Of course you didn't, Giano; it wasn't meant for you to find. Nevertheless, it's there, Signora," Zizola insisted. "You must take that path if either you or Rinaldo is ever to find the center of the maze. Do you understand?"

"A little," Simonetta said. She wiped her hand over her forehead. "It's all so strange in here."

"No stranger than the dreams we inhabit at night," Zizola said. She reached into a pocket in her skirt, pulled up two pale yellow pears, and handed them to Simonetta. "Take the path, Signora. Perhaps we will meet in the center."

"Damn," Giano swore, and glared down at Zizola. "There's another gold piece you've lost. Must you give it away for free like a slut on a market day?"

"Ignore my servant," Zizola said sweetly. "He's never been generous in his life, the grasping old thief!"

"I've never had anything to be generous with!" he countered.

"Nor I, until now," Zizola snorted. "Signora, you are welcome to my knowledge of the maze."

"How do I know you're right?"

Zizola gave her little shrug and adjusted the ribbons on her bodice. "You just do," she replied. "It's your choice, Signora."

Simonetta weighed the pears in her hands and made a quick decision. She bid the odd couple thank-you and farewell. Then she started on her way alone down the path through the cypress trees. A new urgency pricked at her heels. Rinaldo was in the maze. He needed her. And the more she thought about him, the more Simonetta realized she needed him. She started walking quickly and then began to run, the green walls blurring as she searched for the entrance of the cave.

24

Where do you suppose she went? And what happened to Lily? She would never leave my side." Mirabella wrung her hands as she peered down the shadowy path. The high trees arched together in a leafy canopy over the path, tinting the bright sunlight a pale green. With her blurred vision, Mirabella felt like a fish lost in the canals of Venice.

"I don't know," Fabrizio answered. "One moment we were all together. Erminia was beside me. Next to her, Anna and Simonetta. I could hear Lily barking. And then . . . then, poof, they were all gone."

"How could you have lost sight of Anna?" Mirabella snapped.

"Me? Why should I be the one to follow her?" Fabrizio said hotly. "She's your mother."

"But your siren is wearing my spectacles. I can't see anything without them."

"Nothing?" Fabrizio asked.

At once Mirabella was aware he was standing in front of her. She squinted, wondering if he was making faces at her. She couldn't see his features clearly, only the masks of Pantelone and Arlecchino hanging around his neck. They wore worried expressions, like lost children. Tears of frustration welled up in her eyes.

"I can see only color and shapes. Nothing else very clearly unless it's under my nose."

Fabrizio's face loomed suddenly very close to hers. She could see him now, his long blond hair falling over his blue eyes. She could count the tiny freckles that dotted the bridge of his nose and cheeks. The pale golden hairs of a new mustache sprouted above his soft lips.

"How about now?" he asked.

"Yes," she answered, staring into his blue eyes, her pulse quickening. She stepped back into the blur of her nearsightedness. There were no other pilgrims about. Her mother and Lily had disappeared somewhere in the complicated folds of the maze. The siren had taken her spectacles, leaving her half-blind. This young actor, whom she hardly knew, let alone trusted, was her only hope of finding Anna. She fidgeted with the laces of her bodice. Her face felt hot and flushed.

"Come on," Fabrizio urged. "I think if we keep walking, we'll find them. This place can't be that big. Here, Mirabella, take my hand so you don't fall."

"I won't fall," she said quickly.

"But you said you can't see!" he insisted.

"I can't see, but I can walk!"

"Fine," he answered in a clipped voice. "Don't take my hand. Be stubborn."

Mirabella winced at the hurt in the young man's voice. She hadn't meant to offend him; she just didn't feel comfortable taking his hand. It had been all right on the piazza. Her mother had been there, after all. Here, in the quiet of the maze, with the leafy boughs of the trees sheltering them in a private bower, she felt less certain. She had read enough about damsels who had their virtue stolen from them by unscrupulous young men. Boccaccio and Aristo were full of them. True, many of them had found the inevitable experience a pleasant one, but Mirabella wasn't so sure that real life, or at least her life, would turn out to have a happy ending.

Out of habit, Mirabella touched her face, pushing up the spectacles that weren't there. She squinted at the darker shadow of Fabrizio's back moving before her. She could feel his irritation flowing from him with the snap of a whip. He turned his head as though studying the walls of the maze, but Mirabella guessed he was watching her out of the corner of his eye. Perhaps he truly meant her no harm, she thought, and she did rather enjoy the idea of his hand holding hers.

Mirabella smoothed down her hair with a quick gesture and then pretended to trip, flinging her body into Fabrizio's back with a dramatic lunge. "Ow! My foot, my ankle! I've twisted it on a tree root!"

Fabrizio turned smartly and caught her. "There. What did I tell you, Mirabella?" There was a hint of smugness in his voice, but his manner was gentle as he helped her to stand. "Does it hurt?" he asked.

"Oh yes," she lied, a little breathless. Her flesh was tingling where his hands held her. "Rather a lot," she added, surprised and delighted by his charming look of concern.

"Here, lean on me," he offered, and swung an arm around her waist.

"I'm sorry for being such a nuisance." Her legs felt weak, but her heart was hammering with all the strength of a smith pounding at his anvil.

"It's all right," he answered, and flashed her a smile. "I shouldn't have been so rude to you before. I get irritable when my stutter makes it hard to speak. It must be hard on you not to see as well as you are used to."

"Sometimes, it's a blessing," Mirabella said, leaning her weight against his shoulder. She affected a limp on her right ankle. "It makes the world dreamlike. The drabness of the city is transformed when all its colors swirl together like pretty glass. I don't see the dead cats and last night's chicken bones floating in the dirty waters. I see emerald ribbons threaded with diamond sequins of sunlight. When I look at the domes of San Marco, they become mountains of gold, guarded by stallions of smoke. Sometimes when I am utterly bored with my life, which is often, I take off my glasses and pretend to be someone else, traveling through a strange, mysterious land." Mirabella suddenly blushed a furious red. The thrill of the moment had turned her into a gushing fountain of nonsense. He would surely think her a fool now.

"It sounds like the theater," Fabrizio answered earnestly. "The stage, even when it's a primitive board up on a wagon, is a small, magic world where painted domes become mountains of gold and a green cloth looks like an ocean. And best of all, you can be anybody you want on the stage."

Mirabella breathed a quiet sigh of relief and swore not to say any more about herself. This lovely walk, leaning on the arm of a handsome young man, could end in one mortifying moment if she wasn't vigilant.

"How long have you been an actor?"

"All my life," he answered with a grin. "Right from birth. No, it's true," he insisted when she started laughing. "You should have seen the look of rapture on my aunts' faces when they drew me out from between my mother's legs. I bawled my opening lines and they shouted back 'Bravo! Encore!' "

"And did you give them an encore?"

"Yes, certainly. I was a professional even then. I shook my fists, wailed a short speech, and then pissed in the air. They were entranced."

"What about your father? Was he so easily amused?" Mirabella asked. Fabrizio's pleasant smile soured. She felt the arm around her waist grip her savagely.

"Nothing I ever d-d-did amused my-my fa-fa-ther," he stuttered.

"I'm sorry," Mirabella said.

"Ba-ba-bastard, wa-wa-wanted only one th-thing from me-me. To punish my-my mother for re-pu-pu-lsing him, by t-taking me from her and ma-ma-making my life mi-mi-miserable."

"That's horrible. How did you ever manage?"

Fabrizio shrugged, the words knotting up in his throat. They walked silently, the pleasant mood overcast. Stupida, Mirabella hissed to herself. Why don't you just stab yourself in the heart and get it over with?

Fabrizio picked up Arlecchino's mask and placed it over his brooding face. At once his angry mouth broadened into a huge grin. He licked his lips, rubbed his belly, and took Mirabella's hands between his, his tense body grown languid. Mirabella could feel his chest, his thighs resting warmly against her.

"Colombina, my little cheese, do you know that I love you?" the mask asked.

"Arlecchino, my big sausage, tell me the whole of it!" Mirabella answered.

"I love you more than sailors love their cabin boys!" the mask crooned.

"I love you more than girls love rich old men!"

"I love you more than friars love brandy!"

"I love you more than actors love applause!"

"Hold it right there," Arlecchino exclaimed, a finger held up in the air. "That's too much!"

Mirabella laughed and the mask of Arlecchino leaned forward to kiss her. Dazed, she tilted her head up and watched the soft mouth descend toward her.

"Mirabella! Mirabella!" Anna's voice cried out in alarm. "Mirabella, where are you?"

"Mamma, I'm here!" Mirabella jerked her head around, squinting down the green corridor. "Where are you?" She could see nothing. Somewhere in the distance, Lily was barking.

Mirabella bolted from Fabrizio's arms and ran down the path, her hands held out in front of her. "Mamma! Mamma!" she called out. "Where are you?" She turned a corner only to see another blurred wall of green trees, the path forking into two different directions.

"Mirabella! Mirabella!" The sound of Anna's voice was fading. She was moving farther away from Mirabella. Lily barked once or twice more and then fell silent.

"Can you see her?" Mirabella asked when Fabrizio caught up with her. "Is she there?"

"I don't see her anywhere. Only these damn trees."

"Lily! Lily, come to me," Mirabella called out to the dense wall of trees. She waited, hearing only her own breathing.

"Your leg has healed quickly," Fabrizio said dryly.

"My leg?" Mirabella asked, staring distractedly at the two paths before her. Which one led to Anna?

"Be honest," Fabrizio said. "You never really hurt your ankle, did you? You were just pretending."

Mirabella turned from the trees to confront him, her face contorted with sudden, embarrassed anger. "To hell with you," she announced. "I don't need you." She spun on her heel and stormed blindly down the left-hand path, praying that she might avoid slamming into anything at least while she was still in Fabrizio's sight. It was like spitting in the wind and having it all come back in your face, she thought bitterly. She had made a fool of herself with Fabrizio, and she still hadn't found her mother or Lily. Could it be any worse?

Tears welled in her eyes. She wiped one away and saw too late that the path angled sharply to the right. Her foot stepped forward, and off the path. "No!" she shrieked as she toppled over the side of a wall, her arms flailing in the air. There was a brief moment of flight, just long enough for her to recognize the rank smell of the water below her. "Not fair!" she cried, and splashed down hard.

She sank under the cold, salty water. Floating weeds caressed her face and she forced herself back to the surface. She spluttered, choking, her legs kicking fiercely to keep her heavy skirts from dragging her under again.

"Do you need a hand?" Fabrizio asked, leaning over a brick wall.

"No! Go away! I want to die in this miserable canal!"

"Come on, Mirabella, don't be a fool, take my hand!" Fabrizio commanded.

A fool, she thought, defeated. That's what I am. Mirabella thrust her arm out to grab Fabrizio's hand. But instead of letting him pull her out, she jerked him hard into the cold water. If she was going to look like a fool, she wanted company.

Fabrizio dove headfirst into the water, having scarcely the time to utter a word. The masks around his neck looked aghast, their eyes goggled beneath raised eyebrows, their lips pulled into grimaces. Fabrizio sank like a stone and Mirabella watched with a smirk of satisfaction as little bubbles erupted on the surface of the water.

But he did not follow them. The bubbles ceased and only the widening rings were left to mark his entrance into the water.

"Madonna Santissima, I've murdered him!" Mirabella cried out, and dove under the water to find him. She groped around in the murky waters, snatching at handfuls of weeds, brushing them away as she swam in the water. The weeds tangled in her fingers and curled their viscous tentacles around her kicking ankles. Where was he?

Just as she was about to give up, she saw a dark floating shadow hulking in the water. She grabbed the body by the shoulders and dragged it to the surface. As her head broke free of the water she coughed and gagged on the salty water, but she kept Fabrizio's chin above the surface and swam with him to the edge of the canal. Squinting hard, she made out the rusted circle of an iron ring embedded in the canal wall. She grabbed it and tried desperately to rouse the young man. His eyes were closed, his mouth open. She couldn't tell if he was still breathing. Green weeds laced his wet hair.

"Fabrizio! Fabrizio! I'm sorry!" she said, shaking him. "I didn't mean to pull you in. I was mad! Please, Fabrizio, speak to me. Don't drown."

Silence. Water sluiced out of Fabrizio's cold, purple lips.

"O'mio Dio, Fabrizio, please! Speak to me. Don't be dead!" she wailed.

The slack mouth twitched into a grin. He opened one bright eye and winked mischievously. His body came suddenly to life, shivering violently in the water. He reached up, grabbed the iron ring, and floated next to her, blowing little bubbles in the water.

"You—you liar! You deceitful—"

"We're even, now" he said smugly. "You know, that wasn't a bad bit of acting you did back there. You really ought to consider a life on the stage, Mirabella." He spoke as though they were conversing comfortably in a piazza and not bobbing like wine corks in a filthy canal. "Come on, I can see some stairs carved into the wall farther on. Will you take my hand and let me get us out of here?"

Speechless with embarrassment, Mirabella meekly gave Fabrizio her hand. He swam along the canal wall, pulling her through the water until they reached the stairs. Together, they ascended into the maze, dripping like half-drowned dogs and leaving trails of water behind them.

25

*S*o, my beauties, where did I take the wrong turn?" Anna asked. She was lying on her back staring up at the flutter of silvery leaves. The air was redolent with the scent of green grass and spicy olive wood. The sun was warm on her face, easing the panic she had felt at discovering herself quite alone in the maze.

"Leaving Venice," said a miffed Pantelone from inside the bag.

"Not studying the classics!" Il Dottore objected.

"Not bringing enough to eat," complained Arlecchino.

"Not bringing any wine!" grumbled the satyr.

"Loving the devil who cursed us," said the soft voice of the nymph, rustling her leaves.

"Not having a dowry for Mirabella," piped the ingenue.

"Letting the drunkard Spaniard take up space in the bag," groused Pulchinella. "Prickless coward! When I get out of here, I'll give you a hundred whacks where it hurts the most!"

"Wart-faced whelp of a worn-out whore, what do you know of courage!" demanded Il Capitano. "Anna should have chopped you up for the moths to eat."

Anna rolled her eyes and pinched her fingers together. "Madonna della Santa, I didn't ask for your opinions about my life. I only asked where I made the wrong turn in the maze to lose Mirabella?"

The masks were silent a moment before they all started to chatter at once.

"At the cedars, you should have—"

"By the fountain of naked nymphs—"

"The bridge, stupid—"

"What about those dead trees—"

"It's clear that the rountunding ambrage, reticulating the reversals—"

"Get your nose out of my eye—"

"If you rustle those leaves in my face, I swear I'll sneeze them off—"

"Stop licking my cheek, Pulchinella!"

"Basta! Silensio!" Anna cried, holding her hands over her ears. "At

least now I don't feel so bad. Clearly, I'm not the only one to be hopelessly lost."

"Anna, why are we here at all?" asked Pantelone.

Anna waved her hand irritably. "Because I have been cursed by an evil
man, of course."

"Of course," repeated Pantelone skeptically.

"I gave him my love, and he gave me the curse of thorns," Anna said,
clenching her hands.

"You embraced the thorns, Anna," Pantelone said gruffly.

"No, they made me miserable, they tore my heart into shreds," Anna
argued.

"It wasn't your heart," said the ingenue.

"But your womb," finished the nymph.

"And it wasn't he that cast the rake over your flesh. It was you who
scoured with it your rage," said the satyr.

"You let grow in its place a vine of thorns," Pantelone went on dismally.

"And you watered it with wine," Pulchinella intoned.

"Fed it pieces of self-loathing seasoned with anguish," Il Capitano
said.

"And what of the precious seed, already, growing that was lost,
Anna?" asked Arlecchino.

"What slipped out between your legs in the rivers of blood you
sweated for this lost love?" asked the ingenue sadly.

"I didn't know," Anna said softly. "I didn't know, until too late. Until
the thorns had done their worst."

"Bring back the vine that grows the sweet grapes, Anna," the nymph
pleaded.

"That's enough!" commanded Anna, rising. "You are masks! I made
you! What right have you to speak to me thus?"

"It's true, we are masks, Anna," answered Pantelone. "We are limited
to knowing only what each mask represents—cunning, cowardice, bra-
gadoccio, foolishness. The man on whose face we rest, he must change
to suit us. We are always the same. But you Anna, you have changed."

Anna shrugged. "It's the way of all human beings."

"But you no longer know yourself. You wear a mask to hide your true
nature rather than to reveal it, as we do," Pantelone insisted. "You are
afraid, Anna. Of yourself."

Anna sat quietly amid the olive trees, Pantelone's words stinging her
like blown sand. Tears started in her eyes as the thorns began to twist in
her womb. They were her punishment for life, planted there by her

lover's words, fed by her own rage. The masks were right. She laid her
hands against her belly. She pressed, feeling the thorns tear at her soft
interior. They had destroyed everything and she had permitted it. She
might live in a drunken woman's mask or a bawd's mask, revel enough
to drown the shame. Only in her own face did she acknowledge the
truth.

She glanced up at the sounds of tinkling bells. At the far edge of the
olive grove she saw a group of women processing through the trees.
Some clanged little cymbals between their fingers, some beat small
drums or shook metallic rattles. The lead woman held high a thyrsus, an
ancient staff topped with a pinecone and wreathed in ivy. The women
twirled in a slow dance, their feet stamping out a path in the long grass
for a cart, hauled by four women, on which sat a pale naked youth
whose black curling hair was wreathed in vines. The cart was decked with
flowers and clusters of grapes and draped with the skins of spotted
fawns and black panthers. As Anna watched, the youth upended a flask
of wine, sending a thin stream of amber liquid into his open mouth.

Anna licked her parched lips. The sound of the bells chimed louder
in her head. Her pulse quickened to the beat of the drums. She could
smell the heady odor of fermented grapes, a sweet, sticky perfume in the
air, and beneath it, another scent, rank and pungent. Flies buzzed noisily around the animal skins.

The procession stopped and the women approached her, their hands
held out in welcome. Anna saw that their faces and arms were covered
with white clay and that they wore white masks festooned with acorns
and tiny pinecones about the brow. They came close to her, speaking
softly in a language she didn't understand. Their hands stroked her hair,
her shoulders, and her back. One woman touched her belly, and Anna
felt the thorns wither. Another brought forth the skin of a fawn and
bent low to present it to Anna.

She took it, the flies buzzing madly in her face. The skin was stiff, an
unfinished hide with dried blood and threads of sinew still clinging to
the back. She trembled as she placed it over her shoulders. The woman
laughed and passed her a bowl of wine. She raised it to her lips and
drank the dark wine, which washed away all her fear. She looked into the
face of the youth and fell deeply in love. Eyes of polished onyx absorbed
her pain, caressed it, transformed it into a burning desire.

"Will you wear a mask and join our revels?" he asked. He handed her
a peach-tinted mask of a young woman.

Anna stared at it. It was one of hers, but not hers, not exactly. The
arched brows were severe, the nose finished in an arrow point. The lips

had lost their youth, the wide sensual mouth opened in a sardonic leer. She took the mask and weighed it in her hands. Once she put it on, she would not be Anna. She would be this mask of the revel, this creature belonging to the youth, to the band of women, to the animal skin, and to the drunken passion of the night.

"Anna, wait," called Pantelone.

It was too late. She had already slipped the mask over her face and felt the change pour through into her veins. She looked at the youth and knew who he was—Bacchus. The sight of him filled her with cravings. She wanted to drink until she was insensible. She wanted to dance until she collapsed. Her thighs twitched and her feet found the tamping rhythm of the drums. She wanted to couple with the Lord of the Revel. She wanted to hunt, to tear down a running beast with her hands and taste the warm flesh. She took a pair of cymbals and rang them between her fingers. The sharp chime was like a knife, cleaving Anna from the past, from the thorns, from Mirabella. From the masks.

"Anna, wait!" cried Pantelone one last time.

But his voice was an echo, sliced off by the knife edge of the chiming cymbals. Anna turned slowly in a circle, finding her place among the dancers as they moved up the hill of the olive grove.

26

The convolutions of the maze didn't worry Erminia. She knew the moment her feet touched the pebbled path that it would lead her to Orpheus. She felt a concentrated force of magic flowing through the maze like waves crisscrossing an ocean. No matter where Erminia placed herself within it, the waves of magic would carry her to Orpheus.

Erminia blinked through the fractured lens of Mirabella's spectacles and thought how easy it was to mistake the blurred shapes of the trees for the sea depths. It was almost like home. The soft undulating branches of the cedars wavered with the same murky green of deep waters struck through with diffused sunlight. All around her was green and gold, dark patches amid the splashes of light. Birds flitted in the air much as small fish darted beneath the spangled surface of the water. But the stony path and the dry, dusty perfume of the cedars were all too earthbound and hard.

There was no other way to clean a fish but scrape against the scales. She had to reappear before Orpheus and worse, after admitting defeat, she had prostrate herself before his contemptuous head and beg for another chance. With every step she took, her recent defeat stabbed her heels like sea urchin quills. She could already hear the derision in Orpheus's voice.

No, it wasn't his voice that interrupted the silence of the maze, but someone else's, walking unseen ahead of her in the maze. As Erminia bent her head to listen, she discerned three different voices, arguing. With a start she realized that the nasal whine of one of the voices sounded familiar. A second voice answered with a huge guffaw and a third voice—whether a man's or a woman's she couldn't say—bid the others be quiet while it prattled on.

Erminia stopped in her tracks and rolled her eyes. Damn Orpheus—he's sent Ipnos to fetch me. Ipnos, who had one body and three heads, each with its own unpleasant personality: Ipnos the fool, Ipnos the wicked, and Ipnos the boy. When taken all together, they made for one Ipnos the Obnoxious. She was never sure whether it was his wealth of heads that had attracted Orpheus to Ipnos, or the boy's muscular young body, which was immodestly arrayed. Either way, Ipnos returned his master's affection with a surprising loyalty for one so apt to commit mayhem elsewhere.

Erminia braced herself as Ipnos turned the corner. To her surprise, he was accompanied by a man, Italian by the look of his black velvet doublet and hose, wearing a grave expression. Erminia lowered Mirabella's spectacles to see the pair better. Ipnos the boy and Ipnos the wicked were arguing, while Ipnos the fool was content to make farting noises with his tongue pressed between his fleshy lips. That sight was all too familiar.

The man was more interesting. Oddly refined for a pilgrim, tall and slim, carefully dressed, though twigs and small leaves had snagged in his thick wavy hair. A jagged white lock of hair fell over troubled dark eyes. She could see he wanted to interrupt the strange conversations of his companion. Erminia gave a twist of a smile. She recognized the look of frustration on the man's face.

Ipnos stopped his prattling as the fool's face caught sight of Erminia standing on the path.

"Looky, looky, if it isn't the fat tuna herself!" the fool crowed. Ipnos craned his neck to the left and Ipnos the wicked sneered at her. "Couldn't keep your trap shut, eh anchovy head?" Turning right again, Ipnos the boy gave a trilling laugh. He placed one hand on his hip and thrust out his naked chest. "Thought you were better than Orpheus, didn't you?"

Erminia pressed her lips together in a tight frown. She pushed Mirabella's spectacles back up on her nose to shield her sight from the insolent six-eyed stare.

"Oh, now she's quiet!" roared the wicked. "Now she don't have nothing to say!" jeered the fool. "Now it doesn't matter whether she speaks or spits," said the youth. "Orpheus will take back what he gave her for good."

Erminia wanted to sing one last shattering note that would split the three hideous faces and silence their stinging tongues forever. But she forced herself to suppress her rage. It was going to be difficult enough to confront that memento mori Orpheus, without having to match insults with his miserable servant. Besides, the little squid could make it worse for her. All he had to do was complain about her to that besotted head and Orpheus would be nastier than ever.

Erminia turned her head and lifted her chin toward the man. "Who's that?" she asked. The air sighed with the clear sound of her voice. The pilgrim looked up, startled.

"Ah, this is Signor Lorenzo Falcomatta," Ipnos the boy answered sourly. "He's here to see Orpheus because he is an incurable liar."

"That's impossible. I neither know this Orpheus, nor am I capable of lying," replied Lorenzo flatly.

Ipnos the fool sniggered; Ipnos the wicked made obscene smacking noises.

"Tell me, Signor Falcomatta, do you see a three-faced man standing before you?" asked Ipnos the boy, turning his head this way and that so that all three faces were clearly visible.

"No," Lorenzo declared. "I see a man with a strange disfigurement. It makes it seem as though he had three faces, but indeed, he has only one."

"Liar!" Ipnos the wicked guffawed, and with both hands scratched two of his three chins.

"And what's that over there?" Ipnos the boy asked, pointing to a small grotto.

Beneath a sculpture of Eros spouting water into a marble basin sat a naked woman. Her hair was very black and fell the whole length of her body. Her skin was green and yellow like molding parchment. The sun glinted off the pearl grey scales that covered her hips. There was a splash, and a large fish tail appeared over the edge of the basin. The green fins sparkled wetly in the air and then fell with a slap against the surface of the water.

Lorenzo turned away quickly. "It's a woman bathing," he insisted.

"And the tail?" asked Ipnos the boy.

"I saw no tail."

"Liar!" hissed Ipnos the fool.

"What do you see there, then?" Ipnos the wicked demanded. He pointed down the pathway to where the trees parted to reveal a grassy glade surrounded by oaks. A satyr coupled with a nymph, his hairy legs straddling her from behind, his hands clasping her upper torso by her ample breasts. His long tail twirled, the white underside flickering wildly in the cool green shadows.

"It is—" Lorenzo hesitated, his brow drawn into a deep cleft over his eyes. "It is a goat," he announced, pushing the lock of white hair off his forehead with a trembling hand.

"And the other person?" Ipnos the boy asked, incredulously.

"A—a shepherd," Lorenzo replied primly.

"And what is the goat doing?" Ipnos the wicked asked with a leer.

"Grazing, I expect. I know very little about goats."

Ipnos slapped a hand on the forehead of the fool.

"Ouch," the fool bawled. "That hurt!"

The hand slapped again, this time on the forehead of Ipnos the wicked.

"Fuck off!" growled Ipnos the wicked.

"Oh shut up, both of you," ordered Ipnos the boy. He raised his hands and tweaked the noses of the other two faces.

Erminia lifted her hand to hide the grin at seeing the three-faced servant quarreling with himself. And as Ipnos argued and swore at himself, Erminia studied Lorenzo over the rim of Mirabella's spectacles. Lorenzo was brushing minute particles of dust from his doublet. He seemed composed, unruffled by the outrageous visions Ipnos had shown him.

"Do you see how he lies to himself?" groused the boy to Erminia. "Denies the truth of everything around him. He could shit, walk in it, and convince himself it was the mud of the Po."

Erminia pulled the furious servant off to one side of the path.

"Why should it matter what this man admits to seeing?" Erminia asked. The air held the sound of her voice and carried it aloft in a band of gold light.

"Because this chicken plucker was once a liar who could speak the truth," Ipnos the boy replied angrily. "He was a poet. A good poet. Good enough to turn my master's head, good enough that even the strings of Orpheus's lyre would vibrate in harmony with his verses. Good enough that the muse Calliope now weeps over his silence."

"What happened?"

Ipnos shrugged his slim shoulders. "The words are still there. It's just something plugged up the spigot. Nothing comes out any more. When Orpheus sensed his presence near the maze, he sent me to fetch him in and find out why. But this fucker is so closemouthed, it's worse than trying to bugger a clam. All he has to do is admit to seeing just one of the mysteries of our world, and Orpheus believes that this prig will become a man of poetry again."

Erminia glanced over her shoulder at Lorenzo, who was staring blankly out at the nymph and her satyr, whose lovemaking had grown more passionate. They had found a new position, leaning up against a sapling. The ardent thrusts of the satyr caused the frail leafy branches to thrash violently. Lorenzo gave no indication that he saw anything but trees and a goat. His features had hardened into the marmoreal mask of righteousness, eyes glaring with defiance, jaw locked tight against dispute.

Erminia pitied him then, because she could hear very faintly—as did Orpheus, as did they all—the songs that he might have sung had he given his voice license. Behind the silent stone mask he wore she caught snatches of images, lines of poetry that he was shaping in the farthest recesses of his mind. He may have forbidden his lips to speak, but he could not silence the poet's heart. Even now, the satyr and the nymph were being transformed into a lyrical and sensual phrase of poetry. Erminia wiggled her fingers in her ears, but that didn't silence the whisperings of the poet. How the sound must itch like a flea in Orpheus's ear, Erminia thought. And he with no hands to scratch.

"Listen anchovy-head," Ipnos the wicked was saying, tugging her fingers out of her ears. "You've got to help me."

"What do you want me to do?" Erminia asked.

"This Lorenzo is like a man with a seven year hard-on who has forgotten how to come."

"And?"

"And you're a woman. Take care of it!" Ipnos the boy said.

"If that's all it takes, you're as skilled as the next."

"Don't you think I would have tried it if I'd thought I had half a chance?" the boy asked savagely. "I've never felt so limp in my life! Even Bacchus couldn't shove a flax seed up that man's ass with an axe. He's driving us all crazy with his buzzing." Ipnos held his hand over each pair of ears, one after the other.

Erminia reflected. It was true Lorenzo's unspoken poetry whined and moaned and scrabbled its tiny nails trying to claw its way out of the prison of silence.

"What's in it for me?" Erminia demanded.

"I'll speak to Orpheus on your behalf," Ipnos the boy said.

"And . . . ?"

"And I'll suggest that you and your sisters get your voices back if you turn this jibbering dildo into a poet again," Ipnos answered glumly. "Orpheus will not refuse me."

"Agreed," Erminia said, her face wreathed in a cornflower blue cloud. She took Mirabella's spectacles off and folded their bent stems neatly before tucking them into a pocket. She brushed back the dark tangle of her matted hair and let the sunlight warm the sapphire glow of her eyes. "To Orpheus, then, to seal the bargain."

27

Rinaldo crept alongside the stand of cedar trees, stealing a glance over his shoulder. His palms itched and he nervously grasped the handle of the long sword. He was convinced that he was being followed. Every time he spun around, his sword held high, there was no one there. Even the strange man who had pulled him so forcefully over the maze the night before had disappeared by the time Rinaldo extricated himself from the tangled branches of the low-lying shrubs.

In the snowy light of a full moon the cedars had looked like soldiers standing at attention with gleaming spears at their sides. Rinaldo had waited for his companions from the other side to join him. But no one followed him. He called for them and getting no reply, he crouched beneath a tree and decided that it wasn't wise to travel in the strange maze at night. He had no idea who or what might have scared off the man who had helped him over, and he made for an easy target on the bright path. He'd slept sitting with his back against the trunk of a cedar and his sword resting across his knees. In the morning when he awoke, stiff and damp with dew, he found someone had left a silver plate of food by his feet—cold mutton, boiled potatoes, shriveled apples, and a wedge of hard cheese. He ate slowly. There were no signs of footprints; the ground looked as if it had been raked clean with a switch.

Before the sun was well up, Rinaldo had set off through the maze. Either he would meet his companions along the way, or he would not. In the end, it didn't matter to Rinaldo. Roberto and Lorenzo had their own curses to look after. He was there to find Simonetta. He had enjoyed Roberto's company, though. The older man had a gracious air and he'd proved handy with his sabre too. Rinaldo felt a sliver of worry for him, at his age, to be so hopelessly in love with a woman that he would leave the comfort of his home and follow after her. Pazzo, he thought, shaking his head. Crazy.

"But is it any crazier than leaving a safe haven to chase a woman because you claim to hate her?" Roberto had asked.

"I have no feelings whatsoever for the woman," Rinaldo argued. "I seek only to reclaim my honor, my horse, and my sword."

"They make cold bedfellows, Rinaldo," Roberto had replied.

A sudden dark shadow blotting out the morning sun caused Rinaldo to look up. A raven spread its wings over the narrow corridor, blocking the sunlight as it drifted back and forth over the maze. A second raven joined it, and then a third. They flew low, skimming the tops of the trees, their glistening black heads downturned to study something in the maze. One cawed loudly, a sound like glass breaking just before it dove through the treetops. The second banked in the wind and dove after the first. The third circled back, cawing at Rinaldo before it, too, folded its wings and joined its companions.

Rinaldo had marked the flight of the ravens with growing unease. He drew his sword as he waited for the presence he felt lurking beneath the shadow of the ravens' wings to appear.

But no one came to challenge him. He slowly rounded the bend of the cedar trees, feeling the presence, vague as a ghost at his shoulder. As he turned the corner, he saw a huge boulder across the path. Its flat surface was slippery with blood, and around its base a pool was congealing in the dirt, the edges already drying to a brick brown. Flies settled atop the stone, washing their feathered limbs in the thick streams.

Rinaldo approached the bloody stone cautiously. The sides were scratched with spiral markings like the decorations of an ancient altar. He wondered what animal had given so freely of its blood. Beyond the pool, Rinaldo saw a rusty smear along the path. He clutched his sword tighter and followed it. Gradually the dusty perfume of the cedars faded under a cloying stench. Whatever had been killed and dragged along the path could not be far ahead of him. The ravens must have seen it already from their flight above the walls of the maze.

The corridor of trees angled sharply to the left and Rinaldo hesitated before he took the corner. He could hear the harsh cawing of the ravens fighting over their meal. He moved warily, keeping his body well hidden by the bank of trees.

He had steeled himself, remembering only too well the gruesome sight of ravens and crows feasting on the battlefields and on the strange human fruit hanging from blasted trees. What busied the ravens was both less and more shocking—the headless carcass of a dead horse. Rinaldo stared bewildered and then sickened with rage. As he approached, the ravens lifted off the carcass, cawing loudly.

It was then that Rinaldo saw the high wall of pocked, weathered stone that rose behind the horse's body. The path led into the darkened mouth of a cave opening at the wall's base. Mounted in sconces on either side of the cave burned two lit torches, and above it, held fast by a spike, hung Lapone's severed head. The velvet muzzle was stiff with dried blood, the tongue black where it lolled out of the slack mouth. The smoky mane billowed in the wind, lashing the rigid ears. Lapone's blood had stained the stone wall with rust.

"Lapone," Rinaldo called softly to eyes white and lifeless as two moons, then tensed as he felt the presence of someone nearby. The wind whispered through the stallion's mouth, a ghost's voice mocking him.

Rinaldo walked to the headless carcass, tugged open the saddlebags, still tied to the stallion's back, and pulled out the torn fragment of a petticoat wrapped with a sprig of dried rosemary. He brought the cloth to his nose and sniffed, squeezing his eyes shut as a thousand memories flooded him, love and hate twined like biting serpents. Simonetta. Simonetta was here. She had let this happen.

Rinaldo stuffed the piece of cloth into his doublet and with three quick strides came to the mouth of the cave. A hot, phantom-filled air exhaled from the throat of the cliff. Barely visible in the dark inner reaches were stalactites, hanging like fangs from the ceiling. Small yellow flames flickered within the recesses of the cave from torches set all along the pathway. Rinaldo ducked beneath the severed head and entered.

Within the cave, the sense of being watched grew even stronger, as if not one, but many, watched him from silent eyes. They were ahead of him, behind him, on all sides—an army of ghosts, watching. Rinaldo felt them lurking in every shadow, darting behind curved walls, shuffling behind him, hiding in the thin white towers of stalagmites. He could hear them whispering, and once, laughing. An eerie voice called out a challenge. Rinaldo raised his sword to meet it and it died away. He strained to follow the sounds of footsteps scurrying over the sandy floor. His arm arched with the effort of holding his sword at the ready. Sweat beaded his brow and stung his eyes.

"Rinaldo Gustiano," called a rasping voice down one darkened corridor. "Prepare to join your dead."

Rinaldo turned toward the challenge, searching for the speaker in the dim light. A torch cast a wide oval of fitful light into the blackness. Tendrils of smoke curled in the air. A man, half-hidden in the shadows, waited for Rinaldo, his naked sword blazing like a flame.

"Who are you?" demanded Rinaldo.

"One you knew not well, but intimately enough to kill."

The man stepped forward into the light and Rinaldo tightened his grip on his sword. His challenger was a corpse. The skin peeled away from one side of the rotting head to reveal the skeletal remains of teeth. The empty eye sockets refused the light and the head swiveled on clacking vertebrae, following the sound of Rinaldo's breathing. Once there had been lace on the sleeves of the tattered clothing, but it crumbled with every movement the corpse made.

As the corpse swung its sword, Rinaldo backed up, gagging on the draft of putrid air, then moved in swiftly, trying not to let his horror overcome his dueling instincts. He blocked the corpse's stroke and staggered back, rebuffed by the unexpected strength in the skeletal hands. He dodged another strike to his head and wheeled around with a two-handed grip. The long sword hissed in the air and, with a clean stroke, cleaved through the corpse's decaying ribs, which snapped and cracked like dried twigs loosing the desiccated remnants of bloodless organs. The corpse cried out, dropping the sword and falling to its knees to pluck at its own remains scattered on the path. Standing over it, Rinaldo drove his sword down like an axe, hacked off the head, and kicked it against the wall.

Sweating hard, fear stabbing needles of ice in his veins, Rinaldo waited for the corpse to rise. But it remained where it was, shattered in pieces. He bent down to examine it. The thing had called him by name. An emerald ring on the skeletal hand glinted in the torchlight, and Rinaldo recognized the insignia carved into the gem. He had killed this man many years ago in a duel. For what reason? He could no longer remember.

Rinaldo stood up slowly and wiped his sleeve over his sweating face. Along the walls he could now see the faint black slashes of ancient paintings. A crude figure of a man huddled against the wall of a maze. On the other side of the wall waited a monstrous creature, his body that of a giant, his head sporting the long horns and the snout of a bull. He carried in his hand a double-headed axe. Littered at his feet were piles of human bones and broken weapons.

Rinaldo turned and tried to find his way back out of the cave. But the more he twisted and turned in the dimly lit corridors, the more he realized he was lost. The deceptive light, the sameness of each tunnel, and the complicated turnings of the path led him away from the entrance and deeper into the cave. The air here was dense. Fissures in the floor of the cave belched yellow clouds of sulphurous smelling steam. Every so often, Rinaldo saw paintings of the bull-headed monster, more scenes of victims succumbing to the monster's double-bladed axe. Sometimes, nestled in the elbow of two different paths, Rinaldo found piles of bones, a grinning skull placed on top with a finger bone stretched out to suggest the way.

The earth hissed and steamed. A low rumble sounded through the hollows of the rock. The whispering voices returned, taunting him from the shadows. A sudden cold wind cut the yellow steam and Rinaldo saw a second corpse waiting for him on the path. The corpse's sword was tarnished and pocked with decay, the blade a rusted jagged edge.

As before, the corpse called out to Rinaldo, inviting him to meet his death. The silver threads of a crest, a snake consuming a boar, were just visible on the corpse's ragged cloak. Rinaldo knew this one too. A Sforza, who once had challenged him over the right to drink in a tavern. As Rinaldo confronted his challenger a second time, he could only think of Roberto's friendly jibe, spoken in the warm sunlight. "Do you have any wish to see your dead again?"

That was it, then, Rinaldo thought grimly, as he hacked off the corpse's sword arm, spinning the dead Sforza with the force of the blow so that the wind whistled through its empty eye sockets. Death had not tempered his opponents' desire for revenge. Here in the maze their rotting corpses sought one more battle with the man who had killed them. How many of them would he have to face before he was through? He stood over the huddled bones of the corpse. It shuddered, the bony fingers of the severed arm clicking open and shut, unable to rise again.

And what of the monster pictured on the walls? Rinaldo looked up along the wall and saw another painting of the bull-headed giant. It waited at the center of its lair, the double-headed axe resting on the massive curve of its shoulder. To the right of the giant, Rinaldo saw himself drawn in black on the wall, a lone figure standing behind three stalagmites with bones laying at his feet. He glanced down at the fallen corpse. There were the bones. Rinaldo glanced over his shoulder. There were the stalagmites. If he were to pass between them, he would face the bull-headed creature. A bellow rumbled through the dark corridors, vibrated the stones, and caused the stalactites to tremble. The wind blew hot, swirling the sulphurous mist into yellow funnels. Footsteps echoed in the cavernous ceilings. Rinaldo sprinted away from the three stalagmites, running until he found a smaller, darker vein down which to escape. Behind him, the rumbling grew louder, the heavy pounding of footsteps pursuing him as he fled.

Then Rinaldo slowed as ahead of him, he saw another corpse step into an oval of torchlight, swinging a pike with a rotting wooden handle.

"Rinaldo Gustiano, prepare to die!" it shouted.

28

Roberto idly rubbed the scratches on his cheeks and cursed himself for being so stupid. And worse, impulsive. Why had he followed Rinaldo over the wall of the maze in the first place? A captain and duelist might be suited to such rugged activities, Roberto thought irritably, but an old merchant should be more sensible. It was the moonlight, the strange whimsy of the marble faces on the Arch of Dreams, the scent of the cedars conspiring to send him climbing up a tree wall after his love only to be shoved mercilessly down again through the thicket of branches. And then abandoned in a dark wood with no moon or stars to light his surroundings. At least when the sun had crept quietly over the tips of the trees, Roberto discovered that the small wood in which he had landed was in fact an orchard of apple trees. He had eaten some of them and then stuffed a few more in his pockets before setting off on a path he had spent the better part of a day idly following.

"Well, Roberto," he said aloud, "a man like you should know better. A man like you should be wiser." He rubbed at the scratches. "But a man like you can't help being in love with Anna Forsetti," he reminded himself with a shrug of resignation. "Well, at least from now on, try to think before doing anything else stupid."

In the late afternoon sun, the tree-lined path was alive with birdsong. Small stands of blue and white flowers bobbed in the gentle breezes. Robert took one of the apples from his pocket and ate it thoughtfully, wondering how to find Anna. He had assumed there would be people to ask, but there was no one, and it bothered him that the maze seemed so empty and lonely.

As Roberto took another bite of his apple, he looked up and saw a dense black cloud of smoke billowing above the cedars. Lightning sizzled in the smoke and loud roaring shook the ground beneath his feet. Flocks of tiny birds scattered in the air in terror. A second roar clapped overhead, and as new bolts of lightning shot through the dense cloud of smoke, a woman screamed.

"Madonna," Roberto exclaimed, and tossing away the half-eaten apple, ran down the corridor toward the shrill screams. He didn't think about what he might find. He didn't think about the danger. His only thought was that it might be Anna who was screaming.

Around the curve of the maze wall, the trees gathered in thick clumps, oaks and pines spreading their boughs across the narrow path. Blinded by the dense branches, the screams pulled him through the tangle of the trees and brush. As he burst into a clearing he was caught up short by the sight of a dragon rearing up on its massive haunches.

The dragon was perched atop a high mound of soot-covered rocks. Flames from its open mouth shot into the tops of the trees; plumes of thick smoke rose from its serpentine nostrils. Lightning exploded from its carnelian eyes. It was holding in its upraised talons the struggling figure of a woman clad only in a thin shift. Blood streaked her terrified face. She was screaming, her naked white legs thrashing wildly in the dragon's grip.

Roberto dashed forward, uttering a quick prayer and drawing his sabre. His glance traveled quickly upward along the exposed belly of the dragon. The armored plates of the dragon's scales scraped against each other in an impenetrable wall of iron. But Roberto knew there was a soft spot. From his reading of Boccaccio's "Geneologia," he knew that even the mightiest of these beasts had a vulnerable spot. He would have only one chance to find it with his sword before he was consumed by the dragon's fiery breath or torn to shreds on the scythelike talons. Stiffly, the dragon lowered its head from the wreath of smoke and its jeweled eye caught sight of Roberto. It roared again, the sound deafening Roberto as he zigzagged over the rocky mound. New smoke issued from the dragon's nostrils, enveloping him in its gritty embrace.

The woman screamed more shrilly as the dragon waved her captive figure in the air, steel jaws snapping open and shut as it prepared to eat her. Roberto yelled a battle cry and waved his sabre to catch the dragon's attention. He charged up the mound toward the dragon but the stones were covered with slick, oily stuff that caused him to slip and slide. Grimly he plodded on ground that trembled and echoed and quaked under his feet.

As he neared the dragon, the thick cloud of black smoke shredded briefly, and Roberto saw a nearly perfect rectangular opening in the scales of the dragon's belly, throbbing a bright red against the blackened iron. Roberto clambered upward as quickly as he could, sliding on the quaking, oily rocks. Panting, his legs aching, Roberto gritted his teeth and struggled on. He was blinded as the dragon belched smoke and a new thunderclap of roaring rattled his rib cage. With a wild thrust, he stabbed the curved point of his sabre into what he hoped was the blood-red rectangle of exposed dragon flesh.

"Merda! Nessuno me lo ficca in culo!" a very human voice howled from within the dense veil of smoke. "Nobody fucks me up the ass with a goddamn pigsticker of a sword!"

Roberto fell back, surprised and more than a little confused by the explosion of insults that followed. He had never in all his reading encountered dragons that spouted obscenities. He was willing to concede that they might swear—in Latin perhaps, or something more exotic, such as Greek or Arabic. But vulgar Italian, of the kind he was used to hearing in the markets? Never.

The quaking ground had abruptly stopped moving, with a sound of gears grinding to a halt somewhere beneath Roberto's feet. Equally abruptly, the dragin had stopped roaring. The dense cloud of smoke was beginning to thin, as playful gusts of wind blew it away over the tops of the trees. Robert glanced up and saw the body of the screaming woman lying limp as a rag doll in the dragon's talons. The dragon itself was strangely still. Through grit-filled tears, Roberto gaped at the dark red rectangle in the dragon's belly, which was moving, pouring out of the body.

A tiny, crippled man wrapped in a red cloak bounded out of the belly of the dragon, rubbing furiously at his backside.

"What the hell do you think you're doing!" demanded the man. His knobby knees pointed away from each other in twin sharp angles, though his heels touched where they met again on the ground. He had a wizened face with two small black eyes closely set over a humpbacked nose. His red cloak flapped in the wind and little bells on his hood jingled merrily.

Roberto closed his mouth and then opened it again, searching for something to say. "I am very sorry," he mumbled at last. "I thought there was a woman who needed rescuing from this . . . dragon?"

"Of course it's a dragon, you cafone! One of the best!" The bent man stamped his foot. He raised a finger in the air. "Even da Vinci, that cabbage head, would bow before my creations."

"Il Maestro Leonardo da Vinci?" Roberto asked, growing more surprised by the moment. Roberto had heard about da Vinci's inventions—the mechanical lion whose chest opened to reveal a wealth of lilies before the King of France and the bird of comedy that flew on mechanical wings, singing with a strange piping voice. "Did you know Maestro Signor da Vinci?"

"Know him?" the little man glared with hostility. "I was his apprentice! How do you think I got so twisted and broken? Do you know how many flying machines he strapped to my back when I was a boy? How many windows he pushed me out of to test his infernal machines? How many times I landed on the ground? Once I had straight limbs! Once I was tall! Now I am like a bent reed that will not stand up after a storm. But there is nothing wrong with my mind! I'll get back at that shithead for what he did to me! Just wait. The creations of Federigo Pedretti will be famous! I will make da Vinci suffer the humiliation of being replaced by the greater genius of his own spurned apprentice." Again his crooked finger stabbed the air.

"Maestro da Vinci is dead," Roberto said, suddenly wondering how long the man had been living in the maze. "Dead for a good twenty years now."

It was Federigo's turn to looked shocked. First he gaped foolishly and then collapsed on the ground spewing curses. When he grew tired of that, he picked up soot-covered rocks and threw them hard at the stilled dragon. The hollow body clanged and chimed with each assault. The red cloak flapped around him, the bells ringing merrily.

"Your pardon, Signore, but what are you doing here?" Roberto asked.

Federigo answered Roberto, still pitching stones at the dragon's body, which was showing signs of denting. "I came like everyone else. It was my hope to rid myself of da Vinci's curse. He stole my ideas, but no one would believe me because he had turned me into an object of ridicule, with my bent legs and crooked arms. It was easy to get into the maze, but I couldn't find my way out of it, brilliant even as I am. There is a diabolical hand in the making of this place. It is never the same, but constantly changing, as though it were reinvented each time a pilgrim enters."

Roberto sat down wearily on one of the rocks and fumbled in his pockets for the apples. He found one, only slightly bruised from the scramble up the rocks, and tossed it to Federigo. The man caught it in his twiglike hands and took a bite.

"I don't remember how it happened," he went on, "but one day I found myself here in this clearing. Waiting for me were all the tools and materials I needed to build my secret imaginings. It was as if the maze had provided the instruments for their creation. How could I leave, when everything I ever needed or wanted was here? Even the audience."

"I don't understand."

"I am a scenographer, Signore. I make settings for dreams or night-mares. Every drama the human heart experiences must have its stage, its props, its monstrous automatons. The ground rises and falls on my care-fully constructed platforms. Steel-plated dragons blow smoke, their ter-rifying roars born of a simple device—a cord pulled through a cylinder."

"And the woman screaming?" Roberto asked.

"A puppet. I have the controls inside the belly there. You should see how it looks when the dragon takes a bite," Federigo said gleefully.

"But why am I here?"

"Because the maze understands that you are here to play the hero, res-cuing the damsel in distress. You're not the only one, you know. Oh I've done this scene a thousand times. Though I'll admit, I've never been bit-ten in the ass before. Usually they take one look at my pet here, and if they don't piss themselves with terror first, they turn tail and run."

"Are we heroes so worthless?" Roberto asked with a faint smile.

"A true hero is the one who knows that often as not the dragon is in the damsel and not the other way around," Federigo said with a sniff. "Could you love your damsel, even if she showed you her fangs? Could you embrace what is terrifying in her as well as what is lovely? My cre-ations, brilliant as they are, are but props for those who would play the role of the Innamorato. And many do not even pass that challenge. But true love, Signore, must be willing to lift the mask and kiss whatever hides beneath."

Roberto stared up at the limp figure of Federigo's puppet. He won-dered about what lay behind the mask of Anna's beautiful face. He thought he knew her. But there were hidden, dragonlike things that gnawed at her from within. Though he saw their terrible likeness in her haunted eyes, recognized their tyranny over her in the recent barrenness of her artist's hands, she would not speak of them. He believed his love could banish those dragons like a child's nighttime fears. But Federigo's words made him pause. Was he prepared to look deep into their cold, gleaming eyes and acknowledge that Anna herself may have created them?

A goldfinch flitted across the rocky mound and came to light on one of the dragon's talons. It trilled an urgent song and was off, a tiny spark of gold streaking across the sky.

"Well, Signore," said Federigo, "I have been called. It's time for the dragon to perform again. Another hero approaches."

"Where shall I go?" Roberto asked, looking around him in confusion.

"Where your heart leads you, Signore, but you can begin by going that way." He pointed to a small path half-hidden behind the dragon's tail. "Quickly now, get out of sight, or you'll ruin my performance." Federigo scrambled back up over the rocks and ducked into the opening of the dragon's belly. Roberto saw him stand on tiptoe to pull levers down with all the might of his spindly arms. Immediately, the rocky ground began to quiver and shake. The gears groaned to life. The metal joints of the dragon creaked as the gleaming head slowly moved from side to side. The white legs of the puppet twitched. Federigo jerked a cord that was hanging above his head and smoke billowed out of the dragon's mouth. The puppet screamed.

Recognizing his cue to exit, Roberto followed the path through the shifting rocks and down a gentle slope. At the bottom of the slope, the path cut through a field of waist-high ferns. The ground was marshy and wet. Ahead of him lay a forest of blighted oaks, their grey trunks and gnarled branches lifting gloomily out of the verdant ferns. Roberto hesitated at the entrance to the forest, which seemed horribly dreary after the lush greenery of the cedars. But there was only one way to go.

He had not gone far into the dying forest when he saw another figure approach him on the path: a priest, his face hidden in the cowl of his black robes, carrying a bag.

"Good day to you, Father," Roberto called.

The priest stopped and pushed back the hood of his cowl. A handsome face with a clean brow and large expressive eyes stared back at Roberto. Even the new beard could not hide his strong chin nor his sensual mouth.

"You—you!" the two men cried out at the same time.

"What are you doing here?" Roberto asked, recognizing the drunken priest from Anna's bedroom.

"The same as you, I'll wager," the priest answered.

"I'm looking for Anna." Roberto was suddenly full of suspicion. Perhaps this handsome young priest was the reason Anna had fled to the maze. Perhaps her dragon was a lust that Roberto could not satisfy.

"As am I," the priest said. "The Tago told me she was here. I must find her!" He clutched the bag to his breast and Roberto saw that one of his hands was bandaged, blood caked on the dirty linen.

"What do you want with her?" Roberto demanded.

"It is a personal matter."

Roberto's jealousy ignited into rage. The thought of the pretty priest in bed with Anna made the apples churn in his belly. He drew his sword.

"I am here to avenge the honor of Anna Forsetti. Say your last prayers before I dispatch you to hell."

The young priest raised his eyebrows, but otherwise made no move to protect himself. Roberto wanted him to beg for mercy before he drove the sword through the young man's sinful heart. But he found it impossible to do anything while he simply stood there.

"Signore, while our last meeting was questionable, I can assure you that I am not here to seduce Anna Forsetti," the priest said slowly. "Rather, I am here because of a task laid down for me by God, by one of the old spirits, and perhaps unknowingly, by Signora Forsetti herself."

Roberto lowered his sword. "What task is that?"

The priest held up the bag and shook it lightly. It rattled dryly. "I was called here to find these. They are bones, Signore. Very little bones."

"And what do these bones have to do with Anna?"

"They once belonged to her child."

"Anna has one child, Mirabella, and she was widowed just after her birth," Roberto argued. "I know of no other child in Anna's life."

"Yet, see how the spirit of these bones calls to us." The priest pointed up into the trees.

Roberto glanced up, and glowing in the approaching twilight, saw the apparition of an infant swaddled in linen and light.

"We must follow it," the priest said eagerly. "There is one more piece of the skeleton missing. Then we must find Anna."

"I don't understand," Roberto said. In the distance, he could hear the roar of the dragon, catch a whiff of the smoke on the breeze. Anna's dragons, he thought.

"I have no answers to give you, Signore. Only that this spirit will lead us to Anna if we choose to follow. It is to these bones that Anna must be reconciled. Only then will Anna's soul and the soul of this lost child be at peace."

Roberto sheathed his sword and joined the priest on the path. The apparition drifted above them through the trees like a tiny moon. Dragon thoughts roared through Roberto's mind. Anna's hands clutched around her belly, the sack of infant bones, a child's restless ghost. Oh Anna, Roberto thought anxiously, what have you done? What have you done?

29

Haven't we been here before?" Mirabella asked, peering at a pair of trailing willow trees at the corner where the corridor of cedars turned to the right. Even though they were blurred, the swaying pale yellow shapes seemed familiar to her. She could hear the trickle and splash of flowing water. They had stopped to rest by a fountain earlier in the day built near two such willows. Was it possible that Fabrizio had led them around in a circle?

"Of course we haven't been here before, Mirabella," Fabrizio said irritably. "Trust me to lead you through the maze. After all, I'm the one who can see clearly."

"Yes, but those trees—"

"There's nothing but trees in this maze. Is it any wonder that they all resemble each other?" They turned the corner past the willows and Fabrizio stopped, slapping his forehead in frustration.

"What's that big white thing over there?" Mirabella asked, knowing the answer.

"Merda!"

"Unusual color for shit." Mirabella could hear the falling water splash more loudly now. It was the fountain again. It had to be. She could just make out the tall white sculpture of Diana rising naked from the water, her hounds spouting mouthfuls of water. "We've gone in one big circle, haven't we?"

Fabrizio continued to swear under his breath. Mirabella felt a dart of sympathy for his injured pride. He had seemed so certain about their direction. Straight on, he argued, even though Mirabella felt the path curve in an arc. When she said something about it, he had sworn on his mother's love that they were making progress.

"It's possible that there's more than one fountain," he ventured. "Perhaps we're farther along than before, but this is a ruse of the maze, to make us turn around and go in a different direction."

Mirabella walked up to the fountain. Diana's cold, serene face slowly came into focus. The eyes stared down at her with a hint of amusement, the stone lips parted in a smile. She held up one hand as if in greeting. A bow was slung over her shoulder, its arrows grasped in her other hand.

"It's the same one," Mirabella said, and sat down on the rim of the fountain, exhausted. She nudged something shiny among the pebbles with the toe of her boot.

"How can you be sure?" Fabrizio argued.

"Here's one of my hairpins," she answered, leaning down and picking up the silver wire. "I must have dropped it when I leaned over to take a drink last time." She laid the hairpin in her lap and with a heavy sigh began to undo her hair. She uncoiled the braids on either side of her head and raked the tangles from her long hair with her fingers. She was tired, very hungry, and strangely disappointed in her journey. All she seemed capable of doing was going around in circles. Even with a young man to lead her, she got nowhere. Where were the adventures she had hoped to find in the maze? Where was her mother? And Lily—where was Lily?

Fabrizio threw himself down on the ground beside her with a groan. "I'm sorry, Mirabella," he said miserably. "I thought this would be easy."

"It's not your fault, Fabrizio," she said, tugging at a snarl. "I'm used to this. In Venice one never asks for, nor gives, directions."

"Why not?"

"Because the city was built by madmen. It's a more complicated maze than this one. There are all the canals, the narrow calli, some only a finger wide. Then there are the dark tunnels that burrow between two buildings and the bridges that lead nowhere and the doors that open only when the tide is low." She laughed.

"But that's crazy."

"Eh, it's like life, isn't it?" Mirabella waved a hand in the air. "How many times have you awakened in the morning determined that from now on life will be different, only to find that, by day's end, you've returned to the same wretched place? The same misery? The same dead end?"

"That's true only if you follow another's path and not your own," said a girl's voice from the other side of the fountain.

Mirabella spun around and squinted through the cascading water. Standing on the path, hands perched on her hips, was a girl with blond hair and bright red ribbons fluttering at her shoulders. A taller man in a red velvet doublet waited by her side.

"Very true, Signorina," Mirabella replied, cheered by the sudden appearance of the pair. "But how do you know the difference? How do you know when you're following your destiny and not someone else's?"

"You must ask yourself what you truly want," the girl answered. "If you know your own course in life, no one can lead you astray."

"Is that all there is to it?" Mirabella asked.

"Indeed," replied the girl. "It's that simple."

"What do I want?" Mirabella asked herself softly. No one had ever asked her that before and she had assumed that she had never had much of a choice. She had always had to take care of Anna and wait for something better to happen. Her heart's desires were nothing but dreams, impossible, hopelessly romantic dreams. Only a fool could make a life based on dreams.

"I'm Zizola," the girl said. "And this is my servant, Giano. What are you doing here? You aren't suffering a curse."

"My name is Mirabella Forsetti. I came to Labirinto with my mother, Anna Forsetti."

"The maskmaker?" Giano asked, his face brightening.

Mirabella groaned. What was it about Anna that made men go rapt when her name was mentioned? Why couldn't she, Mirabella, inspire such a look?

"My mother and I were separated when we entered the maze," Mirabella explained. "I've been trying to find her. I'm sure she needs me."

Zizola arched one pale eyebrow. "Have you no reason of your own to be here?"

The question was a challenge. Account for yourself, Mirabella, it demanded. But she didn't know how.

"Hey! I know you," Fabrizio blurted, pointing to the servant. "You're the pr-pr-"

"Prince?" Giano supplied, with a modest flourish of his hand.

"Prick. You t-t-tried to se-se-"

"Seduce you? Why you depraved spawn of a donkey! I assure you my prick is busy enough with women."

"S-sell me a ma-ma-ma-" Fabrizio struggled to get it out, though his face was flushed with growing frustration.

"Sell you his mamma?" Zizola hooted. "I doubt he has one. Ruffians like this are hatched from serpent's eggs!"

"A map! Sell me a worthless map of the maze!" Fabrizio shouted in one gasping breath. "You cheat!"

"I wanted those masks," Giano snapped gruffly. "They're wasted on a tongue-tripping cafone like you. I, at least, am actor enough to know how to use them!"

With a strangled cry, Fabrizio flung himself at the taller man, his hands reaching for Giano's throat.

The mask of Arlecchino squawked in terror.

"Fanculo, not again!" bellowed Pantelone, the eyes rolling upward. "I hate the water," he screeched as Giano neatly sidestepped Fabrizio's charge, grabbed him by the front of his doublet, and tossed him into the fountain.

But Fabrizio clung to Giano's arms, and as he toppled over the rim, he used his falling weight and a boot squarely planted in Giano's chest to pull Giano off his feet. Giano shouted as he was lifted into a graceful arc over Fabrizio and plunged into the fountain after him. The two men floundered and splashed in the water, alternately standing up and knocking each other down as they traded insults.

"Plague-louse!"

"P-pig's spit!"

"Pile of rotten straw!"

"Br-brothel-bred, n-northern shithead."

"Syphilitic southern trash sired by a hundred fathers!"

Above them, the cool marble statue of Diana looked on in haughty disdain. The masks spluttered and coughed, Pantelone growling in protest and Arlecchino wailing every time Fabrizio was knocked into the water.

"Basta! Enough," shouted Zizola. "Get out of there, both of you! Get out before I ask the maze to turn you into a pair of dogs, spouting water instead of insults."

Giano quickly put his hand over the young man's open mouth. "She can do it," he warned. "We'll be fucked if we don't shut up."

Fabrizio jerked Giano's hand away, but remained silent, his fury barely suppressed behind tightly pressed lips. He climbed out of the fountain glowering at the older man, whose face had resumed a benign expression.

"That's better," Zizola said. She turned to Mirabella and smiled. "Down this path, you will find the Arch of Dreams and beneath it a table set with food. Stay there tonight, as my guest. And in the morning, think hard about your own journey before you set out again. Otherwise"—she jerked her head to the silent Diana—"you will see this fountain over and over again!" Zizola took off one of her red ribbons and tied it around Mirabella's billowing hair, then pinched Mirabella's cheek lightly. "Che bella ragazza," she said appreciatively.

"And what of me?" Fabrizio asked, shaking the water from his ears.

"Go with her. For I can see that you are fellow travelers."

"How d-do you know all this?" Fabrizio asked.

Zizola raised her eyebrows and shrugged, palms upturned.

"She just does." Giano sighed. He looked longingly at the pair of dripping masks. "And to think they could have been mine, Zizola, if only you were willing to sell what you know instead of squandering it."

"Don't be greedy," Zizola snapped. "Your face is puzzle enough without a mask."

"I am but a simple man," he protested.

"Full of complicated tricks," she finished, wagging a finger at him. She took Mirabella's hand. "You must reach the center of the maze before you can leave here."

"My mother—"

"She has her own path. The way is harder for her, but there are others who may be able to help her," Zizola said gently. "You must think of yourself, Mirabella, and look to your own dreams if you ever want to see the outside world again."

"T-tell me," Fabrizio asked, wiping the dripping water from his brow. "C-c-can I rid my-myself of this stu-stu-stutter?"

Zizola nodded gravely. "Yes, but like Mirabella, you must stop treading on the heels of someone else."

"I am my-my-my own man!" Fabrizio replied hotly.

"Perhaps, but you've someone else's stutter," she retorted. "Come on, Giano, it's time we were away. I can feel the gates opening again."

Zizola tugged Giano by a wet sleeve and began walking down the path. The wall of cedars parted at Zizola's touch and the pair entered the opening. Giano gave a quick wave of his hand and the bank of trees closed around them.

"Well, that was interesting," Mirabella said, and, out of habit, touched the bridge of her nose. "Can you see the way to the Arch of Dreams?" she asked Fabrizio.

He shrugged and pointed. "Over there," he said. "Give me your hand, Mirabella, and I'll guide you."

Mirabella took his hand and gave it a friendly squeeze. He didn't squeeze it back. He was silent, rapt in his bad mood, but the warm feel of his hand over hers was still pleasant. She glanced sideways at him, admiring the way the water droplets in his fair curls captured the light of the sun like jewels. She liked his clean profile and the distant melancholy look in his eyes.

There was one thing Mirabella knew she wanted for certain. She wanted to be in love. And what's more, she wanted to be loved in return. Passionately loved, like all the women in the romances she had read. Like the Innamorate of the stage, whose suitors threw flowers at their feet. She gave a wistful smile at Fabrizio's somber face and thought how ridiculous she was to want anything so foolish. Fabrizio's wish was much more practical.

"What did Zizola mean when she said you had someone else's stutter?" she asked suddenly.

"My fa-fa-ther," he said.

"Did he stutter too?"

Fabrizio nodded. "I never stuttered in my life until I was ten years old and brought from Naples to Urbino. I left my mother's home and my aunts, the sun and the sea, and came to live with that c-c-cold ba-bastard in his wre-wretched ca-castello. I was his only son. He wa-wanted me to be a so-soldier like him."

"But you're an actor! Didn't he understand that?" Mirabella asked.

Fabrizio shook his head violently. "No! He only wanted to bend me to his wi-wi-will. But I wa-wa-wasn't very agreeable. I learned to stutter imitating my fa-father in a rage. I did it to m-m-mock him at first. Bu-but after a while, I couldn't stop. He gave me a weapon, but he won the ba-battle."

"You don't stutter when you are alone with me, unless you're talking about your father."

"I don't stutter around women." He flashed her an unexpected grin. "It must be because I love women. All women."

Mirabella blushed, and wondered if Fabrizio could feel the racing of her pulse.

"It's only in the company of men, or when ta-talking about that ba-bastard that I stutter."

"Then Zizola was right. Whether you meant to or not, you have taken your father's place. You travel on his road. His voice is yours. His speech strangles your words. You must stop this," Mirabella said firmly. "You must forget the hurt he caused you. You must take back what was yours from birth, from that first performance you told me about."

"Easier said than accomplished." Fabrizio glowered.

"It is easy. It's what you want!"

"And what of your path, Mirabella?" Fabrizio asked, rounding on her. "I know what you want. I can see it in your face. I can feel it in your hand." He folded her arm back behind her waist and pulled her close to him.

Mirabella struggled weakly in his arms, suddenly frightened. His grip was hard and her wrist hurt. Beneath his angry eyes, she felt exposed. The scent of his body was overwhelming, his strength greater than hers. He was mocking her. Her mother would have known what to do. But Mirabella was not Anna Forsetti. She was not beautiful or tempestuous or experienced.

"Go away!" she said brusquely.

He leaned his face closer. "From my sight."

"Demon with a mask of love," Mirabella answered without thinking. "Fury with Heaven's face!"

"How I curse—"

"How I detest—"

"The day I set eyes on you!" Mirabella said slowly.

Fabrizio grinned, the dark anger gone from his eyes.

"Do you not see it, Mirabella?" he said softly. "Do you not hear it in your voice? You can't help yourself."

"What do you mean?" she asked, breathless.

"You're an actress. All your life you've been waiting to speak those lines to someone."

"An actress?" Mirabella repeated, dazed. "I'm not an actress." She tried to pull away from Fabrizio.

"But you are!" he answered, holding her firmly in his arms.

"How can that be?" Of all the dreams she had squirreled away, this was the one she had hidden deepest. She was afraid even now to let it escape to the surface. "I'm not beautiful. I'm not like my mother."

Fabrizio kissed her gently on the forehead. "The Innamorata has a passion that glows from within, Mirabella. It makes her shine on the stage with radiant beauty. It doesn't matter whether you have good looks, but whether you love the words and the audience with all your heart, with your mouth, your tongue . . ." Fabrizio kissed her on her eyelids, then the tip of her nose, and then, very softly, on the mouth.

Mirabella closed her eyes and received his kiss. The breath caught in her chest and her heart slammed wildly against her ribs. Her skin was a thin shell holding back the torrent of blood that pounded through her veins. She reveled in the smoothness of his lips, in the cool wetness of his tongue sliding past her teeth. She leaned into him, hungry for this new experience. Her body bent like the willow to follow the curves of his. Every poem she had ever read, every play she had ever seen, crowded into her mind, the passionate words rising like heat from the flame.

Muffled cries of protest came from the masks crushed between Mirabella and Fabrizio's clinging bodies. Fabrizio released her and held her hands at arm's length.

"Brava, Mirabella, brava!" shouted Arlecchino. "You're one of us!"

"Of course she is, you simpleton!" scoffed Pantelone. "Anna made her, didn't she? And I shall serve as her papa! Unless, that is"—Pantelone wheezed with excitement—"you would care to be my wife!"

"You old lecher," declared Arlecchino. "She's not for you. She's mine! I love you like sausages . . ."

Fabrizio and Mirabella gazed shyly at each other, ignoring the chattering masks.

"No more scorn, only melting glances," she recited.

"No more wars, only loving touches," he replied.

"Cupid loves once more!"

"And disdain dies forever!"

Mirabella clapped her hands to her mouth to preserve the memory of his kiss. Then she started laughing, a joyous sound that settled on the trees. Something rare had been released from the stronghold of her fantasy. It didn't matter if she was awkward or plain. She had found a source of power. The Innamorata's words transformed her into a ravishing beauty. Love moved like quicksilver in her veins. She brushed the surface of her skin and heard it chime.

"I'm an actress," she said happily.

"How do you feel?" Fabrizio asked her.

She thought for a moment. "Hungry!"

"Then let's go to the Arch of Dreams! We shall celebrate your first performance."

"Perhaps there will be an encore?" she said, with a suggestive lift of one eyebrow.

Fabrizio flashed her a grin and took her hand. "By all means. Every good performance deserves another."

Fabrizio wrapped Mirabella's arm in his and strolled with her down through the corridor of cedars. She had no doubt of her direction now. She was certain that, in the morning when she woke, she would be journeying to the center of the maze. She bid farewell to the marble statue of the virgin goddess, offered a brief prayer for her mother's safety, and then moved eagerly toward the dazzling white columns of the Arch of Dreams.

30

Lorenzo was having a difficult time walking with his usual calm, steady stride. His legs wanted to bolt, to carry him as far from his unusual companions as he could get. But to run would be to admit that there was something unnatural about them, that they were not simply ordinary pilgrims lost in the maze. To run would be to admit he walked beside a three-faced man and a woman who claimed to be a siren.

Ever since Ipnos had pulled him over the wall of the maze, Lorenzo had been trying to choose which face to confront when he spoke to the querulous servant. But it had been impossible. Whenever Lorenzo spoke to one face, it gazed elsewhere while the other two faces regarded him keenly. And when Lorenzo switched his attention to a different face, then that face would ignore him and he would discover that the first face was now taking an interest in the conversation. Ipnos was one man, Lorenzo told himself firmly. All Lorenzo had to do was figure out which face was the real one.

But Ipnos hadn't disturbed Lorenzo's peace of mind half as much as Erminia. She should not have captured his attention at all. After all, she was ugly, a single black brow across her forehead shading her eyes, her hair an unwashed mat of snarls.

But there was something in the scent of her that made Lorenzo light-headed, something in the glance of her piercing blue eyes that made him feel vulnerable. Every time she spoke, his throat constricted with an unbearable sadness. Her voice tore through the seams of the lawyer's facade, threatening to expose the poet beneath.

No. It was not a facade. It was the truth! He had studied law in Bologna. He was no longer a poet. That conceit had been drummed out of him seven years ago. He had no use for metaphor. Poetry had died with Cecilia and the lie she had made of their marriage. He stole a glance at the heavy-bodied woman beside him. If only he didn't have to hear her voice or travel in the wake of her scent, it would be easier.

"Was she beautiful?" asked Erminia, brushing her tangled black hair out of her eyes.

"Who?" Lorenzo asked. His fingers dug channels in his palms in an effort to ignore the pale blue cloud of steam that evaporated with her words.

"Whoever she was that brought you to this state," answered Erminia. "It had to be a woman."

"It usually is," scoffed Ipnos the boy.

Lorenzo pretended not to see the lavender steam exhaling from her nostrils. Beneath her heavy lids, her sapphire eyes probed for secrets.

"Signora, I have no idea what you are talking about."

"That's Signorina, and you do know what I am talking about. You're just being disagreeable. Do you know what happens when you're disagreeable about such things?"

Lorenzo was silent. His nails dug small tears in his palms.

She sighed and a ripple of blue steam filtered through her tangled hair. "Do you know the story of Orpheus?"

"The poet who went to the underworld to bring his wife back from the dead," Lorenzo said. "A fairy tale told by the Greeks."

"More than a fairy tale, my pretty poet."

"I'm a lawyer."

Erminia shrugged. "As you wish. There isn't one of us who hasn't worn a mask for some reason. Look at me. I, too, am not what I seem. But we were speaking of Orpheus. Do you remember what happened?"

Lorenzo tore his gaze away from Erminia's stabbing blue eyes. Tiny fish of green smoke were swimming around her head. His head hurt from trying not to see them. "Something about losing his wife after all."

"After being instructed not to look back as he led her out of the underworld, Orpheus turned around at the last moment to reassure himself that she had followed faithfully behind him. With that glance, he banished his wife back to the underworld for good."

"Doesn't this duckling know anything?" piped Ipnos irritably. "How can you not know the tragedy of Orpheus?"

"Hmmm, sad isn't it?" said Erminia. "But what came after was much worse, dear poet—oh excuse me, lawyer. Well, Orpheus grieved for a while. But wearying of grief, he decided to pretend that he didn't care that he had lost Eurydice. He banished his wife from his heart. He invented a dull religion, turned his back on women, and gave up music, poetry, and pleasure of all kinds. He did just about anything he could think of that would erase forever the love that he had once felt for his wife and his shame at losing her. Twice murdered was Eurydice—first by a snake and then by Orpheus. To deny one's true nature and the gifts given you by the gods is to tempt disaster. You cannot hide behind the mask forever."

Lorenzo coughed, trying to clear the thickening in his throat. Memories of Cecilia flashed unbidden across his eyes. Her golden hair, the blushing skin of her breasts, the deep pink of her nipples. He had once written sonnets to the smooth skin of her belly. He shuddered.

"What happened to Orpheus?" he asked stiffly.

"Orpheus came to believe so strongly in his own stern mask that he ignored that god who required pleasure as a form of worship. Insulted, Bacchus grew angry and sent the maenads to teach him a lesson. With their bare hands, they tore Orpheus's body from limb to limb and cast the severed pieces in different places. His head drifted downriver. It was fished out, stuck on a pedestal, and Orpheus, never one to keep quiet for long, started to hand out judgments and prophecies to anyone with a coin."

"Until that scumbag Apollo grew jealous, of course, and shut us down," groused Ipnos the wicked. "We were doing a great business until then! Now we're here, just scraping by with these miserable pilgrims. Oh, for the glory days!"

"Signorina," Lorenzo said, "I don't see what any of this has to do with me. I am here to find my servant Giano and then return to my office of law. I'm really pressed for time. I thank you both for your combined interest in my affairs, but I assure you I am in no need of assistance. Now, perhaps we may amiably part company and I can be on my way once more. Good day to you."

Lorenzo scarcely realized that he had begun speaking faster and faster, trying to shove the strange pair and their tales away, trying to remember the simple, real reason he had entered the maze. The path split just in front of him and he was convinced that if he could just keep talking until he reached the fork, he'd be able to escape.

"I wouldn't do that if I was you," warned Ipnos the boy.

"Do what?" Lorenzo asked brusquely.

"Go down that path. You'd find it very unpleasant. Listen, and you can hear the dragon bellowing. Probably gobbling up some poor noddle of a pilgrim. You'd best stick it out with us," finished Ipnos the fool with a wild bob of his head.

Lorenzo pulled nervously on the lock of white hair. He heard a distinct rumbling that might have been thunder or growling. The breeze brought a whiff of peppery smoke. He strained his ears. Was that someone screaming? There were no dragons, he told himself sternly. Just as there were no sirens or three-faced men. But still he hesitated at the fork.

"Come, come, poet, accept your punishment like a man," cajoled Ipnos the boy.

"Punishment?" asked Lorenzo. "Punishment for what? I've done nothing wrong."

"Seven years ago, you committed a crime!" exclaimed Ipnos the wicked.

"You lie in your throat," Lorenzo retorted angrily. He fumbled for a sword that wasn't there. "I killed Giampaolo Vittuci in a fair duel. Who could have known that Cecilia would throw herself between our swords? The tribunal deemed it an accident and my honor was restored."

"Cock's dung on that!" snorted Ipnos the boy. "I don't care about your duels and sluts! Your crime was to fall silent!"

"She wasn't a slut. She was my wife," Lorenzo snapped.

"You killed your wife?" Erminia asked in amazement. The vaporous cloud turned grey around her lips.

"There is no one who can state that with certainty," Lorenzo said, raking his fingers through the lock of white hair. "I found Cecilia in our bed with Giampaolo, my closest friend. Honor demanded that I call him out to duel. While we were fighting, she ran between the blades. His sword struck her first. Mine was the second blow. I never intended to hurt her. She died, but from which of our two swords, it was never known."

"Twice murdered," murmured Erminia. "First by the snake, then by the husband."

"Ah, here we are!" announced Ipnos the boy cheerfully. "My master's home at last."

They had reached a stone grotto surrounded by verdant ferns. Small marble sculptures of fauns and satyrs stood in carved niches all around the rim of the grotto's opening, lit from within by a flickering green light that washed over the rough wall like the sun's rays wavering beneath the surface of the sea. Here and there, nestled in the crannies of the grotto's roof, glimmered tiny, phosphorescent mushrooms. As they stepped into the entrance of the grotto, Lorenzo looked down at his hands and saw that his skin was a watery green.

"Remember your promise." Erminia nudged Ipnos. "I will do this task for Orpheus, but my sisters and I must have the use of our voices."

"Only if you succeed with this dried fig," snapped Ipnos the boy. "But first you've got to take your tongue-lashing."

"What other injury can a man with no arms do me?" Erminia said tartly.

"Keep a civil tongue in your head, Siren, or you'll lose it forever," Ipnos the boy warned, wagging a finger.

Erminia rolled her eyes, but remained silent.

They walked quietly into the deeper recesses of the grotto. Here the air was cold and clammy and smelled of salt and fish. Lorenzo heard Orpheus before he could see him. The light tenor voice echoed through the cavernous grotto, rising and falling with the cadence of sung poetry. Lorenzo felt a flutter of panic as the cool, seductive voice reached into his heart, pulling at his soul, threatening to unravel his lawyerly dignity. He struggled against the voice, training his eyes to study the details of his surroundings as he labored to ignore the power of Orpheus's song.

The head of Orpheus rested on a tall pedestal of white marble mottled with blue veins and rust-colored molds. The head was surprisingly large and commanding, the neck forming a thick, powerful base draped with a linen cloth. The cheeks were long, smooth planes, the forehead was broad beneath the heavy, oiled tresses. The nose was formidable, jutting proudly over a pair of thick, sardonic lips. The eyebrows were combed upward, accentuating almond eyes that at the moment were closed as Orpheus sang.

Placed in smaller roughly hewn niches in the roof of the cavern were other heads, their eyes closed as though listening. As Lorenzo stared up at these busts he realized that not all of them were carved in the style of antiquity. Some were curiously familiar. Wasn't that head up there his old friend Moreto Romaneti? He had been a great poet once, gregarious to a fault, expansive in all his gestures. He had lost everything in a mad passion for gambling and drink. The last Lorenzo had heard, Moreto had disappeared, fleeing angry creditors.

Ipnos and Erminia waited quietly at Lorenzo's side until Orpheus finished his singing. As the last echoes of his voice died away, Orpheus snapped open his eyes, revealing golden pupils. The eyes slid sideways to Lorenzo, whose heart pounded in a burst of panic at the fiery gold stare. The lips formed a sneer.

"Hah! What have you caught in your net, Ipnos? Two stinking herrings! A babbling poet and a slip-tongued siren! By Hermes, Leucosia, you couldn't have made yourself any more ugly. What a fat donkey's behind you've got there! Whoa, I'll bet you were ridden to town often enough!"

"Ever gracious, Orpheus," Erminia said. "A pleasure as always to kneel before you." She bowed low to hide her indignation.

"And what about you, sniveling poet?" The eyes swiveled to Lorenzo's face. "Some unripe plum stuck up your ass, eh? Bunging up the plumbing? And where then does the shit go?"

Lorenzo stood speechless, blood draining from his face. Surely he was dreaming. He could hardly bear to meet the golden stare.

"It all goes to your head, you . . . you . . ." The eyes swiveled again to find Ipnos. "What do the Italians call it again?"

"Testa di merda!" Ipnos the wicked crowed.

"Shithead! That's what you've become," snapped Orpheus. "A head full of shit! You shut off the words like a man closing the gate of his asshole, but they're festering in your head and every time you exhale there's the stench of feces! What do you think about that?"

"I am at a loss for words," Lorenzo replied.

"No! By Hermes, you will answer me!" ordered Orpheus. "What am I?"

"A construct of stone—"

"No! The truth now, poet!"

"A mask—"

"Try again. Pluck the cork!"

"A puppet—"

"Puppet!" shrieked Orpheus. "He calls me a puppet! A crude toy with some peasant's hand up my rear!" The gold eyes narrowed into gleaming slits of malice. "Listen, you wretch, I am the poet Orpheus, son of Calliope, creator of music. When I sing, the world turns as I please, wild animals become meek and even the damned shades are so charmed they cease their endless wailing. You are a stuck-up piece of dried fruit, ignorant from the neck down. Better your head should rest here and I make use of what you squander! Oh to have back those simple bodily functions, to feel the stirring of pleasure even in the relief of one's bowels. I ask you again, poet, and this time answer with your whole self, what am I?"

Words twitched in Lorenzo's mouth and banged against the gate of his clenched teeth. Speak! Speak! a voice whispered in his ear. He touched the smooth velvet of his doublet and remembered the sensation of Cecilia's smooth thighs beneath his palms. He snapped his fist closed, the nails digging into his palms, gripped by a different memory. Cecilia wearing a ribbon of blood around her neck. The words shriveled and crawled back into the empty cavity of his heart. He must speak the truth.

"I am not a poet. I'm a lawyer. And you are a thing such as I have seen on the stage at Carnevale," Lorenzo said. "A hollow thing of paper and wood, a voice piped in from behind a screen. You are a mask intended to frighten and amuse the unlettered."

"And what think you of the heads above me that sit in silent judgment of your follies?" asked Orpheus in a cold voice. "Do you not know some of them?"

Lorenzo glanced up quickly and then away. "No."

"No?" Orpheus said with a sneer. "Can it be that you have uttered your first lie?"

"There is one that might resemble a man I once knew," Lorenzo admitted reluctantly. "Moreto Romaneti. But the likeness is a poor one and so I cannot claim in all honesty to know the face."

"And I tell you, in all honesty," Orpheus sneered, "that it is indeed the head of your friend Moreto. And your head will join him in these ranks of speechless and worthless poets unless you remember what it is to give honor to me and to the art which we both must serve."

"Such a waste it would be to join his noble head to that silent lot," Erminia interrupted. "Perhaps, gracious Orpheus, it would be far better to rescue an admirer than to cut off his head. Haven't you had enough of this dreary lot?"

"Better than having to listen to the cries of their stillborn poetry." Orpheus snorted. "I have some sympathy for those who strangled their work with excess. In the grip of demons, they pickled their verses in wine, or sold them to whores, to gamblers, and, even worse, to publishers. But this one! This one has no vices except to chew on a dried turd he calls truth. Ipnos, come here and use your finger to scratch my ears," Orpheus shouted. "Even now this mute poet torments me with his thoughts."

Ipnos scuttled quickly across the room and gently wiggled his little fingers in Orpheus's ears. Orpheus closed his eyes and sighed with relief.

"Allow me the opportunity to assist in the restoration of this man's poetic voice," Erminia said.

"What? Speak up, I can't hear you!" Ipnos hastily removed his fingers.

"I said, allow me the chance to restore the poet's voice. After all, a siren can be very persuasive!"

"He's deaf, I tell you," Orpheus insisted. "Dried shit instead of beeswax stuck in his ears. Better to let the maenads finish him off! I'll put his head up there, next to his friend."

"But, Orpheus, if the man is truly a gifted poet, his voice must be heard. How long has it been since there was one to sing your praises?" ventured Ipnos the boy. "Why not let the siren try and make of him a believer again?"

"What's in it for you?" Orpheus asked, turning his golden glare on Erminia.

Erminia smiled and bowed slightly. "Pax, oh noble head. The Sirens' voices restored and permission to return to our home."

"You screwed it up last time!"

"Because I was asked to remain silent. A siren's skill is in her voice. Let me use it now to free us both. I will give you back your poet, and you will give us back our songs."

Orpheus chewed his lower lip, considering.

Erminia turned to Lorenzo. "Poet, let me save you!" she urged. "Say yes, and we may both walk away from the maze free! Don't become one of these dried-up heads!" Greenish clouds streamed like serpents from her lips and rose to touch the faces of the stilled heads above.

Lorenzo glanced up, his eyes following the trail of the mist. As it settled on the impassive features of Moreto Romaneti, the lids opened slowly and dull eyes gazed down at Lorenzo. The lips parted with a dry crack, but no sound came out. Lorenzo shuddered and lowered his gaze.

"Speak, poet!" From beneath the siren's heavy dark brow, her sharp crystalline eyes stabbed him, begged him, hungered for him. It was how Cecilia's eyes had spoken to him when she lay dying.

"How did Moreto die?" Lorenzo asked Orpheus, avoiding Erminia's eyes.

Orpheus curled his lip into a contemptuous sneer. "He gambled, and thinking his art of no great worth, put it up as a stake. He lost to the maenads. They tore him apart, as they will you, and tossed the head up there where you see it."

Lorenzo's joints ached as though he could already feel the pulling grasp of the maenads.

"Let me try, Orpheus!" Erminia urged.

"Who better to teach the truth to a poet than the mistress of lies?" said Ipnos the boy. "Aren't you getting tired of these dead heads?" Ipnos the fool asked. "They're so depressing, not to mention creepy! Even a dirty epigram or two would help to liven the place up," said Ipnos the wicked.

Orpheus pursed his fleshy lips and made annoyed smacking noises. "Oh, all right! You know it's hard for me to refuse you, Ipnos, when you scratch my ears so nicely. But you have only two days, Leucosia. If you fail this time, you will not only lose your voice, but your life. I'll stick your head up there along with the rest of the losers!"

Lorenzo saw Erminia touch her neck and then slide her hand to push back her tangled hair.

"I am a siren, Orpheus. My voice will be heard, even if it is only by one man. I will show him the way back to the lie that gives voice to the truth!"

"Just hope he doesn't drown first!"

"I will see to it!" Erminia said.

"Then take him away, for the babbling of his thoughts is driving me mad! Ipnos, my ears! Give me your fingers to scratch!"

Ipnos the fool winked broadly at Erminia as he wiggled his index fingers into Orpheus's ears. "Good luck," he whispered to her.

Erminia shrugged as though she didn't need anything so capricious as luck. Then she grabbed Lorenzo's hand and, jerking the sullen man into motion, dragged him out of the grotto.

They stood again on the wooded path between the cedars. The yellow sunlight was nearly blinding after the wavering green shade of the grotto. Erminia released him, walked a little ways down, and raised her head as she caught the scent of something on the wind. He saw her in-hale deeply, her hands pressed first to her heart, then her cheeks. She turned to him and grinned.

"The sea! It is here! Come, poet, follow me, and I will be the cause of your rebirth. In the salt of your mother's womb, you grew into a poet. You died to yourself seven years ago. But through me and the salt of my womb the sea, I swear on the siren's song, your poetry will live again!"

Lorenzo moved toward her on stiff, wooden legs. His face, his chest, his arms felt encased in a brittle hard shell, but something soft and aching yielded in his breast. Blood gushed from invisible wounds newly opened, and a flood of rusty words clotted on his tongue. He broke out in a drenching sweat and was suddenly, inexplicably afraid that the skin of his face would dissolve with the salty droplets.

Erminia stretched out her hand to take his.

"Have courage, my poet," she breathed, and a pale wreath of golden light encircled his brow.

She clasped his hand firmly and led Lorenzo down the path through the trees to where the sea beckoned her.

31

Zizola!" Giano called, his hand cupped around his mouth to force the sound higher. He could see her feet dangling over the edge of a platform mounted atop a slender pole. Her skirts fluttered nois-ily in the wind. Ravens circled her, their glistening black heads cocked curiously. "Zizola, come down!" he shouted up again.

She bent down and her face appeared over the edge between her feet, her blond hair whipping in the gusting wind. "Come up!" she waved.

"Madonna Santissima, not on your fucking life," he muttered, eyeing the tiny wooden ladder hammered into the slender pole. She was a cathedral wall high in the air, perched on a platform only St. Simon could call home. The pole was shuddering in the stiffening wind. He'd have to be mad to set foot on the ladder.

"Come up here, you scaredy cat!" Zizola taunted.

"I'm not scared!"

"Pulchinella! Stuffed chicken!"

"I'll have you know I've pissed from taller heights!" he boasted.

"Cluck, cluck!" She flapped her arms. The ravens echoed her, cawing harshly.

Shamed into action, Giano started up the ladder, swearing violently under his breath. He clung with sweating hands to the wooden rungs. He refused to look down, but kept his eyes firmly planted on the rung immediately above his hand. As he climbed, the spirited wind played little tricks with his clothes, running cold fresh fingers under his shirt, unraveling the knots of his ties and even the strings that held his hose in place. With his hands clinging desperately to the rungs, he could neither pull up his drooping hose nor pull down his billowing shirt. By the time he had reached the platform he was out of breath, his legs and arms ached, and he felt as molested by the wind as a maid at a crowded market.

Zizola was humming to herself, her legs swinging merrily over the edge of the platform. A raven who had boldly joined her, flew off as Giano's head appeared in view over the edge of the platform. Zizola watched him haul himself onto the wooden boards and crawl over to where she sat.

"Mamma mia, Santa Maria della Grazie," he intoned. "What the hell are you doing up here!"

"Are you afraid of heights?" Zizola asked.

"No!" he snapped. "It's not the height that makes me nervous. It's just the big empty space between me and the ground! Personally, I like it filled with floors and walls and maybe a decent chair or two!"

"Look, Giano! Look at the maze from here!" she exclaimed.

Giano pulled himself slowly into a sitting position, his long spindly legs tucked up close to his body. Over the tops of his knees, he could glimpse the earth spread out below him, wide green bands of the cedar and cypress walls knotted into one enormous and intricate pattern.

"Che bella vista!" Zizola said in awe. "Look, over there." She pointed to a tiny figure running down a narrow corridor.

Peering down, Giano could see that the poor soul was about to encounter a dead end, that the way back to the right turn was a long one.

"That pilgrim has just taken the wrong turn," Zizola said with a note of sympathy in her voice. "How easy it is to see that from up here. To the pilgrim on the ground, there is only the little bit of the path before and the one behind. Nothing makes any sense—it's all so much madness, like luck or a curse. That's how my life has always been. Passed from hand to hand since birth, suffering on one street or another, tossed like one of these blind pilgrims from disaster to disaster!"

"And now?"

"Now I can see my way. Now, for the first time, I know where I am going. I am here above the chaos in a place that is mine. And I wouldn't trade it for any coin in the world."

"It is pretty," Giano said with a grudging admiration. Some time in the past, a master's hand had laid out an intricate pattern of knots with cedar corridors and coiled paths of cypress and oak that encircled grottos, olive groves, and fields. Silvery lines of small streams sliced symmetrical angles from one side of the huge maze to another.

"It seems so orderly from up here. It makes me a little sad for the buggers lost down there. Wait! Is the maze changing?" Before Giano's eyes, a field opened up where none had been before and the entire maze shifted, the walls rippling as it adjusted itself into a different, distinctly new pattern.

"Yes, that's what I've been watching," said Zizola. "It's part of the sorcery of the maze. As each pilgrim enters, he brings to it his own imagination, his own fears, his own twisted path, his own luck, his own curse. The maze replies, like an actor improvising a scene. Dramas and comedies everywhere!"

"Have you become the Maestra? Handing out lines and scenes to be played by the actors in their dramas? Is that why we've been wandering around the maze, spouting advice instead of getting straight to the center?" Giano asked.

"Yes. I can't help it. Look, Giano," she said, pointing. "They seem so small, so helpless from up here. And yet I think each one of them deserves a happy ending. Life should be full of the good things, a warm bed . . ."

"Sex!"

"Food!"

"Sex!"

"You said that already," Zizola grinned.

"Sorry. How about love then? That encompasses all of it. You can love the roasted capon or the pretty wife of your neighbor, the act of sucking on peaches or your neighbor's pretty wife's—"

"Basta!" Zizola laughed. "You've said enough!" She looked down wistfully. "I think it's time to go to the center. I've helped as many as I can, set the stage for enough dramas, now they must help themselves."

"What about you, Zizola?" Giano said.

"Me?" the girl asked, surprised.

"Has your own drama begun? How do you know that you, too, are not taking a wrong turn? From up here, you can see the lives of others. But what of your own life, Zizola?"

"Both." She made for the ladder. "I have already played my role."

"How do you know?" Giano demanded as she prepared to descend.

Zizola laughed. "I just do!" With that, her head ducked below the ledge, leaving Giano quite alone. He chanced one last look at the maze over the edge of the platform. He watched in breathless wonder as the pattern changed again, the green twisted paths giving way to a blue ocean that miraculously appeared on the far side of the maze.

32

Zolfo jogged down the narrow streets of the city Labirinto, clutching his churning belly. This was something about being human that he didn't like. All along the road to Labirinto his body had betrayed him, forcing him to leave behind little pieces of his new self. He had wanted to gather the black piles up, swallow them like coals back into his body. But each time he had reached down to the steaming pieces, he had felt a human shudder of disgust. Leave it, an unknown voice had whispered, and he slunk away from the pieces, upset to be abandoning them.

When he was in the maze, he would change that, he decided. His human body would not do such a thing. And neither would he be commanded by other ungovernable parts of his quarrelsome body, he thought, glancing down at the bulge below his waist. That creature, too, had awakened him on the road, clamoring with terrifying urgency. Only holding it in his hands had eventually pacified it, though in its tantrum it had wept milky tears. Zolfo knew that to make others like himself, he needed his little piece of flesh. But first, he had to teach it to obey.

The dark, narrow alley ended, thrusting Zolfo out into the bright sunlight that spilled over the huge Piazza del Labirinto. He stopped, blinded by the golden glare. He threw up his hand to shield his eyes and entered the piazza. Across the sea of black cobblestones, he could see the towering gates of the maze and the undulating green wall of cedars. Beneath the soles of his feet, he could feel the stones' subtle pulse of power. He knew the pungent scent of the cedars, tasted the pitch of their sap in the air. He began to run.

The piazza was crowded with pilgrims awaiting the opening of the gates. Zolfo shoved past them, knocking some out of his way in his hurry. A chorus of obscenities followed him, but he was oblivious. He had barely seen the woman who slapped him hard across the face. His outstretched hands had brushed against her breasts as he rushed past her. The slap stung, and Zolfo stopped, shocked and outraged.

"What are you?" Zolfo glared at her coarse face. She was taller than he, her body lumpy in the drab clothes.

"A finer piece of business than you'll ever get!" she said, shaking a finger at him. "What are you?"

"I am a man."

"More's a boy, I'd say," she scoffed.

"No! I am a man," Zolfo shouted.

"Only one way to know, amore mio," she said with a laugh, and clapped her hand between Zolfo's legs. He gasped, a shiver running through his body. "How much will you pay me, amore mio, to prove your manhood?" she whispered in his ear.

"Lie down," he hissed between gritted teeth.

"Here, amore? Surely we can find an alley—"

"Not you," Zolfo stammered, trying to edge away from the woman's groping hand.

"Ah," she said with a wicked grin and another squeeze that set Zolfo groaning. "But see where this one has his own ideas. Surely you can part with a coin or two to satisfy him?"

Anger bristled in Zolfo's veins, blood turned to thin ribbons of magma. The pupils of his eyes flashed a brilliant red beneath the blond brows. Heat traveled along the surface of his skin and steam whisked away from his palms. He grabbed the woman's hand and she gave a small scream as his fingers scalded her wrist. She stared into his burning eyes and panic swept across her face.

"Il Diavolo," she cried, and, jerking her hand free from his grasp, fled through the crowds.

Alone once more, Zolfo continued toward the maze, his gaze set on the wooden gates. As he marched across the piazza, he became aware of an old man sitting on a stool near the gate. The man was shabby in every respect except one: a pair of black leather boots trimmed with a band of red and yellow diamonds. The old man was nodding at the younger women, who remained oblivious to his presence, his fingers sketching benedictions to their beauty.

As Zolfo approached the gate, the old man glanced up at him, interest sparking in the beady eyes.

"Going in?" he demanded.

Zolfo placed his hands against the gates, anticipating they would open at his command. They didn't. He frowned and pushed harder, but the gates remained firmly shut. Growing angry, Zolfo let the heat of his rage enter his palms, pressed against the gates. The skin paled and then grew red as flame, but still the wooden gates resisted. Suddenly Zolfo was aware of something that was preventing him from entering.

But what was it? he wondered. It was too small a thing to be counted among the greater elements of magic: earth, fire, air, and water. And yet it was strong enough to deny him entrance. Zolfo snarled and drew more magma into his veins.

At one corner of the gate a Terminus stone groaned to life. Zolfo looked down and saw its rough features carved in the rock face. It was a guardian, a creature fashioned like him out of rock and alchemy, set by the maker's hand to maintain a border of magic around the maze.

"None may enter until the Maestro allows it," the Terminus rumbled.

"I am the master!" Zolfo answered, thrusting his chin high in the air.

The Terminus huffed a slow, rumbling laugh. "No. You are a curse."

"I am a man!" Zolfo protested, and beat against the gates. Carbon ash flaked away from the glowing red skin of his pounding fists, but the wooden gate was uncharred.

"Men have souls," the Terminus said through grinding teeth. "But there is no such light in you. You are a servant, like me. Powerful, but a servant nonetheless."

"Who prevents me from entering?" Zolfo demanded. He kicked the Terminus, furious as a shock of pain traveled up his leg. "Open! I command it!"

The Terminus rumbled with laughter.

"Stai calme!" The old man spoke up in a quavering voice, waving his knobby fingers at Zolfo's reddened face. "Be calm, ragazzo. You aren't the first to beat at the gates of Labirinto and demand to be let in, you know. There's no way of convincing them in there, even if you was to agree to kiss the Pope's arse. Take it from me, the only game is to wait and watch for a chance to slip in."

"Fuck yourself," Zolfo shouted, not knowing where the words came from, but finding them immediately satisfying.

The old man scraped his fingers beneath his chin. "Eh, bravo. A young man's curse to an old one. I would fuck anything you liked if I could get inside those gates that are shut tighter than a nun's hole. Oh, would I fuck. I know they're waiting for me in there. Dozens of beauties, mermaids, sirens, nymphs. When I get my hands on them . . ." He half rose from his stool, grabbing the air with his shaking hands, but the excitement proved too much and he was seized by a coughing fit. Wheezing, he fell back onto his stool.

Zolfo resumed pounding on the gate. After a while, the old man tugged on his shirt.

"Listen, ragazzo, I'll make you a deal!" he panted.

"What sort of deal can a bag of bones like you make with a man like me?" Zolfo sneered.

"Hey, you're not the only one with a prick. The rest of me may be falling down but that, by God, still works! Do you want to get in there or not?"

Zolfo pondered the question, his chin resting on his fist. He riffled through his collection of human thought, searching for an answer to his unexpected dilemma. A thread of words came to him. "Bene. The two will wash the face."

"Eh?" the old man barked, a hand cuffed around his ear. "What nonsense is that you're saying?"

"These two hands," Zolfo said, and reached out for the old man's face.

"Don't touch me!" The old man reared back.

"I have it wrong?" Zolfo asked.

"Santa Madonna, you certainly do. You may be a pretty boy, but I'm no country priest or pope. I don't go that way."

"What way?"

"Where are you from, the South?"

"Amalfi."

"That explains it," the old man said, pinching his fingers together disgustedly.

Zolfo was hopelessly confused. "Are you going to help me or not?"

"That depends. Are you going to help me?"

"Yes. I will wash one hand against the other—"

"Ah! And together the two will wash the face!" The old man grinned, showing his mostly toothless gums. "You help me, I help you. Why didn't you say that in the first place?"

"I thought I did," Zolfo answered irritably.

"Quick now, bend down and let me up on your back," the old man commanded, reaching up his spindly arms to grab Zolfo's shoulders. He pulled Zolfo down and scrambled up on his back. Zolfo wrinkled his nose at the fetid smell of the old man's clothes and the uncomfortable intimacy of his clutching hands. "My knee tells me the moment just before the gates open. It aches something awful, and then I know that the doors to paradiso are about to open." He was whispering loudly in Zolfo's ear, spraying saliva on the word *paradiso.*

Zolfo wiped his damp ear. "Then why haven't you gone in already?" he asked.

"Because I can't walk fast enough. With my limp, the gates close before I can enter, and all these other pricks shove me out of the way. But not this time! No, this time your young legs will carry me into the maze. I'll let you know when to start running."

Zolfo waited, shifting from one tired foot to another. The old man had his legs clamped like a vise around Zolfo's waist. Zolfo heard a low rumble and felt a deep-throated vibration carried through the soles of his feet. The Terminus was laughing at him.

Zolfo was about to kick it when the old man slapped him hard across the rump with his walking stick and shouted: "Go, you ass, go! The gates are opening!"

Zolfo bolted forward, his flank on fire where the old man had struck him. But he quickly forgot the pain as he saw the gates quiver and begin to open with a loud clang. Across the piazza, the pilgrims were seized by a collective panic. They cried out, desperate fingers pointing to the gates, and then they began to run, leaving their belongings scattered over the piazza like the remnants of a sacked village.

"Go, goddamn it! Get in quick!" the old man barked, and twisted Zolfo's ear. "They won't stay open for long!"

Zolfo hoisted the old man higher on his hips and ran along the width of the huge gate as it swung slowly back, trying to reach the opening before the pilgrims crowded it completely. He was knocked to one side by a barrel-chested peasant with a rake. Recovering, Zolfo shoved aside an elderly woman hobbling with her walking stick. He was caught up in the panic of the crowd, a horrible anxiety far worse than the hunger for flesh that tore through his veins. He must enter the gates. He must!

Zolfo reached the lip of the gate and forged a path through the crowd, the old man beating off pilgrims with his walking stick. The Terminus brayed with mocking laughter and the ground quaked as Zolfo inched his way through the crowd into the open space. Halfway through, captured in the thickened stream of pilgrims, he heard a loud clang and the scrape of iron hinges as the gates prepared to close again. Zolfo was nearly lifted off his feet as the crowd surged into the maze.

"You've done it, boy!" the old man cried out. "We're in!"

Zolfo chanced one glance over his shoulder and saw the gates closing behind him. He stopped shoving, rooting his feet to the ground
while he let the desperate stream of pilgrims split and pass on either side
of him. They fanned out in a wide arc, all of them disappearing rapidly
down different paths.

Zolfo felt a moment of vertigo as the power in the maze shifted, ac-
commodating the cursed lives of new pilgrims. Zolfo heard the drum
of a man's heartbeat reverberating through the earth, and if he listened
closely, he heard a second heartbeat, faint and quick. Two sources of
magic at work here—connected, but different—one old and one young.
But which one had tried to keep him out? Zolfo wondered.

"Go on then, boy. Don't lose your nerve now!" the old man ordered,
slapping his walking stick over Zolfo's thigh.

Zolfo took a few steps forward, knowing that for him it did not matter which path he took. He would arrive at the center. That's where
Zolfo would fulfill his purpose as a curse and then reign as a man. The
wind gusted through him like the exhalation of a forge, and he felt the
heat rise in his core.

"No, you ass, that way!" the old man wheezed.

Zolfo, suddenly aware of the unnecessary weight, grasped the spindly
legs around his waist with scalding palms. The old man yelped with the
sudden, searing pain, unlocked his viselike grip on Zolfo's waist, tumbled from Zolfo's back, and fell on the path, swearing. Zolfo didn't turn
around. He kept walking down the cool green corridor of trees, the
shimmering heat of his body withering the tips of the leaves as he
passed.

GLI EORI,
THE HEROES

How true it is that for every plan man makes,
Fortune makes another.

—*Cardinal Bibbiena, "La Calandria"*

33

In the dimming twilight, Anna stood on the bank of the river and scooped out handfuls of white clay embedded in the dark mud. She threw back the fawn's skin from her shoulders and smeared the wet clay on her arms, her legs, and her throat. Excitement threaded her veins. The night was fast approaching when they would begin the ritual of the hunt.

The ritual began by drinking wine until it overflowed the rims of their mouths and stained their white, clay-covered throats with crimson. The drowsy torpor that assailed the maenads during the day would be replaced with a fever born of the quickening breath of the wine and the sting of Bacchus's biting kiss. Then the drums would sound their slow ponderous beat, the leader would cry out her high-pitched ululations, and the hunt would begin.

Bacchus was generous to them, his divine hand guiding wild prey into their snares. Last night it had been a panther, his black velvet coat sleek as the shadows. The maenads followed the trail of his musky scent along the fringes of the dead oak forest until Bacchus lured him into the sacred olive grove. There they had quickly circled the beast, chanting and rattling their spears. The panther had raked the mask from the lead hunter with his steel-grey claws and torn deep furrows in her face. The screams of the fallen woman had joined in chorus with the panther's defiant squalls.

Anna stopped spreading the white clay on her arms. A strange mixture of emotions warred within her: elation and pleasure at the ecstasy of the hunt and horror at the memory of the mutilated panther and the dying woman, her true face drowned in blood. Her broken mask lay on the grass like the panther's legs and paws and tail when the maenads had torn it to pieces. Anna could still taste the raw flesh on her tongue, still smell the strong metallic odor of blood. With painful deliberation, she lifted a hand toward her masked face. If she could touch the unfamiliar face that curved so intimately over her own, these fearful images would stop.

Suddenly Bacchus was there. He caught her hand in his and placed it against his heart. His hairless chest was smooth, the skin warm and oiled. Through her fingertips, she could feel his heart rapping out an invitation to the hunt. He grinned at her, his midnight eyes capturing the doubt in her eyes and banishing it. She tilted her head back and he bit her lower lip and sucked it hard, drawing blood. The taste of wine and his saliva trickled into her mouth with each thrust of his tongue. A fire erupted in her belly and spread its flames to her thighs and her breasts. He released her and was gone.

The solemn drums quickened their pace and the reed pipes played shrilly, calling the maenads together. The lead hunter raised high her thyrsus and shook its dry rattles over the band. They waited restlessly as Bacchus held the bowl of wine above their heads. He gave it first to the leader of the hunt. Head tilted back, she gulped steadily until the wine dribbled down the sides of her chin. She lowered the bowl at last and, with a reluctant sigh, passed it to the next woman, who drank as deeply. And so the bowl passed from hand to hand, from mouth to mouth, and was never emptied.

Anna took the bowl between her white hands and closed her eyes as she inhaled the fragrant wine. Eagerly she tipped the wine down her throat. Like the god's kiss it scorched her lips like a mouthful of flames. Her lungs clamored for air, but still she drank, swallowing rapidly until she felt the wine fill the dark hollow of her belly. She gagged as wine bubbled over her tongue and gushed down the sides of her mouth. And only then did she pull the bowl away from her lips and pass it to the next woman.

Anna staggered, her body quaking with the wine's intoxicating rush. She was flooded with wine, and yet her mouth was hot and dry. She could drink until she drowned in its fiery sweetness and yet there remained a desperate thirst for more.

The leader of the hunt saluted Bacchus. Some of the maenads picked up spears, others carried the small drums and the rattles. A few, like Anna, carried the torches to light the way. The leader shook the pinecones on the thyrsus, the frenzied rattles sounding a warning like a swarm of wasps, and the drums beat out a slow, determined rhythm. Small animals scattered through the underbrush and the shrill pipes flushed the birds from the trees into the darkening twilight.

By the time the maenads reached the sacred olive grove, night had covered most of the sky, leaving only a faint lavender edge on the far horizon. The torches cast bright orange blooms across the twisted trunks of the ancient trees and the small pale leaves flickered like tiny flames. As the maenads entered the sacred grove, the leader caught sight of a young lioness pelting through the trees and whooped loudly. She began to run, her body loping close to the ground. Behind her, the women separated into two strands, circling the grove from opposites sides, closing a ring of hunters around the animal.

They tightened the circle and, with a cry, moved inward to the heart of the olive grove. Anna saw the lioness crouching amid the tangled branches of the tightly packed trees, her round ears flattened against her skull and her lips drawn back in a snarl. Her emerald eyes glowed in the circle of firelight. At her side gleamed a second pair of eyes: a cub huddled against its mother's flank. With a desperate lurch, the lioness twisted away from the trees and the pair began to run, stretched into pale gold streaks against the dark olive trees. Spurred on by the drums and the cries of the other women, Anna ran, following the lioness and her cub. Blood boiled in her veins and she let loose a trilling cry that seemed to explode like a shower of white-hot arrows.

The night had closed quickly around Roberto and Don Gianlucca while they made their way through the dreary forest of dying oaks. There were no stars or moon to light their way, only the faint glimmer of the Tago illuminating the path between the decaying trees. They heard the drums and the first piercing cries of the hunt as they reached the edge of the forest. At the sound, the Tago's incandescent body flared with a blue-white flame.

"Santa Madonna! What is that?" Roberto asked in alarm.

"Maledizione!" Don Gianlucca spat. "Tago, tell me, is Anna among them? Has she taken up the mask and become one of his?"

The Tago nodded, a tiny finger pointing to the olive grove. The shining orb drifted closer and stopped where the boundary of oaks gave way to a grassy field.

"What holds you back, Tago? Show us Anna!"

The Tago shook its head, its childish features mournful.

"You can't leave the forest, can you?" Don Gianlucca asked.

It shook its head, staring longingly out at the olive grove.

"What has happened to Anna?" Roberto demanded, unnerved by the clamoring of women's screams echoing down the grassy hillside.

"We must hurry if we are to save her!" Don Gianlucca grabbed Roberto by the arm and they ran up the hill toward the olive grove, the long-bladed grass slashing at their ankles. "She has taken up the mask and joined the maenads that follow Bacchus."

"The god of wine?" Roberto asked.

"Yes, and at the moment she is in danger of losing her soul as well as her life."

"We must rescue her," Roberto huffed, winded by the sprint up the grassy hillside.

"Not so easily done," Don Gianlucca said. "Once under the spell of the hunt, the maenads will murder any man foolish enough to be caught observing their revels. Even Anna will try and kill you Roberto."

"What's that?" Roberto halted as the grove erupted with a new sound. A cat screamed, its howls ricocheting through the trees.

"They have found their prey," Don Gianlucca answered. "And knowing no fear or caution, they will surround it. Then they will kill it with spears or their bare hands."

"Hurry."

"Beware!" Don Gianlucca cautioned. "We must remain unseen."

The two men crouched low in the high grass and slowly crept along the outer fringes of the olive grove, edging around the slender, twisted trunks, trusting the shadows as they approached the tight circle of women. The animal's fierce snarls were drowned out in the cacophony of drums, pipes, and triumphant shrieks. Don Gianlucca grabbed Roberto by the sleeve and pulled him flat into the grass.

"There." He pointed to a woman bent over the mangled corpse of a lion cub. "That's Anna!" he said thickly.

The woman was twisting the head of the cub, grunting and swearing as she tore at the flesh with bloodied hands.

"It can't be!" Roberto protested. The woman had raised the limp carcass of the cub to her mouth and was using her teeth to tear at the bloodied fur on its neck. The upper half of her face was obscured by a coy, youthful mask. The wide eyes were blackened hollows and the peach-colored cheeks were splattered with blood.

Roberto turned away. That creature wasn't Anna. It couldn't be Anna. It was a monster that hunted and ate raw flesh.

Don Gianlucca shook Roberto hard by the shoulder. "Don't lose your nerve, Roberto! It is Anna! She is the reason you and I are here!"

"But look at what she's become!" he hissed.

"There are none among us, Roberto, who do not harbor demons. All manner of virtues and vices exist within our imperfect breasts. Faith gives us one mask to wear. Bacchus has given Anna a different mask, and it has shaped the grief of her heart into a flesh-eating demon. You must catch her, Roberto, and tear the mask from her face. The woman you love is cowering beneath it."

"I am afraid of her," Roberto said simply.

"As are we all of the darker side of our natures. Will you abandon her because she has one?"

Roberto watched the masked Anna cracking the cub's skull. The pink ruffled tissue of the brain spilled into one of her palms. The mask looked up and gave a crowing laugh. But Anna's hand shook violently and wiped away the soft pulpy mess on her soiled skirts. Roberto saw the hand stray toward her face, and then hesitate.

He knew by that tentative gesture that whatever she was now, driven by the demands of the mask, the Anna he loved was still struggling against it. Every actor believed that to touch the mask was to break its spell. The human hand on the mask accentuated the artifice of the second skin, shattered the illusion, and lessened the power of the mask to perform. Anna was trying. But her hand wavered, unable to reach the blood-smeared cheeks.

"What should I do?" Roberto asked in a hoarse whisper.

"Take these," Don Gianlucca said, handing Roberto the bag of bones. "I'll cause a diversion so that the maenads will follow me. When they do, you must make a grab for Anna, pull her down, and hold her until the others have passed. As soon as you can, remove her mask. Then take her to where the Tago waits."

"And what of you?" Roberto asked.

Don Gianlucca shrugged, his hand waving away the question. His face had grown haggard in the maze, its indolent charm replaced by a tough, aesthetic beauty.

"You have only one chance to rescue her, Roberto. No matter what happens, don't hesitate."

"They'll catch you," Roberto said.

Don Gianlucca gave a twisted smile, and something of the sensual youth returned to his somber features. "I've outrun my share of angry women in the past and even managed to avoid the pots and daggers that they threw my way. Besides, they have already hunted once tonight. Drink and blood will make them slower the second time. Don't think of me, only Anna."

He turned to leave and stopped. "There is one thing more."

"What's that?"

"Tell Anna that God has long since forgiven her. All that remains is that she forgive herself. Tell her that, Roberto."

"I will," Roberto said, and clasped the young priest on the shoulder.

"I go now! Have courage, and may God protect you both!"

Don Gianlucca slipped past Roberto, and his black-robed figure disappeared in the cross-hatching of shadows. Only the soft rustle of leaves and the tired creak of branches marked his passing. Roberto tied the bag around his shoulders and watched Anna with troubled eyes as she gnawed at the skull of the lion cub.

He felt sickened by the gruesome sight, but his resolve to love her remained firm. It was as the crippled scenographer had said, blustering amid his mechanical dragons to scare away the false heroes and timid lovers. Roberto must look beneath the mask and embrace all that Anna was—not just her beauty, but the ugliness that had driven her into the maze.

"Demon with a mask of love," he whispered. And then changed the line to suit the moment. "Love with a demon's mask—"

"Hey ho!" A voice boomed out of the darkness. "You maggot-eaters! You slavering beasts of hell gnawing on the leftovers!"

The maenads looked up, their bodies crouched over the torn remains of the lioness and her cub. They snarled and hissed, the blackened eyes of the masks searching the shadows. The leader raised her chalk-white mask and sniffed the air in all directions. She stood upright and cackled with shrill laughter.

"I smell the stink of a coward! A dog accustomed to the stroke of every cudgel and the kick of every boot in the world!"

"It is your own foul stench you smell," the voice roared back. "Your head's crammed between your legs, you pestilent cunt!"

"Who are you who dares to witness the revels of the maenads? Show yourself, you worthless sardine!"

"I am the fiercest among the fierce, the bravest among the bloodthirsty, a killer of nations, brother to Death, and a longtime friend of Satan himself! I visit Hell often, just to kick the devils in their backsides for fun!"

Catcalling and booing, the maenads rose angrily to their feet and snatched up their weapons again. The primitive eyes of the masks stared hungrily out into the grove, searching out the offender's hiding place. The drum beat a quick tattoo.

What in the hell did that priest think he was playing at? Roberto thought, frantically biting his knuckles. All their lives were in danger and here he was, performing Il Capitano the braggart, boasting to the queen of cannibals. This priest was worse than reckless. He was mad.

Yet when Roberto glanced at Anna, standing unarmed, her body tense with anticipation, he understood the reason for Don Gianlucca's strange choice of diversions. Il Capitano's voice was one that might reach behind the mask and speak to Anna. The Commedia dell'Arte was in her heart, in her blood, in the hands that crafted the masks. She knew their voices as a mother knows the wails of her own children. She was standing away from the others. Her masked face leaned forward, her ear turned to catch the sound of the once-familiar voice.

Roberto inched through the long grass on his hands and knees. He laid his hand down on a bumpy shape and heard a muffled protest. Alarmed, he jerked his hand back. There was another bag half-hidden in the grass. Roberto opened it and peeked inside.

"Hist, who's there?" whispered a voice.

The pale flicker of the maenads' torchlight showed the face of Pantelone, its goat hair mustache quivering. Surprised, Roberto opened the bag wider and saw a second mask of a pretty face, trimmed with lace.

"Buffo!" The ingenue sighed. "Are you here to rescue me?"

"Who's that out there using my lines?" growled the mask of Il Capitano, thrusting his huge nose between Pantelone and the ingenue. "Doesn't even sound like me!"

"Be quiet, all of you," Roberto warned. He didn't have time to think about Anna's masks speaking to him. "I'm trying to rescue Anna!"

"Anna! My dearest sausage." Arlecchino gulped. "They took her, those other ones. Those cruel masks."

"And I'm trying to get her back! Now be quiet." Roberto shut the bag, retied it, and slung it over his shoulder with the bag of bones. Looking up nervously, he saw the maenads moving stealthily through the trees on the far side of the grove. Their leader was shouting insults at the man hidden among the trees. Each time he blasted back an answer, the maenads shifted their position, closing in on him.

Only Anna trailed behind, held back by doubt, or, as Roberto fervently hoped, by love for the voice of an old braggart.

"I shall make you all tremble at my feet, you hyenas! When I'm through with you, you'll be licking my boots and peeling my grapes!" Il Capitano roared.

"We shall crush you like the rotten fruit you are!" the leader called back. She readied her spear. The drums beat faster and louder, setting the dried leaves of the olive trees aquiver. "I'll wear your skin and hang your worthless carcass out for the ravens!"

With a grunt, she hurled her spear into the bushes as the pipes sang out a shrill screaming note and the beating of the drums reached a crashing crescendo. The leader raised her hand and the drums stopped, the pipes fell silent. The maenads waited, hushed.

"I'll have your guts for garters!" came the insult from the shadows.

The leader screamed in rage and the maenads began to tear through the forest.

"Yip, yip, yip," catcalled a voice from the bag.

"Shut up, you foolish servant," Pantelone snapped.

"The cats are out chasing a mouse!"

"On the contrary," puffed the voice of Il Dottore, "the Latin term that amply suggests the inner provarication of such misoginationary extemporare—"

"Stuff the Latin, you old fraud—" growled Pulchinella.

"Anna! Anna come back to us," sobbed the ingenue.

"We who love you," sighed the nymph.

"Throw off the counterfeit, you belong to us!" cried Pantelone.

"Cupid, who has become Lucifer!" said Arlecchino.

"Beauty tricked into falsity!"

"Love shackled by hate!"

"Bread without salt!"

"Madonna, shut up all of you," Roberto whispered fiercely. Anna was hesitating, stalled while the other women were storming the farside of the grove. She turned and glanced behind her. Roberto hunched deeper into the grass to escape the mask's black eyes. Still clutching a bloodied piece of the cub's skull, she took a step toward them. Roberto was certain that her ear had caught the pleading voices of her masks. She raised her torch higher to penetrate the shadows. Then the pipes shrilled loudly, and trapped by the piercing command, Anna spun on her heel to follow.

Roberto seized his chance. Leaping up from the grass, he grabbed Anna around the waist, pulled her down, and rolled over on top of her, pinning her to the earth. Her torch fell and spluttered in the grass, tendrils of smoke and weak flame rising from the ground. Anna struggled fiercely, but he wrapped his legs around her thighs and clamped his hand over her mouth. She snarled beneath his palm, trying to bite his fingers, rocking her hips violently, kicking her trapped legs to throw him off. But Roberto clung to her, embraced her, pressed her hard into the soil.

Removing the mask under these circumstances was an impossible task. To move his hand from her waist would be to lose her. And to move his other hand from her mouth would allow her to call the others. They would be discovered in no time.

Voices began to chorus from inside the bag. "Anna! Anna! It's us! Pantelone! Arlecchino, Pulchinella!"

Anna ceased struggling, and in that instant of stunned quiet, Roberto took his hand from her mouth, ripped the mask from her face, and flung it far out into the grass.

Anna's body went rigid in his arms. She opened her mouth as though to scream, but no sound came. Staring down at her in the flickering torchlight, Roberto knew a moment of terror. Her naked face, shocked with pain, still held the imprint of the mask's features. He watched the frozen expression crumple, the lines reappear at the corners of her haunted eyes, the curve of her cheek clawed by anguish, the soft mouth stretched into the beginnings of a sob. Gradually, Anna's features returned, revealing in their mobile imperfections the scars of her misery. She stared blindly up at the dark sky.

"Anna, it's me, Roberto," he whispered. "I've come for you."

The haunted eyes jerked and she stared at him with deep pain. "Roberto?"

"Si, bella. I've come—"

"Hey, what about us?" spoke a voice from the bag.

"We have come to bring you home, Anna," Roberto said gently.

"It's not possible," she said dismally. "I've done things, terrible things—"

"It doesn't matter. The priest said it was all forgiven."

"Forgiven?" she asked, and he felt her body shrink into itself. "Do you even know what I've done, Roberto?"

"No, and it doesn't matter. Come. We must go. There is someone who waits for you. Someone who will rid you of your sorrow."

"I can't," she said in a tiny voice.

"You must. Let me help you."

Roberto pulled Anna up from the ground, wrenching the stinking animal skin from her shoulders. He gently wiped the dirt and blood from her chin with the sleeve of his shirt. He tried to get her to release her hold on the cub's skull, but she pulled it tighter to her breast, her eyes wild with fear. He let her keep it, choosing to hurry away from the grove rather than argue.

As they reached the bottom of the grassy field, near the edge of the forest of dying oaks, Roberto heard behind him the shrill screaming of the maenads, the thunderous roll of the drums, and the screech of pipes. He thought he heard a man cry out. Half of him wanted to return, to rescue the priest if he could. But Anna had caught sight of the Tago and was pressed against him, whimpering. She needed him too, Roberto thought, and Don Gianlucca had said that this might be Anna's only chance. Roberto crossed himself, sending a quick prayer to the priest, and guided Anna toward the faint glow of the Tago.

"What is it?" she whispered.

"A child's spirit, known as the Tago."

Anna flinched, cowering deeper in Roberto's arms. "No, not that. I cannot face this spirit. Please, Roberto, take me away. Give me back the mask."

"No, Anna. Don't be afraid. The Tago means you no harm."

The Tago drifted down from the naked branches of the dying trees and hung like a star before Anna's haggard face. Tiny glowing fingers caressed her cheeks and the blue eyes gazed lovingly into hers. Tears streamed down Anna's dirty face.

"Anna!" The Tago sighed. "Anna, you are here!"

"I threw you away," Anna answered, her voice breaking. "Into the canals."

"I floated here. I tried to come to you in dreams but you refused me—"

"I didn't want you," she said. "I killed you."

"It wasn't you who caused my death." The Tago sighed.

"But it was me. I let the thorns of hate grow in my womb. I didn't know when he cursed me that you were there. I didn't know. And when he left me, I let the cursed thorns grow so that the pain would keep alive my hate for him. And when I knew you were there, the thorns stabbed until you died. You slipped from my thighs too soon, your face hard as a plum pit. I could not look at you. I could not own that you were of my making and my destroying."

The Tago spread wide its arms, blooming like a lily in the dark.

"I was not meant for your world, Anna. My fate was determined by another, and another's hand drew back early the breath of life. It was not you who killed me. And it was not hate that you felt for me."

"What, then, can you call it?" Anna asked. She fell to her knees, her head bowed. "I threw you into the canals to hide my shame. No one was ever to know that you existed. Was that love?"

"You loved me while I lived within you," the Tago replied gently, "even as you hated another. When I died, in your grief you assumed the blame."

"No," Anna wailed, and shook her head. "I am filled with thorns. They stab, they murder. They killed you."

"No, the thorns came later," answered the Tago. "Planted by the sin of self-hatred."

"Why are you here? Why do you come to me now?" Anna asked, her eyes lowered.

The Tago drifted closer to Anna, shedding a warm light over her distraught features. It waited until she had raised her eyes to meet its serene gaze.

"Because though you cast away my body, your grieving love binds me to the earth. My spirit is not free. You must accept that once you loved me, and then you must let me go. You must give me back my bones and release my spirit so that I may return to the ether from whence I came. You must cut the twisting vine of thorns that binds us both."

"How do I do such a thing?" Anna asked, her voice quavering.

"Take the bones and put them together in the earth. And bid me farewell."

"I don't have your bones."

"But I do," Roberto blurted, and quickly unslung the small bag from his back. He thrust it toward Anna, who stared at it uncertainly. "Take them, Anna. Don Gianlucca gathered them for you in the maze. But Tago, there is still a missing fragment."

"What do you carry in your arms, Anna?" the Tago asked.

Anna opened her arms. Something dry and white tumbled into her lap.

"Look, Anna, and see what is there."

Roberto heard the sharp intake of Anna's breath as she took up the thing she'd dropped with trembling fingers. The matted fur head of the cub had been transformed into the front half of a human skull, a small, delicate face composed of fragile, egg-white bones.

"A mask," said Anna, her bloody fingers tracing the curves of the tiny brow. She held it up for the Tago to see, and taking it, the spirit lowered its own face to fill the void. On the head of the Tago there appeared a child's face with luminous eyes, a plump soft mouth, rounded cheeks, and a snub nose.

"Not a mask, Anna," Roberto whispered. "It's a child's face. It's the missing piece."

"Do you love me, Anna?" the Tago asked.

"Yes." Anna sighed.

"And do you love yourself and the mysteries that abound within you?" The Tago lowered the mask from its luminous face.

Anna clasped her arms around her middle, her eyes averted from the Tago's glowing face. The Tago reached out its tiny hand and brushed her cheeks with streaks of light.

"Am I forgiven?" she asked in a low, sad voice.

"A long time ago," the Tago answered.

"Can it be true?"

"Yes. You are free of this curse, if you choose to be."

"Then I choose it," Anna said with a deep sigh. "Madonna Santissima, I choose it," she repeated. Her hands fell away from her sides and she reached out for Roberto's hand.

"Anna?" He called her gently, squeezing her hand.

She turned to him, as if seeing him for the first time. "Oh, Roberto, how this old shame imprisoned me! How I have missed my art, my daughter, and you, Buffo, my oldest friend. Oh, how I have missed love."

Roberto's heart leapt at the sight of her tired face. Speechless with happiness and relief, he lifted her dirty hand and kissed it.

"And us, Anna, what about us!" Pantelone shouted from the bag.

"How could she forget Il Capitano, the greatest lover and fighter of Spain?" Il Capitano boasted. "Ah, Anna, your nostrils are pieces of artillery, which, firing, have found their mark in this breast—"

"Me, me next! Her most loyal servant," Arlecchino barked. "Anna, let me be the mule you ride upon—"

"Ass is more like it!" snapped Pulchinella. "Anna, my succulent-breasted hen—"

Anna's joyful laughter silenced the masks, though Roberto heard Il Dottore grumble that he hadn't gotten his chance to orate. The sound of her voice warmed the cool night air, brightened the dreariness of the dying oaks as it shivered like rain through the Tago's corona of light.

The Tago waited as Roberto helped Anna to stand. It placed the final piece of the infant's skeleton in the sack while Anna gathered up the bag of masks.

"The day comes and I must leave you," the Tago said. "Follow the path before you. It will bring you to the center of the maze. After that, there is another who will help you. Farewell, Anna."

"Wait, Tago!" Anna called. "Can you give me news of my daughter, Mirabella?"

The Tago smiled. "She is well. No harm has come to her. You will find her on your journey to the center."

"Thank you, spirit," Anna said, her hands clasped together over her breast.

The Tago rose in the air, the bright orb of its body fading with the stars in the coming dawn. Roberto and Anna watched it until it winked out in the rosy blush of the new day.

Together they walked through the forest, marveling as the dying trees gave way to living ones: newly sprouted oaks, sharp scented pines, and knotted shrubs of butcher's broom. The sun lifted over the trees and warmed the air. Tiny white and lavender flowers bloomed beside lush stands of fern and the babbling of water echoed through the woods.

They found the stream and, while Roberto waited on the banks, Anna waded into the water and washed her face and hands clean of blood and clay. They slept for a while, surrounded by nodding ferns. Late in the afternoon, they awoke and resumed their journey, moving in companionable silence, their hands linked together.

A clearing opened in the woods, and they approached the stone remains of a village church. Moss-covered gravestones nestled amid blooming wild flowers and long yellow grass. Anna stopped and turned to Roberto, a question on her face.

"Yes," he said. "It's a good place to leave them."

Leaning against the hull of the church was a rusted spade. Roberto set about digging a hole in the soft, fertile soil while Anna gathered handfuls of wild flowers: yarrow, borage, bright-eye, and wild mints. When the hole was ready, Roberto lowered the sack of bones into the earth and covered them with dirt.

"Look there." Anna pointed to a broken statue of a marble cherub resting on its side in the grass.

Roberto retrieved the statue and placed it over the mound of dirt. A corner of its wing and an upraised hand were missing, but the childlike face was still intact, the features pure and innocent. Anna laid the flowers down at its feet and gave its round cheeks a quick caress. She stepped back from the cherub, a pained expression on her face, and wrapped her arms around her waist.

"How do you feel, Anna?" Roberto asked.

Slowly, she unfolded her arms, laid a hand against her belly, and then smiled. "Empty."

"And the thorns?"

"Gone." Anna turned to Roberto, her smile widening. "What I wouldn't give for a plate of risotto—"

"And scampi in brodetto!" Roberto groaned, his stomach grumbling as it awakened to hunger.

"Roasted sardines!"

"Cake!"

"Blood oranges from Spain!"

"Stop!" bawled Arlecchino from the depths of the bag. "You're making me crazy! I'm going to start eating that dried chicken, Pulchinella."

A second voice from the bag squawked an obscenity.

"Come, Anna, let's hurry," Roberto urged, taking her hand again. "We will find Mirabella again and leave this maze at last! And then, I promise you a feast!"

At the edge of the field, Anna chanced one long look behind her at the quiet grave. The wind was soft, its voice a sigh as it brushed through the long grass. Then, giving Roberto's hand a squeeze, Anna turned and followed him into the cool tree-lined corridors of the maze once more.

34

Rinaldo dodged the swinging pike and clove the attacking corpse from one dessicated clavicle to the hip, shattering its brittle ribs. The skull, with its few chattering teeth, collapsed on the heap of broken bones. In the stillness that followed, Rinaldo leaned against the walls of the cavern.

He had never been so battle weary in his life. Every muscle cried out in agony, and his fingers ached where they gripped the handle of his sword. The sweat that poured from his skin dried quickly in the hot sulphurous air of the caverns. He licked his parched lips and closed his eyes, swollen with grit.

How many more must he kill before this torture was finished? He examined his conscience, trying to understand why his dead should rise to seek revenge on him. He had not sought their deaths, only obliged them in their challenges. Why then should they take such offense when he killed them? Behind his closed lids, he saw the fleeting signs of their identities: the silvery threads of a crest on a rotting cape, a signet ring, the family emblem on the pommel of a sword. Not one of his dead opponents had been a soldier: they were all the nobles, the fencing masters, and the angered husbands that died at his hand after he had left the battlefields. After he had been cursed by the old soldier.

How were they able to find him in the smoke-filled caverns? He scowled at Lucio's heavy sword, hating the awkward feel of it, so different from his own weapon. Clumsy and badly balanced, this pigsticker was more suited for a tavern brawl than a real fight. Under the sulphurous reek, he could still detect the peculiar stench of the blade—like excrement, damp and pungent. He raised the sword and saw thin vaporous wisps float free from the edges and drift like a coiling serpent into the air to disappear down a dark tunnel.

A loud bellowing thundered in the passages until Rinaldo was deafened by the sound. The ground above and beneath him vibrated under the running of something heavy in the deeper caverns. A brilliant yellow light flared and he threw up his arm to shield his eyes from its glare.

"Prepare to die!"

Rinaldo lowered his arm and saw the next corpse waiting for him in the darkened mouth of one of the tunnels. This one was newer than the others, for rotted flesh was still clinging to the sunken cheeks, the soft lips were eaten away to reveal long teeth. Dusty locks of black hair fell over the empty eye sockets. The shirt was stiff with dried blood.

Rinaldo lifted his sword to prepare for an attack. This time he noticed the trailing wisps of vapor curling away from the blade. The corpse waited, the sightless head swiveling from side to side as if searching. But when the vapor circled the decaying head, the corpse turned to face him and attacked.

That was it! Rinaldo sidestepped a careening blow to his head. They found him by the stench of the sword. He had been tricked before he'd even entered the maze. But who had conjured such a punishment? Rinaldo spun on his feet and swung at the corpse's shoulder. Pieces of the corpse's decaying flesh splattered the wall.

And what of Simonetta? Rinaldo asked himself, grunting as he feinted and slashed the attacking corpse. Had she conspired with someone in the maze to see him dead? Or was she, like Lapone, lying dead somewhere in these dark caverns?

At the thought of Simonetta dead, a wave of intense exhaustion crashed over Rinaldo. Pain exploded in his joints every time the swords clashed. Sorrow lodged in his throat like a dagger. Suddenly it seemed as if everything he had ever loved—the sword, the horse, even the woman—was gone from his life forever. The corpse swung and sliced a gash in Rinaldo's forearm. He danced back, and summoning the last of his fading strength, he hacked at the corpse's knees, causing it to buckle and fall forward. With a roar of fury, he raised his sword again and drove it down across the decaying neck, decapitating the dead man. Then he dropped the stinking sword and left it lying beside the headless corpse, whose hands clawed at the ground.

Small odorous tendrils continued to waft from the blade. Holding his bleeding arm, Rinaldo hesitated, trying to decide which corridor to take. Near one, the flickering torchlight revealed another drawing etched into the corrugated wall. Rinaldo peered at it and saw the bull-headed monster standing over a prone figure whose head was bowed in defeat. His eyes narrowed as Rinaldo recognized himself, bent before the monster, naked without a sword. Another figure caught his eye, a dark shape barely discernible in the shadows behind the monster. Rinaldo watched as the drawing slowly emerged on the wall and a sinister hand reached out from the shadowy figure.

The thunderous bellowing began anew. The stalactites quaked and a fine dust filled the air. Without another glance at the developing fresco, Rinaldo, weaponless and exhausted, turned from the wall and ran for his life down a different tunnel.

Simonetta smelled Lapone's rotting carcass long before she saw the ravens circling above. It was an odor that haunted her sleep, one that years of bathing in herbs, squeezing lemons on her skin, and holding garlic beneath her tongue had failed to banish. She shivered, holding the sword close in her arms. What corpse would she find when she turned the corner of the maze? What dead and decaying body awaited her this time? Cheiron had said this was the path for her. The girl with the ribbons had sent her this way as well. Why did the way always take her back to the stench of death?

Simonetta glanced up, hearing the raucous cries of the ravens disturbed by her presence. She picked up a rock and threw it high into the air.

"Le animie maledette! Cursed souls every one of you," she screamed at them as they crowded darkly in the sky above her.

She turned the corner and saw the high wall of weathered rock blocking the path with Lapone's headless body sprawled in front of it. She groaned softly, aware of a rush of relief that it was not Rinaldo's corpse. She walked slowly toward the carcass, hearing the flies buzzing madly in the drying pools of blood. The rotting haunches were pitted with peck marks. A fox gnawing at the hindquarters bolted when it saw her.

"Ah, il mio poveretto!" Simonetta exclaimed when she saw Lapone's head nailed above the cave's entrance. "Look what they have done to you, my brave cavallo!"

A hot wind blasted from the mouth of the cave and whistled through Lapone's stiffened lips.

"Beware," a voice said.

"Of what?" asked Simonetta. "Of whom? Has Rinaldo done this to you! Out of revenge, my brave brute? Does he wait to kill me in there?"

"Beware," the voice whispered again, and fell silent.

Simonetta wondered what to make of the warning. No matter how she sliced it, it wasn't good. Rinaldo was somewhere in that dark cave. Was he a lover, or an enemy like the condottiere, waiting with a sword to kill her for her betrayal? Had he slaughtered Lapone because the stallion had permitted her to ride him? Simonetta weighed her memories of Rinaldo, the gentleness of his touch in bed against the violence that always surrounded him. For all his dueling, she had always found Rinaldo an honorable man. He had never once raised a hand in anger against her. He was proud of the stallion and spoiled the creature with good feed and small sweets hidden in his pockets. Cheiron had said that Rinaldo needed her. The girl had told her the same thing. She had to go, frightened or not.

Simonetta shoved Rinaldo's sword in the belt strapped around her waist. She opened the bag the centaur had given her, hoping to find something that might aid her. There were several small bouquets of dried herbs, all of them good for the treatment of wounds. In the bottom of the bag she found a ball of tightly wound string.

Simonetta pulled out the string and smiled grimly. She tied one end of the string to a stunted tree whose roots had snaked around the boulders of the rock wall, and then she entered the cave, trailing the string behind her.

The light near the entrance was quickly swallowed by the cavernous tunnel. The path grew dark except for flashes of yellow light that flickered like summer lightning across the vaulted ceilings. The air was hot and stank of sulphur. Simonetta tore a strip of cloth from the hem of her shift and tied the rag around her mouth and nose to protect them against the stench. Each time the yellow lightning flickered, she moved a few steps forward, one hand touching the wall for support, the other unwinding the string behind her.

As she rounded a corner, Simonetta found herself plunged into total darkness. There were no more flashes of light. She looked behind her. The mouth of the cave with its pale circle of light had disappeared completely. Simonetta prayed feverishly behind the cloth mask as she moved forward in the dark. Her foot nudged something lying across her path and she jumped back, slamming herself against the wall and knocking the ball of string from her hand. She curled her body against the dry stone, terrified of the utter darkness.

"Madonnina, protect me!" she begged. "Madonna Vergine, save me! Cheiron don't abandon me here! Turanna, help me find my way!" she whispered, calling on the mercy of any saint or pagan god who might be listening.

A thin line of gold light glimmered along the floor of the cave. It was Cheiron's ball of string, glowing in the dark. As Simonetta pushed away from the wall, the ball of string begin to roll forward by itself. It skirted an ancient pile of bones and then continued, unraveling its light down a night-black passageway.

Simonetta followed it, stopping a moment as the faint gold light illuminated the blackened lines of an etching on the cave wall. It depicted two hastily sketched figures, one with the head of a bull with massive horns and a double-headed axe raised high over its head. The other figure was a man, kneeling in surrender. With a cry, Simonetta touched the figure of the defeated man. It was Rinaldo.

She turned away from the wall and sought the thin golden line of unraveling string. Setting her foot alongside it, she began to run, gripping Rinaldo's sword and shouting his name down the dark corridor. Deep in the twisting bowels of the cave, a bull roared in reply.

Rinaldo crouched low in the tunnel. Had he heard Simonetta call his name? Or had it been a dream, the last wish of a doomed man? For doomed he was. The monster on his heels was wearing him down, chasing him through darkened corridors, forcing him to go where it wanted. Twice had he entered a torchlit tunnel and found his old footsteps dug in the dirt, mocking him; twice had he passed the painting on the wall depicting his defeat. He was reaching the end of his strength, his arms feeble as an old man's. He couldn't catch his breath in the hot, gritty air.

Again he heard Simonetta call his name and he straightened, desperately searching the dark.

"Simonetta!" he answered, his voice harsh. "Simonetta, I'm here!"

"Hah! At last I have you!" The voice was not Simonetta's.

Rinaldo swore, realizing that he had fallen into yet another trap.

Light sputtered into being out of the pitch darkness as around Rinaldo torches suddenly flared into life. He was not in a tunnel, but in the middle of a high-ceilinged cavern. All around the walls of the cavern were painted scenes of great battles: horses and men tumbling headlong into one anothers' swords and lances. The painted skies were dark with the flight of arrows. Low stone couches lined the cavern spread with pieces of armor, some badly rusted, some as bright as the day they emerged from the forges. Skeletons, dressed for battle with helmets on their bony skulls and swords gripped in their fleshless fingers, sat propped among the armor. In the center of the cavern was a stone altar, its sides stained rust-red. Littered across the sandy floor were more bones, human legs and arms snapped in two by powerful hands, sucked clean of marrow. Skulls rolled across the floor, those with teeth clacking warnings to Rinaldo, while others, broken and smashed, regarded him dolefully out of shadowed sockets.

At least a dozen tunnels opened black mouths into the cavern and Rinaldo guessed that every passageway in the cave must eventually lead to this one place. From the first moment he had entered the tunnel, he had lost all chance of escape.

He heard the footsteps approaching and saw a huge chest and torso balanced over thick sturdy legs filling one of the entrances. The creature bent down its enormous head in order to pass through the low-arched doorway, the twin points of his horns scraping sparks from its stones. As the creature straightened again in the cavern, Rinaldo felt the blood turned to ice in his hands.

The monster sniffed the air. Steam issued from his nostrils, and he laughed, a fierce guttural sound. "So. Again we meet."

"Never have I seen your kind before," Rinaldo answered.

"But you know me well—well enough to have slain me and sent me to this inferno. You have made me as surely as I made you."

"I swear, I have never laid eyes on you," Rinaldo protested. Yet the guttural voice sparked a distant memory. Something was alerting his senses: the desperate fatigue, the odor of battle and smoke-covered fields, the dead surrounding him. The heavily accented voice.

The creature sauntered toward Rinaldo, the double-bladed axe held in readiness. He reached out and pinched Rinaldo on the ear. The old scar on his earlobe split open beneath the creature's claws and bled down the side of his neck.

"I gave you this, and a warning," the monster said.

Rinaldo clapped a hand to his injured ear and stared into the terrible face. He saw that the bull's features were stiff and immovable, the muzzle frozen open. The rough hide was shedding and the frame of a mask was barely visible beneath the tanned leather. But the eyes of the monster were alive and they sparkled with triumphant hate.

"You cursed me!" Rinaldo spat, knowing the voice at last.

"I warned you. But fool that you were, you didn't listen." The monster curled his fingers into a powerful fist and swung at Rinaldo. Rinaldo tried to swerve out of the way but the blow snapped his head cruelly to one side. Pain cascaded through his body, and the sputtering torches blazed into a single flame of blinding light. Dazed, Rinaldo staggered, his hands raised as he tried to avoid the monster's second blow. But his eyes couldn't focus and the force of the second blow across his cheek spun him around like chaff in a brisk wind. The monster laughed coarsely and then kicked Rinaldo in the side of his knee and sent him crashing to the ground. Rinaldo curled in a heap, clutching his knee and coughing up mouthfuls of warm blood. He sucked at the dusty air, fighting to stay conscious through the fierce pain invading his body.

"Let me explain before I kill you," the monster said.

From the cavern floor, Rinaldo watched the bull-headed creature shoulder his axe.

"The sword was cursed. I found it in an abandoned temple in the

Holy Lands. It had been forged centuries ago when magic was abundant. It seeks blood and will never lose a battle once engaged."

"But I killed you," Rinaldo said.

"Only when an act of bad fortune knocked the sword from my hand. Had I held on to it, you would have died as had hundreds of others before you."

"But why are you here?"

"Because I cannot rest without the sword. I tried to warn you to leave it, but you were too ambitious to understand. You left my body in the fields and took possession of the sword, not knowing that soon it would take possession of you. I awoke here in this cavern, my soul restless, my body alive and hungering for revenge. But I was not alone for long. Your dead, the victims of my sword, soon followed me here, filling these chambers with their tormented rage."

The monster lowered his scornful glance to Rinaldo. "And what pathetic shits they've all been. That sword could have made you into a brilliant warrior, a conqueror of nations, an emperor! But the only blood it feasted on was of these miserable spawn of asses."

"And all this time, I thought it was me," Rinaldo said dryly.

"It was never you," the monster snarled. "It was the sword that made you great."

"And you, too, old man," Rinaldo replied. "All these years I cherished the one memory of our battle as the only honorable fight I'd had. And now I learn that it was nothing more than a trick of sorcery!"

The creature threw back his head and bellowed with rage. The walls of the cavern trembled, rattling the propped skeletons and sending the loose skulls rolling across the floor of the cavern. The monster raised the double-bladed axe and glared down at Rinaldo.

"Rinaldo Gustiano, prepare to die."

Rinaldo stared up at the blade, the hairs of his neck prickling in anticipation. His last thoughts shuffled rapidly together, like a pack of cards. His life was a sham, his duels all lies without honor. A card flipped past his eyes: the queen of spades, a sly smile on her dark face.

"Simonetta," Rinaldo whispered. On his knees before his executioner, with death poised above his neck, Rinaldo suddenly wanted only to possess her one last time. Vivid memories of her numbed the aches of his injured body: her breasts scented of rosemary, her slender waist, her smooth thighs gripped around his hips. Goddamn her, he thought angrily, goddamn that woman. He felt the fierce pain of an erection even as he stared up into the sharpened edge of the axe. In that instant he understood the dying curses of husbands and jilted lovers he had once slain.

"Fuck the whore who has brought me to this," he cried out to the axe.

He heard the hiss of the axe slashing through the air and he tensed, fists clenched, his eyes wide open to meet his death. The axe lost its direction and missed his neck as a different blade severed the monster's head. It rolled off the brawny shoulders and landed with a heavy thud amid the other skulls. Blood erupted in a brilliant red fountain, and the axe slipped harmlessly from the massive hands to the cavern floor. The headless torso swayed over the wobbling legs just before collapsing, raising a cloud of dust. Behind the monster stood a figure gripping a bloodied sword in its two hands, its featureless white face surrounded by a curtain of black hair.

"I shall honor that last request," a woman's voice said.

"Simonetta?" Rinaldo asked in amazement.

She pulled down the cloth covering the lower part of her face. "It's nice to know, Rinaldo, that you were thinking of me even at the end."

"Simonetta," Rinaldo repeated, raising himself from the floor of the cavern. His legs were weak, his injured knee caving in as he tried to stand. "Are you alive, or one of these ghosts?"

"Alive, my captain." She laughed.

Rinaldo limped toward her and clasped her tightly in his arms. She dropped the sword and pressed her body against his, her arms circled around his waist, holding him upright against her. He inhaled the fragrance of her skin, the soft silkiness of her black hair. He kissed her throat, her chin, and then covered her mouth with his.

"Do you still hate me, Rinaldo?" she asked when he released her from his passionate kiss.

"Yes."

"Do you still love me, Rinaldo?"

"Yes."

She laughed. "It's more than I had hoped for." Her expression filled with sad tenderness and she brushed his gaunt cheeks with the back of her hand. "I didn't mean to hurt you," she whispered.

"It wasn't your fault." Rinaldo turned to gaze at the monster. "Fortune long ago designed this journey for me." He released Simonetta and bent down to pull off the bull's mask, revealing the old soldier's face. "But now, it is done, and we are both free from our bonds. If only I knew how to get us out of here."

"I have a way," Simonetta said. She held up a tiny thread, its light glowing faintly in the torchlight. "It was just long enough to reach this chamber." She bent down to pick up Rinaldo's sword, but he stopped her.

"Leave it," he said gruffly.

"But it belongs to you."

"You once told me that the pilgrim leaves his curse in the maze."

"So I was told."

"The sword was my curse, and will be the curse of anyone who possesses it. Leave it be."

"So it shall remain," Simonetta said, and took his hand. "Come, Rinaldo, let's leave this place."

Simonetta wrapped her arm around Rinaldo's waist, he leaned against her shoulder, and together they followed the lighted path of the string out of the caves. When they reached the mouth of the cave they discovered that the maze outside had changed. Lapone's bloated corpse was gone, the pools of blood had soaked into the earth, which was covered over with new, lush grass and profusely blooming violets. When they turned to look at the wall of rock, they saw its solid facade melt like ice in spring. Beyond it the path beckoned, the cedars lined up on either side, their green spears bright against a blue sky.

"Where to now?" Rinaldo asked.

"To the center," Simonetta answered. "And then beyond, to wherever the road takes us."

"Simonetta, do you remember what I asked of you the night—"

"The night I betrayed you?" she finished. "Yes, I remember."

"Well?" he asked.

She nodded. "Yes, Rinaldo, I will marry you, my captain, if ever we find our way out of here."

"I have no fear of that," Rinaldo answered. "Love will lead us as it leads a bride happily to the altar."

"And the groom tripping in fright up the steps of the church!" Simonetta laughed.

35

Erminia walked beside Lorenzo, half pushing and half dragging him toward a crescent shore. Far out in the water, a small island floated on the edge of the blue horizon, waves curling onto its rocky shore. Anthemoessa, she thought longingly. Home. Near enough to swim to, but lost to her forever if she couldn't heat up this frozen icicle of a poet.

What was she going to do with the man? Erminia could sense the frustrated passion that threaded his veins despite the cold fist clamped over his wretched heart. How could he resist what was so obviously his nature that even a siren was affected by his presence? She sighed to herself and a pale fog surrounded her face. She had to rejoin his voice to the music of the spheres. She had to make him forget the past, and she had to do it without allowing him to drown. It was as she had told Fabrizio on the journey to Labirinto: if she took him into the sea unaware of the danger, he would sink under the weight of his memories, pulled down by the arms of his murdered wife. If Erminia could separate the man from his shipwrecked past, then he could swim to her and be whole again.

Erminia glanced sidelong at him. At least he was handsome—a little dour perhaps, but his melancholy air made him all the more appealing. She was charmed by the bleached lock of hair falling over his glowering eyes. She reached out a dirty hand and touched it. He flinched and jerked his head away. The undercurrent of his poet's voice babbled louder. Erminia moved closer to him.

"What is it, my poet? Did your wife once hold you by that white lock?" she asked, and saw the shadow of misery crease his brow. "Did she stroke it and whisper loving words to you?"

"She held it, yes," Lorenzo said shortly. "But there were no loving words. Only a curse."

"The curse of love?"

"The curse of truth."

Erminia laughed. "Is that it, then? Is that why you have silenced the poet's tongue, because your wife cursed you with speaking only the truth?"

Lorenzo nodded, his face glum.

"But whose truth, poet?" Erminia demanded. "The adulterous wife's in the heat of rage or the scheming lawyer's in the cold print of the law? And what about this truth?" She opened her arms wide to the sea embedded within the maze. "And what about me?"

Lorenzo groaned and grabbed at the collar of his shirt, wrenched at the knotted strings and tore at the fabric until his chest was bared to the salty wind. He opened and closed his mouth, gasping at words.

"She lied to me," he whispered at last. "She deceived me with my own friend. And when I found them together, she grew angry at me! She said it was I who had lied, I who had made a mockery of our marriage. She said that God would forgive her taking an attentive lover in place of a distracted husband. How could she say that? I loved her better than any man breathing!"

"Did you?" Erminia asked. Lorenzo's olive skin paled and his brows knitted over his eyes, belligerent with remembered emotions. His hands touched the air before him, shaping the image of his wife. Erminia could see her: tall and voluptuous, honey-colored hair reaching to her heels. Even in the fragile vision, Cecilia exhaled passion and warmth, her face beautiful enough for a noblewoman's and frank enough for a whore's.

"I did not compose one poem that did not praise her beauty, did not cry out the depths of my love for her," Lorenzo answered sullenly. "It was there for anyone to read in my writing."

"What a selfish way of loving, poet," Erminia retorted. "Your wife was right to despise you."

Lorenzo gaped at her, anger and pain contracting his features. He jerked his arms free of his black doublet, flung it violently onto the ground and kicked it, sending plumes of fine white sand into the air. The gusting wind snapped in the sleeves of his torn shirt. With fingers splayed to the wind, he scraped away the vision of Cecilia.

"I loved her!" Lorenzo shouted, his lips white. "And she betrayed me!"

Erminia gazed calmly at Lorenzo, untroubled by his outburst.

"You loved your work, poet. You loved the idea of your wife as she appeared in your poetry. But the woman of flesh and bone, you as good as ignored." Erminia shrugged, her palms turned up. "Mortal women can't live on words alone. They're a poor substitute for deeds. Your wife wanted a man who could love her as a woman, not as some distant . . ." Erminia trailed off.

"Distant what?"

"Distant siren, my poet, whom you expected to exist for the sole purpose of inspiring you to greatness."

Lorenzo's eyes narrowed. He straightened his disheveled shirt. "A siren?" he repeated, contemptuously. "Surely I thought better of Cecilia than that. An angel perhaps, or my own Beatrice. What is a siren? In tales she is a meddling witch, squatting on an island of bones, her counterfeit voice luring lustful men to their deaths."

"Only stupid men search for such shameful and meaningless deaths," Erminia snorted. "Petty men who dare not raise their eyes to meet the glance of heaven. Men so cowardly they stop their ears to the wisdom of the siren's song."

"Meaningless gibberish," Lorenzo replied.

"Divine songs made flesh!"

"Flute-playing whores!"

"Not that again!" Erminia flung herself at Lorenzo, her hands reaching for the white lock of hair, intending to tear it from the roots of his skull. Lorenzo caught her arms and tried to force her away. She reached for the front of his shirt, and with a heave of her shoulders and a kick at his shins, toppled him on the sand. He fell, taking her down with him. They rolled, kicking and grappling as each strained to gain the upper hand.

"Bastardo! How dare you repeat that insult to me! You can't even be original, you dried-up shit," Erminia shouted in his face as she rolled on top. Lorenzo grunted and kicked up his legs. She fell to one side and he covered her with his body, holding her down by her wrists.

"Leave me alone, damn you! I've no use for poetry, or for you," he yelled as she fought beneath him. She slammed her hips hard against his weight and again they rolled, Erminia on top once more.

"Fool! Idioto! Without me, without poetry, the world will have no use for you except as a worthless head on Orpheus's wall, testimony to your failure as a man!"

"Shut up!" he cried, and raising his legs, clinched them around Erminia's hips. He lifted his back and shoved against her hands. Once more she screamed in fury as Lorenzo sat on her.

"Lorenzo, listen to me!" Erminia insisted.

He closed his eyes and shouted, "No, no," to drown out all sounds but his own denial.

But Erminia raised her voice. "Lorenzo, you've crammed wax in your ears and lashed yourself to a ship headed for the rocks!"

Lorenzo just kept shaking his head and shouting, "No!" With a desperate twist of her wrist, Erminia freed one hand and, grabbing Lorenzo by the lock of white hair, jerked his head toward her face, and planted her mouth over his.

It was unfair and she knew it.

Even a frozen poet must thaw a little in a siren's embrace. Erminia's kiss, like her voice, was unique; it was rich and complex, salty with the saliva of the ocean and acidic with the vinegar of exile. With the tip of her tongue, Erminia deposited words on the roof of Lorenzo's mouth and he swallowed them as a man dying of thirst sucks at the dew. He stopped struggling and Erminia laid her other hand against his cheek, while her fingers threaded through the lock of white hair.

Lorenzo closed his arms around her waist and held her tightly.

Erminia pulled her head away, gently breaking the kiss. Lorenzo's eyes remained closed, his lips parted. She smiled at him and waited for him to open his eyes.

He did, slowly. But there was no joy in them. A terrible sadness lingered in his dark pupils, and she read his disappointment as he gazed at her, taking in the contours of her rough face.

"I am not Cecilia," she said flatly.

"No," he sighed heavily. "And you are very ugly. Yet, you make me feel so strange." He rolled off Erminia and lay in the sand gazing up at the dusky afternoon sky.

Erminia chuckled softly. "Bread has a hard, brown crust, Lorenzo. But inside, it's soft, white, and pure. You feel strange because you look at my face and you see the crust. In my kiss, you can taste what's hidden inside."

Lorenzo slapped a hand to his forehead. "I don't understand anything any more. I must be going mad."

"A beginning at last!" Erminia answered.

"It feels like the end."

"The end of your curse, Lorenzo, and the beginning of your life as a poet."

"But why must I be a poet?" he moaned. "Can't I just be a lawyer? Where is the harm?"

Erminia wrapped her arms around her shoulders, drew her knees up close to her chest, and exhaled a grey cloud of dense fog that covered her body like a cloak of sadness. Perhaps, she thought miserably, I could turn to stone here on the beach and let the tide slowly erode what's left of me.

Lorenzo reached a hand through the mist and touched her. She remained silent. What did she have to say to a lawyer? He grabbed her arm and pulled her close. Drops of moisture collected in his dark hair and a fine powder of sand clung to his cheek.

"Erminia, I'm afraid of being a poet again," he said. "As a poet, I destroyed everything I ever loved. My wife, my friend, my work . . ."

Erminia opened her arms and slid them around his back, her head resting against his chest. He shivered in the damp air of her sorrow, but his heart beat furiously.

"And damn it, I'm afraid of you. Every time I hear your voice, I want to weep for the loss of mine; every time I look into your eyes, I feel naked and unmasked."

"You're right to be afraid, Lorenzo. So am I. But there is no other path out of this maze for you, except through me. And there is no other life for me, except through you. We need each other."

"What must I do?" he asked.

Disengaging herself from Lorenzo's arms, Erminia stood, brushed away the clinging mist from the air, and started to undress, untying the laces of her bodice and dropping it onto the sand.

"Do you see that island out there, Lorenzo?" she asked, pulling off her skirts.

"Yes." He leaned up on one elbow to gaze out at the horizon. The setting sun gilded the tiny scrap of land so that it glittered like a gold star on the water.

"You must swim out there to meet me." She yanked the shift over her head and tossed it to one side. Wind gusted over her body, speckling her coarse brown skin with sand.

"I can't swim," Lorenzo said quickly. "I'll drown before I reach you."

Naked, Erminia squatted beside him and rubbed a handful of sand between her palms. She brushed her palms clean against her thighs and raked her fingers through the white lock of hair.

"You must try, Lorenzo. Open your heart to me and follow the sound of my voice. It will carry you over the waves to the island."

"Is that all?" he asked.

"There is one thing more."

"Say it."

"You are making a journey to the edge of the universe. My voice is the path. But it will not bear the weight of your earthly miseries. You must follow me as empty of experience as a newborn infant. Leave behind all memory, all thoughts of anger, of jealousy, of desire and longing. Leave behind, too, the fear of death. These are stones, Lorenzo, that will plunge you below the waves. Forget them, forget yourself, and surrender to my voice. That is how you will lose your curse and be reborn."

"Is it possible?"

"Some have succeeded. Many have not." She shrugged. "It's up to you."

She turned toward the water. If he did not follow her, then this would be the last time she would swim out to her island, the last time she would sing as a siren. She tried to hold fast the image of Anthemoessa, where the water broke against the shore into thousands of tiny shards of light. She shivered as she walked into the surf, the waves stroking white fingers of foam down her thighs. She waded farther out until the sand under her feet began to slip away and she was swimming.

Turning on her back in the deep water, Erminia let the salty ocean burn away her carapace. Fish tugged at the fingertips as it dissolved along its center seam. Freed of the skin, she dove beneath the surface and swam for the island. Shoals of anchovies, their bright bodies glittering in the last burst of sunset, followed in her wake, shaping a golden path through the blue-green sea.

Lorenzo sat on the shore and stared at the golden path trailing toward the island. He was still dazed by the heat of Erminia's unexpected kiss and by her naked body as she knelt next to him. Her breasts were large and pendulous, with a ring of dark hair around each nipple. There were scabs on her shins and dirt in the creases of her knees. The thatched hair of her sex was long and tangled like the pelt of an unkempt animal. He should have been repulsed by her, but he wasn't. A heady scent wafted from her skin, from her breath, from the faint beads of sweat on her upper lip. It carried the clean odor of the sea and a perfumed mixture of apricots, dried roses, and honey. Tension stirred in his loins. But the moment he had reached out his hand to her, she was skimming the waves in the sea.

Lorenzo stood, a hand to his brow. He watched her turn on her back and he saw the moment the skin dissolved away from the shimmering white body beneath. White as the moon, he thought, his throat constricting as he tried to whisper the lines. White and smooth as the flesh of the scallop. Another pain forbade him to speak. The curse imprisoned him and he doubted that he could ever tear through the bonds of hatred that Cecilia had laid upon him.

How could he free his voice again? How had he lost it in the first place? Was it Cecilia's fault, or was it his own selfishness, as Erminia had said? He had loved Cecilia, hadn't he? Yet all he could remember now were the words that had described her, the poems that had surfaced when she drifted into his studio and waited for him to speak to her. He had become famous for his work. Actors took his poems and wove them into their improvised plays. He had heard Isabella Torelli, the great Innamorata of the Libertini, speak his poetry in her exit speeches, capturing the audience with her voice and his words. He owed all of his success to Cecilia. Who could say that he did not love her?

Yet there remained a niggling thought like a stone lodged in his throat. Without Cecilia, could he still be a poet? Was it fear then, and not her betrayal, which had enraged him so on finding her in the arms of his friend? Was it fear that if he lost her, he would lose his words, his fame, his very identity? Perhaps Erminia had been right to say his love was selfish. He had used Cecilia to drive his thoughts into the spheres of poetry where she herself would not, or perhaps could not, enter.

Lorenzo tugged on the lock of white hair and then brushed it savagely out of his face. Cecilia may have cursed him with her dying breath, but he had wrapped her curse about him, silencing the poet rather than confronting his fear of failure. Just as he had used her in life to speak, he used her in death to remain silent.

But could he write as he once had without her? He might, if he could surrender himself and follow the siren's voice across the water. But how does a man lose himself in the ocean, except by drowning. Could the power of the siren's voice truly keep him afloat? And what of the stones of memory, could he free himself from their weight?

Lorenzo shucked off his boots, untied the strings of his hose, and peeled them down his legs. A full moon was rising to take the place of the disappearing sun. For a brief moment it was red and bloody, vivid as a wound in the fading twilight, but as it lifted higher into the night sky its violent hue faded until it was as luminous as a mirror, reflecting the calm of the sea. Lorenzo pulled his shirt over his head and waited for the siren to sing.

It began softly, floating over the water with the hushed undertones of a lullaby. Lorenzo strained to hear it, taking small steps toward the shore. The cold waves slapped at his feet; the warmth of the voice lulled him into the surf. He smiled, entranced by the beat of the waves rocking like a cradle against his shins. A woman's hand seemed to lead him forward. "Trust me," the voice crooned. "I'll not let you come to harm."

Lorenzo waded up to his knees, the lullaby recalling memories of childhood: the lump of dough handed to him as a sweet, the rounded breast against which he laid his head. His mouth parted in surprise as the misty specter of his mother, her arms outstretched to catch him, emerged from the white foam. Her form gathered strength in the moonlight and became solid. Lorenzo held out his hands to greet her and then, remembering Erminia's warning, pulled them back, acknowledging that his mother was dead and his ache for her long past. The pearl face nodded in sad surrender and the ghost turned to a vapor over the water. As he passed through the shredding fragments of mist he shivered at their soft, cold touch.

The song segued into a new melody and Lorenzo waded deeper into the restless sea. His mother's dulcet song became a loud chorus of women's voices, trilling over the water. He heard the chiming of bells and the clash of cymbals as around him the mist coiled into the slender forms of women dancing in a circle. Lorenzo gasped as another memory claimed him. Here was his youth, when the pretty girls of the noble houses laughed and danced around him. Oh, how he remembered the flame of agony when one rejected him, and the flame of joy when another received him. Lorenzo shoved against the waves, thrusting into the deepening water to join them. Their small cold hands pressed against his bare chest and the sand was sucked away from his heels.

He tumbled headlong into the sea, unable to stand, the waves tossing him like a bubble of glass from a fisherman's net. His arms scrabbled to keep his head above the white, foaming water. His teeth chattered as the chorus of girlish voices grew more strident. Their song drove the waves higher around his struggling shoulders as they spun wildly, gathering the white spume into their foaming skirts. The waves whirled and Lorenzo cried out with despair as other memories rose from the ocean floor.

Memories of Cecilia, memories of murder, memories of unbearable grief, rage, and silence.

The currents of the whirlpool strengthened and Lorenzo spun in a hollow cone of white water. With every turn, he sank deeper into the throat of the whirlpool. Animal fear inspired him to kick his legs and paddle his weakening arms against the inexorable tug of the water. And all the while, the women's voices sent arrows of painful memory into his heart. As Lorenzo swallowed water and his limbs became numb, he knew he had been betrayed. It was the siren's voice that had shaped this fierce funnel of water; it was the siren drowning him in the cold, dank waters of his own memory. She had lied to him! She had lied!

"Who has lied?" sang a voice. Lorenzo gazed up through the water and saw a woman whose cloud of hair swirled around her head as she drifted high above him like a shadow.

"Erminia! Help me!" he cried, reaching out through the wall of churning water.

Even as he tried desperately to thrust his body toward her, he was sucked downward into the narrowing neck of the whirlpool. The siren's song rose to the high-pitched howl of a woman's rage. Water cascaded inward from above, spilling into the hollow opening and filling it up like a glass. Lorenzo caught his last gulp of air as the water closed over his head.

The woman's shadow appeared beside him through the moon's slanted light, then sank below him, her hands grabbing at his heels to pull him deeper into the water. Through the rushing in his ears Lorenzo could hear the shrieks of the siren's voice, the hammering of his terrified heart, and the blood pounding in his temples. He looked down and saw a woman's waterlogged face. He fought against her grip as she seized him by the thighs. Small pearls of air escaped through his pressed lips.

In rage and fear, he thrashed wildly. The woman tightened her grip, sliding her body along his torso until her face was close to his.

"No!" his mind shouted as the woman closed her mouth over his to suck away the last of his air. His eyes wide open, Lorenzo saw that it was not the siren who had seized him under the water. It was Cecilia, her beautiful face harrowed by death, her eyes shell-white and her skin eel-grey. And then Lorenzo realized that it had not been Erminia's voice that had brought him here, but the choir of strident voices from his past.

Forget your past, Erminia had warned him, and do not fear death. Forget anger, despair, and even love. Follow my voice.

Amid the lullabies, the chorus of girlish tauntings, and the howling of his dead wife, Lorenzo prayed that there was one voice that did not belong to his memory. But to make out the siren's voice amid the cacophony of his scattered life, he had to forget himself. Twirling defenselessly in the foaming water, Lorenzo understood. Death was the only path to such forgetting, the only way to hear the voice of the divine.

Abruptly, Lorenzo stopped kicking his legs and let his arms go limp. He let Cecilia hold him, her legs clamped around his waist as she pulled him down. Her hair formed a clinging shroud over his face and her tongue darted like a fish in his slack mouth, stealing air. Dimly Lorenzo heard the multitudes of voices collapse into one pounding roar that he realized was the last protestation of his heart.

Out of that thundering noise, his ear plucked the fragile voice of the siren.

It was a single, serene note, clear and pure as the light from distant stars. Memory could not cling to its smoothness and all mortal yearnings were fulfilled by the divine completeness of its sound.

Lorenzo tuned his ear to its call and surrendered his life. Pain ebbed from his body as he allowed himself to die. Distantly, he sensed Cecilia's watery body grip him harder as he slipped through the tight clench of her embrace, buoyant and free. They separated, though their bodies were still trapped by the spiraling current of the whirlpool. Lorenzo no longer heard Cecilia's howls, no longer remembered the grief or the shame of her death. The voice of the siren bore him slowly through the water in a net of silken notes. Cecilia drifted past him, the features of her face eroding, her hair a dusky shadow. A pale hand of bleached bones clutched at him, but the fingers dissolved before they could reach him.

The sea went dark and Lorenzo breathed in the cold salty water of the ocean. As he exhaled, remorse and bitterness, love and ambition, escaped from his throat in a thin stream of white bubbles. He floated aimlessly in the rocking water, carried by the siren's voice, that one sustained note, without pause, without breath, without end.

Out of the darkness of the sea, a pinpoint of light sparkled and then another and another until the sea had evaporated into a velvet sky, brimming with radiant stars. Lorenzo gazed at them with quiet wonder. Had he left the sea and the maze? Was he only a spirit now? The siren's voice shaped wings, and he felt his sluggish arms lift from his side and he was flying, his fingertips brushing the streaming light of the stars and setting them to ringing. Chords of music chimed, one vibration harmonizing with another, until the whole night was crisscrossed with glimmering ribbons of sound. Lorenzo flew through the bands of light, his body pierced by the music of the spheres.

Suddenly she was there beside him, the white flash of her body curving around him like the arc of a dolphin's back. She circled him, her skin slippery where it brushed him, her body gleaming in the darkness. Leucosia, the shining one. She floated before him, bright as the moon, and he saw her parted lips smile as her song continued to hold him in its silvery net. He was no longer flying, but floating upright in the night sky, twirling slowly, his skin glistening with the silvery dust of the stars. She draped her arms around his neck and he stared into her sapphire eyes, dazed as something returned to him, something he had abandoned in the dark sea below. It was an emotion, stowed away in the far corners of his heart and now released. Happiness. Tenderness. Love.

And then came the words, solid as clay, giving him weight and density.

Suddenly weighted, Lorenzo plummeted from the sky, his passing a bright streak across the darkness. Down he fell, burning in the dark, his mouth open in soundless surprise as the sea reached up with white foaming limbs to receive him. He felt the cold shock of water and the heaviness of the sea as it reclaimed him. He sank quickly, a hot fragment of heaven cast into the water, the steam boiling around his diving body.

Almost at once, Erminia was there reeling him in by his white lock of hair. She tugged at it and Lorenzo thrashed in sharp pain like a hooked fish. His heart was pounding again and his body clamored, awake to its need for air.

Erminia tucked her hands into his armpits and pulled him quickly to the surface. He broke through the foaming waves with a loud gasp. He coughed and spluttered, the sea rushing from his mouth. Erminia swam with him toward a rocky shore where the waves rattled over pebbles. His limbs felt cumbersome as the sand floor of the sea lifted under the soles of his feet. He tried to stand, but his knees buckled in the surf and the rocks cut the tender soles of his feet.

Lorenzo staggered drunkenly in the shallow surf, gasping and sneezing saltwater. He heard the clear ringing sound of Erminia's laughter and turned to find her floating easily in the water like a seal.

"Well, my poet, what say you now?" she asked.

Lorenzo gazed down at her blazing face, dizzy with the tangled rush of emotions and words. All the poetry that he had denied now roared in his thoughts demanding to be shouted aloud to the world.

He threw back his head and laughed. Then he lunged through the water, stamping his feet and slapping at the waves until a veil of white rain showered his head.

"Chiara soave angelica divina!" he shouted, snatching at handfuls of sea spray.

"An angel indeed. Some have called me so!" Erminia cheered, and rolled her body in the water.

Lorenzo sent a fresh spray of foam into the air. Then he held his hand aloft, his gaze fixed on the star-bright eyes of the siren. More words came to him.

"With her, there is a different kind of love; in all others, spears of hope and fear murder the heart. In her, desire seeks no further than to be content in her presence!"

"Bravo." Erminia laughed. "But perhaps I may be honored by more than a worshipful glance?"

She coiled around him, her face half-hidden in the water, blowing bubbles. Lorenzo felt her body bump into his legs.

"O'Dio," he shuddered, as she slithered between his legs and then rolled to face him and spouted a fountain of water over his stomach.

Lorenzo dropped to his hands and knees and crawled forward in the shallow water toward Erminia's shimmering body.

"Breasts of snow, thighs succulent as the flesh of scallops, skin more radiant than moonlight blinding the lover to all else but her glory—"

"Bella, bella," she encouraged.

"Sweet song of binding, life in the seas of man's bitter drowning . . ."

He couldn't stop talking, the words like a fever heating him. Waves rippled around him, pushing him toward Erminia until he was beached on her outstretched legs. She raised herself on her elbows and, gazing down the length of her body, gave him a frank grin. Lorenzo felt her legs part. She raised her knees out of the water, reached down, and drew him up to her chest.

He groaned a line of poetry, his body delighted by the cool sensation of her breasts against his chest, the wet press of her thighs around his buttocks, and the curved mound of her belly filling the hollow beneath his stomach. Words came faster and more passionately to his lips. Her eyes sparkled and she planted small kisses on his chin, his throat.

"Oh, divine hand erecting proud masts, carry me from the torment of death into your celestial spheres!"

Erminia gave a happy shriek of pleasure as Lorenzo, guided by his poetry, entered her.

For an instant the words faltered in his mouth, unable to express the astonishment of his body awakened again to the intensity of sex.

"Don't stop," Erminia commanded, digging her fingers into his shoulders.

"Love exerts its force on me—"

"Oh yes." She sighed.

"And rocks my life with storms upon the deep—"

Erminia arched her back out of the water and clung to him, the sand churning beneath them.

"And drives my fleeing spirit, rising from death into this tranquil harbor—"

"Not so tranquil now!" she countered, and bit her lower lip.

Lorenzo couldn't decide which was reaching its crescendo first, his body or the poem that wouldn't stop unfolding from his lips.

"And I, encircled by such storms of gripping sighs—"

Erminia's legs tightened around Lorenzo's waist and he moaned, struggling to speak the next lines.

"Lose my way in the dark shroud of night. But howling winds are calmed by her divine tongue's sound—"

Erminia licked the sea spray from his neck.

"And I, my spirit roused by her singing voice, ascend into a star-flamed heaven—"

If there was more to the poem, Lorenzo had lost the ability to speak it. The water steamed from the heat of Erminia's thrashing limbs. Her gasps and sighs surrounded them in a green mist that turned blue and finally flared into a dazzling white curtain. Her embrace boiled away the edges of Lorenzo's physical awareness and transformed his body into waves of light. It flamed so fiercely in his belly that he cried out in delirious agony, and for one long moment, he imagined himself dying again and transported to the edge of the universe by the workings of the siren's body.

He returned from those spheres slowly, gradually regaining the edges of his body, the cool water slapping against his thighs, his cheek resting on Erminia's wet and glowing breast.

"Am I alive?" he asked.

"Very much so." Erminia chuckled and sprinkled cool water over his back.

Lorenzo closed his eyes, a profound weariness settling in his limbs. He felt Erminia turn him over in the surf and tow his weary body into deeper water. His hands sculled the water weakly and he tried to open his eyes.

"No, my poet, sleep," she whispered into his ear. "I will bear you back to the far shore. Tomorrow, when you wake, we will continue through the maze."

"Must we leave here?" he mumbled.

"Yes, my poet. This island is only an illusion of the maze, and no more home to me than the rude village where I lived in exile. Sleep, tesoro mio, sleep."

"As you command," Lorenzo answered, and let the arms of the siren bear him across the rocking waves of the open sea.

36

Convinced that he had heard his mother singing, Fabrizio awoke from a deep sleep and stared perplexed at the stars hovering above the Arch of Dreams. Night-cloaked trees swayed in the breeze. The song lingered in his ear, the voice so achingly pure that he could feel tears burning in his eyes. At his side, a woman stirred, and the lingering voice of his mother faded into the sound of her soft breathing. Fabrizio wiped away a tear with the back of his hand and turned on his side to gaze at Mirabella's sleeping face.

He studied her in the moonlight, noticing the subtle changes in her features since he had first met her in the Piazza del Labirinto. Her cheeks were still round, her nose snubbed, but there was a new sensuality in the fullness of her face, the kissable pout of her mouth, the curve of her shoulders, and the rippled tresses of her loosened hair. Full and ripe like a nymph, he thought, and traced a finger across the fine arch of her eyebrows. When she gazed at him without her spectacles, the intense, myopic stare of her beautiful blue eyes completely distracted him. He loved the musical sound of her voice reciting poetry. He let his fingertip follow the slope of her nose and brush against her parted lips. She kissed his finger in her sleep. He smiled, his fingers continuing their journey over the soft mound of her chin and down her neck. She hummed lightly, her throat vibrating against his fingertips, but she didn't waken.

How easy it would be to make love to her, he thought, letting his hand float over her breast without actually touching it. He was certain she would surrender to him. Even if her maidenly pride required that she protest, he knew he could overcome her with his passion. He was, after all, irresistible to women.

"Merda!" he muttered, returning his wandering hand to rest on his warm forehead. He turned on his back again and frowned at the columns of the arch, curved in the moonlight like a woman's thighs. He could fuck this girl, he announced brashly to himself. It would be easy. Except that he loved her too. And a girl like Mirabella didn't want the temporary pleasure of sex; she wanted everything else as well: companionship, marriage, family. And Fabrizio wanted to be the one to give them to her. So, if he was going to make love to her, he was going to have to marry her first. He held up his hands, faced them to each other, and whispered a duet of lines.

"What spell holds me back?"

"What sorcery of love prevents me from fleeing you?"

"Ah, you are too strong."

"Your power too hypnotic."

He grinned as he made his two hands entwine in a passionate kiss, the fingers interlaced. Abruptly, one hand pulled free from the tangle and rapped the other on the knuckles.

"Naughty fiend. How dare you touch me," he whispered in a falsetto voice.

The other hand curled up, shamed by its reckless abandon.

A third and smaller hand snaked up to the cowed hand and began noisily kissing the curled fingers.

"Now, now, my pretty, don't despair," said the small hand sweetly. "I am your true love, not that calloused brutta over there." The small hand waved away Fabrizio's other hand, which was stiff with injured pride.

"Mirabella, I'm sorry. Did I wake you?" Fabrizio asked, lacing his fingers through hers.

"No, your hands did." Mirabella chuckled. "What is it, Fabrizio, can't you sleep?"

"It's this place." He shrugged. "Everything is changing. I feel like I don't know who I am any more."

"You're an actor," Mirabella answered. "And a good one."

"But how can I be an actor if I can't speak the lines? Why am I cursed with this stutter? And how am I supposed to lose it in the maze?" he asked, trying not to sound as desperate as he felt.

Mirabella sat up and leaned her back against one of the columns. In the moonlight her face was serious, her chin tucked into the palm of her hand. Then she looked up and smiled at him.

"Give me Pantelone's mask," she said.

"What do you have in mind, Mirabella?"

"A little theater. A little practice. A little fun." She giggled as she lifted the mask to her face. Fabrizio saw Pantelone's horrified expression as it gagged in protest.

"But, but . . . I'm not a woman," the mask stammered.

"Hush now," Mirabella told the mask. "I don't ask you to be a woman, Pantelone, but that you make me a man. Fabrizio needs to learn how to speak to men without stuttering. Surely you can lend me your sex for a moment?"

The mask leered, the eyes growing rounder with anticipated delight. "Help yourself to my sex, Mirabella. It may be my only chance for a while!"

Mirabella adjusted the mask to her face, coughing a few times as Pantelone's voice invaded her throat.

Fabrizio glowered, watching Mirabella's round, feminine body altered by the persona of the mask. She stood up and strutted, her shoulders pulled back. A manly chest puffed arrogantly and her pouting lower lip jutted stiffly under the bristled curtain of Pantelone's mustache. Her girlish voice was gone, replaced by the gravelly pitch of a quarrelsome old man.

"So, you impudent rascal, you want to get married!" Pantelone's voice accused Fabrizio.

"I ne-ne-never said that," Fabrizio retorted quickly. He flushed, sweat prickling his forehead under the severe gaze of the mask.

"Ah, I know from the squint in your eye, you cockerel, and the bulge in your hose every time Mirabella flounces by. And I know it by the itch in my fingers at the thought of her handsome dowry! Say. That gives me an idea!" Mirabella's shoulders hunched with greed and she clapped a hand between her legs and then to her sides, searching for Pantelone's money bag. "I'll marry her myself and keep the gold and the girl!"

"Fa-fa-ther, you can't!" protested Fabrizio.

"And why not!" Pantelone roared back. "Am I not a virile specimen?"

"A p-p-pig's squeak," Fabrizio muttered to the imaginary audience.

"Eh?"

"A f-fine physique, Fa-father."

"Why, my physician told me this morning that I didn't look a day over forty . . . six."

"Did he l-l-look at your face?"

"What's that, boy?" The mask glared at Fabrizio.

Though he was sweating under its blunt stare, Fabrizio concentrated on forcing the words to form a single unbroken line.

"Your pace," he improvised, more loudly. "Why it's that of a race-horse—"

"Indeed."

"Heading for the barn," Fabrizio muttered.

"The what?"

"A lion, sir."

"Better," Pantelone growled.

"With no claws."

"How's that?"

"No flaws in you, sir. Perhaps a rich widow would be more suited to your needs, Father. A big bottom that's broken to the saddle and a fat purse just for the taking." Fabrizio winked at the mask. He smiled, flushed with the unexpected pleasure of success. If he spoke loudly enough, he thought, forcefully enough, then he could make the words come without their stutter.

"Say, not a bad idea, boy. We'll double our income. You get those brains from me, you know," Pantelone boasted.

"Randy old goat."

"What are you saying to me, scamp?"

"A new coat, Father. You would do well to buy a new coat to impress the widow."

Pantelone's mask mouth gaped, addled at the thought of spending money.

"Bra-bravo," a deep voice intoned from the dark covering of the trees. "The in-in-ingrate can speak for himself a-a-after all."

Fabrizio stepped backward, his arms spread wide to keep Mirabella safely behind him. The blood drained from his head, leaving him dizzy and nauseous.

"Who's th-there?" he called, but he knew the answer already. Che cazzo, he swore to himself, just when the words were starting to flow. The man had tyrannized him in life, and now his ghost wouldn't leave him alone.

"Hah, f-f-fool, sp-spawn of a ja-ja-jackass."

Fabrizio saw a lambent form slipping through the dark trees. The ghost of a tall knight appeared at the edge of the clearing, his body en-cased in silvery armor, his head covered by an elaborate helmet. Plumes of black feathers crowned his metal skull. A lance protruded from his bloody chest, and at the small of his back, the punctured cuirass bent inward around the shaft of wood. He made no noise as he advanced to the Arch of Dreams, his feet gliding over the ground.

"Fabrizio, who is it?" Pantelone asked.

"Gh-ghost of my-my father," Fabrizio whispered miserably.

"And just when you were doing so well," Pantelone replied irritably. "You weren't stuttering at all."

"Not to you, a mask. But this is di-di-different."

"I'm more of a man than that one," Pantelone grumbled. "He's dead, remember."

"And you're not really a man, remember?"

"No need to insult me," Pantelone snarled.

Fabrizio closed his eyes in confusion. Pantelone's brash voice in his ear was arguing with him, but Mirabella's soft hands were on his shoulders, her womanly body pressed against his back. Before him the ghostly image of his father rippled in the wind, but his voice was solid, the stutter like the jagged sounds of a rock slide.

"I'll get rid of him for you," Pantelone offered. "Tell me what to say."

Fabrizio's shirt was stuck to his back with sweat, but his hands were unbearably cold. He tried to think of what to say to the man who had terrorized him most of his life and who died so violently a year ago. Should he be rude? Should he be meek?

"Say, Is it well, with you, Sire?" he whispered to Pantelone.

"How's hell, Sire?" Pantelone shouted at the ghost.

The ghost hesitated, fluttering like a pale flag over the grass. One hinged hand slowly raised the visor of the helmet. A man's face peered out, a single, heavy black brow furrowed over a long nose. The lance bobbed up and down in the wind, the jointed tasses of his thighs creaking with the motion.

"Wh-what's that you say, you d-diaper-assed b-boy?"

"Ask him if he's all right," Fabrizio prompted.

"Is your arse still tight?" Pantelone barked.

"I didn't say that," Fabrizio hissed to the mask.

"Eh, what do you want me to say?" Pantelone sniffed.

"I don't know," Fabrizio answered, shaking his head in frustration. "I don't know. No, wait. I just want to know why the bastard's haunting me. Why can't he leave me alone?"

"Hey, bastardo, how dare you taunt me! Why don't you piss off?" Pantelone shouted, shaking his fist at the ghost.

"Madonna, I didn't say that either," Fabrizio squeaked.

"You're afraid of him, aren't you?" Pantelone murmured.

"No—yes," Fabrizio answered glumly. "Aren't you? Look at him, with that thing sticking out of his chest." Fabrizio gave a small shiver. "Even dead, he's in his armor. I don't think he ever took it off, even to shit. He wanted me to be like that. Ask him why he's here."

"Hey, you old queer—" Pantelone called.

Fabrizio slapped his hand over Pantelone's mouth and turned to face the ghost. Remember, he told himself, just be loud.

"Why have you come to Labirinto, S-sire?" Fabrizio shouted. Damn, almost made it through a sentence.

"I was doing fine." Pantelone sniffed, after he pried away Fabrizio's hand.

"Shut up," Fabrizio snapped. "You're no help at all."

The ghost was gliding closer to the Arch of Dreams, the dark, pleated face wearing a look of surprise.

"How s-say you again, you pile of d-d-dung?"

"When will I be fr-free," Fabrizio moaned.

"Fuck off, you flea," Pantalone roared at the ghost.

"No!" Fabrizio cried to the mask. "I must speak to him!" Fabrizio stepped up to the rippling ghost of his father. With his hands balled into fists, he forced an avalanche of words from his mouth, praying that volume alone would be enough to prevent him from stuttering.

"Free! I said. Free! When will I be free of you, old man?" he demanded. "You and your curse of stuttering? You and your fucking s-soldiers. You and your tournaments, you and your ar-armor. Why did you ever send for me if you despised me so? Why didn't you leave me w-with my mother? She at least loved me!"

The ghost's mouth fell open with loud guffaws. The armor rattled and clanged as his metallic shoulders shook violently.

"I di-didn't send for you, pi-piss p-pot. She didn't w-want you."

"That's not true."

"Oh b-b-but it is, you limp rag." The ghost sauntered closer to Fabrizio. Fabrizio tensed, nausea gripping his stomach at the sight of his father's broad, toothy grin. Dried blood was caked on the withered lips. "I was f-fighting in Naples and for my-my rest I went to the s-sea. There, I was be-be-be-witched by three mermaids. Evil cre-cre-atures," the ghost spat. "They used th-their voices to ench-ch-chant me. I was unable to m-move from the s-sand. They claimed me for their lover and I ca-can't tell you which one of the th-th-three that mounted me th-that day was your m-mother."

"Why are such blissful fates wasted on pigs like that?" Pantelone complained.

Fabrizio stumbled backward. It was the first time his father had ever spoken of this. His mind raced, gathering images as the sea washes everything on the shore into its arms: the fragments of his momentous birth, his mother and aunts cavorting in the waves, and even the night when Erminia's voice encased a village in coral. Why did he not feel more surprised to discover that he was a child born of a man and a mermaid?

No, he thought, hearing his mother's voice as she sang him to sleep and remembering Erminia's white body lifting out of the sea. His father was wrong. His mother and his aunts were not mermaids; they were sirens, like Erminia.

Knowledge, warm as the noonday sun, burst in Fabrizio's heart and poured its heat into his frozen hands. He was the child of a siren. And as miserable and worthless as his father's ghost made him feel, Fabrizio felt an equal thrill of happiness and that divine confidence he had experienced at the moment of his birth.

He was certain. His mother had bequeathed him the siren's gift of song. It was there in his voice, in his speech—he had only to open his mouth and use it. And yet, he found it curious that his mother would have sent him away to be with this cold, humorless man. Unafraid for the first time, Fabrizio spoke to his father's ghost.

"Why did she send me to you? Why did you accept me as your son?"

"Sh-sh-she sent a ca-ca-casket full of g-g-gold. I was wi-wi-widowed twice and had n-no other heirs."

"Probably killed them trying to screw in his armor," Pantelone quipped.

"Without me-me, you w-would have b-been nothing! A b-b-beggar of N-naples, c-cast off sh-shit. B-b-but I ga-gave you a na-name and m-made you a m-man, weakling though y-you are."

It was Fabrizio's turn to laugh, seeing the glimmer of his mother's dream and recognizing his father's utter ignorance of the gift the sirens had given him. He realized that his mother and aunts, like Erminia, must have suffered under the same curse of silence. They had discovered a man on their beach and allowed him to plant within one of them a last hope for their future. Fabrizio's mother had sent him to Urbino as a gift to the human world, a creature enough like his mother to bring sublime joy through his voice, yet able to speak so that men did not go mad. She could not have known how deaf to music his father was and how willing to beat the song out of his son. And yet Fabrizio had survived.

Fabrizio's laughter filled the night, echoing beneath the Arch of Dreams. The ghost teetered backward as though the sound hurt him and ground his teeth until Fabrizio's laughter died away into hiccuping gulps of air.

"Sire, how little you know me. Neither your name nor your iron fist did anything to make me a man," Fabrizio said quietly. "It was forcing me to be like you that nearly cost me my manhood. I could imitate you in no part of your life except your crippled speech. As I allowed you to make me feel worthless, so, too, did I allow you to strangle me with your stutter. But no more. Though you gave me humanity, it is my voice, my mother's gift that serves me far better than your weapons served you."

"Ba-ba-bastard whelp!" the ghost wheezed.

Fabrizio shrugged good-naturedly. "We're not all born on the right side of the cradle. But fewer still can claim to be born with a golden throat. I am content with who I am, Sire. Now begone, ghost, for your part is over and this scene has ended."

The ghost raised his arms high as though preparing to crush Fabrizio's skull. Fabrizio waited, holding his breath as he watched the wind tear apart the fragile light, disintegrating the ghost of his father. The armor's clanging softened into a distant pinging as the ghost faded.

Fabrizio puffed out his cheeks in a long, relieved breath. He heard Mirabella shift behind him and turned around. She had removed the mask of Pantelone and was smiling. With Pantelone tucked under her arm, she clapped her hands.

"Bravo, Fabrizio."

Fabrizio bowed, one foot pointed in front, with a flourish of his hand.

"Is it true?" Mirabella asked. "Was your mother really a mermaid?"

"No, a siren," Fabrizio announced. "My father, of course, couldn't tell the difference. But I can clearly recall the wonder of my mother's voice. It's strange. I could have sworn I heard her singing tonight."

"Maybe it was Erminia?" Mirabella suggested.

"Of course." Fabrizio clapped his hands together. "She must have freed herself from whatever curse bound her to silence."

"Is it possible that Erminia is one of your aunts?" Mirabella asked.

The more Fabrizio thought about this, the more grateful he was that the darkness hid his furious blush. Erminia might be his aunt, but all he could think of was his unrequited desire for her luminous breasts floating on the surface of the sea and the dark, secret cavern between her thighs. Enticing and utterly sinful. It would be almost like sleeping with his mother.

"Fabrizio, are you all right?" Mirabella asked in the silence.

Fabrizio nodded. He had wanted Erminia, but she had always gently resisted him. There was no shame in desiring her, he decided, and good fortune had prevented him from doing anything more embarrassing. Still, it couldn't hurt to move in the right direction. He pulled

Mirabella into his arms, held her tightly, and kissed the soft skin of her earlobe.

"Will you marry me, Mirabella?"

"Yes," she answered. "Yes, I will."

Fabrizio held her close for a long time, not wanting to break the fragile skin of this spell of happiness, love, and a future. But Pantelone grew restless on Mirabella's arm, yawning loudly and then snoring.

Mirabella retied the mask around Fabrizio's neck, then lay down with him beneath the Arch of Dreams, their arms wrapped around each other. Gazing up at the night sky, they cast wishes on a handful of shooting stars that blazed brightly in the darkness and then were gone, carrying the wishes with them.

37

Don Gianlucca crawled on his hands and knees through the dark tangle of the forest underbrush. Thorns and twigs gouged his palms. His chest ached; his cracked, bleeding lips gasped for air. With each expansion of his lungs, two halves of a snapped rib bone scraped together. He coughed, folded around the waves of pain, and gagged as blood bubbled into his mouth. One leg dragged behind him, oozing blood down his thigh. He could hear the whooping cries of the maenads, beating the bushes with their hands and spears. He curled into a knot of agony and lay as quiet as his ragged breathing would allow. The leaves shuddered violently overhead, battered by the tempest of searching hands. And then the hands passed over him without finding him. In the stillness, he heard the maenads depart, the drummers trying to keep pace with the hunters.

He waited a long time, lying in the merciful dark. His nostrils were filled with the scent of humus and the sweet sap of crushed leaves. As long as he took shallow breaths and didn't move, he could endure the scorching pain in his chest. The blood trickling over his lips was warm, but his body shivered with cold. He closed his eyes, exhausted. In his mind he saw the maenads circling him, their rigid, white faces alive in the torchlight, the glowing, orange eyes hunting him with a bestial madness. Hands had grabbed him and thrown him to the ground. As he turned over, a cast spear had entered his thigh, nearly pinning him to the earth. He had fought them off from the ground.

A woman had clubbed him twice on the chest before he had succeeded in wrestling the cudgel from her. He had swung the knobbed wood into the side of her head, exploding her mask into small, chalky pieces. Beneath the mask, Don Gianlucca saw a woman's ravaged features contorted by madness. She reeled back, clutching her naked face, her lips forming a taut circle. With blood streaming between her fingers, she ran screaming among her sister maenads, grabbing at their weapons and plucking wildly at their masks. Amid the confusion, Don Gianlucca wrenched the spear free from his thigh and escaped into the underbrush.

In the silence of the forest, Don Gianlucca could hear the labored beating of his heart. He wondered if he was dying. His thigh throbbed and he felt dense liquid thickening in his veins, paralyzing the muscle of his leg as it moved upward toward his groin.

Poison, not intended to kill him outright, but to keep him from escaping. He struggled to rouse himself. He didn't want to die like a beast, hiding in the undergrowth. He wanted to see the stars, the moon, even if they were only an illusion of the maze. He wanted to believe that he looked upward to the dome of heaven and sent his soul soaring over the walls of the maze and into the freedom of the night. Groaning, he raised himself on his knees. He pushed away the stubborn twigs and crawled through the gnarled mat of branches until he reached a small clearing around a blighted oak tree. Using the rotting trunk for support, he managed to stand, his weight resting uneasily on his good leg.

He gazed around him in the stilled night and smiled grimly. The olive trees were gone. He had returned to the dying forest again. The oaks were ghostly in the moonlight, their pewter arms nearly naked of leaves. The wind gusted, lifting the stiff boughs and rattling the few dry acorns. As Don Gianlucca was seized by a spasm of coughing, he wrapped his arms across his chest, the pain tearing like a jagged knife through his body. He wept with agony, the salt from his tears stinging in the scratches of his face.

When he had stopped coughing, he wiped away a trickle of blood from his chin. He glanced up at the fragments of sky visible between the etched lines of entwined branches. One star glittered like a woman's jeweled earring hanging from one branch, while on another limb, the moon rested in a nest of twigs. It was as much as he was going to have of the sky's freedom, he decided. He was too weary and in too much pain to find an open field. His soul would have to find its own way through the tenebrous maze of branches.

Don Gianlucca sat down again, grimacing as his wounded leg buckled uselessly beneath him. His back rested against the rough bark of the tree and his hands lay palm up on either side of his body. He panted, hearing the air squeak in and out of his throat like a tattered bellows. He thought he should pray and tried to remember the words that would proclaim his sincere contrition and cleanse his soul of sin.

But memory played tricks on him. He wanted to express repentance for his misdeeds, but the thought of those deeds recalled their pleasures not their sinfulness. The cool night breeze brought him the cloying scent of a woman's perfume. He licked his lips, and through the metallic sting of blood he imagined the sweet taste of wine. His upturned palms recalled the weight of a breast, the soft mound of a woman's furred sex, the firm density of her backside. He chuckled and coughed painfully, blood speckling his chin. Here he was, dying an unrepentant sinner while the whores of Venice appeared to keep him company. Even close to death, Don Gianlucca realized he was hard-pressed to renounce his passion for them. Despite the pain, he shrugged. Were they not God's handiwork too? Weren't their kisses a Vin Santo, their white outstretched limbs, their long supple torsos a cross on which he had crucified himself over and over again?

A girl's solemn face appeared in his mind, her large somber eyes holding him captive. Vittorina, whom he had loved, but not well enough.

"Forgive me," he whispered and closed his heavy eyelids.

"Ego te absolvo a peccatis tuis," answered a feathery voice.

Don Gianlucca forced his eyes open and saw the faint outlines of a small woman standing near his feet. In the sketchy moonlight, she gazed at him with sorrow. He smiled, believing her to be an angel and was pleased to know that heaven had not abandoned him after all. As she approached, her white skirts drifting weightlessly over his broken body, he recognized her. She bent, touched her fingers to the bloody wound on his thigh, and put her reddened fingers to her mouth. Her transparent form became opaque. Her dark eyes were solid wells of grief, but her face was as sweet and childlike as the morning he had left her with a worthless promise of marriage.

"Vittorina." He sighed. "Have you come to taunt me in death, I who wronged you in life?"

"No, I am here because it's my forgiveness you have begged for, Gianlucca, and not God's. I grant it to you, amore mio, though a whore's forgiveness counts for little."

"It's much more than I deserve." The maenads' poison had numbed his body up to his waist. He could no longer feel the ground beneath him or close his hands into fists. Soon the poison would arrest the fitful labors of his torn lungs. Anguish swept over him, and shame at his selfishness that had made this sad ghost.

"Vittorina, I absolve you from your crime against God."

She shook her head. "Too late, Gianlucca. Since my suicide, my soul has wandered lost, my spirit trapped by the thicket of these dead woods. I cannot enter heaven."

"I will bring you there," he declared.

"How?"

"My soul is still mine, and it shall carry the burden of us both. Come, climb into me, possess me, and at the moment of my death, my soul will release us both to God."

She looked away, refusing the offer. "My haunted spirit will drag you down into these woods."

"No," Don Gianlucca said. It was getting harder to move his mouth and speak. The poison was folding over him like a heavy cloak. "We will not be abandoned by heaven. I am ready to be relieved of this body. It's no more than a dark shell that covers God's purest radiant light. Climb deep into me, Vittorina, dig below the mortal shell and find that well of light. At death, it will be released like an arrow, returning to its celestial target."

Vittorina's pale cheeks burned bright with hope. Delicately, she sat astride him, the weight of her fragile ghost settling on him like fog. She closed her arms around his neck, her legs around his hips. She pressed her rosebud mouth against his and moaned. Gianlucca inhaled a long ragged breath and felt her misty form sucked into his mouth, his nostrils, and the corners of his eyes, damp with tears. Like a fine mist, she soaked into his pores and settled in the hollows of his broken frame: the cavity at the base of his throat, along the narrow ledge of his collarbones, in the valley of taut skin beneath his sternum. She stretched her being into the span of his hips and wrapped her misty limbs around the tendons of his knees and elbows. His paralyzed fingers contracted with a sudden spasm, shocked to life by her presence in him.

Still she traveled, merging with his innermost self. He felt her hands stroke his heart, brush against his liver, his spleen, cradle for a moment his torn lung. Feathery sighs cooled his heated temples from within the pulsing skin. She invaded his bones, squeezed herself into the rich pulp of his marrow. For a moment he felt a shift in his body, a vague sense of a woman's broad hips, the curve of breasts, the cheeks free of stub-

ble. He felt in his aching heart her relief at escaping solitude and the
dark woods of the maze.

Don Gianlucca stared out at the dying trees and managed a smile. He
too would not die alone.

The smile lingered as the poison paralyzed his face. He wanted to
speak the words of contrition aloud, but could not move his tongue.
Around him, the pale trees gradually receded, falling farther back into
darkness, until they were shafts of moonlight. They had become angels
he thought, lined up around him like heavenly soldiers, guarding his soul
as it entered heaven. They would not let him slip and fall with his precious double burden.

Between the shafts of light, he saw the luminescent figure of Christ
approach, arms opened to receive him, His form burning brighter than
the sun. The warmth of that divine light surged over him, penetrated the
dying husk of his body to touch the last filaments of his nerves with fingers of fire. Odd, Don Gianlucca thought, that Christ was so . . . so
short. This blazing form, embraced by a corona of pure light, was no
bigger than a boy.

"Give me your soul," Christ said, and held out a blazing hand.

I render it unto you, my Lord, Don Gianlucca thought, tears of joy
evaporating on his withered cheeks. There was a tugging at his breast as
a hand reached in, searching for the root of his soul. Don Gianlucca exhaled, freeing the last of his breath to give passage to his soul and the
ghost of Vittorina into the hand of God.

Zolfo backed away in alarm from the recumbent man as the soul slipped
over his fingers, snaked up his arm, and entered his flaming body
through his ear. He cried out, shocked by the explosion of light behind
his eyelids and the sudden roaring of voices. The soul turned and turned
in his brain, wings battering the walls of his skull, protesting this false
prison that was not its intended resting place. Unable to flee, it grew as
heavy as a pure drop of molten lead and descended into the core of
Zolfo's fiery being. His spine shuddered, a stiffened cord stringing together dowels of bone. His skeleton clenched into a hard, brittle frame.
His muscles grew dense, his flesh like a sponge absorbing the constant
flow of blood. Organs shaped themselves into single purposes, unwill-
ing to be transmutable. His heart beat quickly, the rhythm no longer that
of the earth, but of a man in terror.

The corona of light around his fiery body dimmed and died as the
soul embedded itself where Zolfo could no longer feel it. Zolfo stared
at his hands, touched himself over the front of his chest, slowly realiz-

ing how the soul had altered him. In making him a man, it had permanently congealed his malleable form into immutable flesh around it. He
staggered back and for the first time felt a strange emotion that bowed
his shoulders and made his flesh stink.

Fear, his memories told him. Humans know fear as well as ambition.
Zolfo glanced back at the dead man, surprised to see a pile of ashy
bones, not completely burned away. Too many bones for one man. He
peered at the smoldering pile and kicked one skull away from another
lying next to it. There were two humans here, Zolfo thought, though he
was certain there had been only one man. He picked up a slender rib and
then found a second, bigger, rib, cracked in the middle. The bones broke
into sooty crumbs in his hands, and he flung them away with a snarl of
disgust.

Who these bones and the soul had once belonged to didn't matter.
The soul was his, and now, he was truly a man. Though he was human,
Zolfo sensed that he could still draw strength from the source of his
power. He could no longer change himself, but he could change the
world around him. Zolfo whispered a phrase taken from the cries of the
stolen soul.

"The strong man shall turn to tow, and his work shall become a
spark; both shall burn together and there shall be none to quench the
flames."

Zolfo glared at the dying trees and gave a smirk of satisfaction as
leaves of fire unfurled along their dry branches. The wood crackled and
burned, smoke rising into the air. One tree lit another and then another
as the fire spread. He would cleanse the maze of all others save himself
and those few he chose to save, who would be his to command. Zolfo
created in his mind a circular path for the fire, moving first along the
outside of the maze, slowly spiraling in to the center. He turned on his
heel and walked away from the flaming forest, heading through the olive
grove toward the path that would lead him directly to the center of the
maze.

At the edge of the dying oak trees he stopped. Beneath the roaring
of the fire, he could hear another voice crying in outrage. He sensed a
new wave of resistance, almost like the one that had met him at the gate,
swirling around him, pressing hands against his shoulders, preventing
him from traveling further on the path.

He snarled and pushed back. This one who fought against him would
burn in the flames the same as everything else. Zolfo continued his
journey, his eyes flickering like candles through the rolling clouds of
drifting smoke.

38

oberto, look over there!" Anna called excitedly. "That looks like Mirabella's dress. Madonna mia, is she all right?" Mirabella was stretched out, belly down, on the grassy bank of the small stream Anna and Roberto had been following. Mirabella's loosened hair billowed in the wind, and her faded green skirts exposed a length of leg.

"Mirabella! Mirabella," Anna and Roberto shouted, and hurried toward her.

A high, musical laugh rang over the stream's babbling. Anna stopped, clutching Roberto's doublet, and listened, a scowl creasing her forehead. Mirabella seemed to be conversing with someone who lay almost out of sight beyond her. Anna and Roberto glanced at each other and then proceeded more cautiously. Anna's pulse quickened as she recognized something familiar in the sultry sound of Mirabella's voice and laughter—a throaty, intimate sound that was not so different from Anna's own voice when she was in the company of—

"A man!" Anna snapped aloud. "She's lying with a man! Hurry, Roberto, and pray that she hasn't lost her honor along with her good sense!" Furious, Anna bunched her skirts in her hands, holding them up to clear the long grass. What sort of ruffian would take advantage of an innocent child like Mirabella? What kind of devil would seduce such a cherub, her cherub?

"Take your hands off her, you scoundrel, before I thrash you into the dirt!" she commanded as she neared Mirabella and saw the long dark form lying next to her on the grass and the arms wrapped around her waist. Mirabella gave a squeal and bolted upright. She turned and Anna gaped, shocked to see her daughter's face half-hidden by a mask of the elderly Pantelone. One of her masks no less. Anna shook her finger at the old reprobate.

"Mamma! Roberto! O'Dio," Pantelone exclaimed in a girlish voice, the blue eyes innocent in the dark, wrinkled skin of the old man's face. "It's not what you think!"

At her side, Anna heard a choking sound. She turned to see Roberto strangling his laughter, which ended in a fit of coughing at her furious glare. Roberto attempted to restore his composure by smoothing down his wayward locks and straightening his doublet. Then he glanced up at the angry woman and shrugged.

"What is it about you Forsetti women and masks? Some sort of aphrodisiac?" he asked.

"Boh!" Anna exhaled, waving his question away. "Get up! Get up, both of you!" she ordered the couple. "And take off that mask, Mirabella!"

"Mamma, we weren't doing anything! I swear it," Mirabella protested, pushing the mask of Pantelone on top of her head. Next to her, Fabrizio stood up slowly, brushing grass and leaves from his hose. The mask of Arlecchino was balanced on the crown of his head. He glanced sheepishly at Roberto and then Anna.

"I find you lying in the grass with this man, and you tell me you're doing nothing? What kind of stupid tale is this? Do you think me a fool? Have you lost your mind, Mirabella?" Anna railed, not waiting for the blushing girl to answer. "Would you give away your virginity to this . . . this . . ."

"Actor?" Fabrizio finished. He tried to say more, but Anna held up her hand to stop him.

"Be quiet!" Anna commanded. "Roberto will deal with you later."

"Me?" Roberto blurted.

"Buffo, help me," Anna pleaded.

"Help you do what, Anna?" Roberto replied, annoyed. "What can you have in mind this time?"

"My daughter is being seduced by this . . . this . . ."

"Actor," Mirabella finished.

"Mirabella, don't interrupt. I am trying to stop you from making a horrible mistake."

"No. You're trying to stop me from doing what you do all the time."

"And what does that mean?" Anna snapped.

"You know what it means," Mirabella said coolly. "How many men have lingered in your bed, Mamma?"

Anna staggered back. "Viper!" she hissed. Then she lunged forward, a hand raised to slap Mirabella.

"Anna—Mirabella," Roberto and Fabrizio cried, grabbing the two women and pulling them apart.

"Anna, stop this! She's your daughter," Roberto commanded.

"Mirabella, please. It's her blessing I want, not her curse," Fabrizio pleaded.

"Why my blessing?" Anna demanded, surprised.

"I don't want to seduce Mirabella," Fabrizio answered earnestly. "I want to marry her."

"Marry her? But she's not old enough."

"Mamma, I'm past sixteen," Mirabella exclaimed.

Anna stared at her daughter. In the years that she had buried herself in her own private grief, her daughter had grown and blossomed into a woman.

"Sixteen, can it be so soon?" Anna repeated softly.

"Yes, Mamma. Please let me marry Fabrizio," Mirabella said.

Anna had married at sixteen. But that had been different. Forsetti had been a respectable man, with a profession and an income. She herself had a dowry to protect her. This handsome but completely inept young man Mirabella had set her heart on couldn't have been a worse choice.

"Be reasonable, Mirabella," Anna said. "How can you marry this . . . this . . ."

"Actor," Roberto supplied. "Why not, Anna? The girl has been around the Commedia all her life. What did you expect of her? To marry some old man of Venice with shriveled calves and a fat purse?"

"But how will you live?" she asked the couple.

"We want to form our own Commedia troupe," Mirabelle answered breathlessly. "I intend to perform as well."

"You, an actress?" Anna asked. The girl was mad! Love had made her mad! Anna slapped a hand against her forehead. "And what about your stutter, Fabrizio, eh?" she asked angrily.

"Cured," Fabrizio answered proudly. "Left behind in the maze. I know, Signora, that I don't look like much, but I assure you my parentage has given to me some unique gifts. I will be an actor, a great one, and Mirabella, as my wife, will be the most celebrated of the Innamorate!"

Mirabella beamed at Fabrizio. "It's true, Mamma. Fabrizio is truly great. And as for me, I want to play all the roles—the Servetta, the Innamorata, Colombina, Isabella. I have never wanted any thing more in my life. Except, of course, your blessing at this moment."

Anna stared at the couple in amazement, their youthful confidence, their exuberance, and simple joy in each other's presence eroding her anger. Not even the weight of money could forge such a strong bond. And she had to admit that they made an attractive couple. Fabrizio had lost the furrowed brow and clenched jaw his stutter had given him.

But it was Mirabella who dissolved the last of Anna's resistance. Gone was the coltish awkwardness and the habit of keeping her shy face turned toward the ground. She stood next to Fabrizio, poised and determined. Even in the badly cut dress, Anna had to admit her daughter was pretty enough. A light glowed in the depths of her blue eyes, sparked by the heady potion of young love.

"All right," Anna said, breaking the silence. "What else can I do when confronted by such faces? I give you my blessing, Mirabella. I've nothing to pay in the way of a dowry," she told Fabrizio ruefully, "but I can promise your troupe masks and a home in Venice."

Anna stretched forth her arms and Mirabella flew into them. Anna sighed deeply, holding her daughter, willing herself to accept the changes in Mirabella.

"And you, Mamma?" the girl whispered in Anna's ear. "Will you be able to work again at your beloved masks?"

Anna released her daughter and gently brushed back the wild strands of hair from Mirabella's face.

"The thorns no longer torture me," she answered softly. "My curse, too, has been buried at last—with Roberto's help. You know, he rescued me."

"Roberto, how happy I am to see you here," Mirabella said, kissing the older man's hand passionately. "You got my letter, didn't you? And then you came after Mamma. You were worried for her, weren't you?"

Roberto nodded. "Yes, well, both of you, really."

"How romantic."

Roberto grinned as pink spread across his forehead.

"How heroic!" Mirabella sighed.

Roberto waved his hands about to show it had been nothing.

"Anna! Mirabella!" a woman's voice sang out from the trees. "Help me, please!"

At the sound of their names, the two women turned and saw Simonetta stumbling toward them over the brow of the bank, supporting an injured man in bloody bandages slumped over her shoulder.

"Rinaldo!" Roberto called, and started up the bank, with Fabrizio close behind.

The two men relieved Simonetta of her burden and, carrying the injured Rinaldo between them, returned to the riverbank where they laid Rinaldo down in the grass. "I need water to wash his wound," Simonetta said wearily, sitting down next to him.

Mirabella tore a strip from her shift which she soaked in the stream and handed to Simonetta, who used it to wash a wound on Rinaldo's arm.

"Simonetta, what has happened to you?" Anna asked. "You look as though you have suffered a terrible battle."

Simonetta gave a wry smile. "More than one, I'm afraid, since I last saw you."

"Poveretta! And do you still search for the waters of youth?" Anna asked.

"No. I found them," Simonetta said thickly. "But I refused to drink when I learned that, along with my sorrow, I would also forget the few things in my life that I hold dear."

Roberto laid a hand on Rinaldo's shoulder and called his name. Rinaldo's lids, smudged with smoke and dirt, fluttered open and his red-rimmed eyes stared back at Roberto. "It's me, Roberto. I'm glad to see you alive, my friend."

"And I, you, Roberto." Rinaldo squinted past Roberto's shoulder to Anna, who was sitting by Simonetta. "You found her?" he asked with a small grin.

Roberto nodded and then jerked his head toward Simonetta. "And I see you, too, have found the woman you sought. It seems, my friend, that you have changed your mind about her."

Rinaldo chuckled and then grimaced with pain. "How is it that a man can be both ruined and saved by a woman's love, Roberto?"

"Happy for us is the truce that follows. No more scornful glances . . ." Roberto quoted.

"Look, over there," Anna said, pointing to the bend in the stream. "Here come two more pilgrims. The woman looks familiar."

"It's Erminia!" Fabrizio cried, and began waving his arm.

"But it can't be," Anna said. "The woman's skin is too fair."

"She has shed her disguise," Fabrizio explained, "and returned to her true siren's form. But who is the man?"

"I know him," answered Roberto, "though he too has changed since last we met." Roberto noticed Lorenzo's loose-limbed gait, his arm draped languidly around the woman's waist. His stiff black doublet was gone, his immaculate white shirt torn open at the neck, and his long, black hair was tangled except for the white lock that lay curled neatly over his forehead.

"Don't tell me," croaked Rinaldo, struggling to sit up. "It can't be."

"But it is," Roberto replied. "The tight-assed lawyer, Lorenzo Falcomatta, looking rather . . . unlaced."

"Undone," Rinaldo quipped.

"Unraveled." Anna laughed.

"See how the siren leads him on—" Fabrizio said.

"By the strings of his hose," Simonetta added.

"Oh he's definitely in the grip of love," Mirabella finished, squinting.

"And what a lovely white hand it is that has seized him," Roberto added. "Lucky man."

"Roberto! Rinaldo! My friends, how it warms my soul to see you again," Lorenzo greeted them. "And in the company of such beautiful women," he added, bowing.

"You seem well, Lorenzo," Rinaldo said. "Did you find the servant you were seeking?"

"I was waylaid by the servant of Orpheus, a three-faced, skinny little prick. Had this divine siren, this most extraordinary muse"—he kissed Erminia's hand—"not saved me from my wretched fate, I'd be a headless fool instead of standing before you, a new man."

"And had I not met this sublime poet, this extraordinary man who gave me everything I asked for and more," Erminia added, little clouds of silvery fish floating from her mouth, "I might well be as silent as the stones on the beach."

"You can speak again!" Fabrizio exclaimed, and embraced her. "Zia Erminia!"

"What did you call me? Since when did I become your aunt?" she asked, emitting a thin stream of green-misted seaweed. "And where is your stutter?"

"Departed, even as your voice has returned," Fabrizio announced. "And there is more to tell—"

"I'd bet a bag of florins that between all of us there are enough tales to keep even Boccaccio amused," Roberto interrupted. "But does anyone have any food that might sustain us while we listen?"

"Yes!" Mirabella bubbled. "At the Arch of Dreams, where we slept last night, our hostess saw to it that we were well fed. When we set out today, we took the remains of the meal with us. Come, share it with us!"

Mirabella unwrapped a length of purple cloth, producing several loaves of bread, two thick wedges of cheese, a string of sausages, a bundle of cured olives, a cold breast of fowl heavily seasoned with saffron and cinnamon, a pair of roasted peacock legs, figs, and some crumbling cakes. Fabrizio lifted two leather flasks of wine from the stream, promptly uncorked them, and passed one to Simonetta and the other to Erminia.

"This is quite the feast!" Roberto said delightedly as he broke the bread and handed a piece to Anna.

"Who was your hostess?" Anna asked Mirabella. "Until I was taken by the maenads, I saw no one else in the maze."

"A strange girl, really," Fabrizio answered. "A bit of the gutter in her stance. Eyes sharp as a stiletto, but the rest of her face like a Botticelli angel's."

"Fair-haired?" Simonetta asked, sucking on an olive pit. "With red and yellow ribbons?"

"Yes," Mirabella said. "And she was accompanied by a peculiar servant. A tall man with shifty eyes, rough-spoken. Do you remember, Fabrizio? He annoyed you very much."

"Che buffone," the young man grumbled.

"Called Giano, the two-faced?" Lorenzo asked, his eyes narrowing.

"The very same."

"My wayward servant," Lorenzo announced to Roberto and Rinaldo. "I should have known he'd survive in here. The man is a cat with nine lives. I just hope the girl can handle him better than I could."

"Who will tell their tale first?" Simonetta asked, as she shaved off a slice of cheese and dropped it into Rinaldo's mouth.

Rinaldo swallowed. "If I may be so bold," he said, and gestured to Simonetta to help him stand. Food had revived him and the wine had restored a ruddy color to his gaunt cheeks. He swung the purple cloth over his shoulders like a regal cape and his eyes glittered with dark humor as he planted his feet well apart and thrust out his chest. He stroked the ends of his mustache into twin curls, twisted his mouth into an arrogant sneer, and glared ferociously. Mirabella giggled nervously.

"Hah, you may laugh!" Rinaldo boomed. "Look well, young woman, on this preeminence of a man, this preponderance of strength, this killer of Turks—"

"Wait!" Anna shrieked happily. "Wait, I have the very thing!" She fished into her bag and pulled out the mask of Il Capitano. With a respectful bow, she handed it to Rinaldo, who laughed dryly as he tied it on.

Il Capitano's long bulbous nose stabbed the air, and beneath the heavy pleated brow, the fierce triangular eyes stared aggressively.

"Hear me now as I recount the valiant deeds of a man so brave, so bold and fierce, that he sprung from his mother's womb fully clothed in armor—"

"Oh the pain!" muttered Simonetta to Anna.

"Clothed in shining armor—" Rinaldo repeated more loudly.

"Though his undergarments are tattered rags—" Fabrizio whispered behind his hand.

"Tatters caused by the incredible virility of my body hairs which, when I am enraged, burst through those feeble garments," Rinaldo shouted. "Men quake in the fiercesome presence of Il Capitano, the magnificent. Women everywhere swoon—"

"Due to the stench of his rotten teeth," murmured Anna.

"I am the greatest lover of all time. My sword is enormous."

"And limp in the scabbard—" Mirabella added.

"I have satisfied the lust of cannibal queens—"

"And made them puke with indigestion, the old sardine—" Simonetta said, pretending to gag on a finger.

Unable to hold up under the rigorous demands of Il Capitano's inflated personality and the audience's derisive asides, Rinaldo started to laugh. He slumped down into the grass again and slipped the mask off his face, revealing a more thoughtful expression.

"Even with your mask, Signora, I'm not much of an actor. And yet, my curse was to play the role of a violent man and a slave to the power of a charmed sword. This, then, is my tale."

Between draughts of wine, Rinaldo recounted the story of the mercenary's sword, of its curse, and how his own youthful foolishness had bound him to its devilish purpose. When he spoke of the caverns, Mirabella and Anna shuddered at his description of the battling corpses. They clung to each other, as Rinaldo described the bull-headed monster in the black heart of the cave. He kissed Simonetta's palm before relating how she had arrived like an avenging angel to bring him salvation. And when he was finished, he bowed from where he sat and the audience applauded with loud bravos.

"Who's next?" Mirabella asked, plucking a sliver of roast fowl.

Lorenzo leaned over to Anna. "Tell me, Signora, have you the face of that fraudulent, Latin-mangling lawyer, Il Dottore, in your bag? I believe it's my turn."

Laughing, Anna retrieved Il Dottore's mask and handed it to Lorenzo. Then she looked up at the others. "Who else would like a mask with which to tell their tale?"

"Give me Pantelone! I, too, am not much of an actor, but this is one character I know very well," Roberto said, wiping the peacock grease from his fingers onto his hose. He hummed happily as he tied on the mask of the old Venetian miser and propped it on the top of his head in readiness.

"I'll take the ingenue," Mirabella said.

"I will keep the face of Arlecchino," Fabrizio said, stroking the cheeks of the fool's mask.

"This one is for you," Anna said to Simonetta, handing her the nymph. "Beware of the satyrs!"

"Oh, I have no fear of those randy goats!" Simonetta said, and took the mask.

"Erminia, what mask will you wear?" Fabrizio asked.

"None! I have already suffered too long from wearing one. It's good to be myself again. No, wait. I have the very thing." She pulled up Mirabella's spectacles from the pocket of her shift and put them on. Her sapphire eyes grew huge behind the glass.

"And you, Mamma? Will you wear a mask?" Mirabella asked.

Anna's smile froze at the memory of Bacchus extending a peach-colored mask to her. Her face paled and she shook her head wordlessly.

"Anna will play the Innamorata," Roberto answered for her. "She wears no mask, save what the look of love gives her."

Anna smiled weakly and squeezed his hand.

"Now that we have our parts, let us begin again," Roberto said cheerfully. "Il Dottore, the stage is yours."

Lorenzo slipped the lawyer's mask on his face, adjusting the huge bulbous nose over his own. Bushy eyebrows of lamb's wool concealed his dark eyes. He rose to his feet, spouting incomprehensible Latin as he turned in a small circle to face his audience, which segued into a lecture in heavily accented Bolognese.

"A man who is sick, can be said to be unwell," he intoned, a finger in the air. "He who is wrong is less right than any others. To cure a toothache, place an apple in your mouth and your head in the oven. Before the apple is cooked, the toothache will be gone!"

"Beautifully put." Fabrizio nodded.

"If I put my mind to it, I could do worse," Ill Dottore replied.

"I believe you!" Fabrizio cried.

"Matrimonium requiritur—"

"Who will save us from this insufferable pedant!" moaned Roberto.

"I shall save you, gentle people!" Erminia chimed, a pearly mist circling her kelp-black hair. She stood and raised her white arms to the sky.

"Listen, good people, and learn how the siren's song transformed the loquacious lawyer into a lusty poet!"

"Show us! Show us!" shouted the audience.

With Fabrizio agreeing to improvise alternately the part of Ipnos and the head of Orpheus, Erminia and Lorenzo recounted their adventures in the grotto of the ancient poet. Then Lorenzo spoke of his perilous journey into the depths of the sea, his near drowning in the arms of his dead wife, and his surrender, body and soul, to the siren whose voice carried him aloft to the edge of the universe.

Lorenzo removed the mask of Il Dottore and stood before the audience as himself. Softly, he began to recite.

> *"Fammi amor qual voi offersa*
> *S'io dovesi e ben morire!*
> Strike me, Cupid, with thy dart, even if I should die of it.
> If I should lose her, at least my noble desire will
> Show great courage!"

"Che bella." Mirabella sighed, and the rest of the audience applauded enthusiastically.

Lorenzo and Erminia gave dignified bows and then resumed their place on the grass. Roberto coughed nervously into his palm to clear his voice. With all eyes suddenly turned on him, he rose, lowered the mask of Pantelone, and stepped into the center.

Pantelone strutted like a cock, his neck snaking back and forth as he walked, his hands flapping in the air. "I know how old I am, there is no need to point this out to me," he snapped at Rinaldo as he passed by him. "But, although I am no longer young, I am bursting with health, fit as a stallion, a dog in the prime of life! All I need to fulfill my wants is a woman. Someone beautiful, lusty—"

"And rich!" Anna shouted.

"Oh yes, there is no harm in a lovely fat dowry. Oh, the thought makes me swell. Now who will serve as wife to Pantelone? Will it be you, sweet dove?" he asked, bending down with an old man's grunt to chuck Mirabella under the chin. "Eh, you'd like to make Pantelone happy, wouldn't you?"

"Oh, no, Signore, you're old enough to be my father! And may well be, for all I know!" the girl exclaimed wide-eyed.

"Shh, don't let the others know!" Pantelone hissed, waving the girl away. "How about you, my lovely creature, with your risotto-scented skin?" Pantelone asked, sniffing Simonetta's hair.

She gave a husky laugh and stroked the immense length of Pantelone's nose, inspiring him to shake his leg like a hound scratching itself.

"I'm only too familiar with your kind, old man, and would sooner wed an ass. At least the ride would last longer! Besides, I've no money to my name."

Pantelone squeaked and shuffled quickly away. "How about you, my melon-chested beauty? Let me thump you and see if you're ripe!" he wheezed, reaching to grope Anna's breasts.

"Oh I'm past ripe, good sir." Anna laughed, swerving to avoid him. "I am a lonely widow—"

"Better still. Shoes that are broken in fit more comfortably."

"And my husband left all his worldly goods to me."

"Ah, Signora, you are making me faint with desire. What, besides yourself, is there to acquire?"

"A bed, slightly broken—"

"A promising sign of vigor." He drooled, rubbing his hands together.

"And a French disease," Anna grinned wickedly.

"He must have been quite a man," humphed Pantelone. "Excuse me, but perhaps I will dine alone tonight, Signora, for I am a chaste man—"

"Yes, a cheap man," Fabrizio agreed.

"A solitary soul—"

"A sodomized hole—"

"A man who prefers sitting to doing—"

"Shitting to screwing—" Fabrizio's head continued to bob in agreement.

Now it was Roberto's turn to laugh. He slipped off the mask of Pantelone, his face flushed, mopped his sweating brow with a handkerchief, and returned the mask to Anna. Sitting down beside her, he took her hands in his as he addressed his audience.

"What makes a man leave the comfort of his table, take to the road, brave dragons and savage women that threaten to tear him into shreds? It isn't the promise of thumping ripe melons or acquiring a widow's wealth," he said good-humoredly. "It's the power of the woman herself. It's the force of her glance that penetrates like the arrows of Eros. It's the silk of her skin, the sweet scent of her breath, the strength of her hands. I could do nothing else but follow. When Anna left Venice, nothing else in Venice existed."

In a quiet voice, Roberto recounted his journey from Venice, the brigands on the road, his fortuitous meeting with Rinaldo. He told of the wonders he had seen in the maze, the scenographer's dragon, the pale ghost of the Tago, and the ravaging maenads. He held his arm tightly around Anna's waist as he said that he would go through it all again for the sake of her love. Anna and Mirabella shed a few tears, each taking turns daubing their eyes with Roberto's handkerchief.

Then it was Simonetta's turn. She lowered her face to put on the mask of the nymph, arranged her black hair to fall behind the wreath of dried leaves, and looked up. The audience inhaled sharply. The early twilight softened the stark lines of her body, which looked supple as a willow. The thin creases of her long neck were hidden by the mask's rounded chin. Behind the youthful features of the nymph, Simonetta recounted the brutal death of her family and her flight into the walled city, numbed by grief and overcome with shame at having survived where others had suffered and died.

"On that plain, amid so much carnage, I ceased to be young," the nymph said, her arms crossed over her breasts. "And in the city, I sacrificed myself and my honor on a barren bed. It was a death without dying."

Simonetta removed the mask and gazed at it sadly. The hard, chiseled features of her own face looked haggard after the nymph's wild beauty. But a spark remained in her eyes, and she grinned as she handed the mask back to Anna. Her hands on her hips, she tossed her head as she confronted the audience.

"Are not all men cruel creatures?" she declaimed. "They will do almost anything to get us on our backs. Liars, every one of them!" Simonetta wagged her finger at each man.

"Colombina! Colombina!" Fabrizio wailed, groveling at Simonetta's feet.

"Humph, that is my name, but how you stretch it until it would tear," Simonetta replied sharply. She arched an eyebrow at Rinaldo and pursed her lips. "At first, I am the new lover to be conquered by lies. Once tricked into a wife, I am changed into a servant. All day long, from every corner of the house, my ears ring. Colombina, where's my hat! Colombina, bring me food! Colombina, clean my ears! Colombina, I want my pipe! Colombina, get naked!

"And yet, there is worse. For a man gets hungry and believes it is his right to sample other women just as he samples different cheeses. But if I wink at the fishmonger or blow a kiss to the baker or bat my eyes at the boys in the market, then I will feel his fist to my ear or his boot to my backside, and consider myself lucky that he doesn't murder me.

"Listen to me all you women. If I, Colombina, were made Queen tomorrow, I would make it a law that all unfaithful men must carry a green switch. Believe me when I tell you that in no time our cities would resemble forests!"

"Brava! Brava!" shouted Anna and Mirabella, clapping. "Colombina for Queen!"

"But how will you live without men, Colombina?" Rinaldo demanded. "Will you be an Amazon?"

Simonetta shook her head. "Oh no, my captain," she said in her own husky voice. "I have seen their world and find it as brutal as any ruled by man. Listen when I tell you of the death disguised as perpetual youth that almost befell me among the Amazons."

Simonetta related her encounter with the Amazons on the field of battle against the centaurs and she told them of Cheiron and his offer to exchange her lost youth for everything else that mattered in her present life.

Simonetta couched the rest of her story over Rinaldo's tale of the cavern like gold threads on a cloth: the yellow-haired girl who told her Rinaldo needed Simonetta, Cheiron's gift of glowing twine that led her through the dark tunnels. With her hands clasped in front of her, Simonetta recalled the sudden unnatural surge of strength that caused her to lift up the sword at the right moment and cleave the monster's head from its shoulders. Simonetta, caught in her memories, opened her hands, released the imaginary sword, and drew a trembling hand over her eyes.

"How glad I was to let go of that cursed sword," she whispered. "And even more glad to see Rinaldo alive."

Simonetta bowed shyly and sat down next to Rinaldo again. He embraced her, kissing her to drive away the gruesome memories until she laughed and begged him to stop.

"What strange and terrible sights we have witnessed in the maze," Roberto said thoughtfully.

"And yet here we are, sitting on the grass with the ones we love, eating and drinking, and what's more, able to amuse each other with cautionary tales and deeds of valor," Lorenzo said.

"It's time for a tale of young love. Let the Innamorati take the stage." Fabrizio stood and held out his hand to Mirabella, who took it and rose. With tiny graceful steps, she positioned herself in the circle, her hands clasped before her bosom, one dainty foot extended. Her face was rapturous. Fabrizio bowed to the audience.

"My friends, today you will hear how a young woman trapped in a rioting crowd on market day fell madly in love with a handsome young swain who rescued her."

Mirabella laughed merrily. "And you will learn how the young man, completely smitten by the girl's beauty and grace, led them around in circles in the maze."

"Not fair, my goddess. The one time I let you lead, we wound up in the canal," Fabrizio protested.

"Tesoro mio, if it wasn't for that girl we'd still be cooling our heels in Diana's fountain!" Mirabella pointed out.

"Beloved cloud of desire, I am certain that it I was who led us to the Arch of Dreams."

"Oh no, pillar of masculine beauty, it was I who saw to our safety whilst you were still treading the heels of your wretched papa."

"But sweetness and light, I bravely confronted the ghost—"

"Only, breath of life, after I taught you to speak—"

"Oh no, my garden of delight, you are wrong."

"My true love, I am never wrong."

"One would think they were already married," Roberto said.

Mirabella and Fabrizio developed their own lover's duet, a tart argument, in which each shed a small bit of information about their journey, while the other pleasantly, but firmly, contradicted it. Eventually they succeeded in recounting the entire tale, and well before they had reached the conclusion they were reciting once more promises of undying love.

It was full twilight by the time the young couple had finished their performance. The rising moon cast a silvery light over the gathered couples. The cedars filled the moist air with their pungent scent, and dew weighted the grass. In the growing dark, the pilgrims huddled closer together, seeking comfort and shelter in each other's arms.

"It's your turn, Mamma," Mirabella said.

Anna stood slowly, reluctantly, brushing the dew from her skirts.

"I am more used to making the masks that allow others to speak. But I shall relate my story, though it is a sad tale, a ghost story that this heavenly light renders all the more fantastic. Hold on to the one you love while I speak. Cherish the warmth, the companionship, and the joy. For that is all the wealth that matters in this changeable world."

The moon floated higher, creating a silvery halo around Anna's head. She opened her hands, as though to catch the raining light of the stars, then she lifted them to shape the light into a child's face.

"Once I loved well, but not wisely, a man of great beauty," she started. "And although at first he returned my love, after a while, he scorned me. His love turned to poison and his words into a curse of thorns. Foolish and angry woman that I was, I allowed the thorns to take root in my body, to remind me of my hate."

Shadows drew across her eyes as she bowed her head to avoid the audience's pitying glances. "When our child died, born too soon, I believed it was my hate that had murdered it. And I accepted a curse of thorns as my punishment."

She raised her head again, her face bathed in the silver wash. "We are cursed not by others, but by our own weakness that blinds us and drives us down the wrong path in the turning of a maze. It's strange, isn't it, that out in the world, where everything is real, we were wandering, lost, while in the maze, where nothing is as it seems, we have once again found our selves."

"But not alone," Lorenzo pointed out, gazing at the siren.

"No man was ever meant to live alone," Roberto said.

"Nor woman, either," answered Simonetta. "It's like pasta without sauce."

"Meat without salt," Fabrizio added, grinning.

"Cheese without bread!" Mirabella laughed.

"Sweets without raisins!" Anna exclaimed.

"Squid without ink." Erminia smacked her lips and kissed her fingertips.

"Stop! I'm getting hungry again and we've eaten everything!" cried Fabrizio, putting his hands over his ears.

"Basta, then, it's enough," Anna said, and sat down next to Roberto.

They continued to talk for a while longer, their voices growing thick and drowsy with the night. Finally, beneath the soft whispering of the branches and the faint glimmer of the distant stars, the weary pilgrims fell asleep. They lay huddled together, each couple intertwined, their faces pressed close together. The stream's babbling grew more quiet and a wind rustled through the grass. But the pilgrims heard only the sounds of their own exhalations as they sighed in their sleep.

Erminia startled awake in the false grey light of a coming dawn as the field of magic beneath the maze ruptured. She sat up, inhaling gritty mouthfuls of ash-laden wind. She squinted through the fractured lens of Mirabella's spectacles and saw clouds of black smoke rising over the tops of the cedars. She could just hear the roar of fire and the crackle of wood being eaten by flames.

"Get up! Everyone quickly get up!" She moved rapidly among the sleepers, shaking them roughly. "The maze is on fire! Something has gone wrong. If we stay, we will be destroyed. Hurry!"

Fabrizio and Mirabella woke groggily, their eyes sticky with unfinished sleep.

"What are you saying?" Mirabella asked, getting to her feet.

"We are cooked, dead, finished, if we don't get out of here. Now!" Erminia said, helping Simonetta to stand.

"Where do we go?" Rinaldo asked.

"To the center. It's the only place where I can sense safety," Erminia answered.

"And how do we find it?" Roberto asked.

"Follow me through the stream. The water will take us there," Erminia said, and stepped into the rushing stream. "Take hands, so that we will not lose each other in the smoke."

Lorenzo took Erminia's hand and gave his other hand to Anna, who extended her free hand to Roberto. One by one, they clasped each others hands, forming a chain of pilgrims. With Erminia leading the way, they stumbled over the rocks and rushing water, moving with panicked haste through the billowing clouds of smoke and ash.

Around them in the tree-lined corridors, they heard the terrified cries of other pilgrims and the bleating of wild animals fleeing fire. As they ran, a flock of starlings, their singed wings smoking, fell like a rain of heavy ash. Mirabella screamed as the burnt offering of birds pelted her head and shoulders. Her feet stumbled, but the hands that held hers kept her upright and forced her to keep moving.

39

Giano, something's wrong here," Zizola said. "Don't you feel it?" She halted in the middle of the path and stared worriedly at the green walls of the maze.

"Yes," Giano agreed, and grabbed two handfuls of his paunch. "It's my stomach. It's hungry."

"No, something worse."

"Worse than an empty stomach? Impossible."

"Do you smell smoke?"

Giano lifted his nose to the air and sniffed. He turned in a slow circle, gathering scents from all sides. "Now that you mention it, there is a smell of wood smoke like the forno in the Piazza del Labirinto where I used to buy focaccia. Perhaps your papa is roasting us a little capon to welcome us on our arrival."

"Come on," Zizola said gruffly, pulling at Giano's sleeve. "Let's get there and find out."

Zizola walked quickly, glancing nervously behind her, seeing only the parallel line of trees. She had been feeling strange for a while now. A foreboding of trouble itched behind her left ear, prodded her spleen, and pierced the ball of her foot.

It was always that way with her, she fumed. Every time something good came into her hands, there was always a wolf ready to snatch it back again. She could never hold on to good fortune. And yet, in the maze, she had experienced a measure of security for the first time in her precarious life. The unexpected familiarity of the place made her want to weep with relief, like a long-lost foundling finally arriving home. Even Giano's ambiguous friendship didn't bother her, for in the maze, for once, she had the advantage.

Security and comfort were intoxicating gifts to one who had never known them before. And now that she knew what it was like to belong somewhere, she didn't want to be cast out again.

Before dawn that morning, Zizola had sensed a tremor of anxiety spreading through the corridors like oil over water. She couldn't grasp its source, nor even its cause. Throughout the day, as the sense of foreboding deepened, Zizola had grown increasingly worried, then afraid, then angry.

The closer to the center they traveled, the more strongly the static charge of dread crackled in the air. Zizola could almost see the knotted corridors of trees contracting around a new and dangerous curse. The roots of cedars quaked in the soil alongside the path, poised for something awful to happen. It worried Zizola that she could only sense the danger of the curse and not its shape.

"Look," Giano called out. "I think we have arrived."

A closed gate blocked the path ahead of them. Stone walls curved away from the gate through the crush of trees. Zizola knew the walls enclosed the center within a protective circle of stone. The gate was similar to the gate of the maze itself: a pair of huge wooden doors, closed and bolted. A small stream ran by the wall like a miniscule moat, spanned by a narrow bridge. As they crossed the wooden bridge, they heard an explosion of raucous voices.

A line of grotesque marble heads embellished with stucco wreaths of ivy and acanthus leaves stared down goggle-eyed from the top of the stone wall. Some of the carved heads were male, others female, but all of them wore expressions of malice and stupidity. One female head was cross-eyed and her hair swept upward on her brow into two horns. A squat, masculine head flapped his thick lower lip over broken teeth and made rude noises. Another, decorated with a long phallic nose, stuck out its tongue and licked its chin while it rolled its eyes.

"Pus face, nose knockers, slack jaw, puny brains," the chorus of grating voices taunted Zizola and Giano. "Get away from here! Piss off, skinny-ass crow bait!"

"Hey, shut your beaks or I'll knock you all into bits!" Giano replied angrily, and shook his fist at the stone faces.

A thick-jowled head puckered up its lips and made a wet, farting sound. The others burst into hilarious laughter, one female with a sour expression honking like a goose.

"Somehow it's not as dignified as I had imagined," Giano complained. He picked up a stone and hurled it at the row of heads.

"Ow, ow," the heads chorused as the stone chipped the tip off the phallic nose and ricocheted into the cross-eyed female face. "Get him!" the heavy-jowled face roared, and all the heads started spitting at Giano, who flung up an arm and danced back out of the way.

"Who wakes us from slumber?" demanded a guttural voice. "Who dares disturb us?"

The stone walls undulated with a grinding sound like the turning of a millstone. Mortar cracked and loosened as the wall bulged outward. On either side of the gate, two long rows of armored knights emerged with their carved hands crossed over their chests, holding stone swords. Grey-green mortar outlined their armor and sculpted the contours of their stern faces; lichen grew into crests on their breastplates. They opened their eyes and Zizola gasped to see granite pupils brightened by flecks of mica staring back at her. They stood shoulder to shoulder, elbow to elbow, their backs firmly embedded in the wall as if they could not free themselves entirely from the stone.

"Who dares approach?"

Zizola edged back in alarm. But Giano pushed her forward, though her heels dug tracks into the soil.

"She dares," he announced. "Zizola of Labirinto! Daughter of Graziano!"

"Who?" croaked a knight.

"Gaetano, you idiot," Zizola muttered.

Giano cleared his throat and tried again. "Zizola, daughter of Il Maestro Gaetano! Can't you blockheads see that for yourself! Isn't the resemblance to Il Maestro striking?" he asked, lifting Zizola's chin to give them a better view.

"I'll strike you," Zizola muttered. "Let go of me." She kicked Giano's shins and he released her quickly, retreating to rub his injured leg.

"Well, do you want to get in or not?" he asked irritably. "Isn't this what you came for?"

"I'm not so sure, now," Zizola said. The stone knights stared back at her, their flecked eyes expressionless. They were waiting, she thought, for her to do something. Even the grotesque heads above the gate had grown quiet, muttering among themselves.

"I am here to see Il Maestro Gaetano," she announced with a confidence she didn't quite feel.

The knights were silent, only their eyes following her as she stepped up to the wooden doors.

"Let me in," she demanded.

A low moan rose near her feet. "Rosalba, my queen. Why have you returned?" Zizola looked down and took a step backward. Hunkered into the earth at the base of the wall were two huge stone giants, one on either side of the wooden doors. They were bent over on their hands and knees, their heads cruelly pressed down between their forearms. Across their broad backs they supported the weight of the gate's pillars. One turned its head with a scraping sound, and its dull, grey eyes regarded her sadly.

"Why have you returned, Rosalba?" the stone giant asked again.

Returned? Zizola thought. When had she ever lived here? And who was Rosalba?

"Because . . . because it's home," Zizola said carefully.

"So you could not stay away. See how he has used us, we who helped you to flee. With every passing year our punishment has grown heavier."

"I'm sorry," Zizola stammered.

The giant shrugged and the wooden gates shuddered at the gesture. "You should have stayed away, Rosalba. After all this time, he has not forgiven you. He waits behind the gate, still full of fury. He may yet harm you, seeking his revenge. The curse, like the maze, remains."

Zizola swore silently at the closed gates, imagining the man behind it. So the wolf was here, in the center, waiting to take back her good fortune. She should have known that it was too easy. She bit her thumb angrily at the locked gate, holding back tears of frustration. What should she do now?

Zizola glanced at Giano, wanting the quirky man's advice, but he was busy tossing stones at the heads who were hawking up mouthfuls of phlegm and spitting back at him.

"Giano, basta! Leave them alone," Zizola snapped, and grabbed the servant by his throwing arm.

"Wait!" Giano protested. "I won't stand here and be insulted by bad art." He pitched another stone, starting up a new round of spitting and shouting.

"Saint's hell," Zizola swore. "Be quiet, all of you!"

The carved heads cowered, some turning to hide their ugly faces in the mantle of ivy.

"Madonna, who put such pazzo creatures up there?" Zizola asked irritably.

"Il Maestro Gaetano did," groaned the giant. "They are what remain of the court. He did that to punish those that once supported you against him. He stuck their heads up there, and in all these years they have forgotten everything they ever knew except the basest of human speech."

"The court," Zizola whispered to herself, eyeing the cowed heads. "And you? Who were all of you?" she asked the wall of silent, attentive knights.

"We were your army, loyal to your cause."

"My army?" Zizola repeated, more astonished. "And you?" she asked the pair of stone giants.

"Your servant and your groom. How could you forget us, Rosalba? It was we who plotted your escape and guarded the hidden doors that allowed you to escape from his curse. Have you returned to free us from his spells? Tell us, that we may hope to live again as men."

The heads began to shout, whining and pleading, demanding that Zizola free them from their miserable ledge. The stone knights strained against the wall, causing alarming cracks to appear in their armor.

"Madonna mia, what have I gotten myself into?" Zizola said. She shook her head, her resolve crumbling in the rising noise of their cries. "This is beyond me. Courts, armies, sorcerer's spells. Ah, Dio, I'm too simple for this. Listen to me," she told the giants. "I don't know who you think I am, but I'm not her. I'm just a beggar from the streets of Labirinto."

Giano clapped his hand over her mouth. "Shut up, Zizola!" he whispered savagely in her ear. "Don't give us away, girl!"

Zizola peeled off his fingers. "I'm not here to rescue people from evil spells. It's hard enough keeping my own skin whole. I can't do this."

"You can," he insisted. "Play the part of Rosalba, Zizola. Put on the mask. Be whatever it is they need you to be: a queen, a sorcerer's daughter, a jilting wife. For the love of Christ and my stomach, Zizola, play the role they have handed you that we may eat again."

"Or be killed, you fool."

"Death is a certainty, whether we starve or eat well. Let's gamble on winning the feast."

"I have no luck."

"You have skill—that's more reliable. I've seen you convince an audience on the piazza. Come, Zizola, perform for them."

Giano released his hold and gave her a quick shove toward the gates. Frightened though she was, Zizola had to admit that the old fool might be right. What else could she do? Where else could she go? Stelladonna and her spoon, Ruggerio and his knife, hunger and the streets were all waiting for her outside the maze. In the maze, she might gamble for something better. As long as she played her role, she had the satyrs, an army of stone knights, a row of silly heads, two giants, and one fool of a servant to back her up if she faltered.

Furthermore, curiosity whined like a mosquito in her ear. Rosalba the Queen, the giants had called her. Zizola smoothed the front of her bodice down over her waist and adjusted the ribbons at her shoulders. Queen it was then.

She addressed the closed gates with a haughty expression on her face. Giano gave her a wink of approval.

"Open," she ordered.

"As you command," mumbled the giants.

The ancient bolt squealed as it slid back. The hinges moaned, releasing brown puffs of rust into the air. The gates lurched opened and the wall undulated, stone grating against stone as the knights turned to salute her. It unnerved Zizola to see only half of their formidable figures. On top of the gates, the marble heads had already turned and were gazing into the unseen center of the maze. The gates moved inward as far as their rusted hinges would allow, then ground to a halt. A stale wind blew out, driving dried leaves and bits of colored paper out onto the path.

"Nella bocca del lupo," Giano whispered at her elbow, giving her the Commedian's version of good luck.

Into the mouth of the wolf, Zizola thought, repeating Giano's words sarcastically to herself. This was it, time to step onto the stage. Zizola squared her shoulders and tried to look regal. She was going in there to snatch back her good fortune from the mouth of the wolf.

40

izola's heart was racing as she stepped through the parted gates. The wind circled and blew as though opening the gates had released it from its prison. It riffled through her skirts, fretted the ribbons at her shoulders, and tossed handfuls of grit into her eyes. She hesitated, a hand held before her eyes to ward off the swirling dust.

"Go on, Zizola." Giano prodded her in the back. "Don't stop now."

Furious at being frightened, Zizola slammed the point of her elbow into Giano's stomach. He snarled an oath, which made her feel somehow better. She sucked in a breath behind her palm and holding it, stepped through the blustering curtain of dust. Two long strides and she found herself clear of the grit-laden wind.

"Saint's hell." She groaned, turning her head slowly to take in her surroundings. The angry fear on her face melted into disappointment.

Behind her, Giano coughed loudly as he batted the dusty wind away.

"What's all this miserable—" He stopped abruptly, bumping into Zizola. "Well, well, now," he said, and whistled under his breath. "Quite a palace, Rosalba. No wonder you wanted to return."

The gates shuddered, and with a rusty moan, slammed shut again, enclosing Zizola and Giano within the center of the maze.

They were standing in the cortile of an old palazzo. The ground was cobbled with smooth, black and white stones that formed constellations of planets and stars beneath their feet. Tufts of grass had sprouted between the stones and weeds had splintered and obscured the pattern with their insistent roots. Along the broad back of the cortile, the wall showed the skeletal frame of a decaying loggia, flanked by the crumbling ruin of the palazzo's walls. The maze's cypress forest was visible through the paneless, arched windows of the palazzo's remaining wall. Vines, their spiked leaves tinted red and orange, strangled the columns of the windows. From their spindled stems hung the shriveled pellets of dried grapes. Small trees had sprouted along the base of the wall, their gnarled roots cresting from the paving stones like the humped backs of sea serpents. Slender, leafless branches poked through gaps in the wall. Closer to the gate, the stone walls were embedded with terra-cotta plaques and the remnants of Roman slabs chiseled with the erod-ing faces of the old gods. Here and there along the wall hung moth-eaten tapestries showing faded scenes of a unicorn hunt, a wedding feast, a battle of angels. There were shafts of sunlight falling randomly in the cortile, spearing the decaying arches of the loggia as they slanted over the walls. But they weren't enough to brighten the gloomy silence, nor warm the autumnal chill.

Zizola shivered and rubbed her arms. She wished she had a cloak. In the maze, it had been full summer, the sunlight hot and bright where it fell on the trees. In here, the air was cool and damp, the light somber as in an old church.

In the center of the cortile, a huge horseshoe table had been set with an extravagant feast. But it had happened a long time ago, and the moun-tains of lavishly prepared food had undergone a curious transformation. Some dishes resembled petrified wood, others clay, covered with dust or stained by rainwater. Zizola recognized a tall-sided torte stuffed with birds. The pastry was burnt amber; the surface was deeply cracked around the black-mottled wing of a bird arrested in its attempt to es-cape its hot pastry. There were platters filled with dirty yellow ribbons of tagliatelle under an array of roasted meats; a hard, brick-red haunch of venison wreathed with wizened carrots; the peeling flesh of a white peacock, its flamboyant feathers faded and drooping with dirt. Brittle twigs of aromatic herbs were still stuffed in its beak. A whole roasted boar, its skin black and withered into coal, slept on a bed of shriveled arugula, erbette, and wild dandelions. In its wrinkled maw, there was a stuffing of acorn and hazelnut into which small black beetles bored busily. Its soot-colored tusks sported blasted apples. There were platters of split figs, their juicy interiors long dried out; blood oranges from Spain shriveled into dense, pale balls; and golden pears shrunk into brown commas. There were bowls of condiments turned to crystals or blanketed with bright molds. A stiffened cake of spun sugar collected a thick grey icing of dust.

There were place settings of tarnished gold plates and silver finger bowls dusted with the remains of rose petals. Damask napkins folded into birds and flowers disintegrated alongside cracked and chipped crys-tal goblets filled with rainwater. Forks with blackened tines and cracked bone handles rested unused beside rusty knives.

In the seats, leaning back wearily or slumped to one side, were the headless bodies of the court, dressed in the faded remains of their fine clothing. Starched lace collars circled the white stumps of their necks. Squared and plunging necklines revealed the waxy bosoms of the women. Ermine, black velvet, and faded red doublets covered manly chests. They were propped in their chairs like broken dolls, their finely shod feet splayed out beneath the table. On the wall, the marble heads looked down and whimpered.

"Madonna." Zizola breathed and touched her own neck. She walked slowly toward the table. "A wedding," she guessed, nodding at the curved center of the horseshoe; a wind-torn, red silk canopy had been raised over two elaborately carved thrones.

"It didn't happen," Giano whispered to her. "What a waste of food, eh?"

"Hard to eat without your head," she replied. "Look," she said softly. On either side of the bride's throne were seated two men who appeared to be sleeping. One had his head thrown back, leaving only the thatch of his grey-bearded chin visible above the swell of his broad chest, while the other rested his head in the cradle of his arms crossed on the table. Zizola couldn't see their faces, but she was glad that they at least had heads. One must be Ill Maestro Gaetano, Rosalba's papa. The other, she guessed from the white doublet, was the jilted bridegroom.

Zizola crept closer. If the two sleeping men were dead, then perhaps there was no danger here. She would simply order her servant to clean up the mess and start over. She glanced sidelong at Giano, who had made his way over to the seated and headless court. He was humming quietly while he slipped off their gold chains and examined the heavy cut dia-mond rings, emerald pins, and ruby bracelets before tucking them into secret pockets in his doublet.

"Giano," she snapped. "Leave them alone! Don't steal from them."

He looked at her with hurt innocence. "But why? They don't need their jewelry," he argued. "And I can always find a use—"

"Thief! Pickpocket!" shouted two of the heads. "Molester!" shrieked the woman with the horned headdress. Giano had just plucked a pearl pendant from between the waxy breasts of a headless woman and had been unable to stop himself from giving her round bosom an experi-mental grope.

The marble heads started shouting loud insults. Giano wheeled around, picked up a handful of dried tortellini, and hurled them one after another at the heads, who continued to shriek. Angrier still, he strained to pick up the petrified lump of venison in both hands, and pre-pared to catapult it at the shouting heads.

Zizola was about to demand that they all shut up when one of the men at the table abruptly coughed, yawned, and sat up. Giano put down the venison, and the marble heads fell silent, except for some whispering. Zizola stared at the white-cloaked bridegroom. He yawned again and blinked like a newborn.

He had a long, angular face with a wide, pale brow and weak chin. His nose was aquiline and almost noble except for the nostrils, which flared out as though catching some unpleasant scent. The matte brown eyes were a shade too close together, and the dark eyebrows had been combed upward, giving him a perennial look of surprise. The thin line of his lips had been rouged and his cheeks were dusted with white powder. A black mole had been coyly placed on his cheekbone and his dark hair had been oiled and curled into heavy, stiff tresses.

His eyes roamed bewildered over the table and settled at last on Zizola. His painted lips broke into a leering grin.

Zizola flinched at the yellowed, vulpine teeth.

"Rosalba, my turtledove," he said in a nasal voice. "You have come to your senses at last. See how I have waited for you, my pigeon. Come kiss your beloved bridegroom, Brigante!"

The marble heads immediately began making loud vomiting sounds, and their sleeping bodies stirred at the table, rocking from side to side. One man's legs jerked violently as though he might stand at any moment. Even Giano looked aghast.

"Shut up, all of you worthless shits," Brigante snapped, and stood up. He wavered on his feet and clutched the table for support. He was wearing the white silk doublet of a bridegroom, with smears of dirt streaking the gold embroidery. A bird had left a grey-green splotch on his split sleeve as he slept. Brigante pursed his ruby lips together and placed his hands on the table, clearly intending to vault over it. His gangly legs made it only halfway over before his arms gave out and he crashed heavily into the dishes, landing on a platter of rotting sweetmeats that left a brown, sticky mess on the right flank of his white hose.

"Damn, damnit," he swore as he scuttled clumsily to the other side of the table. The heads hooted in derision, while Brigante attempted to scrape away the gooey sweetmeats with a napkin. But the napkin shredded into worthless rags. The sweetmeats remained on his hose, layered with lint and broken threads from the old napkin. He chose to ignore the mess and lurched toward Zizola, his thin painted lips puckered in an amorous kiss.

"Madonna, you can't be real," Zizola declared. "That most certainly can't be real!" She pointed a finger to the huge, padded, velvet codpiece, completely overworked in gold bullion stitch, which parted the folds of the short skirt of the doublet. It protruded like an enormous golden horn, absurd and obscene on the man's thin-shanked and slope-shouldered body. A hand belonging to a headless woman snapped out, sending a knife flying in the air toward Brigante. He gave a little scream and shielded his golden bulge from the weapon with his hands. The knife fell far short of its mark, but the heads on the wall began a new round of raucous laughter.

"Shut up, or I'll have the maestro turn you all into dried turds," Brigante warned.

"Is it any wonder Rosalba fled?" Giano whispered in Zizola's ear.

"You there, get away from her, I say." Brigante was waving a hand at Giano.

"Fuck yourself!" Giano growled.

"You are a dog, and I shall beat you like a dog!" Brigante exclaimed. Wheezing with excitement, he pulled his sword from the scabbard and began waving it around dangerously. The blade, having spent the years in the protection of the scabbard, was still sharp and deadly looking.

Giano yipped in surprise and bolted backward as the enraged bridegroom attacked, swinging the blade from side to side. Brigante pinned him against the table, slashing the blade down on either side of the servant as he rolled one way and then the other to avoid the blows. Swearing loudly, Brigante lifted the blade with both hands to slash the servant's legs. But Giano hoisted himself onto the table and, by kicking the dishes at Brigante, managed to escape. He ran down the table, Brigante in pursuit, the keen edge of the sword once nicking Giano in the back of his calf. With a roar of pain, Giano jumped off the edge of the table onto the high ledge of the wall to join the clamoring heads.

"Come down, you coward! Spawn of seven whores!" Brigante yelled.

"Eat my farts, you whey-faced puffball!" Giano shouted back. He picked up one of the marble heads and cast it toward Brigante. The head, mouth agape, flew over the table. Well before it could pound Brigante like a cannonball, two hands reached up from the table, grabbed it out of the air, and stuck it on the stump of a headless neck.

"Ah hah!" the thick-jowled masculine head shouted jubilantly, finding itself once more attached to a living body. The hands slapped its cheeks and pulled happily on the ears. However, its joy at being reunited with a body was short-lived when it looked down and found itself attached to a very feminine body. Beneath the neck, a pair of breasts heaved with emotion, and slim white hands fluttered with agitation.

To the heads on the wall, their fellow's distress didn't matter. "Me next! Me next! Throw me! Take me!" they shouted in unison. Giano obliged, picking them up one by one and throwing them down into the cortile, where waving, desperate hands reached up to receive them. Brigante was howling in outrage, his sword dragging behind him as he ducked and swerved to avoid getting hit by the flying marble heads.

Zizola had quickly sidled out of harm's way behind a spindled tree along one wall. She watched in increasing amazement as the courtiers assumed their chance-caught heads and made a havoc of what remained of the ruined wedding feast. The somber, sleeping cortile came alive with a riot of shouting, weeping, and quarreling. One woman screeched when she discovered she was riding the body of an elderly man. Her mouth curled in a rictus of disbelief as she looked down at what she had become, lifting and lowering the bowed legs. Angry clashes broke out between pairs of mismatched heads, each demanding the return of its rightful body. But, once affixed, the heads would not be removed, and though they tugged at their chins and grabbed one another by the ears and pulled, the heads remained where they had landed. Giano, perched on the wall, guffawed with laughter until his eyes ran with tears.

"Don't touch me, you miserable worm!" screamed the woman with the horned headdress. She was shouting at the thick-jowled man whose head crowned her former body. He had one hand beneath the bodice squeezing her breasts, the other riding up between her plump legs. His squat features wore a stupid grin, the eyes rolled back in his head with lust.

"Caffone!" she shrieked defiantly. "How would you like me to shorten you!" She snatched a knife from the table and stuffed her hand inside the hose of her man's body. She held the knife over the bulge in the hose and glared at the thick-jowled man. He let out a wail and jerked his wandering hands free from the woman's garments.

"You bitch, leave my parts alone!" He lunged for the woman who wore his body, grabbing for the knife. The pair struggled, slamming into the table, knocking over the dishes, and scattering the remnants of the figs and pears to the ground.

"Saint's hell," muttered Zizola, uncertain of how to stop the insane rioting. It was like a macabre dance, couples locked into pointless struggles, grabbing at their heads, demanding back their bodies, inflicting injuries on themselves in an effort to taunt their rival's head. The woman on the old man's body just stood and wept, tears springing like twin fountains from her eyes, while her former body, wearing another man's head, was engaged in yet another battle elsewhere. The peacock carcass was trampled on the ground, the venison haunch was pressed into use as a club, the brittle ribbons of tagliatelle were ground into fragments between the stones, and knives and forks flew through the air like lethal hailstones.

Madonna mia, Zizola hissed to herself, suddenly aware that Brigante had shoved his way through the battling courtiers and was rapidly making his way toward her. "And just when I thought it couldn't get any worse!"

Brigante was panting and wheezing, his mouth hung open with the effort, though his pallid face showed no sign of his recent exertions. Even his hair remained perfectly coifed. Zizola hiked herself away from the tree, not wanting to get trapped, just as Brigante reached for her, his arms spread wide. As she dashed past him, he caught a handful of her skirts.

"Let go!" Zizola screamed, her arms windmilling as she strained to pull herself free of Brigante's grasp.

"Not—until—you—have—kissed—me—" he wheezed, pulling her hand over hand toward him.

Enraged, Zizola turned and punched Brigante hard in the face. At the impact of her punch on his nose, they both screamed and fell away from each other: she at the sharp pain in her battered knuckles and he as his face broke into thick pieces of wax.

Zizola's jaw dropped open as the bridegroom struggled to catch the broken pieces and fold them over his face again. Blood flowed between the cracks and dripped off his chin. The helmet of stiff hair slipped to one side over the wide, cracked brow.

"Fake! Liar!" Zizola shouted, suddenly understanding the man's peculiar pallor. She batted Brigante's hands away from his face. The waxen mask fell to the ground, revealing a wrinkled and aged face and a tuberous, bloody nose. When Zizola reached up and yanked at the stiff hair, a wig came away in her hands.

"Oh no, no, no . . ." Brigante protested, trying to cover his bald and deeply freckled pate. He was wheezing desperately now, as though, having lost the mask of youth, old age had welled up in him with a terrible vengeance. He was drowning in his years, his brown eyes growing rheumy, his shanks quavering with the effort of fending off Zizola's attack. She pushed him away from her and he fell against a tussling pair of courtiers, who paid him no attention.

"Basta! Enough, all of you!" Zizola yelled as loudly as she could. "Madonna Santissima! Stand still and shut up every one of you or I'll—I'll—"

"You'll what?" inquired a grave voice from the table.

Zizola's mouth continued to work, silently. The timbre of the new voice flickered down her spine like a claw scratching along the bones. The courtiers fell into a hush, drawing back along the wall, every face stiff with fear. Even Brigante hunched down beside the drooping table-cloth. Only Giano looked out from his perch on the wall with interest.

"You were always one for a dramatic scene, Rosalba," the deep voice continued, heavy with sarcasm.

At the table, the second sleeper slowly adjusted the bulk of his large body over his chair and rested his elbows on the table. He ran a massive hand over his face, wiping centuries of sleep from his eyes. Then he looked up and glared at Zizola from beneath a bushy fringe of black and grey eyebrows.

His head, like his girth, was huge. Long, heavy waves of wiry black hair made him look like a beast wearing the half mask of a man. His lower features were hidden by a full beard of greying curls. The matted hair fanned out around his wide jowls and cascaded down over his portly chest and shoulders. Above the beard his nose sat like a monument, brown and mottled as a porcini mushroom. The nostrils flared when he inhaled, and he gave an ugly, satisfied smile.

"Well, Rosalba, I cannot guess at what arrogance returns you to this long-forgotten table," he said. "Can it be that you are no longer able to hide from my curse? Have you come at last to beg my forgiveness?"

Zizola kept quiet, her mind rapidly sorting through the possibilities of escape. Her eyes shifted to the cracks in the wall, wondering briefly if she'd fit through them. She recognized the threat in this man's voice, the cold violence of his gaze. The habits of the street twitched in her fingers and her feet. Not a wolf, she realized looking at Gaetano, but a bear ready to eat her in a single bite.

"Nothing to say now to your father? You, who was never at a loss for words?"

Maestro Gaetano heaved himself from his chair and lumbered down behind the table, his eyes on her face. Creatures had joined their lives to his in the time he had slept, making nests in the thick fabric of his long black cloak. A litter of pink, hairless mice rolled away, dislodged from the hem by the swaying of his cloak. Lichen had spattered pale fronds over his broad shoulders, and staghorn moss had raised a miniature for-est of green fruiting trees down his back. The sticky filaments of long-abandoned spiderwebs lay like couched threads across his chest. Two courtiers whispered nervously together and the maestro growled to si-lence them.

At the far end of the table, he turned the corner, and came toward Zizola like a malevolent black wave.

When Maestro Gaetano reached Zizola, he planted his feet wide apart, casting his towering shadow over her. She stared at his creased leather boots, the moth holes in his cloak, the solid emerald ring that circled his thumb, shivering in the chilly darkness of his shade.

"Hey, who the hell do you think you are, scaring her like that!" Giano complained loudly.

Zizola heard Giano jump down from the wall and land with a solid huff, and her lips twitched into a half smile. She saw the little clouds of dust swirl away from his shuffling feet. Don't get too close, she prayed.

"Back off, bully," Giano continued. "No one—"

Giano's words choked off in midsentence. Zizola's head snapped up to see the maestro's massive hands around her servant's throat, throttling the words out of his mouth. Giano was gagging, his face turning pink, red, blue. His hands scrabbled uselessly at the maestro's sausage fingers. As Gaetano shook him, the stolen rings and necklaces rained out of his pockets and clattered across the stones.

"Leave him alone!" Zizola commanded, angrily. "I said, leave him alone!" She slammed the heel of her foot hard onto Gaetano's instep. The huge man bellowed and Zizola stamped on his other foot as well. She continued stamping until he released Giano, who staggered back and fell over the table, gasping and retching.

"How dare you attack me?" Gaetano roared. "How dare you, you miserable wretch!" He clamped his hands on Zizola's shoulders and shook her violently. Zizola's vision blurred as the world wagged back and forth. Gaetano clenched his hands in the fabric of her bodice and lifted her high into the air. She screamed and kicked and flailed her arms, but it was useless. He held her aloft, proving to her that she was helpless and at his mercy. He shook her until she almost lost consciousness. Dazed, she dangled from his hands, her stomach heaving, purple and yellow flashes of pain skating across her eyes.

Slowly, he lowered her to face him. She grimaced at the putrid odor of his breath, the lice crawling through his beard, and the fierce glare of his eyes. "I have cursed you, Rosalba," he spat. "Cursed you with all the love turned to hate that a father can have for his child."

"Well, there you're wrong," Zizola said thickly. "Your curse means very little to me."

His eyes narrowed into obsidian shards. "And why is that?"

"Because, goddamn it," she blurted out, "I've been cursed, beaten, and starved already by a lot worse than you, old man! You think I give a donkey's prick about your curse? Hah! And anyway, you old fart, I'm not Rosalba! So go on, curse away. I hope you choke on it."

"Who are you, then?" Gaetano demanded coldly.

"A thing, a flea on the ear of a mutt, a boil on your arse, old man. Zizola di Labirinto, that's me."

Gaetano raked his dark glance over her studying her angry, flushed face as if trying to peel back the folds of a mask. He brought her closer and sniffed her hair and her sweat-soaked temple. Zizola shuddered with disgust.

And then, he let her down slowly and moved his hands from her bodice to her shoulders. She wasn't free yet, but at least she wasn't swinging like a helpless rag. The stones felt good beneath her feet.

"Not Rosalba," he growled softly, his tone puzzled. "But Rosalba all the same. It's in the blood, in the sweat. I know my own child." He placed his hand alongside Zizola's cheek. She flinched, anticipating the crack of a blow, but he touched her lightly. He held her face in his palm, as though he might feel the pulse of his own blood coursing beneath her skin. It was a gentle touch, as full of tender sadness as it had been full of vengeance. Confused by it, Zizola stepped back to avoid him.

"I've told you, old man, I'm not Rosalba," she said gruffly. "Though I can understand why she didn't want to stay. What girl would marry that ridiculous bit of mutton dressed up as lamb?" she said, jutting her chin at Brigante.

The bridegroom huddled closer to the tablecloth, his wizened head tucked into the valley of his hunched shoulders.

"It wasn't my idea," he whined. "I didn't want to go through with it. It was all the maestro's doing."

Zizola frowned at Gaetano. "Now why would you do that, old man? She was your daughter. He doesn't even look all that rich. Everything about him is fake!"

"To punish her," Gaetano said in a heavy voice.

"What was her crime?"

"Treachery and betrayal. She was my right hand, my apprentice in the art of sorcery, and my blood. But I saw it foretold in the entrails of a goat, in the shift of the stars, and in the swirling patterns of quicksilver that she was to be my downfall."

"Why didn't you confront her before you cursed her? Give her a chance to mend her ways?" Zizola asked.

"I did. She denied that she was plotting against me. She said she was loyal, obedient. She said that she had nothing but love for me. And still the stars shrieked of danger. Rosalba had the gentle face of her dead mother, but she was well schooled in the arts of sorcery. I had reason to believe she was skilled enough to overthrow me."

"Why the limp noodle?"

"Rosalba was well loved by the court. I could not risk imprisoning her without first providing just cause for the punishment. I contrived this wedding to test her obedience."

"Uffa," Zizola exhaled noisily. "What an ass you are, old man. You tried to shame your daughter with this tough bit of leather all because of a goat's twisted gut and a star wheeling in the wrong direction? I'll bet she wasn't so stupid as to fall for your prank."

Gaetano snarled behind the veil of his beard. He reached into the voluminous folds of his black cloak and pulled out a tiny gilt-framed portrait. He studied it, his voice rumbling discontentedly.

"The stars augured right. On the day of the wedding, Rosalba defied me. While the court provided a distraction, she disappeared from the cortile almost before my eyes. I knew then I was too late to smother her influence. The court had rebelled against my authority and the knights were preparing to rise up against my rule. In a rage, I first punished all those who had assisted Rosalba in her betrayal. I tossed their heads onto the gate, turned them into stone, and embedded them into my walls, or made them kneel at my threshold.

"Then I cast a spell to trap Rosalba, a spell that would shape her deception into a maze from which she could not escape. I pulled every thread of power from the depths of my soul and wove it so tightly that she would never again know freedom. For three days I sat at this table, without food, without water, while I cast my spell."

Gaetano looked up from the portrait and his barrel chest rose and fell in a sigh. A small, pearl-white spider scuttled down his shoulder, trailing a thin thread of silk. Gaetano turned slowly in the cool, autumn air and surveyed the ruins of the cortile. His eyes beneath the dark brow were unreadable.

"How was I to know that my own curse would serve to entrap me as well as Rosalba in its web? Only after I had roused myself from my trance on the third day did I realize what I had done. The maze had grown beyond my abilities to control it. I can't prevent the flow of magic that twists every cursed life that enters the maze through an endless knot of winding paths. I cannot leave here, for I know that the moment I step from this cortile, I, like all the others lost in the maze, will be condemned to wander down those corridors forever."

"Do you mean that no one leaves here? That none of the pilgrims who have entered the maze have ever succeeded?" Zizola asked.

Gaetano shook his head. "No one leaves here. They join their curse to mine and the maze grows deeper and more confounding."

Anger flared in Zizola's cheeks, red on white. She listened to the low murmurs of the maze beneath her feet, felt it writhe like a serpent digesting a century of misery. For all that, something was missing, and a tiny spark of hope flared.

"Rosalba wasn't trapped in your maze, old man," Zizola said with conviction. "She was too smart and too fast for you."

"How do you know?" he rasped.

"I just do." She took the portrait from Gaetano's hand and looked down at it, touching the fine lines cracked into the thick patina of paint. It was like her own face, all right, only happier and better fed, the yellow hair dressed with ropes of pearls. The familiar hollow curve of her cheek was there, her dagger eyes and her pointed chin. It could have been Zizola, or some past version of her.

Suddenly the details of Rosalba's story didn't matter. It could have been pirates, it could have been a nobleman, it could have been bad luck, it could have been the plague. Whatever Rosalba's history once she left this bridal feast, nothing in her life or in the life of her descendants had gone well since the maestro had set his curse in motion.

"Rosalba didn't fare much better outside your maze, old man," Zizola said tartly. "Maybe she was my grandmother, or my great-grandmother, after all, no one knows for certain how long the maze of Labirinto has existed. But I can tell you that fate was not generous to her, nor to those of us in her line. I was born on the street with memories of cold and hunger, but no mother. As a baby, I was passed from hand to hand, a prop in a play of begging. And when I could finally toddle, I became a beggar myself. A hard life, old man.

"You looked at the stars and decided that Rosalba was to be your downfall. But in the end, it was your curse that ruined us all. If you had only believed her when she said she loved you, we might all have been spared the misery."

Zizola felt a sickening lurch in her stomach as she looked around her at the decaying cortile, at rotted food scattered over the stones, at the quarreling courtiers with their grotesque heads, and the bestial, moth-eaten bulk of Maestro Gaetano. That was all her journey in the maze had brought her: a prison of ruin and sadness, inhabited by a man who resembled a Carnevale bear.

Her cursed life had led her here. Gaetano's maze had merely plucked the threads of her own troubled thoughts and laid down for her a tangled path to nowhere. She had had only two dreams in her short life. The first was to eat well and that dream had almost succeeded in killing her. Failing that, she supposed the maze had constructed another, more insidious trap. Her second dream was to belong to someone, to be loved, to be the mislaid jewel, found and returned to its golden setting.

Zizola fought back a wave of despair. None of her good fortune had been real. Even her miserable attempts to help people along the path had been nothing more than a ruse, a trick of the maze. And now everything was coming apart, the promise of the maze, the fulfillment of dreams, the wild hope of belonging. The wolf was herself, and the world was ending for her.

She flung the portrait to the ground as though it scalded her fingers. She turned from Gaetano, her face white with panic, and ran toward the closed gates.

"Zizola, wait for me!" called Giano, sprinting after her.

"Daughter, wait!" Gaetano barked.

"Rosalba, don't leave us," the courtiers wailed, their backs pressed against the wall.

Zizola reached the gates and pulled on the rusted bolts. She had to get out or she'd be stuck forever in here, going mad like those stupid courtiers or turning into a moldering old maid, beating off the attentions of that dried-up stick of a bridegroom. At least among the cedars and cypress, she'd be free to go mad in private.

"Out! I command you to let me out!" she shouted, pulling at the bolt until her arms ached.

"Rosalba, do not leave us again," pleaded the giants at the gate's threshold. "Stay, we beg you."

"Where are we going, Zizola?" Giano asked, straining hard as he added his strength to hers, trying to pull back the bolt. It wouldn't budge, but remained firmly locked in its channel.

"Anywhere but here," she answered, pounding on the wooden gates. "Out, let us out, you thick-headed pile of rocks!"

Almost at once, a distant pounding answered her. She stopped and backed away from the gate. The pounding grew louder, more insistent. Its force vibrated the planks of wood, rattled the bolts, and knocked clouds of brown dust from the hinges. It sounded like an army of fists was beating against the wood on the other side of the gate. Over the top of the stone walls, the wind carried the sounds of desperate voices.

"In! Let us in!" Zizola put her ear to the shuddering wood and listened, trying to understand who was out there. Men shouting for help and the guttural bleating of satyrs. Women, shrill with panic. And, amid the riot of sound, an ethereal voice pouring like light through the knot-holes of the gate, beseeching Zizola to let them in.

"Open the gates," she commanded to the giants. "Open and let them all in!"

"Do as she says," Gaetano commanded.

The bolt slid back on its own with a thunderous crack. The hinges scraped with a shriek, and the gates parted inward. Zizola and Giano moved to one side, allowing the gates to grind open. Almost at once the entrance was flooded with pilgrims streaming into the cortile, and the air grew dense with their coughing and sobbing. A heavy, hot wind chased them through the gates and blasted the cortile with thick, black ash and fiery cinders.

The satyrs rushed in, their pelts smoking. In their arms and on their backs they carried their children, or supported the frightened nymphs, whose rosy skin was dirtied with soot. Zizola recognized the girl Mirabella, whom she had met by Diana's fountain. With Mirabella was the young man with the stutter. And over there, staggering beneath the weight of a wounded man, was the tall, dark-haired woman Zizola had met in the forest. Zizola wiped her hand across her sweating forehead as a boy with three faces arrived, puffing obscenities as he lugged an enormous sculpted head in his wiry arms. A crippled man, his red cape flapping over his hunched back, scuttled sideways like a startled crab into the center.

"Anna, take my hand, let me guide you" an older man called. Zizola watched him help a woman, her undone hair cascading down her back like flax, to a chair at the wedding table. She sat down, wiped her eyes free of the grit, and promptly screamed when she saw a woman's well-dressed body wearing a man's grotesque head offering her a handkerchief.

"Lorenzo! Lorenzo!" a white-skinned woman called through the swirling crowds of frightened pilgrims. Her voice threaded into a green light, shaping into a tendril of sea grass as it searched.

"Erminia! I am here!" the man answered, raising his hand above the milling crowd. The green tendrils of sea grass circled his wrist like a bracelet and pulled the woman closer to him. He was helping a nymph and her child, who had fallen in the crush to enter.

Zizola looked beyond the gates and saw a bank of black, smoky clouds draped over the trees. Far in the distance, she could see the orange flames licking up the branches.

"Do something, Zizola! Do something!" Giano shouted at her.

"Me! What am I supposed to do?"

"How did these people find their way here?" Gaetano demanded gruffly, shaking her by the shoulder. "The maze should have prevented that. They should have been lost in their own journey."

"I told them," Zizola said. "I told them where to go. And they helped each other."

"Then it's true," Gaetano said, standing very still amid the tumult. He was gazing at Zizola and she saw the spark of longing in his dark eyes. "You are my daughter, or my daughter's daughter. For only one of my blood could have altered the paths of magic in the maze."

Beneath the distant roar of the flames and Gaetano's growling voice, Zizola heard the sound of laughter—cruel, arrogant, triumphant. She felt a wave of intense nausea as magic was sucked into the fiery furnace of the burning maze. In a short time, it would all be gone: the cypress, the cedars, the forest of dead oaks, and the sacred olive groves. There would be nothing left.

"Stop this," she begged Gaetano. "Don't hurt these people! They have no part in your revenge!"

"I can do nothing," he answered. "This is beyond my power to change. It's Rosalba's revenge on me. She survived long enough to create your line and to pass on her power through her blood. Only you could have started this inferno. And unless you can now stop it, we are doomed."

Zizola shook her head. How could she have done all this? She was only a beggar from the streets, beaten and bested by bigger ones in the world. But even as she tried to deny it, Zizola remembered the cold night of stars, the beating, the pain in her face, and the whispered curse as she leaned her back against the wall of the maze. "Curse them all," she had whispered to the stars. The maze had heard her and had complied. She looked over at Gaetano, grief crumpling her features.

"What can I do?"

"Find the source," Gaetano said grimly.

"And then?"

"Call back the curse."

"Is this before or after I'm turned into ash?" she snapped.

Gaetano didn't reply.

"Saint's hell," Zizola swore. "Why me?" She looked out over the huddled groups of pilgrims, their clothes stained with ash and dirt, their faces wan with fright. She saw the courtiers hiding their ugly heads out of shame, the anxious flock of satyrs trying to comfort their weeping nymphs and children. A thought flickered across her mind, a memory of the Piazza del Labirinto, of the wretched pilgrims gathered there, as full of hope as anguish.

And all at once, Zizola knew that Gaetano's dreary cortile was not where she should be. The cortile was the blasted heart of Gaetano's curse, a closed fist where time had crawled at a snail's pace to a halt. She would have no power in here to do anything.

"Can you keep them safe in here for a little while?" Zizola asked Gaetano.

"I can try," he rumbled. Smoke curled up the sides of his cloak. "But I must close the gates."

"Va bene," she agreed with a shrug. "I'll be back if I can." Without another word of explanation, she darted through the open gates into the burning corridors of the maze.

"Wait for me, Zizola!" Giano called after her and started running. "Where are we going? We're going to be turned into cooked sausages heading that way."

"Follow me!" Zizola shouted. Zizola sprinted through the thick haze of smoke, allowing the maze to lead her through the burning cedars back to the one place she had ever loved, the one place she had called home, both outside and inside the maze. She was going home to the source of her own power, which lay beneath the white columns of the Arch of Dreams.

41

For the first time since he had entered the maze, Zolfo slowed his steps, uncertain of his direction. The green corridors were shrouded in a veil of smoke, and the path before him parted into two different directions. Standing in the fork of the path, he hesitated and turned his face to the right. The center of the maze lay in that direction—he could taste the particular mustiness of its air, feel the pull of its power like a coil of rope around his ankle. Yet he was also aware that a second and equally strong rope of power tugged him toward the left. It threatened him and anger tempted him to turn left. But the force of his nature as a curse compelled him to the right.

While he stood contemplating, the soul trapped in his breast awoke and renewed its struggle to free itself. Zolfo stumbled in a circle, surprised by the strength of the beating wings. He hugged himself hard around the chest, his breath sucked in to keep the light of the soul from escaping through his mouth. He could feel it slamming against his ribs, chipping the bones of his pelvis, expanding and contracting like a fetus misplaced in his stomach. A whirring wind deafened his ears and his vision was blinded by bright flashes of light across his eyes.

"Stop! You are mine! You are my soul. Lie still!" he commanded. But the soul would not lie still, and Zolfo sensed its panic and its urgency as though they were his own.

Blindly, Zolfo bolted down the left-hand path, trying to outrun the soul's panic. He kicked his legs hard against the ground, pumped his arms, and worked the bellows of his lungs. The soul weakened once more and slipped deeper into Zolfo's body, folding beneath his heaving chest. Zolfo kept running until he could no longer feel the ground under his heels, nor hear the soul's wings striking against his eardrums.

When he finally staggered to a stop, the narrow path had opened into a small clearing. Still panting, his face hot and sweating, Zolfo walked into the clearing, warily searching the quiet trees for danger. The smoke had not yet reached this place. The sky was pale blue and a gold summer sunlight tinted the leaves. A skillful hand had built a marble fountain in the clearing, the wide circular basin filled with sparkling water that lapped at the foot of a tall marble statue of the goddess Diana. She was naked except for a bow slung over one shoulder and a pair of arrows in her left hand. Her right arm was raised as if in a greeting, the smooth fingers translucent in the sunlight. At her feet, marble hunting dogs barked sprays of water into the basin.

Zolfo stared at the woman's face, transfixed by its cool, distant beauty. The sensual mouth carried the hint of a smile, a slight curve of invitation at the corners of her full lips. Her eyes stared boldly back at him, unafraid. There was the promise of strength in the carved muscle of her sinewy arms, the long, pale length of her thigh, the rounded bowl of her calves.

Zolfo staggered toward her, captivated by emotions he didn't understand, but which he knew came from his new soul. Staring into the woman's face, he was overwhelmed by memories of other women's bodies: of the soft texture of their inner thighs, the dimpled hardness of their nipples, the wetness of their tongues, the extreme heat of their hidden folds. Zolfo licked his lips, imagining the press of a kiss there. Desire clamored in his rapid pulse and his breath quickened.

Distracted from his journey, Zolfo climbed over the low wall of the fountain. He was awed by the physical sensations the sight of the naked woman teased from his flesh. His legs trembled, a thin coil of pain compressed down his spine like a spring, and the fickle creature be-

tween his legs sprang to attention. Zolfo stood close to the woman and
her smile seemed to invite him further. Beneath the stone lashes spangled with drops of water, the pearl-colored eyes watched with amusement as he reached for her. He placed his hand over the damp mound
of her breast and groaned as her nipple stabbed the hollow of his palm.
He leaned against the woman, ran his hands down her waist, over the
curve of her hips, back up to her breast, and the damp hollow of her
armpit beneath the outstretched arm. He closed his eyes and pressed his
lips to her cool mouth.

Memories told him there should be an opening there, a warmth waiting to receive him. He probed her parted mouth with his tongue, tasting only the dank, wet stone. His hands continued to wander, touching
her, trying to warm the cold hardness of her flesh with his eager fingers.
A part of him knew that she was made of stone, birthed out of the elements of the mountains even as he had been. He could hear the dull
whisper of her infinite pulse in the striation of blue veins across her
breasts.

"I will make you like me," he promised. "I will get you a soul and then
we will be together."

The soul fluttered in Zolfo's throat. It knew that it too had once lied
like this just to be near a woman's nakedness, to seduce some reluctant
stone-faced virgin into parting her marble thighs. Zolfo's breath came
in shallow pants, the air hot on his lips, his face, his scalp, the tips of
ears sweating despite the cold water swirling around his feet. All he
understood was that he needed this woman. He needed to possess her,
to enter her.

But though he ran his hands over her taut, wet skin and beseeched her
with whispered promises, her smile never changed. He kissed her breasts,
her ribs, the rippled muscles of her stomach, and her rounded belly. But
her legs would not part; her strong thighs clenched together continued
to deny him. He kneeled before her, breathless and in pain, his groin
throbbing. His eyes fixed hungrily on the sloping mound of her sex,
half-hidden between the press of her thighs. Only the tiny cleft of her
navel, on the hill of her smooth belly, offered a suggestion of entrance.
Zolfo leaned forward, his eyes half-closed in mounting rapture, and
placed the tip of his tongue inside the miniature folds.

Her navel was slick with the dew of the fountain and it seemed to
him that it closed itself around his tongue. He shuddered, racked by intense waves of pleasure, planting his mouth more firmly against her
cold skin. Zolfo clutched the woman by her cool hips, moaning and
thrashing against her legs, heat coursing through him in waves.

When he felt the heated waves of pleasure ebb, he pulled his head away from the woman's navel and gazed up at her face. She was still wearing her faint smile, but a drifting, smoke-filled cloud hid the sun, eroding her sharp-hewed features into an expression of disappointment. The white marble sheen of her skin turned a dirty grey, flecked with the blowing grit and ash in the wind. Tears leaked from the corners of Diana's eyes and trickled down her cheeks. Water poured out of her ears, and twin rivers streamed from the corners of her mouth and spiraled around her neck.

Zolfo pulled back, startled. A small fountain of water gushed from the folds of her navel. Zolfo caught the flow in his palm and touched it to his lips, tasting salt and fish. The soul told him he had opened a virgin to receive him, but instead of blood, it was the sea flowing through the veins of her marmoreal flesh.

Zolfo grew alarmed, hearing the sea taunt him for his arrogance, for his foolish decision to imprison his elemental power in a weak human body. The curse that had been created out of the living heart of fire was about to be drowned by the sea just like any mortal.

A gout of rushing water poured out of Diana's navel, striking Zolfo in the chest and shoving him on his back. He lay prone under the plume of white spray as the cold salty water rapidly filled the basin. A crack echoed in the air and the body of the virgin goddess began to split in half below her breasts. Her head and right shoulder sheered off at the collarbone and the beautiful face tumbled into the basin with a splash. Her left shoulder and the arrows in her hand shattered under the force of the water, scattering sharp fragments that cut his hands as he crawled to her drowned face. Out of ruins of her body, the sea gushed, roaring, and lifted Zolfo out of the overflowing basin on a curling wave, depositing him on the path again.

Sprawled in the rushing water, Zolfo struggled to stand in the fast current. When he found his footing, he ran from the flooded clearing with the sea chasing after him along the ground, turning the dry paths into mud. Behind him, he sensed the sea invading the paths of the maze, water confronting fire. Steam hissed and new white clouds billowed high to mingle with the thick shelf of black smoke hanging over the treetops.

Zolfo could taste the tang of the sea in the enveloping, blinding mist. But he had no need of sight to find his way through the haze of smoke and steam. A river of lava far beneath the surface of the earth guided his steps.

"Forget your love," the fiery lava scoffed. "You must not think like a man. You are my progeny. You are the curse."

"What must I do?" Zolfo asked.

"Destroy the Arch of Dreams," it answered. "And with it the girl, Zizola. She is the one who has sent the sea. She is the one who tries to prevent you from fulfilling your destiny."

Zolfo ducked his head and ran faster. He would do as the molten blood of the earth had commanded, but he would not surrender his love. He would not forget the cool, slick skin of Diana's breast, nor her mysterious smile, nor his promise to transform her once the maze was his. Behind him the sea howled and pumped itself into the knotted corridors of the maze, gradually transforming them into tree-lined canals.

"Hey, Zizola, stop! My lungs are bursting!" Giano panted breathlessly.

"I can't stop now! It's all coming apart!" Zizola cried. "I tried to slow it down, but I think I've made it worse!"

"What did you do, Zizola?" Giano puffed.

"I sent the sea into the maze to find it and put out the fires. But the sea has begun to flood the outlying parts of the maze. Look, already the ground is growing wet. It'll be on us soon."

"Why did you do that?" Giano squawked. "Zizola, I can't swim! I'll drown if the water finds us here!"

"You'll float just like a rotten carcass, you old gasbag," she snapped. "Saint's hell." She grunted as her foot caught on a small root. She managed to prevent herself from stumbling, but Giano, running close behind her, could not stop fast enough to avoid a collision. With a cry of surprise, he struck her in the back, knocking her to the earth and sending them both rolling into the lower branches of the cedar trees. Zizola yelped as she bumped and slid over the muddy earth. Giano blasted an obscenity every time a branch slapped him hard across the face as he rolled.

"O'Dio, why me?" Zizola asked when she had finally slid to a stop beneath a clump of cedars. She raised herself up on her hands, scratched, aching, and wet. The front of her bodice was plastered with rotting leaves and a thin coating of mud.

"Why does this always happen to me?" she said miserably. "I get a servant and he nearly kills me with his stupidity. I find my great-great grandfather and he nearly kills me with his old man's fear of losing power. I have a line of grandmothers and mothers who nearly killed me with their desire to wreak vengence on someone already cursed. And then of course my own mouth has gotten me into more trouble than a cat in a kennel. A cursed life, that's what it is."

"Zizola, are you all right?" Giano asked, pushing the branches aside and offering her a hand.

"No. I'm not. But help me up anyway." She sighed and took his hand.

Once up, she brushed the dirt and leaves from her skirts and hobbled out onto the path again, Giano limping at her side. She could just make out the columns of the Arch of Dreams ahead through a curtain of trees. She wiped her face with the back of her hand and thought how from here the arch resembled a stage set for a performance.

"You were right, Giano," she said.

"Yes, of course." He gave her a puzzled look. "About what, Zizola?"

"It's time for me to play a part in my own drama. I moved the others all over the stage, like the maestra of the Commedia, giving instructions to this one here, telling that one there where to stand. Now I'm in my own scene, lost because I don't know how the play ends."

"How do you want it to end?" Giano asked.

"As best it can, I suppose."

"No," Giano said sharply, "that's not good enough. If you don't know, Zizola, another will steal the scene and leave you with a knife in your chest, performing the corpse. You must decide now how this is to end. You must be the one to set the stage. Be the maestra, the sogetto is yours. Play the scene as you intend it!"

They walked through an opening in the wall of trees, and Zizola inhaled deeply. She drew strength from the clean white lines of the arch and the victorious grins of the ancient comic gods. "Don't be afraid, Zizola," they seemed to be saying, "the fool gets hurt, but he never dies."

She patted a marble column affectionately and tried to imagine what she would say to her curse. How would she fight it? What weapons did it have? Was she strong enough to confront it? The last time she had performed beneath these columns, Ruggerio had nearly killed her and she'd been forced to swallow the good fortune she had found. Maybe Giano had the right idea. Like Arlecchino on stage, Giano was always one stumble ahead of disaster as though he had designed the plot in his favor.

Zizola wondered if she was always taking the pratfalls because she had never allowed herself a place at center stage. On the street she had struggled beneath the thumb of others. Stelladonna and Ruggerio had given her the beggar's mask, and not believing herself worthy of anything else, she had worn it until it fit like her own skin.

"Zizola, any chance of a bite to eat?" Giano asked, giving his belly a friendly pat.

"Is that all you can think of?" Zizola asked, astonished.

"I remember a time when it was all you thought of," Giano answered dryly. "Besides, I do think of other things. But it's hard to be imaginative on an empty stomach. A bottle of good red wine goes a long way to fermenting my thoughts—"

"Pickling your tiny brain—"

"Inspiring my cunning—"

"And bludgeoning you into a drunken stupor."

"Zizola, you wound me," the servant said with a pained expression, his hands clasped over his chest.

In spite of her anxious mood, Zizola smiled at him. Clouds of smoke drifted over the afternoon sun, staining the marble arch various shades of grey. Zizola watched the muted light scud over his mobile features. One moment he was a loose-lipped imbecile, and the next, he was sharp-nosed and fanged like the fox. He had only a few desires and the animal cunning to achieve them. She had been like that until she entered the maze, when a yearning for something more had taken hold of her heart. But how exactly had she changed? What did it mean to belong to this place, to this line of miserable sorcerers and their curses? She looked at Giano's shifting face and saw hunger written on every expression.

"All right, let's eat. If you need to eat to think, then you'll do me no good on an empty stomach."

She stood beneath the Arch of Dreams, one small hand against the column's cool flank. She glanced up at the expectant faces of the ancient comics and said, "A table set for a feast, and chairs, please."

"Brava!" Giano cried, clapping his hands. He backed out of the way to avoid the long wooden trestle table covered with a white cloth that immediately appeared beneath the arch. Silver plates floated out of the air, followed by goblets of pink and gold Venetian glass, silver-tined forks, and bone-handled knives.

"What do you fancy?" Zizola asked, amused by the idea of feasting on the verge of disaster. We shall drink a toast to long life, she thought wildly, to health, to pleasure, to companionship, to staying alive in a muddled world and snatching back hope from the midst of flames.

"What do you want to eat?" Zizola asked Giano again.

"Well, if it's to be my last time, I guess a bit of everything would be nice." Giano sat down, tucked the draped edge of the linen tablecloth beneath his chin, clutched a fork in one hand and knife in the other, and waited for the food to appear.

And it did, winking out of the smoky air on huge gold platters. Clams nestled in a mountain of pasta, a creamy risotto blackened with squid ink, nuggets of bark-brown porcini dotted with a mound of golden polenta, a browned rabbit surrounded by roasted bulbs of sweet fennel, and a boiled haunch of veal waited on a bed of macaroni scented with rosewater.

"Che buono!" Giano shouted as a lasagna di Ferrara appeared, the ribbons of pasta soaked in a white cream sauce spiced with almonds, cinnamon, and raisins. He thrust his fork in turn into the lasagna, the veal, and the polenta, his cheeks puffed to bursting with his prodigious mouthfuls. His eyes rolled back in his head and he groaned with ecstasy every time he swallowed.

Following the meat dishes, there appeared a wealth of vegetables: braised, roasted, stuffed into pastries, and scented with saffron, garlic, cinnamon, capers, and fiery peppers. There were sweets, dates, and figs, lemon-flavored tortes and cakes of white flour and spun sugar. Split pears were filled with gooey Gorgonzola, blood oranges were sprinkled with sugar, grapes were folded into pots of mascarpone, and apples were baked to a woody brown with honey and balsamic vinegar.

Zizola sat back in her chair, picking at a pigeon breast studded with walnuts, and grinned at her servant, who was shoveling food into his mouth with gusto.

"And the wine?" he asked, one cheek full of risotto.

She nodded, and at once the table was set with a selection of different red and white wines: ruby chiantis and sangioveses, a blood-red Sangue di Giuda, pale albanas, and golden orvietas. There was a chestnut vin santo and a clear grappa, its fumes pungent as tree sap.

"Enough?" she asked, pointing to the wine.

"A good start," he answered, and pulled the cork from a chianti with his teeth. He upended the bottle and took a long swallow, his throat bobbing wildly. He sighed when he was done and wiped his mouth with the back of his hand.

"What exactly was your curse, Zizola?" he asked, ripping a browned leg off the rabbit.

"I cursed my whole line, wished they'd all been put to the flame, and myself cold ash," she said flatly.

Giano flung himself back against his chair, his mouth gaped open. "But, Zizola," he gasped, the fingers of one hand pinched together, "why?"

"How was I to know someone would take me up on it?"

"Eh, the very point," he said, twirling the rabbit leg. "Those who make themselves sheep, Zizola, will be eaten by the wolf! Why give up on yourself before you know for certain that you're dead? Unless the hangman's knot is at your ear, you've always got a chance."

Zizola shrugged and shook her head. She remembered too keenly the razor's edge of Ruggerio's knife at her neck, the pain in her jaw from the beating, the constant emptiness of her belly, and the lonely desolation in her heart.

"Didn't you ever get tired of just trying to stay alive, Giano? Didn't you ever get weary of the game?"

"I never knew anything else," the man answered quickly. Then he gazed down at the abundant plates of food and his brow creased in thought. He laid down the stripped rabbit leg. "Though, there have been moments . . ."

Zizola held her breath as Giano's vague features folded into deep craggy lines and crevasses cross-hatched the high, smooth brow and pleated the long flat planes of his cheeks. His fool's mask slipped and the gaunt face of an aging thief appeared. She saw the weight of his years hanging on his jowls and the dark pouches like empty coin sacks beneath his muddy eyes.

"I'm a long way from Bergamo," he said huskily, and dug his fork into a dish of pasta. "There is no return from the maze that marks my life. I am what I am, and so I will remain."

Abruptly his face changed, flattened as he hid it once more behind his fool's mask. His lips produced a smile, but his eyes remained cloaked beneath his drooping lids.

"And what about me, Giano?" she asked, earnestly. "Am I lost in my own maze too? Am I always to be Zizola, the crumb left over from the feast?"

Giano's smile stretched into a wide, loopy grin and he slapped his thigh. "You're a kitten, Zizola. The tip of the tail, the first stitch in a shirt, a snip of a girl. There is still time for you to choose your direction." He sat back in his chair and gestured to the Arch of Dreams. "This remarkable maze belongs to you, Zizola. It'll do as you command. You won't be cursed by a lack of choices! It's entirely up to you how you decide to play this scene—a dirty-faced child of the gutters or"—he leaned forward and gently wiped the mud from Zizola's chin with his thumb—"a dirty-faced child of sorcerers."

As he pulled his hand away, a searing blast of wind struck Zizola across the cheek. She turned away from its stinging heat and inhaled an acidic mouthful of burning ash. Her eyes narrowed as she glanced above the line of cedars and saw the low shelf of black smoke brushing the spires of the trees. Throughout the maze she could hear water rushing through the corridors and steam hissing from the newly formed canals between the smoldering trees. A pale green mist was gathering above the cedars as though the sea were being sucked into the clouds.

"Get out, Giano," she snapped.

"Hey, wait a minute," he protested, grabbing a couple of pears.

"Get out now! Save your skin. It's coming," Zizola said.

Giano bolted to his feet and scrambled away from the table. But instead of fleeing as she had expected, he bounded up the stairs to the crest of the arch. She heard his boots scraping the stone as he settled himself just over her head.

"I'm here if you need me!" he said.

"Fool," Zizola whispered, her gaze riveted to the line of swaying trees on the far side of the clearing. Waves of heat struck her skin with scorching slaps as the curse approached. The platters of fruit puckered and creased in the hot air; sauces dried to a brown crust along the edges of the golden plates. Water, she thought, swallowing dryly, I need water.

Zizola wasn't certain what she expected to see, but it still surprised her when she heard the hard thud of feet beating a warning on the packed soil. She sensed the sea, unrolling like a watery carpet, chasing the curse's fiery heels. The green mist thickened into dense rain clouds and moisture condensed into pearly droplets on the columns, beaded into sweat on the marble faces of the comics. At her feet, the soil grew soft as water seeped through the pores of the earth and, bubbling up through wormholes, trickled into thin rivers beneath the table. The legs of Zizola's chair sank a few inches into the muddy soil.

As she waited, Zizola tried to gather her wits into the shape of a plot that would save them. She thought about Gaetano and Rosalba's story, and all the other stories she had heard in the maze of pilgrims whose lives had been corrupted by the misery of a curse.

What is a curse? she asked herself, watching the trees bow before the wind's hot breath. An utterly worthless form of revenge. It was nothing like the honorable confrontation of a duel, or even the devious strategies of cowardice, the poisoned wine, the assassin on a dark, moonless road. No, a curse was a gob of spit launched into the wind that returned to strike the spitter in the face.

Look at Gaetano. With all of his power he had managed only to imprison himself behind a wall of stone. And Rosalba's revenge against her father had only not destroyed her, but all her descendants after her, down to Zizola, abandoned to the streets and a life of poverty. So the curse had come full circle.

"Those who commit a hundred misdeeds must expect one in return," Zizola whispered aloud. She herself had uttered the words that were about to destroy her, Gaetano, and everyone else in the maze.

Zizola shook her head. No, she would have to be different if she was to survive her own ill-conceived spell. She would have to call back her words, undo the tangled knots of misery. She would have to change the elemental nature of the curse into something better: a blessing, a promise, a fragile hope. She had to reweave the patterns of the maze with new threads of power, to replace pettiness with generosity, cruelty with love, and revenge with forgiveness.

"Keep your wits about you, Zizola. I see someone coming," Giano whispered from above.

"I see him, too," Zizola answered. She watched as a boy slouched through a break in the trees into the clearing, his head thrust forward, one arm wrapped around his chest as though he were wounded. His sullen features were contorted with pain. He staggered in circles, clawing the air with his free hand. He was shouting to someone, but Zizola couldn't make out the words.

"Who's he talking to?" Giano asked.

"I don't know."

"He's crazy. They're the worst, the crazies."

"You should know," Zizola muttered.

"Hey, that's not nice."

"Shut up," Zizola whispered. "He's coming."

The boy had finally succeeded in silencing whatever invisible demon taunted him and was walking toward the table with long, swift strides, water seeping into his muddy footprints. Zizola studied his face. His brow was familiar, as was his narrow pointed chin, his petulant mouth, and his slim, upturned nose. His hair, though filthy with splattered mud, was the color of threshed wheat.

"Looks like your twin," Giano called down softly.

Just what I was thinking, Zizola said to herself. Madonna mia, what have I created? A curse wearing the mask of my face. She could see now in his boyish features the same ravenous expression she had worn most of her life: sharp, feral eyes raking over the platters of half-eaten food like a weasel let loose among the chickens. His skin was a pale olive beneath the smudges of mud, his neck a slender stalk rising from his hunched shoulders. He clenched his fists, as though trying to keep his secrets locked within his grasp.

Zizola leaned back in her chair, whose legs sank deeper into the mud. She spread her hands flat on the table and realized that she wasn't afraid of him any more. Instead, an immeasurable sadness coated her throat, cloying as incense and honey. The curse was a mirror of her short life, wearing her starved, belligerent face, her wary, hunched shoulders, her clenched fists.

Was that how she had appeared to others? Was there no grace, no softness, no tenderness anywhere in this mirror image? He looked brittle and sharp as the rusted edge of a stiletto.

"Who are you?" she asked.

"Zolfo di Labirinto," he crowed.

"Are you hungry?" she asked calmly, and saw the answer flame in his eyes. "Come, Zolfo di Labirinto, eat." She gestured to a chair.

Still glaring, Zolfo edged cautiously toward the table, found the empty chair, and sat. His nostrils flared as the aroma of food seized him. He quickly reached across the table and snatched the carcass of the rabbit. Holding it in one hand, he tore off large mouthfuls of its roasted flesh and chewed them noisily. With his other hand, he sneaked apples into his doublet, followed by stuffed fennel and artichokes.

Zizola said nothing as she watched Zolfo gorge himself. She could feel the pain of his starvation like an ache in her own bones, saw her own vulnerability in the furtive, hostile glance of his eyes. A strange tenderness warmed her as she watched Zolfo shovel food rapidly into his eager mouth. It was as if, by this simple act of generosity, she had reached back into her past and offered comfort to the memory of her miserable childhood.

"Zolfo," she said, leaning her elbows on the table.

He recoiled at the sound of his name, alert, as if ready for an attack.

"Zolfo, stop this destruction. Call back the fire and I'll drain the sea. Let's not destroy each other," she said. "We can share the maze."

He scowled at her, uncomprehending. Then a light of understanding gleamed in his eyes. He swiped his teeth with his tongue and sneered.

"You're scared, aren't you?"

"No, I'm not scared. I just don't want to see anyone hurt."

"You can't hurt me," he guffawed. "I am Zolfo di Labirinto. I am the curse come to end your life."

"I created you out of angry words and Gaetano's sorcery," Zizola explained. "And I can end you by calling back the words."

"No, you can't," Zolfo said, shaking his head. He tossed the carcass of the rabbit over his shoulder and reached for the polenta. He picked up a big handful of the yellow mush and lapped it out of his palm.

"Yes, I can," Zizola snapped, irritated by his arrogance. "I made you! I can end you, right now. But it doesn't have to be that way."

"Silly bitch. Go ahead and try it!" Zolfo taunted, licking the sticky cornmeal off of his fingers.

Zizola stood swiftly and raised her hands to the span of marble over her head.

"Here beneath the Arch of Dreams, I call back the words I spoke in anger. Let my curse dissolve like the wine in a drunkard's throat, like money in a whore's hand, like the truth on a man's tongue, like . . ."

Zizola stopped, uncomfortably aware that nothing was happening. Zolfo continued to lick his fingers, unchanged and untroubled by her performance.

And yet she could feel the current of magic rearing up from the damp earth beneath her feet, swirling around her legs like the rising tide of the ocean. It circled restlessly, dense as a newborn storm. She tried again.

"I wish the bonds of the curse to be unknotted, unraveled like a king's charter of peace, unspoken like a priest's vow, and forever banished like a maid's virginity."

And still Zolfo sat untouched and smirking.

Zizola's pulse began to race as the storm of sorcery gathered around her, swept upward in an invisible wave, and crashed over the table. It slammed into Zolfo like a frenzied surf, broke harmlessly against him, swirled back across the table, collected itself, and struck again while Zolfo smugly licked polenta from his fingers.

"Saint's hell," Zizola swore, her stomach tightening. Whatever power she had once had to change the curse, it appeared she had lost it, even here beneath the Arch of Dreams.

"Are you finished?" Zolfo asked with a nasty smile. He stood up and placed a hand on his chest. "I see you are confused. Your words no longer touch me, Zizola, because I am much more than a curse. I am a man. A man, do you hear? And my fate is no longer yours to command. There is no one alive who can stop me from taking what I want."

He threw back his head and started to laugh. And then abruptly, his laughter was choked off as he began to retch.

Zizola watched astounded as he clutched his throat, his teeth clamped hard on his tongue. He fell against the table, his body convulsing.

"What is it?" Zizola demanded as she moved closer.

"Get away," he shouted. "Don't touch me!"

"Madonna." Zizola gasped. A white film slid across Zolfo's dark eyes, moving from one pupil to another. His mouth snapped open and a dagger of gleaming light pierced his tongue. Beneath his chin, his neck swelled, round as a burl on a tree trunk. He clacked his teeth together and swallowed hard to force down the rising bulge.

Zizola ran to his side, ignoring his waving arms. She didn't understand what was happening to him, only that she shared his terror. Her heart pounded with the same wild panic she saw carved in her features on his face.

"Let me help you," she cried.

"No," he shouted. "I am a man. And you are mine!" he snarled, spitting out the white foam that had gathered at the corners of his mouth. Zolfo pressed on his chest with his left hand as though to keep his heart from bursting through the cage of his ribs. He groaned, his body spasming as his right hand reached for a knife on the table and snatched it up.

"No," he snarled to the hand clutching the knife. "I won't allow it!" With his other hand he tried to pry the knife loose from his fist. "Stop it," he shouted as his hands grappled over the knife.

Zizola lunged forward, and seizing Zolfo tightly around his shoulders and chest, pinned his arms flat against his sides. He fought against her, and as they wrestled, they crashed and rolled along the table's edge, knocking over the half-filled goblets and spilling the opened bottles of wine.

"What is it?" Zizola cried out, clinging to his arms. "Who's trying to hurt you?"

"The soul. It wants to go away. But it's mine," Zolfo whined, as a child. "It's mine! You can't have it!"

Locked in a tight embrace, her face inches from his, Zizola searched his wide-open eyes and saw first the flutter of a radiant wing, then the ghostly face of the priest, his mouth open in a scream of silent fury. Within Zolfo's chest pressed so close against her, Zizola felt the soul churning and rippling.

"You stole the priest's soul?" she asked, aghast.

"It's mine! It's my soul," he spat at her.

"Monster!" she shouted. "A man's goods are yours for the taking. But only God or the devil may harvest a soul. How could you be so cruel!"

"Let go of me!" Zolfo roared.

He bucked in her arms, thrashing his head as she fought to hold him. His right hand twisted free, and Zizola shrieked as the knife stabbed through her skirts and into her thigh. Her arms snapped opened immediately so that she could clutch the fierce pain in her leg. She staggered back, trying to keep herself upright. Zolfo swayed on his feet, the bloodied knife waving in the air. He watched her closely, sweat dripping into his eyes, his breath labored. Blood stained her skirts. She leaned against the table and her eyes began to close.

Zolfo shook his head to clear it, and then, grinning, attacked her again. Zizola saw him and twisted her body away from the slashing knife. The blade tore through the fabric of her sleeve and left a long trail of blood on her arm.

Reaching out over the table, Zizola grabbed a plate of pasta with clams and hurled it at Zolfo. He swerved but she quickly followed it with a torte filled with ricotta and erbette and then the remains of the cream-soaked lasagna di Ferrara. She thought she heard Giano cry out in anguish above her as the lasagna plopped into the mud.

Zolfo succeeded in ducking each messy cannonball. Panting hard, he continued to pursue her around the table, his knife passing restlessly from hand to hand. Using the table for support, Zizola edged back from him as quickly as her wounded leg would allow, flinging plates, goblets, and bottles of wine at his head.

"Any time now, Giano," she shouted, hoisting the heavy platter of risotto in one hand.

"Hey, you plague boil! You gutter rat! You piss pot" a voice taunted from up above. "Eat this!"

A pear filled with Gorgonzola sailed from the top of the arch and exploded against Zolfo's chest. It was followed by a second pear that smacked Zolfo in the temple. Dazed by the direct hit, he shook his head, smears of blue cheese clotting in his eyelashes.

In that unbalanced moment, when he was shaking off the pulped remains of the pear, the soul revived its struggle for freedom. Zolfo's right hand snatched back the knife from the left and his right arm jerked high in the air as if pulled by a string. While Zolfo watched, eyes widening with disbelief under his mask of Gorgonzola, the knife plunged into his breast, deep into the soft flesh below the sternum. Zolfo staggered, screaming a high-pitched shriek as his right hand forced the blade down his torso in a long jagged cut.

Zizola threw down the plate of risotto and scrambled as fast as her injured leg would allow to catch the swaying Zolfo. She was too late, and he fell sprawling over the remains of their feast.

"Madonna, Madonna mia," she muttered, turning him gently on his back. Her hands shaking, she pulled the knife free and cast it away. A warm stream of blood poured out of the long, gaping wound and spread like spilt wine along the table. Steam curled from his torn skin. Zolfo whimpered and tried to press the sides of the wound closed with trembling hands.

Giano leaped from the Arch of Dreams onto the table. He ran down its length and jumped to the ground to help Zizola lay the boy down on the muddy grass.

"What's happening to me? Why do I feel so weak? What is this pain?" Zolfo asked bewildered.

"Quiet now, or you'll die," Zizola said, and wiped the Gorgonzola from his face. The pupils of his eyes were huge and black, with strands of radiant light hovering at the edges.

"Die," he said. "I know that word, but no one has told me what it means."

Zizola looked up at Giano, a silent question in her eyes.

Giano gave his head a tight shake.

Zizola gazed down at Zolfo, grieved at the sight of her own face frightened by pain.

"No one alive can tell you what it is to die," she said simply. "It is a place mortals travel to but never return from."

"Am I dying?" Zolfo said, his lips grey against his sallow skin.

"Yes," Zizola answered softly.

The color was draining from his face, washing out of his body with the blood that seeped beneath him into the grass. It seemed to Zizola that soon he would have no more substance than the smoke hovering in thick clouds above them. He wrapped his blood-slick fingers through hers and clung tightly.

"What good is being human if you die?" he asked.

Zizola sighed, and didn't know how to answer him. He was a creature, created out of sorcery, of harsh words, a spell of bitter anger and vengeance. But to be human was also to love, to have compassion, and to dream. What did the curse know of these things? And how could she tell this twisted mask of herself anything of the pleasures of being human?

"Zizola, I'm afraid," Zolfo rasped.

"Don't be. I'm here," she answered, and stroked his pallid brow.

"My soul . . ." he coughed. "It escapes! How can I love her if it leaves me?" he asked, squeezing Zizola's hand. "Oh, Diana," he wailed. "Diana!"

On his cry Zolfo's head pitched back and his spine curved up from the ground, impossibly bent, to lift his chest to the sky. Riding on the flow of his last exhalation, a ray of gleaming light shot from between his teeth and arrowed into the grey sky.

Zolfo's skin stretched tautly over the fragile bones of his skeleton. More rays of light pierced his torso from within, bright spears that tore the fabric of his skin and his clothes on their passage from his body.

Giano and Zizola turned away, shielding their faces from the radiant light that blistered from Zolfo's wound. Through the cracks between her fingers, Zizola saw a diamond-bright orb rising slowly, and a perfumed scent of roses overpowered the stench of wood smoke, blood, and wet earth.

The orb slipped free of its corporeal cage and hovered in the sky, a white-hot star suspended above the trees by spears of light. A pair of shimmering wings unfurled silently across the sky. The spears of light extended out on four sides of the star like the arrowed points of a celestial compass. One spear, thinned to the fineness of a silk thread, thrust down into the lifeless husk of Zolfo's body and plucked a shadow that lay hidden behind the ribs. Zizola heard a sigh and saw a wisp of smoke curl up out of Zolfo's wound. It coiled itself around the starlight strand and twisted toward the diamond orb.

And as the shadow reached the center of the hovering star, Zizola saw a second face, a woman's profile etched in dark lines against the soul's brilliance. And then it faded, absorbed by the flaring heat of the soul's light.

The soul turned slowly in the mist, its wings rustling like shining sails, looking its last upon its earthly home. Then it folded its wings and launched itself into the grey bank of clouds, its passage marked by narrow bands of glistening dust.

"Well, that's that then." Zizola pulled her hand away from her eyes and watched the last of the celestial dust ripple out of sight.

"I don't think so," Giano warned. "Look!"

Zizola looked reluctantly. She had no particular desire to see the bloodied remains of a corpse that in life had resembled her too much.

But the boy Zolfo was gone. His bones were disintegrating into lumps of ocher mud, and sulphurous fumes curled away from the peeling leather of his burning skin. His blond hair sizzled into thousands of tiny red flames that expired quickly into minute puffs of grey ash. As his dissolving form sunk into the earth, the ocher mud spread into a churning, oily-black mass. Zizola crawled backward on her hands, sliding her feet away from the edges of a black pool that simmered like a puddle of boiling pitch.

"What is it?" she asked Giano.

"Trouble," he answered dourly, wrinkling his nose at the rotten stench.

Bubbles rose and broke on the surface with small yellow hisses, then gradually settled until the pool was smooth and flat as a mirror of polished obsidian.

Curious, Zizola leaned forward on her hands and knees to gaze into the pool. Her opened-mouth reflection gazed back, frowning and puzzled. What did it mean? Was the curse gone? It didn't feel that way.

Warnings still clamored in her head, the spot behind her ear itched, and the bones of her little finger ached. But she couldn't guess what they meant. The soul had fled. Zolfo was gone.

She turned her head to address Giano. "Perhaps—" she started to say, but never finished.

Giano snatched her by the ribbons at her shoulders and heaved her roughly back from the pool's edge.

"Saint's hell, what are you doing?" she snapped, the pain of her knife wound flaring in her leg.

Giano grimly continued to drag her away from the pool. Zizola yelped and swore as she bumped over rocks and scraped her heels over broken goblets and platters of spilt food.

"Let go, you fool!"

"Basta, Zizola!" he growled. "I'm trying to save us! Look!"

Zizola stared past her bouncing body and saw an almost human form rising from the pool. The head had no face, no features except a tongue of fire in a wide-open mouth. The withered grass around the pool was burning as the mud churned and the simmering pitch widened.

"You killed the boy, but not the curse!" Giano shouted.

"I didn't kill him," Zizola protested.

"Then try your luck with the curse, and be quick about it!"

"Help me get up the arch," Zizola commanded, and was relieved when Giano stopped dragging her and helped her to stand. The curse was wading through the boiling, black pool. In Its wake, a bed of lava burned bright red beneath a broken crust. It turned a head toward them, and blazing eyes opened in the black skull.

"Curse," It announced itself.

With an arm around her waist, Giano helped Zizola to mount the stairs, half dragging her to the top of the arch.

"What are you going to do, Zizola? Quickly, before the curse burns us up in his cauldron!" Giano shouted.

"I don't know," she snapped back. "I have to think!"

"There's no time. It's eating up everything! The table is gone! And we're next."

The black pool had spread out beneath the arch into a shallow lake of magma, swallowing everything in its fiery depths. A scorching wind howled, carrying the hot breath and ashy rain of a volcano. The chairs exploded into flames, and were gone. The long wooden table floated for a time, the wood crackling and splintering as it blackened with the heat, and tiny gold bubbles swirled on the black surface, the last mementoes of the golden plates.

"Zizola! How does the play end?" Giano shouted, grabbing her by the shoulders.

Zizola closed her eyes and thought of how love might have saved them from this destruction. A father's love for his daughter might have kept him from loneliness; a mother's love for her child might have kept her from despair; and a sister's love for a brother might have kept her from dying in a furnace built of centuries of anger. Tears of frustration trickled down Zizola's face. She touched the salty droplets with her tongue and tasted the possibility of salvation.

Zizola raised her head and looked out at the destruction of the maze. The cedar sentries were barely visible through the dense haze of smoke. The oaks showed only blackened skeletal arms raised in anguish above the waterline. The silvery leaves were stripped from the branches of the sacred olive trees as fire coursed along every slender, twisted branch.

"Bring me the sea," Zizola called into the driving, scorching wind. "Send to me all the tears shed by the pilgrims cursed and lost in the maze and let their ocean of weeping wash away this last curse."

"Tears of Christ, I never thought I'd end up a grilled piece of meat," Giano complained.

"You're too tough to burn anyway," Zizola retorted.

"Very well then, you be the cutlet!"

"Listen!" Zizola interrupted. "Do you hear it?"

A low rumbling vibrated through the ground, shaking the columns of the Arch of Dreams. Thunder rolled across the sky and the wind began to keen and twist into a cyclone of ash and mist. Zizola pressed against Giano, her hands clutching his sleeves as she bent to protect herself against the wind. Lava swirled beneath the Arch of Dreams, leaving black smears along the white columns.

"We're finished!" Giano cried, his lanky frame bent to shield her from the wind. Together they struggled to keep their balance on the slippery roof of the quaking arch. "Here comes the inferno."

The curse had mounted the stairs of the Arch of Dreams. With each step It took, the lava rose higher around the columns, weakening the arch. The carved faces of the Roman comics were pitted by corrosive drops of lava and their white marble brows were stained a sulphurous yellow. The curse stepped onto the crest of the arch, planted Its feet, and turned Its nearly featureless face to Giano and Zizola, Its crystalline eyes blazing through the dense clouds of smoke.

Hunched against the burning wind, Giano and Zizola crept backward as far as they could go. Zizola glanced down and saw the broken staircase melting into the furnace of lava.

"This is not a good ending," Giano argued, shouting into the wind. "Can't you improvise something else, Zizola?"

Zizola peered out from the shelter of Giano's arms into the driving wind and shouted joyously.

"Look where it comes!" she cried, and pointed a finger. "Brace yourself!"

The thunder had grown louder, booming like a field of cannons through the clouds of smoke. Out beyond the remains of the dying oaks, the pair on the arch could glimpse the flooded canals of the maze, and see how the water rose like a herd of stampeding horses. Waves roared through the narrow corridors, swallowing up mouthfuls of earth and trees, drowning the patterned lines of the maze. Glistening green walls of water crested and crashed in sprays of foam and then gathered themselves to surge and roll across the maze to Zizola.

"This is better?" Giano shouted.

The ocean burst though the cedars, flooded into the clearing and over the lava pool, exploding into steam. Smaller waves reared and wound like serpents around the columns of the arch, cooling the seared stone.

"It's making me seasick!" Giano yelled.

Debris of all kinds swirled aimlessly under the arch, captured in the coursing water. Gnarled olive trees, pulled out by their roots, slammed against the columns before being carried away by the riotous swells. The hinged head of a metal dragon bobbed in a whirlpool, chased by a tail of iron scales. A goat cart, its sides decorated with a fawn's spotted skin, smashed against the jagged edge of the arch's broken stairs. A boisterous wave heaved a bronze mask and a lance onto the crest of the arch. They skittered across the wet surface, and before they could come to rest, were swept away by another wave.

The curse stared expressionless at the rising water. Waves licked Its feet and steam hissed a warning.

"Curse," It repeated, Its crystalline eyes unmoved. It turned Its blank face to Giano and Zizola. The red veins of lava flared brightly in Its blackened face. It opened Its mouth, and the black crust cracked along the cheeks in a burning grin. It started toward them, moving stiffly, as though the water had cooled It enough to thicken the molten flow of lava and slow It down.

"O'Dio, look. There's a woman out there in the water!" cried Giano, pointing behind the curse. "Look!" he urged.

The curse sniggered and took another step.

"Stupid trick," Zizola spat. "What makes you think It would fall for that!"

"But I'm serious, Zizola! Look."

Zizola craned her neck around Giano's arm and saw a slender marble arm raised above the surging water as if pleading for help. The unruly waves tossed the figure closer and Zizola saw the arm was attached to the carved head of a woman, her eyes staring up out of the foaming water, her mouth still holding the faint promise of a smile.

"Diana!" Zizola shouted, the serene face jolting the memory of Zolfo's last human cry. "Look, it's Diana!" she repeated, pointing.

This time the curse faltered. It turned, mouth open in a howl as It gazed across the water and saw the drowning fragment of Its beloved. Her strong arm reached out of the foam, appearing to beseech the curse to save her from the cruel waves. Then Diana's head disappeared under the water, and the curse collapsed howling to Its knees at the edge of the arch and searched the churning water for her face. Waves crashed against the arch, striking off shards of black cinder from the kneeling figure.

"There, she's over there!" Giano pointed on the other side of the arch.

Diana's upraised hand was visible again, lifted above a seething dirty-white froth. Another wave scooped her up and tumbled her farther from the Arch of Dreams. Soon she would be lost.

The curse straightened Itself and stared at Zizola, the crystalline eyes bleeding red tears.

Shivering in the cold wash, Zizola clung to Giano and held her breath. With a howl, the curse tore Its gaze from Zizola and flung Itself far out into the churning sea toward Diana's upraised hand.

"Bravo! Bravo!" shouted Giano as the curse plunged into the sea like a falling meteorite. A circular wall of white water lifted out of the sea around It and showered salty rain over Zizola and Giano. When the white curtain fell back into the ocean, Zizola caught her last glimpse of the curse.

It had wrapped Its arms around Diana's face, Its coal black cheek pressed against her white skin. The water boiled around the couple as they bobbed on the heaving surface, the cold sea stealing heat from the veins of the curse, hardening Its molten flesh into rock. Zizola felt the power of her angry words unravel as her curse cried out Its love for the marble face. Weighted by the head of Its beloved, Zizola's curse sank with her beneath the waves.

Zizola struggled out of Giano's arms and came to the edge of the arch.

"Calme. Stai calme," Zizola cried, her hands held out to the angry, coursing waves.

The sea resisted her at first, swells smashing into one another as they charged over the surface of the water. But Zizola continued to whisper words of quiet and peace, and the rolling swells settled back into the body of the sea until only small waves lapped the faces of the comics on the Arch of Dreams.

"Look at my maze," Zizola mourned, her hand pressed forlornly against her forehead.

"There's nothing but water and the tops of trees, and this little shelf where we sit, like the leftover cheese," Giano said glumly.

"Not true," Zizola said. "The center holds."

"How do you know?" he demanded.

She cocked her head at him with a faint grin. "I just do," she declared. "Arch of Zizola's Dreams, bring me a boat to carry us to the center."

A small barca came bobbing over the water toward them, a pair of oars sticking out on either side of its hull like whiskers on a cat.

They climbed into the boat and Giano took the oars. He groaned as he pulled the boat smoothly through the water.

"Giano, I am amazed," Zizola declared in surprise as she clutched the wobbly sides of the boat.

"Eh, why's that?" He panted and pulled on the oars, sending the boat gliding over the water.

"I never knew you could work!"

"Boh," he exhaled. "I did it once before and it seems I haven't forgotten how! More's the pity," he muttered as he bent over the oars.

LE CHUISETTE,
THE CLOSING SPEECHES

For all am I Prince, Lord of land and main,
save for my public,
Whose faithful servant I remain.

—*Pulcinella's chuisette*

42

Zizola and Giano heard the siren singing long before they saw her. The pure sound of her voice drifted over the water, calming the ocean, recalling it to the wombs of the dozen different seas from which Zizola had drawn it. Around them, the corridors of cedar and cypress slowly reemerged, their trunks scorched black and their upper branches green. Flocks of birds swooped through the shredding clouds of smoke over hills newly risen from the water, along whose slick flanks, olive trees pried free twisted boughs from the mud.

Giano had ceased rowing the moment the siren had begun to sing. He drew the oars in and let the seductive magic of her voice carry them, drifting quietly through the canals of the maze, turning one way and another through the wet, glistening trees. Once, Zizola pulled the boat to a stop beside an old door, torn from its hinges by the waves, on which a little dog, looking more drowned than alive, shivered miserably. But as Giano leaned over to pluck her off the floating door, she bared her teeth and snarled.

"Come on you, wretched bitch," Giano growled, trying to grab ahold of the snapping dog without getting bitten.

"Let me," Zizola said gruffly. "You're scaring her, Giano. Come, little one, come, bella, don't be afraid. Come to Zizola," she crooned, and held out her hand.

The dog's fury deflated. She laid her ears flat against her head and whimpered, her shaggy tail thumping on the wooden door. She crawled on her belly to Zizola's hand and started licking her fingers. Zizola quickly scooped her up and set the dog down between her feet in the bottom of the boat.

"There. Isn't that better, bella?" she asked.

The dog wagged her tail and began to puke up mouthfuls of water.

"I hope we get there soon," Giano said, with a heavy sigh as the dog continued to retch at their feet.

The sky was a clear blue when their boat slid through a final wave and bumped against a rocky, muddy shore. Giano jumped out of the barca and tugged the prow higher up the bank to anchor it in the mud. Zizola picked up the little dog by her scruff and deposited her on the land. The dog wagged her tail so furiously that her whole body shook. Zizola moved to get out of the boat, wincing at the pain in her wounded leg. Dried blood cracked on her skin as she swung her leg over the side of the boat and tried to put weight on it. Clinging to the side of the boat, she swore at the fresh waves of pain.

"Look, here come your satyrs, Zizola!" Giano said.

Zizola looked up and saw the huge satyr trotting down a narrow trail to meet her. Behind him, three of the smaller satyrs bleated out their greetings, their tails flicking like white flags.

"You're all right," Zizola said relieved, as the huge satyr lifted her into his arms. She embraced his powerful neck and asked, "The nymphs? The children?"

He smiled at her, his pink tongue pressed between his teeth.

"Good." She sighed and leaned her head on his shoulder. "I didn't ruin everything."

Giano and the little dog followed close behind the satyrs, walking in single file through a wood of young poplars. Beneath the slender trees, oak saplings and ferns created a soft green carpet.

"Look, Giano, how the center has changed!" Zizola cried out.

The high stone wall concealing the ancient palazzo had crumbled, tearing wide gaps between the stone columns, like a Roman arena. Through the gaps, Giano and Zizola saw people collected around makeshift fires, drying clothing or bent over steaming cooking pots. Others had gathered into consoling knots, applying bandages to wounds and goose fat to burns. A nymph seated on a throne next to an ancient oak called to the satyr. Even clothed only in her rose-colored skin, she looked like a noblewoman, so elegantly did she sit, holding a handful of red grapes like jewels.

"Go on, put me down now," Zizola said. Gently the satyr released her, bowed respectfully, and trotted over to the nymph.

"Where are the knights who used to hold up the wall?" Giano asked.

"Over there." Zizola pointed to a group of soldiers, clad in mail and leather jerkins, relaxing around a campfire. Strewn across the ground were the discarded pieces of their armor: a helmet upturned like a beetle, a breastplate heaped with pasta. They were laughing, eating, their faces human and ruddy. They stretched their stockinged feet to the fire, scratched their noses, and leaned back in the grass on their elbows. Rinaldo, his red hair like a cardinal's cap, was standing talking to two of the knights, who held their swords in front of them, inspecting the blades.

"He certainly looks at home," Zizola exclaimed. "And look, there, the woman with the black hair," Zizola said.

Simonetta was deep in conversation with a crippled dwarf in a tattered brick-red cape. They seemed to be shaping something large with their hands, to be built over the rubble of the old palazzo.

"No, no, I want a good oven for baking. Like a hive, not one like a dragon," she was insisting.

"Ma, Signora, please. It will be so dull that way."

"I don't intend to put my hands into the mouth of a dragon every time I want to bake bread. No. Make it look like an oven."

"What about the water spouts and the sinks? Can I design them to look like dolphins leaping out of the waves? Please, Signora, let me do something interesting. I am a scenographer. A kitchen can be more than a kitchen," the little man pleaded with both hands pressed together in front of him. "A fantasia, an extravaganza!"

"Madonna, all right," Simonetta said wearily. "Just make sure it all works."

The little dog that Zizola had rescued pricked up her ears and started barking wildly. She dashed through the sitting knots of people and scattered the ashes of various campfires, leaving a wake of cursing behind her.

"Lily! Lily!" Mirabella cried, bending down to receive the ecstatic little dog in her arms. "Where have you been, you naughty creature? I was so worried."

"Ah," said Giano, holding a finger to the side of his nose and nodding toward Mirabella, "the Innamorati. Look how happy they are. Old and young love together. Which flame burns the brighter?"

Zizola followed Giano's glance and smiled at the two couples sitting together, their backs to the wall of the palazzo, catching the warmth of the sun streaming into the cortile. Mirabella sat close to Fabrizio, leaning against his side with his arm around her shoulder. They were both petting Lily, who was nestled in Mirabella's lap, but their eyes were firmly locked onto each other's faces. Even from here, Zizola could see them whispering the words to the lover's duet, punctuating each pause with a quick kiss. Next to them were Anna and Roberto, their heads touching, their hands entwined. Roberto was talking, and Anna was smiling, sleepy in the sunlight, agreeing to everything he said, without speaking.

"And who would have thought the old stick had the juice left in him to be a poet?" Giano said. Lorenzo was perched above the two couples on the wall of the loggia. His back was against a slender column, his white shirt torn open to expose his chest. He was staring at the siren beside him with a sensual, melancholy gaze. Erminia, clad only in her rough-spun shift, was reaching out her white arms to the watery canals of the maze as she sang. Her shining black hair fluttered in the gentle breezes and her face was decorated with Mirabella's broken spectacles.

"What has happened to the others?" Zizola asked, looking around. "The nobles with stone heads? The groom and the valet? Where is Ill Maestro Gaetano?"

"Come," said Giano, "I think I see them beneath that tree over there."

Giano strolled and Zizola limped toward Gaetano, who was sitting on a stool beneath a huge spreading oak. He was patiently lifting a woman's head from a man's body and replacing it onto her own body. At the woman's feet, the man's stone head whined and shouted insults at the woman's head. On the far side of the tree, the nobles already made whole were sitting and fanning themselves, while a young groom with a bemused face offered them cloths with which to wipe their faces clean of dust and sweat.

"Zizola, you have arrived!" Gaetano called, waving her closer. He laid his massive hands on another carved head and pulled it from the shoulders of a woman seated next to him. The body tapped its feet nervously as Gaetano sorted through the other nobles gathered around him, looking for the right head. "Ah, here it is," he rumbled, finding a young woman's head on the body of a short elderly man. "Excuse me, my dear," he said, plucked her head like a rosebud, and reset it on her body. Then he looked up at Zizola.

"The curse?"

"Gone," she answered.

"You must tell me how," he said gravely.

Zizola remembered how Zolfo had died in her arms and how the curse had died, clinging to Diana. She shrugged, her hands spread wide.

Gaetano looked up at her, a sad smile showing through the curling strands of his black beard.

"Am I forgiven the foolishness of an old man?" he asked her.

"Yes. As long as I can stay here," she added.

"I would be honored. But that is an easy request to grant, for no one has ever been able to leave the maze."

"Not quite true," Zizola said. "You couldn't leave the maze. That was your curse. You couldn't see that there was always a door out. Forgiveness and love would have turned the key and released you from your curse-made prison."

"How do you know this?" he asked, standing gruffly.

"How else did Rosalba leave?" Zizola answered with a shrug. "Follow me." She gestured with her hand and slowly made her way over to one of the remaining walls of the palazzo, Gaetano treading heavily behind her. Others in the cortile, sensing something important, gathered around, murmuring excitedly.

Zizola stopped in front of the tapestry depicting the wedding banquet with the bride and groom beneath a canopy of red silk holding their wedding rings aloft. She ran her hand over the smooth woolen stitches and smiled. Then she pulled the frayed tapestry to one side and revealed a door.

"Where does it lead to?" Fabrizio called out.

"Anywhere you want," Zizola answered.

"Venice?" Anna asked.

"Yes."

"Milan?" Rinaldo asked.

"If that is where you wish to go," Zizola said evenly.

"Has the door always been here?" Gaetano asked.

"While you remained unforgiving, you could never find it. And while Rosalba remained revengeful, she could never find her way in again," Zizola explained.

"But you are here; you made it inside again," Gaetano argued.

"Yes, but I had the help of fools, for they never cling to hate when they can cling to a good leg of mutton, and they never plot revenge when they can plot seduction. So come, who wants to go home again?" she asked the gathered crowd.

"We want to return to Venice," Mirabella said, stepping forward with Fabrizio, Anna, and Roberto.

"Promise you will return with a troupe and Signora Forsetti's masks to give a performance here in the maze at Carnevale," Giano begged.

"It will be our pleasure," Fabrizio said, bowing graciously.

Mirabella turned the latch and the door opened smoothly. She gasped and turned to the others crowded behind her. "It's the Campo San Bernabo. We are home!" She leaned down and gave Zizola a quick kiss on both cheeks, tears misting her blue eyes. Then she turned and stepped through the doorway, Lily barking happily at her feet. Fabrizio kissed Zizola's hand quickly and rushed after Mirabella. Anna and Roberto paused at the door, staring out in awe at the Campo San Bernabo on the other side of the threshold.

"Until Carnevale!" Anna cried out, and waved a hasty farewell. "Oh, my studio." She sighed, stepping through the doorway.

"And you, Lorenzo, my friend," Roberto said, turning to the poet. "Will you join us? A troupe can always use a man of letters."

Lorenzo touched Erminia on the arm, a question on his face.

She shook her head. "No, my poet. Where I am going you may not come. Here we must part, you to your world and I to mine." Lorenzo gave her one last, lingering kiss and then scrambled down the wall of the loggia and joined Roberto.

"Come, my friend," Lorenzo said, clapping Roberto on the shoulder. "Venice awaits."

Together they stepped through the door into the sunlight of the distant piazza.

"I wish to remain in the maze," Simonetta said quietly. "I have no real home to return to. Perhaps, Signorina, you have need of a good cook?"

Zizola glanced over at Gaetano, who nodded. "Consider it done," she answered. "I myself am partial to risotto," she added, licking her lips.

"Will you allow me to serve you as well, Maestro?" Rinaldo said, stepping forward. "I have experience as a captain, and perhaps the maze may have need of my skill."

"My army has been stone long enough," Gaetano answered. "It would be well for them to train again under your command, Captain."

"And me," Giano said, touching Zizola on the shoulder. "Can I stay?"

"Of course," she said. "Who else offers me so much amusement?"

"Your humble servant," Giano said, smiling.

"And you, my lovely siren?" Gaetano asked, taking Erminia by the hands. "Can we convince you to remain with us? I am sure that Orpheus is prepared to put aside his rancor. Your songs would be welcomed here."

"No, Il Maestro," Erminia answered, graciously. "I shall return to Anthemoessa—to my sisters and the sea that I love."

She knelt down and embraced Zizola, brushing the girl's blond hair back from her face. "He has found his Diana," she whispered in Zizola's ear. "They are welded together, stone upon stone, far off the coast of Africa. No one will ever disturb them."

She turned to the door and stepped up to the threshold. A gust of salty air blustered into the cortile, and as it chased out again, Erminia was gone.

"Well, Zizola, I think we should have something to eat to celebrate," Giano said, rubbing his hands together. "And a little something to drink."

"And why not?" Zizola grinned as she shut the door and covered it with the tapestry.

Erminia stood poised on the edge of the cliffs. Below her in the moonlight the sea rushed up the stone walls and besought her with arms of white foam.

"I am coming," she said to the waves. "In a moment."

She turned her head to listen to the faint sounds of laughter coming from the village of Camogli. Arlecchino was rolling across the stage, Isabella was fainting prettily into the arms of Lelio, and Pantelone was chasing after the serving girl, Silvia. Soon the play would finish and the applause would break like the waves rasping against the shore.

It had not been difficult to sing the song of unbinding. She had reversed her spell slowly, transforming the moment of their fear into the vague memory of a distant dream. Coral fell away from their eyes and they moved their limbs, unaware of the time they had passed in their hardened state. On the stage, the actors woke and spoke the lines that had frozen on their lips in shards of coral.

They would not remember Erminia. They would not remember the terror of the night she sang. They would remember only the play, the masked faces of the actors holding their rapt attention, the sound of Isabella's voice as alluring as the siren's. They might dream of a song and a shepherdess, but that was all.

Erminia heard the sprinkled applause, followed by the low murmur, the couplet that signaled the end of the play. She heard her name called, and as she looked out at the moon-spangled sea, she saw her sisters swimming out beyond the rocks, waving at her to join them.

At once, Erminia leapt off the cliff. And with a shriek of delight, plunged feetfirst into the dark sea below.